THE MORMON PROPHET

MORE WILDSIDE CLASSICS

THE MORMON PROPHET

LILY DOUGALL

WILDSIDE PRESS

THE MORMON PROPHET

This edition published in 2006 by Wildside Press, LLC.
www.wildsidepress.com

PREFACE.

In studying the rise of this curious sect I have discovered that certain misconceptions concerning it are deeply rooted in the minds of many of the more earnest of the well-wishers to society. Some otherwise well-informed people hold Mormonism to be synonymous with polygamy, believe that Brigham Young was its chief prophet, and are convinced that the miseries of oppressed women and tyrannies exercised over helpless subjects of both sexes are the only themes that the religion of more than two hundred thousand people can afford. When I have ventured in conversation to deny these somewhat fabulous notions, it has been earnestly suggested to me that to write on so false a religion in other than a polemic spirit would tend to the undermining of civilised life.

In spite of these warnings, and although I know it to be a most dangerous commodity, I have ventured to offer the simple truth, as far as I have been able to discern it, consoling my advisers with the assurance that its insidious influence will be unlikely to do harm, because, however potent may be the direful latitude of other religious novels, this particular book can only interest those wiser folk who are best able to deal with it.

As, however, to many who have preconceived the case, this narrative might, in the absence of explanation, seem purely fanciful, let me briefly refer to the historical facts on which it is based. The Mormons revere but one prophet. As to his identity there can be no mistake, since many of the "revelations" were addressed to him by name—"To Joseph Smith, Junior." He never saw Utah, and his public teachings were for the most part unexceptionable. Taking necessary liberty with incidents, I have endeavoured to present Smith's character as I found it in his own writings, in the narratives of contemporary writers, and in the memories of the older inhabitants of Kirtland.

In reviewing the evidence I am unable to believe that, had Smith's doctrine been conscious invention, it would have lent sufficient power to carry him through persecutions in which his life hung in the balance, and his cause appeared to be lost, or that the class of earnest men who constituted the rank and file of his early following would have been so long deceived by a deliberate hypocrite. It appears to me more likely that Smith was genuinely deluded by the automatic freaks of a vigorous but undisciplined brain, and that, yielding to these, he became confirmed in the hysterical temperament which always adds to delusion self-deception, and to self-deception half-conscious fraud. In his day it was necessary to reject a marvel or admit its spiritual significance; granting an honest delusion as to his visions and his book, his only choice lay between counting himself the sport of devils or the agent of Heaven; an optimistic temperament cast the die.

In describing the persecutions of his early followers I have modified rather than enlarged upon the facts. It would, indeed, be difficult to exaggerate the sufferings of this unhappy and extraordinarily successful sect.

A large division of the Mormons of today, who claim to be Smith's orthodox following, and who have never settled in Utah, are strictly monogamous. These have never owned Brigham Young as a leader, never murdered their neighbours or defied the law in any way, and so vigorous their growth still appears that they claim to have increased their number by fifty thousand since the last census in 1890. Of all their characteristics, the sincerity of their belief is the most striking. In Ohio, when one of the preachers of these "Smithite" Mormons was conducting me through the many-storied temple, still standing huge and gray on Kirtland Bluff, he laid his hand on a pile of copies of the Book of Mormon, saying solemnly, "Sister, here is the solidest thing in religion that you'll find anywhere." I bought the "solidest" thing for fifty cents, and do not advise the same outlay to others. The prophet's life is more marvellous and more instructive than the book whose production was its chief triumph. That it was an original production seems probable, as the recent discovery of the celebrated Spalding manuscript, and a critical examination of the evidence of Mrs. Spalding, go far to discredit the popular accusation of plagiarism.

Near Kirtland I visited a sweet-faced old lady—not, however, of the Mormon persuasion—who as a child had climbed on the prophet's knee. "My mother always said," she told us, "that if she had to die and leave young children, she would rather have left them to Joseph Smith than to any one else in the world: he was always kind." This testimony as to Smith's kindheartedness I found to be often repeated in the annals of Mormon families.

In criticising my former stories several reviewers, some of them distinguished in letters, have done me the honour to remark that there was latent laughter in many of my scenes and conversations, but that I was unconscious of it. Be that as it may, those who enjoy unconscious absurdity will certainly find it in the utterances of the self-styled prophet of the Mormons. Probably one gleam of the sacred fire of humour would have saved him and his apostles the very unnecessary trouble of being Mormons at all.

In looking over the problems involved in such a career as Smith's, we must be struck by the necessity for able and unprejudiced research into the laws which govern apparent marvels. Notwithstanding the very natural and sometimes justifiable aspersions which have been cast upon the work of the Society for Psychical Research, it does appear that the disinterested service rendered by its more distinguished members is the only attempt hitherto made to aid people of the so-called "mediumistic" temperament to understand rather than be swayed by their delusions. Whether such a result is as yet possible or not, Mormonism affords a gigantic proof of the crying need of an effort in this direction; for men are obviously more ignorant of their own elusive mental conditions than of any other branch of knowledge.

L.D.

MONTREAL, December, 1898.

BOOK I.

CHAPTER I.

In the United States of America there was, in the early decades of this century, a very widely spread excitement of a religious sort. Except in the few long-settled portions of the eastern coast, the people were scattered over an untried country; means of travel were slow; news from a distance was scarce; new heavens and a new earth surrounded the settlers. In the veins of many of them ran the blood of those who had been persecuted for their faith: Covenanters, Quakers, sectaries of diverse sorts who could transmit to their descendants their instincts of fiery zeal, their cravings for "the light that never was on sea or land," but not that education by contact with law and order which, in older states, could not fail to moderate reasonable minds.

With the religious revivals came signs and wonders. A wave of peculiar psychical phenomena swept over the country, in explanation of which the belief most widely received was that of the direct interposition of God or the devil. The difficulty of discerning between the working of the good and the bad spirit in abnormal manifestations was to most minds obviated by the fact that they looked out upon the confusing scene through the glasses of rigidly defined opinion, and according as the affected person did or did not conform to the spectator's view of truth, so he was judged to be a saint or a demoniac. Few sought to learn rather than to judge; one of these very few was a young man by name Ephraim Croom. He was by nature a student, and, being of a feeble constitution, he enjoyed what, in that country and time, was the very rare privilege of indulging his literary tastes under the shelter of the parental roof.

In one of the last years of the eighteenth century Croom the elder had come with a young wife from his father's home in Massachusetts to settle in a township called New Manchester, in the State of New York. He was a Baptist by creed; a man of strong will, strong affections, and strong self-respect. Taking the portion of goods which was his by right, he sallied forth into the new country, thrift and intelligence written upon his forehead, thinking there the more largely to establish the prosperity of the green bay tree, and to serve his God and generation the better by planting his race in the newer land.

The thirtieth year after his emigration found him a notable person in the place that he had chosen, with almost the same physical strength as in youth, stern, upright, thrifty, the owner of large mills, of a substantial wooden residence, and of many acres of land. He was as rich as he had intended to be; his ideal of righteousness, being of the obtainable sort, had been realised and strictly adhered to. The one disappointment of his life was the lack of those sturdy sons and daughters who, to his mind, should have surrounded the virtuous man in his old age. They had not come into the world. His wife, a good woman and energetic helpmeet, had brought him but the one studious son.

Ephraim was thirty-two years of age when a young girl, strong, beautiful, impetuous, entered under the sloping eaves of his father's huge gray shingle roof. The girl was a niece on the maternal side. Her New England mother had, by freak of love, married a reckless young Englishman of gentle blood who was settled on a Canadian farm. Pining for her puritan home, she died early. The father made a toy of his daughter till he too died in the fortified town of Kingston, on the northern shore of Lake Ontario. No other relatives coming forward to assume his debts or to claim his child, their duty in the matter was clear to the minds of the Croom household, and the girl was sent for. Her name was Susannah, but she herself gave it the softer form that she had been accustomed to hear; when she first entered the sitting-room of the grave Croom family trio, like a sunbeam striking suddenly through the clouds on a dark day, she held out her hand and her lips to each in turn, saying, "I am Susianne."

That first time Ephraim kissed her. It was done in surprise and embarrassed formality. He knew, when the moment was past that his parents had perceived that Susannah needed more decorous training. He concurred in believing this to be desirable, for the manners that had surrounded him were very stiff. Yet the memory of the greeting remained with him, a thing to be wondered at while he turned the whispering leaves of his great books.

Susannah had travelled from the Canadian fort in the care of the preacher Finney. He was a revivalist of great renown, possessing a lawyer-like keenness of intellect, much rhetorical power, and Pauline singleness of purpose. That night he ate and slept in the house.

The original Calvinism of the Croom household had already been modified by the waves of Methodist revival from the Eastern States. Finney was an Independent, but Martha Croom had an abounding respect for him; his occasional visits were epochs in her life. She had prepared many baked meats for his entertainment before the evening of his arrival with Susannah, but while he was present she devoted herself wholly to his conversation.

The feast was spread in the inner kitchen. In the square brick fireplace burning pine sticks crackled, bidding the chill of the April evening retire to its own place beyond the dark window pane. The paint upon the walls and floor glistened but faintly to the fire and the small flames of two candles that stood among the viands upon the table.

The elder Croom sat in his place. He was burly and ruddy, a wholesome man, very silent, very strong, a person to be feared and relied on. Ephraim believed that force went forth from his father's presence like perfume from a flower. There were many kinds of flowers whose perfume was too strong for Ephraim, but he felt that to be a proof of his own weakness.

Martha Croom, also of New England stock, was of a different type. At fifty years she was still as slender as a girl—tall and too slender, but the small shapely head was set gracefully on the neck as a flower upon its stalk. Her hair, which was wholly silvered, was still abundant and glossily brushed. Her mind was not judicial. She was more quick to decide than to comprehend, full of intense activities and emotions.

"I have heard," said the preacher slowly, "certain distressing rumours concerning—"

Mrs. Croom gave an upward bridling motion of her head, and a red spot of indignant fire came in each of her cheeks. "Joe Smith?", she cried. "A blasphemous wretch! And there is nothing, Mr. Finney, that so well indicates the luke-warmishness into which so many have fallen as that his blasphemy is made a jest of."

Ephraim moved uneasily in his chair.

Mr. Croom made a remark brief and judicial. "The Smiths are a *low* family."

Mrs. Croom answered the tone. "If the dirt beneath our feet were to begin using profane language, I don't suppose it would be beneath our dignity to put a stop to it."

"It is the Inquisition that my mother wishes to reinstate," said Ephraim.

The master of the house again spoke with the *naïveté* of unquestioning bias. "No, Ephraim; for your mother would be the last to interfere with any for doing righteousness or believing the truth."

Mrs. Croom's slender head trembled and her eyes showed signs of tears at her son's opposition. "If God-fearing people cannot prevent the most horrible iniquities from being practised in their own town, the laws are in a poor condition."

"You have made no candid inquiry concerning Smith, mother; your judgment of him, whether true or false, is based on angry sentiment and wilful ignorance."

The preacher sighed. "This Smith is deceiving the people."

"His book," said Ephraim, "is a history of the North American Indians from the time of the flood until some epoch prior to Columbus. It would be as difficult to prove that it was not true as to prove that Smith is not honest in his delusion. We can only fall back upon what Butler would call 'a strong presumption.'"

Mrs. Croom, consciously or not, made a little sharp rap on the table, and there was a movement of suppressed misery like a quiver in her slender upright form. Her voice was low and tremulous. "If you'd got religion, Ephraim, you wouldn't speak in that light manner of one who has the awful wickedness of adding to the words of the Book."

Ephraim continued to enlighten the preacher in a stronger tone. "Whether the man is mad or false, almost all the immoralities that you will hear reported about him are, as far as I can make out, not true. He doesn't teach that it's unnecessary to obey the ten commandments, or beat his wife, nor is he drunken. He's got the sense to see that all that sort of thing wouldn't make a big man of him. It's merely a revised form of Christianity, with a few silly additions, that he claims to be the prophet of."

Mrs. Croom began to weep bitterly.

The elder Croom asked a pertinent question. "Why do you wilfully distress your mother, Ephraim?"

"Because, sir, I love my mother too well to sit silent and let her think that injustice can glorify God."

It was a family jar.

Finney was a man of about forty years of age; his eyes under overreaching brows were bright and penetrating; his face was shaven, but his mouth had an expression of peculiar strength and gentleness. He looked keenly at the son of the house, who was held to be irreligious. And then he looked upon Susannah, whose beauty and frivolity had not escaped his keen observation. He lived always in the consciousness of an invisible presence; when he felt the arms of Heaven around him, wooing him to prayer, he dared not disobey.

He arose now, setting his chair back against the wall with preoccupied precision. "The spirit of prayer is upon me," he said; and in a moment he added, "Let us pray."

Susannah was eating, and with relish. She laid down her bit of pumpkin pie and stared astonished. Then, being a girl of good sense and good feeling, she relinquished the remainder of her supper, and, following her aunt's example, knelt beside her chair.

The two candles and the firelight left shadowy spaces in parts of the room, and cast grotesque outlines against the walls. Nothing was familiar to Susannah's eye; she could not help looking about her. Ephraim was nearest to her. He was a bearded man, and seemed to her very old. She saw that his face looked pale and distressed; his eyes were closed, his lips tight set, like one bearing transient pain. At the end of the table her uncle knelt upright, with hands clasped and face uplifted, no feature or muscle moving—a strong figure rapt in devotion. On her other side, as a slight tree waves in the wind, her aunt's slim figure was swaying and bending with feeling that was now convulsive and now restrained. Sometimes she moaned audibly or whispered "Amen." Across the richly-spread table Susannah saw the preacher kneeling in a full flickering glare of the pine fire, one hand upon the brick jamb, the other covering his eyes, as if to hide from himself all things that were seen and temporal in order that he might speak face to face with the Eternal.

It was some time before she listened to the words of the prayer. When she heard Ephraim Croom spoken of by name, there was no room in her mind for anything but curiosity. After a while she heard her own name, and curiosity began to subside into awe. After this the preacher brought forward the case of Joseph Smith.

Before the prayer ended Susannah was troubled by so strong a sense of emotion that she desired nothing so much as relief. It seemed to her that the emotion was not so much in herself as in the others, or like an influence in the room pressing upon them all. At length a kitten that had been lying by the hearth got up as if disturbed by the same influence, and, walking round the room, rubbed its fur against Ephraim's knee. She saw the start run through his whole nervous frame. Opening his eyes, he put down his hand and stroked it. Susannah liked Ephraim the better for this. The kitten was not to be comforted; it looked up in his face and gave a piteous mew. Susannah tittered; then she felt sorry and ashamed.

CHAPTER II.

Two quiet years passed, and Susannah had attained her eighteenth birthday.

On a certain day in the week there befell what the aunt called a "season" of baking. It was the only occasion in the week when Mrs. Croom was sure to stay for some length of time in the same place with Susannah beside her. Ephraim brought down his books to the hospitable kitchen, and sat aloof at a corner table. He said the sun was too strong upon his upper windows, or that the rain was blowing in. The first time that Ephraim sought refuge in the kitchen Mrs. Croom was quite flustered with delight. She always coveted more of her son's society. But when he came a third time she began to suspect trouble.

Mrs. Croom stood by the baking-board, her slender hands immersed in a heap of pearly flour; baskets of scarlet currants lay at her feet. All things in the kitchen shone by reason of her diligence, and the windows were open to the summer sunshine. Susannah sat with a large pan of red gooseberries beside her; she was picking them over one by one. Somewhere in the outer kitchen the hired boy had been plucking a goose, and some tiny fragments of the down were floating in the air. One of them rode upon a movement of the summer air and danced before Susannah's eyes. She put her pretty red lips beneath it and blew it upwards.

Mrs. Croom's suspicions concerning Ephraim had produced in her a desire to reprove some one, but she refrained as yet.

Susannah having wafted the summer snowflake aloft, still sat, her young face tilted upward like the faces of saints in the holy pictures, her bright eyes fixed upon the feather now descending. Ephraim looked with obvious pleasure. Her head was framed for him by the window; a dark stiff evergreen and the summer sky gave a Raphaelite setting.

The feather dropped till it all but touched the tip of the girl's nose. Then from the lips, puckered and rosy, came a small gust; the fragment of down ascended, but this time aslant.

"You didn't blow straight enough up," said Ephraim.

Susannah smiled to know that her pastime was observed. The smile was a flash of pleasure that went through her being. She ducked her laughing face farther forward to be under the feather.

Mrs. Croom shot one glance at Ephraim, eager and happy in his watching. She did what nothing but the lovelight in her son's face could have caused her to do. She struck the girl lightly but testily on the side of the face.

Ephraim was as foolish as are most men in sight of a damsel in distress. He made no impartial inquiry into the real cause of trouble; he did not seek Justice in her place of hiding. He stepped to his mother's side, stern and determined, remembering only that she was often unwise, and that he could control her.

"You ought not to have done that. You must never do it again."

With the print of floury fingers on her glowing cheeks the girl sat more astonished than angry, full of ruth when her aunt began to sob aloud.

The mother knew that she was no longer the first woman in her son's love.

It was without doubt, Mrs. Croom's first bitter pang of jealousy that lay at the beginning of those causes which drove Susannah out upon a strange pilgrimage. But above and beyond her personal jealousy was a consideration certainly dearer to a woman into whose inmost religious life was woven the fibre of the partisan. As she expressed it to herself, she agonised before the Lord in a new fear lest her unconverted son should be established in his unbelief by love for a woman who had never sought for heavenly grace; but, in truth, that which she sought was that both should swear allegiance to her own interpretation of grace. In this prayer some good came to her, the willingness to sacrifice her jealousy if need be; but, after the prayer another thought entered into her mind, which she held to be divine direction; she must focus all her efforts upon the girl's conversion. In her heart all the time a still small voice told her that love was the fulfilling of the law, but so still, so small, so habitual was it that she lost it as we lose the ticking of a clock, and it was not with increased love for Susannah that she began a course of redoubled zeal.

The girl became frightened, not so much of her aunt as of God. The simple child's prayer for the keeping of her soul which she had been in the habit of repeating morning and evening became a terror to her, because she did not understand her aunt's phraseology. The "soul" it dealt with was not herself, her thoughts, feelings, and powers, but a mysterious something apart from these, for whose welfare these must all be sacrificed.

Susannah had heard of fairies and ghosts; she inclined to shove this sort of soul into the same unreal region. The dreary artificial heaven, which seemed to follow logically if she accepted the basal fact of a soul separated from all her natural powers, could be dispensed with also. This was her hope, but she was not sure. How could she be sure when she was so young and dependent? It was almost her only solace to interpret Ephraim's silence by her own unbelief, and she rested her weary mind against her vague notions of Ephraim's support.

One August day Mrs. Croom drove with her husband to a distant funeral.

In the afternoon when the sunshine was falling upon the fields of maize, when the wind was busy setting their ribbon-like leaves flapping, and rocking the tree-tops, Ephraim Croom was disturbed in his private room by the blustering entrance of Susannah.

The room was an attic; the windows of the gable looked west; slanting windows in the shingle roof looked north and south. The room was large and square, spare of furniture, lined with books. At a square table in the centre sat Ephraim.

When Susannah entered a gust of wind came with her. The handkerchief folded across her bosom was blown awry. Her sun-bonnet had slipped back upon her neck; her ringlets were tossed.

"Cousin Ephraim, my aunt has gone; come out and play with me." Then she added more disconsolately, "I am lonely; I want you to talk to me, cousin."

The gust had lifted Ephraim's papers and shed them upon the floor.

He looked down at them without moving. Life in a world of thoughts in which his fellows took no interest, had produced in him a singularly undemonstrative manner.

Susannah's red lips were pouting. "Come, cousin, I am so tired of myself."

But Ephraim had been privately accused of amative emotions. Offended with his mother, mortified he knew not why, uncertain of his own feeling, as scholars are apt to be, he had no wish then but to retire.

"I am too busy, Susianne."

"Then I will go alone; I will go for a long, long walk by myself." She gave her foot a defiant stamp upon the floor.

He looked out of his windows north and south; safer district could not be. "I do not think it will rain," he said.

A suspicion of laughter was lurking in his clear quiet eyes, which were framed in heavy brown eyebrows and thick lashes. Nature, who had stinted this man in physical strength, had fitted him out fairly well as to figure and feature.

Susannah, vexed at his indifference, but fearing that he would retract his unexpected permission, was again in the draught of the open door.

"Perhaps I will walk away, away into the woods and never come back; what then?"

"Indians," suggested he, "or starvation, or perhaps wolves, Susianne."

"But I love you for not forbidding me to go, cousin Ephraim."

The smile that repaid him for his indulgence comforted him for an hour; then a storm arose.

In the meantime Susannah had walked far. A squatter's old log-house stood by the green roadside; the wood of the roof and walls was weathered and silver-gray. Before it a clothes-line was stretched, heaved tent-like by a cleft pole, and a few garments were flapping in the wind, chiefly white, but one was vivid pink and one tawny yellow.

The nearer aspect of the log-house was squalid. An early apple-tree at the side had shed part of its fruit, which was left to rot in the grass and collect flies, and close to the road, under a juniper bush, the rind of melons and potato peelings had been thrown. There was no fence; the grass was uncut. Upon the door-step sat a tall woman, unkempt-looking, almost ragged. She had short gray hair that curled about her temples; her face was handsome, clever-looking too, but, above all, eager. This eagerness amounted to hunger. She was looking toward the sky, nodding and smiling to herself.

Susannah stopped upon the road a few feet from the juniper bush. It occurred to her that this was Joseph Smith's mother, who had the reputation of being a speywife. The sky-gazer did not look at her.

"Are you Lucy Smith?"

The woman clapped her hands suddenly together and laughed aloud. Then she rose, but, only glancing a moment at the visitor, she turned her smiling face again toward the sky.

Into Susannah's still defiant mood darted the thought of a new adventure. "Will you tell my fortune?"

"Who am I to tell fortunes when my son Joseph has come home?"

Again came the excited laugh. "It's the grace of God that's fallen on this house, and Lucy Smith, like Elizabeth, the wife of Zacharias, is the mother of a prophet."

"He isn't a prophet," said Susannah, taking a step backward.

"Seven years ago was his first vision, and all the people trampling upon him since to make him gainsay it, but he stood steadfast. I dreamed it—when he was a little child I dreamed it, and it has come true." Then, seeming to return into herself, her gaze wandered again to the sky, and she murmured, "The mother of a prophet, the mother of a prophet!"

On the other side of the road a few acres of ground were lying under disorderly cultivation. In one patch the stalks of sweet maize had been fastened together in high stooks, disclosing the pumpkin vines, which beneath them had plentifully borne their huge fruit, green as yet. At the back of this cultivated portion an old man, the elder Joseph Smith, was digging potatoes; his torn shirt fluttered like the dress of a scarecrow. Behind him and all around was the green wood, close-growing bushes hedging in the short trees of a second growth which covered a long low hill. Above the hill ominous clouds like smoking censers were being rolled up from the east; the waving beards of the corn stooks rustled and streamed in wind which was growing colder. Susannah's dress and bonnet were roughly blown, and the clothes on the line flapped again around the tall figure of the witch in the doorway.

Susannah contradicted again with the scornful superiority of youth. "I don't believe that your son is a prophet."

Lucy Smith, having the sensitive receptive power of an hysteric, was sobered now by the determination of Susannah's aspect. She looked almost repentant for a moment, and then said humbly, "If you'll come in and see Emmar—Joseph and Emmar have come home—Emmar will tell you the same."

A gray vaporous tint was being spread over the heavens, folding this portion of earth in its shadow and darkening the interior of the cabin which Susannah entered.

Upon a decent bedstead reclined a young woman. Everything near her was orderly and clean. She belonged, it would seem, to a better class of the social order than the other, certainly to a higher type of woman-hood.

"What have you got? Is it a kitten?" asked Susannah. Advancing across the dark uneven floor, she perceived that the reclining woman was caressing some small creature beneath her shawl.

"Emmar, Emmar," said Lucy Smith, "tell Miss from the mill about the angel that appeared to Joseph."

Emma Smith was a nobly made, dignified young creature. She looked at Susannah's beautiful and open countenance, and straightway drew forth the young thing she was nursing for her inspection. It was an infant but a few days old. Surprised, reverent, and delighted, Susannah bent over it. The child made them all akin—the squalid old hysteric, the respectable young mother, the beautiful girl in her silken shawl.

Some minutes elapsed.

"Emmar, Miss here doesn't know nothing about Joseph. She says it ain't true."

The young mother smiled frankly. "I suppose it seems very hard for you to believe," she said, "but it's quite true, and the Lord told Joseph where to find the new part of the Bible that he's going now to make known to the world. Shall I tell you about it?"

Susannah looked at her dazed; she had heretofore heard of the Smiths' doctrines as of the ravings of the mad. It had not occurred to her that a sane mind could regard them seriously.

"It was seven years ago," said Emma, "at the time the big revival was here and Joseph was converted; but he heard all the Methodists and Baptists and Presbyterians disputing together as to which of them was right, and he felt so burdened to know which was right, and he felt a sort of longing in him to be a great man, bigger than the revival preacher that had been here that all the people ran after, and Joseph felt that he could be bigger than that, and preach and tell all the people what was right, if they would all come to hear him. And he was so burdened that one day he went out into the woods, and he began crying and confessing his sins and calling out to God to show him what was right and make him a great preacher. Well, when he had been crying and going on like that for a long time, he just fell right down as if he was asleep, and it was all dark till a light fell from heaven and an angel came in the light." Emma went on to tell of Smith's vision and first call, of his backsliding and final commission.

Susannah stared. The young mother was a reality; the baby was a reality. Could the statements in this wild story bear any relation to reality? The old woman stood by, nodding and smiling. The young girl's mind became perplexed.

"It was just before he began to translate the gold book that he came to board at my father's in Susquehannah County, and he told me all about it, and I believed him; but my father wouldn't, so I had to go away with Joseph to get married; but since then father's forgiven us; and we've been back home this last summer, and we've been to Fayette too, living with a gentleman called Mr. Whitmer, who believes in Joseph, and all the time Joseph's been translating the book that was written on the gold plates that he found in the hill. It's been very hard work, and we've had to live very poor, because Joseph couldn't earn anything while he was doing it, but it's done now, so we feel cheered. And now that it's going to be printed, and Joseph can begin to gather in the elect very soon, and now that baby's come—"

Emma stopped again; the last domestic detail seemed to involve her mind in such meshes of bliss that she lost sight of the end of her sentence. All her words had been calm, and the baby that lay upon the bed beside her stretching its crumpled rose-leaf fists into the air and making strange grotesque smiles with its little red chin and cheeks was undoubtedly a true baby, a good and delightful thing in Susannah's estimation. Had the Bible in the hill been a true Bible? Susannah intuitively knew that Emma Smith, bending with grave rapture over her firstborn, was not trying to deceive her.

"It seems to me," she said, "that it is terribly wicked of you to believe about this Bible." Her utterance became thick with her rising indignation. "How can you sit and hold that child and say such terribly wicked things?" She could not have told why she referred to the child; the moment before it was spoken she had not formulated the thought. She was not old enough to reason about the sacredness of babies; she only felt.

The tears started to Emma's eyes. She clasped her child to her breast. "Yes, I know how you feel. I felt that way too myself, and sometimes even yet it frightens me; but, you see, I know it is true, so it must be right. But I've given up expecting other people to believe it just yet, until Joseph is allowed to preach, and then it's been revealed to him that the nations shall be gathered in. Only you looked so—so beautiful—you see, I thought perhaps God might have sent you to be a friend to me. I have no friends because of the way they persecute Joseph."

Susannah turned in incredulous wrath and tramped, young and haughty, to the outer door. The first drops of a heavy shower were falling; she hesitated.

"But tell her about the witnesses, Emmar." Old Lucy stood half-way between the bed and the door, making nods and becks in her excited desire that Susannah should be impressed. "For when the dear Lord saw that folks wouldn't b'lieve Joseph, He didn't leave him without witnesses."

Susannah, stopped by the weather, felt more willing to conciliate. She returned gloomily within the sound of Emma's gentle voice.

"It was Mr. Cowdery and Mr. Whitmer and Mr. Harris," Emma said. "Mr. Cowdery and Mr. Whitmer saw the gold plates held in the air, as it were by hands they couldn't see, but Martin Harris he had to withdraw himself because he couldn't see the vision, and he went away by himself and sobbed and cried. But Joseph went and put his arm around him and prayed that his faith might be strengthened, and then he saw it. So they three have written their testimony in the front of the book that's being printed."

A storm had now broken upon the house in torrents. The door was shut. Emma wrapped her child closer in her shawl. Susannah sat sulky and disconsolate. She had a vague idea that the vengeance of heaven was overtaking her for merely listening to such heresy. Over against this was a shadowy doubt whether it might not be true, roused by Emma's continued persistency.

"Is it any easier to believe that those things happened to folks when the Bible was written? Don't you believe that God appeared to Moses and Samuel and told them the very words to write down, and showed them visions; and isn't He the same God yesterday, today, and for ever? It's just what it says in the Bible shall come about in the latter days. It's because of the great apostasy of the Church, no one really believing in Jesus Christ, that a new prophet had to appear—that's Joseph."

"They do believe," Susannah spoke sullenly.

"Well, there's your aunt, Mis' Croom. Now she's as good as there is in the modern Church, isn't she? She's doing all she can to save her soul. She can't do it, for she don't believe. Why the Lord, He said that signs and wonders should follow them that believe. Have they any signs and wonders up at your place? And He said that believers must forsake all, houses and lands and all; what have your people forsook? And as to its being hard to believe about Joseph—you just take the things in the Bible, Elisha and the bears, for instance, and Paul bringing back Dorcas to life, and just think how hard they'd be to believe if you heard they happened yesterday, next door to you. And with God all times and places is the same. Souls is only saved by believing; the Lord says so, and accepting the things of faith to come to pass, and being baptized and giving up all and following; and it's an awful thing to lose one's soul."

At this reiteration of the doctrine of the soul as a thing apart from the development of reason and character, Susannah rose, ready to cry with anger. Her aunt's agitation on the subject had left a sore to which the gentlest touch was pain.

"I don't believe it," she cried. "I don't believe God wants us to do anything except just good. That's what *my* father told me. I'm going home. I don't care how it rains."

Emma did not hear her. Over her pale young face had come the peculiar expression of alert and loving listening. She had detected the sound of a footstep which Susannah now heard coming heavily near.

A large man of about twenty-five years of age entered from the bluster of the storm. As Susannah was trying to push out past him into its fury, he paused, staring in rough astonishment.

Lucy hung on to her arm. "Stay a bit! Joseph must hold the umbrella over Miss. Emmar, tell her she can't no wise go alone."

Susannah fled into the driving sheets of rain, but Joseph Smith, umbrella in hand, followed her.

CHAPTER III.

The umbrella was a very heavy one. Susannah certainly could not have held it against the wind. Joseph Smith held the shelter between Susannah and the blast, looking at her occasionally with a kindly expression in his blue eyes, but merely to see how far it sheltered her.

They walked in silence for about a quarter of a mile. The rain swept upon her skirt and feet; she saw it falling thick on either side; she saw it beating upon Smith's shoulder, upon one side of his hat, and dripping from his light hair. The wind was so strong that the very drops that trickled from his hair were blown backward. His blue coat was old—not much protection, she thought, against the storm.

The false prophet had hitherto appeared quite as terrible to her imagination and as far removed from real life as the wild beast of story books; now he appeared very much like any other man—rather more kind in his actions, perhaps, and distrait in his thought. Susannah began to think herself a discoverer.

"You are not keeping the rain off yourself."

"It don't matter about me. I don't mind getting wet."

His tone carried conviction. After a while gratitude again stirred her into speech.

"I'm afraid you find it awfully hard holding up the umbrella."

He gave a glance downward at her as she toiled by his side. "Why you're most blown away as it is. You couldn't get along without the umbrellar." Regarding her attentively for a minute, he added, "Emmar will be vexed when she hears that your dress got so splashed."

They were both bending somewhat forward against the wind; the road beneath them was glistening with standing water. When they passed by the woods the trees were creaking and cracking, and over the meadows hung shifting veils of clouds and rain.

"I guess I'd better not take you farther than Sharon Peck's. Your folks would be pretty mad if you walked through the village with Joe Smith."

The lines round Susannah's mouth strengthened themselves; she felt herself superior to those whose attitude of mind he had thus described.

"You have been very kind to come with me. I'd like better to go home than stop, if it isn't too far."

"I guess not. If you'd lived here longer you'd know that there was all manner of evil said about me, and the worst of it is that some of it's true. I've been a pretty low sort of fellow, and I hain't got any education to speak of."

She looked up at him in astonishment; the expression of his face was peaceful and kindly. "Then why do you go about preaching and saying—"

"I hain't got nothing to do with that at all. If an angel comes from heaven and gives me a partic'lar revelation, calling me by name, namely, 'Joseph Smith, Junior,' tain't for me to say he's made a mistake and come to the wrong man, though goodness knows I hev said it to the Lord often enough; but now I've come to see that it's my business just to do what I'm told. But as to the low ways I hed—why, I've repented and give them up, and as to the education, I'm trying to get that, but it won't come in a minute."

Her conscience was not at rest; to be silent was like telling a lie, and from motives of fear, too! At length she burst out, "I don't believe you ever saw an angel, Mr. Smith. I think it's very wicked of you to have made it up, and about the gold Bible too."

They were still half a mile from the nearest house. Susannah gasped. When she had spoken her defiance she realised that if she had nothing worse to fear, she at least deserved to be left alone among the raging elements. She staggered somewhat, expecting a rebuff.

"I guess you'd better take my arm," he said. "It ain't no sort of a day for a woman to be out."

When she hesitated, flushed and frightened, a smile came for the first time across his face. "You're almost beat back by the wind. It won't hurt you to grip hold of my sleeve, you know, even if I am a thundering big liar. I don't know as I can expect you to believe anything else. Emmar didn't for a long time, but then, after a spell, she gave up all the comforts of her father's house just to stand by me, and no one's ever had a word to say against Emmar."

They stopped at a farmhouse on the outskirts of the village.

Smith had said to Susannah, "There's a gentleman I know stopping at Sharon Peck's. I'll pass the umbrellar on to him, and he'll take you home. He's been a Quaker, but I guess you'll find him a pretty nice young gentleman. Mrs. Peck, she isn't to home."

He left Susannah standing upon the lee side of a wooden house amid treeless fields. The eaves sheltered her. She stooped down and with both hands wrung the water from her skirts. She was busy over this when the promised escort joined her.

The remnants of his forsaken Quakerism hung around him; his coat was buff, his hat straight in the brim, his manner prim, and when he spoke it was in the speech of his people. His complexion was very light, hair, eyebrows and lashes, and the down on his chin—almost flaxen; his face was browned by exposure to the weather, but so well formed that Susannah found him very good to look upon, the features pointed and delicate, but not without strength.

"Thou wilt walk as far as thy home with me?" he asked.

He held Smith's huge umbrella, but he did not hold it with the same strength, nor did he show the same skill in keeping it against the wind.

He spoke as they walked. "Thou hast walked a long way. Art weary?"

"Yes—no—I don't know." What did it matter whether she was tired or not? Baffled curiosity was exciting her. "You are a stranger here. Are you a friend of the Smiths?"

"I have experienced the great benefit of being acquainted with the prophet for the last fourteen days."

"But he's not a prophet," said Susannah resentfully.

"Did'st thou never find thyself to be mistaken when thou wast most sure? Hast thou not perceived that thy Bible tells thee in many different ways that God chooses not as men choose?"

Then with great ardour he preached to her the doctrine of this new Christian sect. He was a convert; his preaching was rather the eager recital of his own experience, which would out, like some dynamic force within him, than pressure brought wilfully to bear upon her.

He said, "I do not ask thee, friend, if thou art Methodist or Baptist or Presbyterian, but I do ask thee, canst thou read the promises of thy Lord to his church and be content with its present low estate?"

Susannah was habituated to some recognition of her beauty; she missed it here, not knowing what she missed. Smith had known that it was important for her to be sheltered from the wind; he was sorry that her skirts were splashed; his manner, casual as it had been, had at least had in it that element of "because you are you," the first essential of any human relationship. But Susannah liked the young Quaker much better than Smith; he was of finer fibre, and her heart was agape for young companionship; so, unconsciously, she resented his indifference, not only as to her sect but as to her sex.

"My father was an Englishman," she replied with dignity, not knowing why this seemed sufficient answer.

The Quaker proceeded eagerly with his own story. He had searched the Scriptures diligently, and found in them no warrant for believing that the age of miracles and direct revelations would ever pass from the church. Then upon the gloom of his deep despondency a star had arisen. He had heard of a young man, poor, obscure, illiterate, who had dared to come forth saying again, as St. Peter had once said, "This is that which was spoken by the prophet Joel." He had come far to hear the word, and, upon hearing it, he had found rest for himself and a hope for the world.

His ardour was beginning to tell upon Susannah's mind. The desire awoke within her for some fellowship with his enthusiasm. Stronger was the desire to receive personal recognition from the fair-faced youth.

"I am English," she repeated, "and of course I think it very wicked to add anything to the Bible; it says so in the Revelation."

"That to me also was a stumbling-block for a short time; but if thou wilt consider, friend, that the Book of Mormon is the history of God's dealing with the wild races of our own continent from the time of Noah until the time of Maroni, which would be about three hundred years after the first coming of the Lord, and that this sacred history, so necessary for the instruction of us who must now dwell in the same land, could not be given until this continent was known to the world, thou wilt cease to cavil, and wilt in all humility believe that that which is done of the hand of the Lord cannot be wrong."

Faith begging the question is a sight to which the eye of experience becomes accustomed, but Susannah, standing upon the threshold of life, blinked and failed to focus her vision, feeling vaguely that during the last phrase some one had turned a somersault, and that too quickly to be watched.

"Thou wilt think upon these things?" The young Quaker stood in the storm and looked earnestly upon Susannah, who was upon her uncle's doorstep, within shelter of the brown pent house.

Susannah smiled. It was a perfectly instinctive smile, not one self-conscious thought went behind or before. She smiled because the young man was comely, and because she was young and wanted companionship.

"I don't know," she said with perfect frankness; "my aunt will be so vexed with me when she hears that I've been to the Smiths that I don't believe I'll be allowed to think of anything this good while."

Her smile, her girlishness, seemed at last to pierce beneath the armour of his devout abstraction. Fortune at work chooses her a fine-edged instrument, and Joseph Smith, with unerring but probably half conscious instinct, had sent the right messenger. The cloud of serious intent on the youth's face broke now into a sudden admiring glance, half playful yet fully earnest. His gray eyes held for a moment gracious parley with hers. "Wilt thou," he asked, still smiling, "give it as excuse in the day of judgment that they would not let thee think?"

"N-n-no." She was more struck with the inadequacy of the excuse than with the fact that she had a better one if she had chosen to give it.

He was again grave, but he was not now unappreciative. "Thou art very fair, and beauty to a young woman is, no doubt, a great snare. I will wrestle in prayer for thee."

He was going down the brick walk between the masses of drenched flowers. "Don't," cried Susannah faintly, "don't do that." But he did not hear her.

CHAPTER IV.

The wind that in the hurly-burly out of doors had been a cheerful if boisterous enemy, seemed suddenly transformed into a wailing spirit when Susannah was making her way up the stairs of the darkening wooden house. Its master and mistress had not yet returned from burying the dead. The girl made her way up to Ephraim's room. The books were left open upon the table; no one was there.

It was a new thing that Ephraim should breast a storm.

Susannah trudged downstairs again and dried her bedraggled skirts at the fire—an empty house, a dreary wailing wind, and gathering twilight for her sole companions.

At length a step was heard. Ephraim came in bearing Susannah's rain cloak and goloshes. He was wet, pale, and breathless, but he would not betray his weakness and excitement by a word.

"You were looking for me, Ephraim, and some one told you that I had come home. Did you hear who brought me? O Ephraim! I have been out walking with the false prophet, and then with one of his disciples." Susannah, sitting by the fire, looked at him trying to smile through his gloom.

She began again, then stopped; how to impart the full flavour of that which had befallen her she did not know. It seemed to her that the difficulty lay in Ephraim's silence. She was not aware that she had not even a distinct thought for a certain interest in her late companion which she most wanted to put into words. "Ephraim, it's all very well for you to stand there drying your feet, but—but—they were just like other people, as you told Mr. Finney, you know."

"Did you expect them to have horns and tails?"

"I don't think they are very wicked," said Susannah. She looked down as she said it, speaking with a certain undefined tenderness of tone begotten of a new experience.

"Well?"

"That's all."

"How could you know whether they are wicked or not?" he burst out angrily. "Do you suppose that they would show *you* the iniquity of their hearts?"

"Why, Ephraim, you've always stood up for them before!"

He gave a sort of snort. "I never stood up for them by making eyes at my hands and cooing out my words."

She looked up in entire bewilderment.

"It doesn't matter what I mean," he added. "What did they say? What did they do? Tell me. If I'd known these fellows had come back, do you suppose I'd have let you go?"

"You are so strange," she said. "They did nothing but just bring me home and hold the umbrella, and Joseph Smith said he knew he'd been a bad man and didn't know anything. I thought you'd be interested to hear about them, Ephraim."

"I should have thought you'd had too much self-respect to allow him to talk to you like that. Of course he was trying to work on your feelings."

"No, he wasn't, Ephraim. You are quite as unjust as my aunt today. He wasn't trying to work on my feelings. He was just—well, he was sorry that my frock got so wet, and he just happened to say the other thing. I am sure—"

Her conviction concerning the naturalness of Smith's conduct and the Quaker's sincerity had arisen in the presence of each, and was not now to be ascribed to any particular word or action which she could remember and repeat.

"Oh, he was sorry your frock was splashed, was he? And the other fellow they call Halsey, was he concerned about that too?"

"Who told you that his name was Halsey?" The interest of her tone was unmistakable.

"That is his name, and he must be a degraded fellow to take up with Smith."

She saw that Ephraim's clothes were very wet; he must have walked far. She attributed his exhausted look entirely to fatigue, and his ill-temper to the same cause. "Mr. Halsey seemed quite good and in earnest, like the people that come to see Mr. Finney when he stays here, asking about saving their souls, as if their souls were something quite different from the other part of them; and, Ephraim, I have often wanted to ask you, but I didn't like to. You don't believe what aunt and uncle do, do you? Aunt talks as if you didn't believe. Do you think"—her voice trembled—"do you think that I ought to think about my soul—that way?"

Ephraim never perceived the nature of her difficulty. He thought she questioned the earnestness of life. He leaned back against the jamb of the chimney, vainly trying to dispel his anger and bring his mind under the command of reason. He looked at Susannah steadily; she was somewhat pale with weariness and excitement; she could never be other than beautiful. How perfect was the moulding of the strong firm chin, of the curving nostrils! The breadth of the cheek bone, the height and breadth of the brow, beautiful as they were in their pink and white tinting, conveyed to him almost more strongly the sense of mental completeness than of outward beauty. He did not dare to look at her questioning eyes; his glance travelled over the amber ringlets, damp and tossed just now, drooping as if to say "Susannah is lonely and perplexed, and she needs your help." Ephraim, proud, and mortified to think how ill he compared with her, laughed fiercely within himself. This was a young woman of distinction, and just now she knew it so little that she sat looking up with respect at his ill-conditioned self. How long would that last? How long would she remember any word that he chanced to say to her?

"Susannah, I think you are very ignorant. Were you never taught anything when you were a little girl?"

"My father and his friends were always polite to me." She spoke with grave, rather than offended, dignity.

"She is entirely sweet," he said to himself; "she will never answer me in anger." Then he went on aloud, "And I am not polite; I am ill-trained and ill-bred. Well, listen, Susannah. Whatever my mother may or may not tell you about my peculiar opinions, whatever *I* choose to believe or to do, remember this, that I tell you that *you have* a soul to be eternally lost or saved, and it behoves you to walk carefully and concern yourself about

THE MORMON PROPHET ☞ 25

your salvation." There was a vibration of intense warning in his voice. He was thinking of the life that might be so noble if will and reason sided with God, and of the snares that the world lays for beauty, and the light way in which beauty might walk into them; and, as with all dreamy minds, he was too absorbed in his thought to know how little it shone through the veil in which he wrapped it.

Susannah grew a shade paler. She had struggled in a blind child-fashion to maintain a religion that would embrace her manifold life, but now it appeared that, after all, Ephraim endorsed the general view; his refusal to comply openly with it came of wilfulness, not unbelief. The stronghold of her peace was gone. "My papa never spoke to me about religion in that way, but I don't think he believed that."

Ephraim thought of the weak and reckless young father, of the careless life broken suddenly by death.

"He has learned the truth now," he said shortly.

After a pause, in which she did not speak, he betook himself to his own rooms, leaving Susannah to the companionship of the lonely house, the howling wind, the gathering night, and a new fear of a state eternal and infernal, into which she might so easily slip. Ephraim said so, and he would never have proclaimed what he would not comply with unless its truth were very sure.

As for him, his self-despite was pain that rendered him oblivious of her real danger. Where was his boasted justice? Gone before a breath of jealousy. The neighbours had told him that she had smiled on Halsey, and the abuse of the Smithites, in which his mother indulged in the blindness of religious party-spirit, had fallen from his lips as soon as his own passion had been touched. Had his former candour, then, been the thing his mother called it, *indifference* to, rather than reverence for truth?

This was the travail of soul that Susannah could have as little thought of as he had of hers. It held Ephraim in its fangs for many days.

CHAPTER V.

The return of Smith and his few followers, and the speedy publication of the first edition of the Book of Mormon, stirred anew the flames of religious excitement. All other sects were at one in decrying "the Mormons," as they now began to be called by their enemies. There was perhaps good reason for intelligent disapprobation, but Understanding was left far behind the flying feet of Zeal, who, torch in hand, rushed from house to house. It was related that Joseph Smith was in the habit of wounding inoffensive sheep and leading them bleeding over the neighbouring hills under the pretext that treasure would be found beneath the spot where they would at last drop exhausted; and there were dark hints concerning benighted travellers who, staying all night at the Smiths' cabin, had seen awful apparitions and been glad to fly from the place, leaving their property behind. There was a story of diabolical influence which Smith had exercised in order to gain the young wife whom he had stolen from her father's roof, and, worse than all, there were descriptions of occult rites carried on in secret places, where the most bloody mysteries of the Mosaic priesthood were horribly travestied by Smith and his friends, Cowdery and Rigdon, in order to dupe the simple into belief in the new revelation.

Ephraim Croom had again withdrawn himself out of hearing of the controversy. Judging that Susannah was sufficiently guarded by his parents to be safe, he became almost oblivious of conversation which he despised. He did not reflect that Susannah knew nothing of his hidden conflict, that she could only perceive that, after uttering an ominous warning, he had left her to work out its application alone.

It was at first not at all her liking for the Smiths, but only her unbiassed common sense, which convinced her that the wild stories told concerning them were untrue. When she became enraged at their untruth she became more kindly disposed toward the young mother, whose baby had made a strong appeal to her girlish heart, and the big kindly lout of a man who had sheltered her from the rain. This benevolent disposition might have slumbered unfruitful but for the memory of the fine and resolute face of the young disciple who had promised to wrestle in prayer for her. There was novelty in the thought. The gay witch Novelty often apes the form of Love. Susannah did not know Love, so she did not recognise even the vestments falsely worn, but they attracted her all the same. Her young blood boiled when her aunt, dimly discerning some unlooked-for obstinacy in her niece's mind, repeated each new report in disfavour of the Mormons. It was the old story about the blood of the martyrs, for ridicule and slander spill the pregnant blood of the soul; but they who believe themselves to be of the Church can seldom believe that any blood but their own will bear fruit. Every stab given to the reputation of the Smiths was an appeal to Susannah's sympathy for them. Mrs. Croom, with a sense of solemn responsibility, was at great cost bringing all her influence to bear upon the young girl whom her son loved. She drearily said to herself, after many days, that her influence was weak, that it accomplished nothing. The strength of it pushed Susannah, who stood faltering at the parting of the ways, and the impetus of that push was felt in her rapid and unsteady step for many and many a year.

One day, when the men were out cutting the maize, Susannah rode with her uncle to the most distant of his fields, and found herself on the hill called in Smith's revelation Cumorah.

The sound of the men at work and the horses shaking their harness was close in her ears while she strayed over this bit of hilly woodland. It is one of the low ridges that intersect the meadows on the banks of the Canandaigua, and here Smith professed to have found the golden book. It was because of this that Susannah had the curiosity to climb it now.

The beech wood grew thick upon it; the afternoon sun struck its slant sunbeams across their boles. Once, where the beeches parted, she came upon a fairy glade where two or three maples, fading early, had carpeted the ground with a mosaic of gold and red, and were holding up the remainder of their foliage, pink and yellow, in the light. The beauty wrought in her a dreamy receptive mood. Climbing higher, she came upon a very curious dip or hollow in the ground. In its narrowest part a man was lying prostrate; his face was buried in his hat, which was lying upon the ground between his hands; the whole expression of his body was that of attention concentrated upon something within the hat. When she came close he moved with a convulsive start, and she saw that it was Joseph Smith.

His look changed into one of deference and satisfaction. He rose up, lifting his hat carefully; in it lay a curious stone composed of bright crystals, in shape not unlike a child's foot.

"It's my peepstone," he said. "It's the stone I look into when I pray that I may be shown what to do." Exactly as one child might show to another some worthless object he deemed choice, he showed the stone to her.

"I don't know what you mean. How could a stone help you?"

"All I know is that when I've been lying for a long time, feeling that I'm a poor fellow and haven't got no sense anyway, and the tears come to my eyes and gush out, feeling I'm so poor and mean, then when I lie and look and look into this peepstone, I see things in it, pictures of things that is to be, and sometimes of things that are just happening alongside of me that I didn't know any other way. I can't say how it may be; I only know when I see it that I am 'accounted worthy.'"

"You couldn't see anything in the stone."

"No more I couldn't. The stone's nothing, an' I'm nothing, and that's why, when I do see the pictures, I know it must be either God or the devil that sends them; and it's not the devil, for I always work myself up to a mighty lot of praying first, and why should the pictures come after that if it was the devil?"

"What do you see?"

"I'll tell you one thing I have seen. Mebbe you'll know what it means; mebbe you won't. I don't know myself rightly yet. I've often to study on those things a long while before I know what they mean, but lately I've seen you."

"Me?"

"Yes, you, miss. The things I see are like small tiny pictures inside the stone. Your bonnet was off. You were inside a room. There was tables and chairs, and there was a man there. He wasn't very old; he had light hair."

"What had he to do with me?" she asked, astonished.

"I just saw you stand there, and him a-sitting, but a voice in my own heart seemed to say—"

"What?"

"It was one of my revelations. If I tell you, you won't believe it. Howsomever, I think it's my duty to tell you, although you may tell your folks, and they may persecute me." He paused here, and when he began again it was in a different tone of voice and with a singing cadence. "The voice said, 'I say unto thee, she shall see the white stone, and shall be told the thing that she shall do for the salvation of her soul; and I say unto thee, Joseph Smith junior, that thou shalt say unto her to look upon the stone, for she is chosen to go through suffering and grief for a little space, and after that to have great riches and honour, and in the world to come life everlasting.'"

As he spoke he was holding up the stone, which glistened in the sunlight, before her eyes.

Susannah stared at it to prove to herself that there was nothing remarkable about it. The feeling of opposition seemed to die of itself, and then she had a curious sensation of arousing herself with a start from a fixed posture and momentary oblivion. That afternoon as she was going home, and in the following days, phrases and sentences from the prophecy which Joseph Smith had pronounced in regard to her clung to her mind. In disdain she tried to tell herself that the man was mad; in childlike wonder she considered what might be the mystery of the vision within the stone and the prophecy if he were not mad. She had never heard of crystal-gazing; the phrase "mental automatism" had not then been invented by the psychologists; still less could she suspect that she herself might have come partially under the influence of hypnotic suggestion. The large kindliness of the new prophet, the steady sobriety and childlikeness of his demeanour, the absence of any appearance of policy or premeditation, were not in harmony with fraud or madness. Her gentle intelligence was puzzled, as all the candid historians of this man have since been puzzled. Then, tired of the puzzle, she fell again to contemplating scraps of his speech, which, having a Scriptural sound, suggested piety. "She shall be told the thing that she shall do for the salvation of her soul," "She is chosen to go through suffering and grief for a little space." How strange if, impossible as it might seem, these words had come to her—to her—direct from the mind of the Almighty!

CHAPTER VI.

Some days after this Susannah sat alone at the window of the family room, the long white seam on which she was at work enveloping her knees.

Far off on the horizon the cumulous clouds lay with level under-ridges, their upper outlines softly heaped in pearly lights and shades of dun and gray. Beneath them the hilly line of the forest was broken distinctly against the cloud by the spikes of giant pines. That far outline was blue, not the turquoise blue of the sky above the clouds, but the blue that we see on cabbage leaves, or such blue as the moonlight makes when it falls through a frosted pane—steel blue, so full of light as to be luminous in itself. From this the nearer contour of the forest emerged, painted in green, with patches and streaks of russet; the nearer groves were beginning to change colour, and, vivid in the sunlight, the fields were yellow. From the top of a low hill which met the sky came the white road winding over rise and hollow till it passed the door. Who has not felt the invitation, silent, persistent, of a road that leads through a lonely land to the unseen beyond the hill?

Susannah was again alone in the house; this time Ephraim was absent with his mother, and her uncle was at the mill. On the white road she saw a man approaching whose dress showed him to be Smith's Quaker convert, Angel Halsey, a name she had conned till it had become familiar. He did not pass, but opened the gate of the small garden path and came up between the two borders of sweet-smelling box. In the garden China asters, zenias, and prince's feather, dahlias, marigolds, and love-lies-bleeding were falling over one another in luxuriant waste. The young man neither looked to night nor to left. He scanned the house eagerly, and his eyes found the window at which Susannah sat. He stepped across the flowers and stood, his blonde face upturned, below the open sash. Under his light eyebrows his hazel eyes shone with a singularly bright and exalted expression.

"Come, friend Susannah," said he, "I have been sent to bring you to witness my baptism," and with that he turned and walked slowly down the path, as if waiting for her to follow.

Susannah, filled with surprise, watched him as he made slowly for the gate, as if assured that she would come. When he got to it he set it open, and, holding it, looked back.

She dropped the long folds of muslin, and they fell upon the floor knee-deep about her; she stepped out of them and walked across the old familiar living-room, with its long strips of worn rag-carpet, its old polished chairs, and smoky walls. The face of the eight-day clock stared hard at her with impassive yet kindly glance, but its voice only steadily recorded that the moments were passing one by one, like to all other moments.

Susannah went out of the door. The sun drew forth aromatic scent from the borders of box, and her light skirt brushed the blossoms that leaned too far over. Outside the wicket gate at which the young man stood was a young quince tree laden with pale-green fruit. Susannah let her eyes rest upon it as she spoke: she even let her mind wander for a second to think how soon the fruit would be gathered.

"Why should I come to see your baptism?" she asked, with her voice on the upward cadence.

The young man blushed deeply. "I am come to thee with a message from heaven." He glanced upward to the great sky that was the colour of turquoise, cloudless, serene.

"It is a strange errand." There was a touch of reproof in her voice, and yet also the vibration of awe-struck inquiry. Her mind rushed at once to the memory of Joseph Smith's prophecy.

"Come, friend," said the young Quaker very gently.

"I can't possibly go."

His strange reply was, "With God all things are possible."

The text fell upon her mind with force.

"Come," he said gently, and he motioned that he would shut the gate behind her.

"Not now; my shoes are not stout; I have no bonnet or shawl."

"Put thy kerchief over thy head and come, friend Susannah, for 'no man, putting his hand to the plough, and looking back, is fit for the kingdom of heaven.'"

At this he walked on, and she was forced to follow for a few steps to ask an explanation. She tied her kerchief over her head and the thick white dust covered her slender shoes.

"What do you want me to come for?" she asked.

He looked upon her, colouring again with the effort to express what was to him sacred. "It has been given to me to pray for thy soul. Today, as I prayed, it was borne in upon me that thou shouldst be with me in the waters of baptism."

Susannah paused on the road, planting the heels of her shoes deeply in the dust. "I will not," she cried. "I will never believe in Joseph Smith."

"And yet it has been revealed, friend, that thou art one of the elect. The time will come very soon when thou wilt believe to the salvation of thy soul."

He walked slowly onward, and after a minute Susannah, with quickened steps, followed him, in high anger now. "I do not believe in the revelations of Joseph Smith," she cried. And because he did not appear offended she spoke more rudely, catching at phrases to which she had become accustomed. "If the salvation of my soul should depend upon it, I would rather lose it than believe."

But when she had said these last words a little gasp came in her breath, and her heart quailed in realising the possibility of which she had spoken. Her own angry words had diverted her attention from questioning the reasonableness of the new faith to the fearful contemplation of what might be the result of rejection.

If she quailed at her own speech, the grief of the young Quaker was more obvious. He put up his hands as if in fear that she should add to her sin by repeating her words. Quiet as was his demeanour, the emotional side of his nature had evidently been deeply wrought upon today, for when he tried to speak to reprove her, grief choked his utterance. It was not at that time a strange thing for men under the influence of religious convictions to weep easily. On the contrary, it was accounted by evange-lists a sign of great grace; but Susannah, accustomed only to the reserve of English gentlemen and her uncle's stern Puritan self-repression, seeing this young Quaker weep for her sake, was greatly touched. She became possessed by an excited desire to console him.

The young man turned, weeping as he went, into a little wood that here bordered the road. Susannah followed, full of ruth, thinking that he merely sought temporary shade.

They had proceeded under the trees a few paces when Emma Smith came up from the bank of the river to meet them. Halsey controlled him-self and spoke to Emma.

"She has refused. For this time she has rejected the truth."

Now to Susannah the matter for amazement was that she had come so far from home (although, it was not very far), that she had actually arrived, as it seemed, at an appointed place. The sting that this gave to her pride was greatly eased by perceiving that she had not by this fulfilled his hopes.

Emma Smith had a pale, patient face, which was at this time made peculiarly dignified by a look of solemn excitement. Young as she was, she turned to Susannah with a protecting motherly air.

"Perhaps next time the opportunity is offered the young lady will embrace it and save her soul." She spoke consolingly to Halsey, but looked at Susannah with encouraging and respectful eyes. "You will see this young man baptized?" she asked.

Under the protection of Emma Smith, Susannah stooped under the willow boughs and found herself upon the bank of the river in the pres-ence of Joseph Smith, his mother, and some half-dozen men.

Lucy Smith was muttering somewhat concerning a vision of angels, and the suppressed excitement of them all was manifest. Susannah was infected by it; she was now tremulous and eager to see what was to be seen.

Joseph Smith advanced into the flowing river and stood in a pool where the water was well up to his thighs. Standing thus, he began to speak in the same formal tone and with the same solemn expression that Susannah had marked when he spoke the revelation concerning herself, but more loudly. "Behold! we have gathered together according to the revelation which has been given to me—"

Here a dark young man called Oliver Cowdery groaned and said "Amen." A tremble of excitement went through the group upon the shore.

Loudly the prophet went on—"Knowing well that there is nothing in me, who was wicked and graceless to a very high degree, and wanting in knowledge, but was yet chosen, upon this sinful earth and in these last days, when wickedness and hypocrisy is abounding, to open to all who would be saved a new church which is such as that which the angel hath revealed to me a church should be, and all them which shall receive my word and shall be baptized of me or of Mr. Oliver Cowdery, whom the angel Maroni, descending in a cloud of light, has ordained with me to the priesthood of Aaron, which holds the keys of the ministering of angels and of the gospel of repentance and of baptism by immersion for the remission of sins. And this shall never again be taken from the earth until the sons of Levi do offer again an offering unto the Lord in the new Jerusalem."

The loud voice carried with it an impression of strong personal feeling; the effect on the bystanders was such as the words alone were wholly inadequate to produce. Cowdery, who during the speech had frequently groaned and responded, after the Methodist fashion, now shouted and clapped his hands towards the heavens, whereupon Lucy Smith fell into a convulsive state between laughter and tears, and the men standing beside her dropped upon their knees. Emma Smith remained standing; upon her face was a rapt triumphant expression. She put her arm round Susannah protectingly, and Susannah did not repulse the familiar action.

Joseph Smith now in the same voice called upon his father to be baptized. He addressed him formally as "Joseph Smith senior." The old man had, as it seemed, a great fear of the water. It took both priests of the new sect together to lift and immerse him. There was more splashing than was seemly. The baptism of a farmer named Martin Harris, which followed, was more decorous.

The sunlight lay bright on the other side of the flowing river, and the shadow of the willow tops above them was outlined on the stream. On the sunny bank opposite there was a thicket of sumac trees reddening to the autumn heat; the wild vine was climbing upon them, making their foliage the more dense, and at their roots, by the edge of the stream, the golden rod was massed. On the bank on which they stood the colouring was more quiet. A few ragged spikes of the purple aster were all that grew under the gray green willows, which with every breath turned the silver underside of their soft foliage to the wind. The place for the baptism had no doubt been chosen because of the depth of the water, and because the bank here was comparatively bare.

It was about four o'clock in the afternoon. The steady sound of the mattock in a neighbouring field was the only token of the common bustling world that lay close around the curious isolation of the hour.

It was time that Angel Halsey should be baptized. In his Quaker clothes he waded into the water. His manner now was entirely serene, his face full of joy.

A thought was struck wedge-like into Susannah's understanding. If Halsey, who was so manifestly on a higher plane of education and refinement than these others, could so triumphantly embrace the new faith, it must surely contain more of virtue and reason than she could see. The influence of what he was, being so much greater than the influence of what he had said, caused her mind to work with solemn earnestness as she followed him in sympathy through the symbol of death and resurrection.

When the prophet came back to the shore he appeared for the first time to recognise Susannah, and stopped before her, but at first with a distraught manner, as if he were trying to recollect some dream that eluded him. He still had his hand familiarly on Halsey's arm, for he had been conducting him out of the water.

"This is the elect sister?" Smith asked in a hesitating tone, as if still striving with memory. "Does she desire baptism?"

"Not yet," answered Halsey, "but I have asked the Lord for her soul, and I believe that it has been given."

In Halsey's mind up to this moment there was, no doubt, only the solicitude of the missionary spirit; but Smith was a man whose mind was cast in a different mould; he had already marked the solicitude and given it his own interpretation, and he had already opened his own eyes upon her beauty. How far this had conscious connection with the condition of actual trance into which he now fell cannot be known. It is probable that what the Psalmist calls the "secret parts" are not in such minds as Smith's open to the man's own eye.

Smith became wrapped in a sudden ecstasy. Oblivious of all around him, he looked up into the heavens, and it was apparent that his eyes were not beholding the material objects around. Those about him gazed awestruck, waiting and listening, for he began to speak in a low unknown tongue, as if holding converse with some one above.

Susannah shrank back, but was held by Emma's encouraging arm. Halsey stayed perforce, for the prophet's grasp had tightened convulsively upon him.

In a few moments the vision was over, and Joseph Smith opened his eyes and smiled in his own slow kindly way upon the frightened girl and upon Angel Halsey, who stood with steadfast mien.

"It has been revealed to me in heaven that the soul of the elect sister is indeed given to be united to the soul of this young disciple, that thereby she may obtain salvation."

He took Susannah's hand, and she felt no power to resist him; he clasped Halsey's almost more timid and reluctant hand over it.

"Wherefore in the sight of God and in the sight of these elect saints now present I declare that these two are joined together in the mystical union of a most holy marriage which God himself has revealed from heaven."

For some moments Susannah gazed fascinated; then she snatched away her hand; dignity sought to maintain itself; pride rose up in anger. Her growing awe of the prophet numbed to a certain extent both these sentiments, but stronger than pride and self-respect and awe was some tender shame within her heart which was hurt beyond enduring, so that she put her hands before her face and wept, and walked away from them weeping, followed by Emma, who began, as they walked, to weep in sympathy.

Tears bring relief to the brain, a relief it is hard to distinguish from comfort of soul. When Susannah could check her unaccustomed sobs, when she found herself walking quietly homeward with only the weeping Emma by her side, the spirit of long suffering and patience stole upon her unawares.

"Why do you cry?" she asked gently.

"I think it must be so hard for you," said Emma; "it's been very hard for me, although I love Joseph with all my heart; but you are so childish and so good-looking, it seems someways as if it came harder on you; and then that Mr. Halsey hasn't got the warmth of heart that Joseph has."

To this astonishing reply Susannah found no answer. Emma was too respectable, too honest in her sympathy, to be derided, but Susannah's understanding could ill endure the thought that the incident of the hour was important. As the outcome of honest delusion, she might forgive it; something in the pathos of Halsey's strained face as she remembered his look when she turned away weeping, urged her to forgiveness.

"Mr. Halsey is nothing to me," said Susannah at last; she spoke with a falter in her voice, for Emma's unfeigned grief touched her.

"Oh! don't say that. Some judgment might come on you that would be worse than any suffering that would come from obedience to the word of the Lord; and besides, it's the will of God, you see; and of course He'll see that it's done, so you'd be punished for rebellion, and you'd have to obey all the same."

Susannah was beginning to be infected by this steady assumption that God had indeed spoken. Could it be possible?

CHAPTER VII.

How much better humanity might have been had we been at the world's making we cannot tell, but as it is, the Creator knows that a woman whose veins are pulsing with youth does not know, as she stands between her lovers, how far influences not born of reason are affecting her understanding. Ephraim remained neglectful, and Susannah remembered with more and more distinct compassion Halsey's wistful face and the touch of his trembling hand. But the emotion which is deeper than human love was also in ferment. The shock which she had received, aided by the pressure at home, had effectually worked religious unrest. She was certain now that she must do some new thing to obtain peace with God. Long monotonous days ripened within her this altered mind.

On one of the warm days that fell at the end of the apple harvest, when such vagrant labourers as had collected to help the farmers were loitering at liberty, Smith held his first and last public meeting in the place where his boyhood had been passed. It was near the cross-roads on the old highroad to Palmyra, where a small wooden bridge carries over a creek that runs through the meadow to the Canandaigua. Here in the leisure time of the afternoon Smith lifted up his voice and preached to an ever-increasing crowd, composed first of men, and added to by whole families from most of those houses within touch of the village.

The elder Croom, his wife, and Susannah were returning from the weekly shopping at Palmyra's store; they came upon the crowd, and stopped perforce. Wrath was upon the faces of the elder couple, and nothing less than terror upon Susannah's white cheeks.

Susannah would have run far to have been saved the awful interrogation of opportunity. Perhaps all that she knew just then, in her childlike bewilderment, was that the slanders of the persecution were wrong, and her untrained mind jumped to the conclusion that the God of truth must therefore be with Smith. Beyond this there was unnamed wonder at the influence that Smith held over her, and more curious thoughts, stretching out like the delicate tendrils of an unsupported vine, concerning Halsey, his prayers and warnings, and the strength of selfless devotion that she had read in his innocent eyes.

Old Croom, deacon and magistrate, was not one to tarry at such a gathering longer than need be. When he perceived that some of the planks of the bridge had been taken to support the dam he alighted and broke down a log fence in order to drive his horses through meadow and stream to join the road nearer home. His women must needs walk over the scanty beams. Mrs. Croom, stately and well attired, could make her way through the crowd; no one there was so rapt but that he let her pass when, with eyes flashing in righteous indignation, she tapped him on the shoulder and bid him stand aside. Susannah followed in her aunt's wake, the crowd of neighbours and strange labourers closing behind them again as they worked their way, of necessity slowly, nearer and nearer the preacher and the little band of adherents that stood steadfast around him.

Susannah heard the words of the sermon in which open confession of his own past sin, bold persuasions to Christianity and righteousness, were strangely mingled with the claim of the new prophet. She could not remember one moment what he had said the last. Low hisses and muttered threats of the angry men about her fell on her ears in the same way, making their own impression, but not on reason or memory. A sickening dread of a call that would come before she got away was all that she fully realised. It came when, in her white gala dress, she stood still at last near to, and under the eye of, the preacher.

The sermon was finished. There was a silence at its end so unexpected that none in the crowd broke it. It seemed for those moments to reach not only into the hearts of the crowd, but into the wide, empty vault of sunny blue above them, and over the open fields and golden woods. Then, before the wrath of the crowd had gathered strength to break into violence, Smith went down into the water and called loudly to all such as felt the need of saving their souls to enter upon the heavenly pilgrimage by the gate of his baptism. His adherents had cast themselves upon their knees in prayer. Susannah saw the strong, dark face of Oliver Cowdery looking up to the sky as though he saw the heavens opened, and she saw Angel Halsey look at herself, and then, clasping his hands over his fair young face, bow himself in supplication.

A man, ragged in dress, and bearing the look of ill deeds in his face, made his way out of the crowd into the water. He was a stranger to the place, and the spectators looked on in silent surprise. Before Smith had dipped him in the stream and blessed him another man came forward, pale and thin, with a hectic flush upon his cheeks. He was a well-known resident of Manchester; all knew that his days on earth must be few. A low howl began to rise, loudest on the outskirts of the crowd, but the fact that the man was dying kept many silent, feeling that the doomed may surely have their own will.

Before Joseph Smith had spoken his benediction over this trembling, gasping creature, when Halsey had left his kneeling to spring forward and lead him to the shore, Susannah began to move forward to the water. No one who saw her move at first dreamed of what she sought. Her aunt had pushed on some distance farther and stood waiting, almost too astonished at this last baptism to notice that she was separated from her charge. Now, when she saw Susannah pushing forward, she only wondered with others what she would be at, and spoke to her ineffectually, without the shriek and struggle which she made when the girl was beyond her reach.

So Susannah, moving like one in an agonised dream, came to the edge of the pool. Among the praying band there was no doubt as to her intention, no astonishment; the kneeling men gave instant thanks to God for her decision, and Halsey, having helped the feeble man to land, led Susannah down into the water, his face illuminated by the victory of faith.

Susannah heard now her aunt's wild shrieks; she heard too the surging of the crowd, but the meaning of neither sound came to her. She waded on to where Smith stood, with only the dazed sense of a goal to be reached. She was perfectly passive in his hands as he dipped her beneath the surface and raised her up, but she listened to the blessing he pronounced with a sudden leap of the heart, feeling that now at last the misery of fear was past and the demand of God satisfied—it must be so because it had cost so much.

When she came to herself she saw that the crowd, like a wild beast, had sprung downward upon the disciples. Even in her first terrified glance she was impressed by the strange and awful difference between the distorted and hideous faces of the mob and the exalted calm of the few men who had at this time fixed their minds on the unseen rather than the seen. She looked up to Smith in the swift appeal of terror, and felt once for all the huge courage by which his life was marked. His hand, helping her to the shore, never trembled. He calmly directed her steps into the quiet meadow before he gave himself to the battle.

When her person was no longer there to be protected, the Mormons gave way at once before the gathering strength of the mob. She saw them beaten down mercilessly; she saw Smith himself beaten and thrown prostrate in the water. The still, warm air that a few minutes before had seemed instinct with prayer was now vibrating to the howls and taunts and curses of the mob. Susannah had no doubt that these, who were now her friends, were being killed; their sufferings justified her to herself and produced a fierce exaltation in the step which she had taken. In her experience of life she thought that the mob would turn upon her next, and stood waiting, every muscle tense, her hands clenched, feeling excitedly that she would rather die than live to see such intolerable wrong.

This tension of nerve relaxed somewhat when her uncle lifted her forcibly into the waggon. With eyes wide open with horror and lips trembling, she asked, "Did they kill them, uncle?"

"No, child, they only gave them a good trouncing in their own pond." He choked here, out of pity for her, keeping back the torrent of his anger.

Even at this early date it was bruited that Joseph Smith exercised some unseemly force of will by which he distorted the reason of his converts. This report explained the fact that for the first day after the shock of Susannah's baptism her aunt and uncle did not lay the blame of it at her door, did not argue or persuade, only watched her as one recovering from a strange disease. But in the afternoon of that first day the pent-up fever of the aunt's wrath against those whom she thought to blame broke forth, and almost in delirium.

The last hot weather of the autumn still held; in the same still hour of the afternoon, the hour in which Susannah's baptism had taken place the day before, Angel Halsey, pallid with his yesterday's beating and ill-usage, but steadfast and even joyful of face, walked up to the front door of the magistrate's house.

This door opened upon an unfrequented entrance-hall. Susannah heard the knock, heard her aunt move with the dignity befitting an expected visitor. Then she heard Ephraim's step on the stair for the first time that day, and reflected dully that he must have seen the advent of some important person from his window to be thus answering the call of the door.

After that she heard words that had the sound of suppressed screams in them. She realised that the house mistress was ordering some enemy from her door. These commands were not obeyed, and Susannah, hearing that the intruder remained, began in fear to suspect the meaning of the intrusion. As she rose the report of a fire-arm startled her from all the remnants of her selfish dulness, causing her feet to fly.

From within the sitting-room she saw the entrance-hall. Its door was open to the wide sweep of land that lay in floods of sunshine. In the light, half turning now to go as he had come, stood Angel Halsey. Her eager eyes drank in the sight of him, because last night she had thought to see him die. She saw his quietness even while, it seemed to her, the gun still echoed, and it was Ephraim who held the gun! Beside Ephraim her aunt stood, like one in a frenzy, her very garments twitching and her gray hair fallen loose. None of them looked to see the girl within the shaded room.

"Friends," said Halsey, "I came to say 'Peace be with this house,' and to speak with her to whom God has given the spirit of obedience to his truth, but it is written that when any house refuses to receive us we must depart."

His voice was for some cause growing fainter, but Susannah was certain that the cause was not fear.

He took a letter from his breast. "I wrote it," he said, "in case I might not enter to speak with her."

He gave the letter to Ephraim, who took it reluctantly, as one impelled by some strong sense of right.

Halsey went out. He tottered upon the path, but he opened the gate and walked on. Ephraim, still holding the gun and the letter, turned and saw Susannah.

Ephraim's face was gaunt and haggard as she had never seen it before; his eyes were large, and she thought she read unutterable distress in them, but could not understand. She held out her hand for the letter, but as he gave it both she and he perceived for the first time that it was stained with blood; they felt mutually the thrill that the sight gave.

He put his hand out suddenly and pushed her within the room. "Go," he entreated, "for God's sake, Susy, go to your own room; take his letter with you if you will, but go."

Susannah went amazed, but she began to think that Ephraim's distress had not been a gracious sorrow, but remorse for his own crime. He must have shot Halsey as he would have shot at some evil beast. When she had time to remember that Halsey had tottered when he walked, she fled back, straining the blood-stained letter to her breast, and tore open the closed door. Her aunt was sitting in a low chair sobbing. Ephraim, bareheaded in the sunshine, was standing on the path shading his eyes to scan the road. Susannah ran out, not to him (her shame and grief for him were too deep for any word), but with intent to run after the wounded man and nurse his wound.

"It can be but a slight flesh wound," said Ephraim mechanically.

She looked first where he was gazing, and saw that some distance down the road Halsey was stepping into a chaise. Another man took the seat beside him and they drove away.

Then she looked at Ephraim. He did not appear as though he felt his guilt; he had the mien rather of one who was striving bravely to endure hardship. Then indeed she felt that the gulf of thought must yawn wide between them; she could even yet have pitied Ephraim's contrition, but he was not contrite. In indignation she retired, sitting in the privacy of her little bedroom.

It was a strange letter, not alone because the ink was blurred by blood that, still warm, soaked it through in parts, but because, coming from a young man to a maid, in the first flush of her strength and beauty, it offered love and marriage, giving only as his reason, urging only as her motive, the service of God.

"If," the letter read, "thou canst see thy way, dear friend, to hold fast that thou hast in the house of thy friends, if thou canst see thy way, by steadfast confession and by the grace of thy demeanour, to strive among them for their conversion, it would be well while thou art still so young to remain with them for a time—at least so I think. But our prophet thinks, and I also greatly desire to think, that the strain upon thy faith would be too great, that thou mightst fail; and remembering that it has been revealed to him that our union has been sealed in heaven, he thinks that thou wouldst do well to commit thy tender life now to my keeping."

The phrase "and I greatly desire to think" was almost as strong as any in a long letter to tell which way his delight would lie, and Susannah's was not a mind upon which this indication of reserve force was thrown away. She trusted, vaguely in thought but implicitly in heart, to that which lay behind—something which did not alarm her, which in her inner vision wore no warm nor obtrusive colouring, but which she knew to be intense and of enduring quality. And she saw herself alone, beaten by adverse winds and without other shelter.

Halsey touched upon the fact that Smith and his disciples (he did not say himself) had suffered greatly from yesterday's ill-usage, and said that, having given their message to the people, they were that day leaving for a place called Fayette, in Seneca county, where it had previously been determined that the new church should be organised. He himself would wait either until Susannah saw her way to come with him, or until he knew that she was at peace, having chosen of her own accord to remain. He would bring a chaise, in which she could travel if she would, near her uncle's house at dawn upon the next morning. He would take her, he said, to the house where the Smiths were in Fayette, but it was implied through all the letter that the mystic marriage which Smith had solemnised was considered by Halsey as valid, and that if she joined her material fortunes now to those of the persecuted sect, it would be as his wife.

In speaking of the future he did not gloss over the persecution; he did not even promise, as Smith had done, a sure and material reward. The mind of the young Quaker convert was fixed upon the things that are unseen. This was not hidden from the girl. The thought of being with him in his faith and resignation gave her peace. Poverty and persecution seemed as nothing compared with the torture of being surrounded by people whose thought and actions aroused in her young heart whirlwinds of passionate opposition. Even Ephraim, instead of rising in his strength to condemn the outrage of yesterday, had attempted today to wound or kill. Her amazement and dismay at this drove her out as it were with a scourge.

Halsey had told her to pray, and she had tried to pray. Halsey had told her to search the Scriptures for guidance, and she read. Text after text came home to her heart, bidding her leave her kindred to share the fortunes of the persecuted children of faith.

CHAPTER VIII.

At break of day Halsey was waiting upon the road with a fairly good horse and a comfortable chaise. Susannah never forgot the light that came to his eyes when he saw her approach; it was like dawn in paradise.

Angel Halsey was not without shrewd worldly wisdom. He turned into a cross corduroy road that led through the woods, passing only some small clearings to the west of Palmyra, and thus by a detour avoiding that village, he returned again to the highroad between Canandaigua and Geneva. The pursuers, upon failing to hear that the chaise had passed through Palmyra, might turn back, or if they had gone on they might have outstripped them on the road, and be in front rather than behind. This danger peopled the long lonely road with possible enemies both before and behind. The strain upon the imagination was very great. The road was heavy and rough.

Susannah perceived that Halsey's apprehension of being overtaken was almost solely on her account. He was so upborne by his religious enthusiasm as to be oblivious to the pain which his wound of yesterday gave him, and was perfectly willing to encounter the violence of her kindred again if need be, yet, seeing her terror with a quickness of sympathy which roused her gratitude, he took every possible precaution that could allay her fears. All through the weary, weary day she hardly spoke to him, never addressed him by name.

They reached the new town of Geneva at sundown. When they had set forth again, it was a great comfort to Susannah that grayness had succeeded to sunshine. She was weary of the yellow light, of the dull glare from the stubble fields, of the obtrusive colours of the autumn foliage, of the blueness of the sky, of everything, indeed, that she had seen and heard during the wretched hours of the day. They now travelled through a very flat tract; little of the land was cleared; the road was straight. It is hard to explain the mental weariness produced by a straight level road. The hope and interest inspired by undulations or curves are lost. The distance ever gives a farther reach of the weary way to the view, as if by a parable it would impress on the traveller the knowledge that the future was to be barren of delight.

About two miles from Geneva, before the daylight was quite gone, they were both startled by hearing a rushing, crashing sound coming toward them in the woods. Were their pursuers upon them after all? Had they chosen this, the most lonely part of their road, to fall upon them?

They did not speak their thoughts to one another. Angel struck the horse, and it galloped forward perhaps about a hundred yards, and then, of its own accord, stopped suddenly.

Upon the side of the road, pushing itself backward among the bushes, the better to gain space for its run, was a bull. Its eyes were bloodshot, its head lowered for a long moment to measure its distance ere it made the attack. The horse seemed palsied with terror. It moved backward with tottering steps, trembling all over, heedless of whip or rein.

The backward movement prolonged the hesitation of the bull, which turned itself to take another aim. The horse uttered an almost human cry.

In the moment of hearing that cry Susannah felt that she had already gone through some shocking form of death. Halsey brought down his whip, striking the horse with all his might; it leaped forward, lifting the chaise almost into the air; then it was rushing madly on, dragging the wheels behind it with terrible velocity.

They had caught sight of the rush of the bull. They felt the animal's heavy side just graze the back of the chaise, and they heard behind them a bellow of rage that seemed to fill all the solitary place with diabolical echoes.

The body of the chaise was bounding upon its leather bands, jolting cruelly against the axle. Susannah cried out that she should be thrown from her seat. The swift-falling darkness encompassed their path. Their hope lay in the straightness of the road, and their chief fear was that by some greater roughness of the way the chaise, which was now swaying fearfully, might be overturned.

Gradually the sound of the bull's galloping became less distinct. The chaise was still upright. The horse, beginning to falter in his pace, took more kindly to the accustomed control of the rein. It was then Susannah found that she had been clinging to Halsey for support, and that he, by bracing himself with one arm to the side of the chaise and holding her with the other, had prevented her from being thrown out.

In gathering her shawl about her she wrapped herself again in a certain amount of her former reserve, but the excitement that she had been through made her former silence impossible.

Halsey at first received her remarks in silence, then as he essayed to answer, his voice grew low and faint, and a sudden suspicion of the cause pierced through her mind.

In another moment he sank, leaning against her. Putting her hand beneath his coat, she found to her dismay that the strain of holding her had opened his wound; his clothes were again wet with blood.

The reins slipped from his hands. Susannah tied them loose to the front of the chaise and, putting her arms round the fainting man, drew the bandages tightly but with unskilful hands; she lessened the bleeding and caused him such acute pain that he lifted his head and spoke.

"What shall I do?" she asked piteously. The blood, diverted from the brain, had left it without healthy circulation, but she did not know yet that this was affecting his mind.

"Friend," he whispered, "that was in truth no bull; it was the devil himself."

"The devil?" she asked faintly.

"He almost succeeded in his cruel attempt to cause us to be discouraged from the way."

"It seems to me he only succeeded in causing us to take the way with greater vehemence," she replied in some scorn.

In the next minute she heard him whisper eagerly, "Look up; look between the branches; quick! Do you not see the face looking at us?"

The branches of the overhanging tree were black with night. She looked up in the direction that his feeble hand indicated, and with indescribable terror scanned the blank spaces in which no human face could possibly be.

"Look!" he whispered again impatiently. "Don't you see it? It is the face of a man. A white face! It is the face of thy cousin as I saw it yesterday when I was counted worthy to suffer. Look! look! does thou not see him?"

His words had the effect of producing in her that maddening fear of the dark which ghostly tales induce, and now he fainted again. She was afraid to cry for help, afraid even of the rustle of her own garments. She did not know how far she was from any house. And it seemed to her that this lover, who was almost a stranger, was dying in her arms. The misery of this hour governed her action in the next.

Halsey in the bottom of the chaise lay with his head against her knee, and soon, holding the bandages of his wound close upon it with one hand, she took the reins with the other and urged the horse forward. She had had no thought all that day but to go, as Halsey had said, to Emma Smith's protection. She hoped now that there was but one road; that when she came to the first settlement she would be with the Smiths. This was not the case. She travelled an hour, obliged to pass more than one cross-road because she dared not turn down it. At length she found herself in front of a large house with lighted windows, which was evidently an inn.

The door opened, letting out a stream of candlelight. A man stood in the doorway. "What place is this?" cried Susannah's voice from the darkness.

"It's John Biery's hotel."

"Will you have the kindness to tell me if you know of any one called Mr. Joseph Smith?"

There was some talking within. "No, we never heard of Mr. Joseph Smith."

"Or Mr. Oliver Cowdery?" Again there was talking.

"No, it don't seem that we've any of us heard o' those names before. Be you alone?" The deep bass voice of John Biery was becoming more insistent in its rising inflection.

For some half-minute Susannah did not answer, and then fear of being compelled to retake the road made irresolution impossible.

"Indeed, sir, I am not alone. I have in the chaise with me a sick man, and I fear that he may be dying. I thought to find friends, but it seems in the darkness I have missed my way. I must beg of you to assist me to lift him into the house and give us shelter for the night."

The men had remained perfectly still, drinking in her every syllable with that fierce thirst for news which is a first passion of dwellers in such desolate places; then, aroused by what they heard, they came forward across a rough bit of ground to the road. The burly form of John Biery came first, and he called for a lantern, which was instantly produced by one of those who followed. They held it up over Angel's crouching form and death-like face. Then they held it higher and stared at Susannah. Her shawl had fallen from off her shoulders. The handkerchief upon her neck was loose, and underneath the pink border of her bonnet the ringlets had begun to stray. Her resolute face, so young and beautiful, startled them almost as an apparition might have done.

"I'm dead beat," said the hotel-keeper under his breath, "if I ever seed anything like that!" But with the ready suspicion of a prudent householder he questioned her. Where had the man come by the wound? For they saw the blood-stained bandages she clasped.

Yesterday, she explained, he had received a slight bullet-wound by accident, and today, in their long travel, the loss of blood had disabled him.

"Does he belong to you, young lady?"

Susannah busied herself with the bandages for a moment, but terror had carried her far. She replied with gentle decision, "He is my husband."

CHAPTER IX.

"It is our fault."

That evening Ephraim Croom stood in his father's sitting-room, near the door of the dark stair that led up to his own rooms. His shoulders were drooping. His face was gray and haggard. Even his hair and beard, damp, unkempt, seemed to express remorse in their outline. He stood doggedly facing his father and mother, repeating the thing that he saw to be true, but with no further words to interpret his insight.

To his parents his opinions, his attitude, appeared as an outrage upon reason. His father looked at him with greater severity than he had ever before exercised upon his only child. "I reckon, Ephraim, that you speak without using the sense that the Almighty has been mercifully pleased to give you. You know, Ephraim, the girl has been as a daughter in this house. When has it been said to her that her father, dying in his worldly follies, left her destitute, the pittance she gets needing to go for his debts? She's had about as good a home as any girl should want, and your mother and the ministers have dealt faithfully with her concerning her soul."

Ephraim made a movement of the head as if for a moment he could have stood upright, feeling in one respect innocent; then again there was nothing but the droop of shame visible.

His mother looked at him with eyes that were red with weeping. She had been wiping them with fierce furtive rubs of her handkerchief; now she was rubbing the handkerchief, a hard ball, in the palm of one hand. Perhaps grief at Susannah's loss had been dominant until Ephraim's accusation had fanned her anger. "She'd better have gone with him openly from the baptising. I never thought then that it was love-making she was after." Deep scorn was here expressed. "Religion! 'Twasn't much religion she had in her mind. And we treated her real kindly, Ephraim, thinking 'twas the hold of delusion they had upon her. 'Twould be very small use to bring her back even if you or your father could have found out which way they'd gone. 'Tisn't likely she'd stay long if you fetched her, seeing she's that sort of a girl, with a hankering for the man. There isn't a place in this house to lock her into unless it is the cellar."

It was perhaps the thought of the unspeakable degradation it would be to the worthy house to hold a girl as prisoner in the cellar, perhaps the dismal knowledge that that which had already befallen them and her was not much better than this, that caused his mother here to lose her self-control entirely and weep bitterly. Ephraim shrank under her words as if they had been the strokes of a whip striking him. When she had ended he went on heavily up the dark stair.

Both the men were in riding-dress. The elder man, when he had comforted his wife as best he might, laid aside his boots and whip determinedly, believing that the use for them, as far as concerned the search for his niece, was at an end. Upstairs, sitting between the three windows that looked east and north and south, Ephraim sat as long as exhaustion made rest necessary. He was still equipped for the road, thinking only which way it behoved him to travel, and when.

CHAPTER X.

The next day, toward afternoon, Joseph Smith stood by the bedside of Angel Halsey. Susannah, wan and weary with a long night's nursing, was sitting beside the pillow. Smith looked upon them both benevolently. It was some minutes before he spoke. Susannah was too much in awe of him to say much, but his presence was welcome. Since Halsey's rational self had been lost in his delirium, loneliness like darkness that could be felt had pressed upon her.

"Our brother will be healed," said Smith at length. "It is given to me to know that he will be healed." He then spread his hands over the sick man and made a short prayer. There was much fervour in his words and his voice was loud.

"Give him to drink," said Smith.

"Biery's wife told me as long as he was in fever not to give him water."

Smith looked down upon her kindly, but he spoke in a tone of absolute authority. "My sister, I say unto thee give him water. It is given to me to know that he must have water and that he will do well."

"It is never done in such cases," said Susannah. "I remember when my father—" She had not the faith that Smith required of her.

Without a frown, with perfect gentleness, Smith fetched the water and, lifting the sick man's head, allowed him to drink eagerly. Halsey was obviously comforted.

Smith had something else to say. If he had not been who he was Susannah might have perceived that he was somewhat perplexed, even embarrassed. Just as a child does not easily attribute to the adult such hindering emotions, so she supposed him to be upon a plane above them.

He lingered by the bedside, apparently watching the sufferer. At length he said, "You set out with this young man—yesterday morning?"

"Yes, very early."

There was another pause, then he said, "Did you go before a justice of the peace?"

"A justice of the peace?" Then she added inconsequently, "My uncle is a justice of the peace." She had never heard of a civil marriage; she did not know in the least what he meant.

"Or—or a minister?"

She began to understand now.

"I married you myself, sister, and it was sealed in heaven, but I haven't got a license to marry, so that the Gentiles would say—that the knot wasn't tied, ye know." The last words were a lapse into common parlance. She had grown accustomed to the hybrid nature of his mannerism.

He had expected and feared to see her white face flame into excitement, but to Susannah it seemed a small thing now what the Gentiles might say. If the marriage was indeed sealed in heaven, then all was well. And if it was not, worse could not be. She was too weary now to respond to the prophet's worldly solicitude for her. Looking at the still unconscious Halsey, she felt that there was time enough for further action.

Smith said, "Emma would have come, but the child has spasms."

"We meant to go to you," said Susannah. "We lost our way. I only heard today where you were."

After a while he said, "I might stop here with our sick brother and send you to Emma, but there is a congregation called for tonight. Mr. Cowdery would have come, but he was at the baptising."

"Did you leave the baptising just to come and see us?" It occurred to her that from his point of view two stray disciples such as herself and Halsey could be of little importance compared with his appearance at the solemn function.

Smith busied himself giving Halsey more water. That done, he went away without further words. Susannah heard his horse gallop from the door. She knew that he had travelled some five miles to pay this visit, and she supposed that he desired to return if possible before the converts had come up from the water. His visit had undoubtedly brought her comfort. His response to her message had been prompt and kind. She knew now that his thoughts and Emma's were busy concerning her. And then, too, the sick man was better. He had gone quietly to sleep.

The woman of the house brought her for food an unusual delicacy. Smith had ordered this. Mrs. Biery made some remarks concerning him. She said that his coat seemed very old, but that he had given her money and bid her attend diligently upon the sick man and his wife. Susannah, who knew how little money the Smiths had hitherto possessed, how many things they must want for themselves, was touched.

As her spirits revived, her faith and hope in the new sect revived also. She looked among the few possessions Halsey had brought with him for the precious copy of the Book of Mormon, and sat reading it by Angel's bedside while the autumn sun was sinking.

Sometimes she heard a traveller stop at the inn door and pass on again. At dusk there was a sounds of horses coming with speed. To her surprise Joseph Smith came into the room again. He looked as if he had been riding hard, but he spoke as quietly as though he had gone only from that room to the next.

"I have brought a gentleman who can marry you according to the law of the State." Susannah had gone forward to greet him, but now she looked suddenly back toward the unconscious man, whose form was almost indistinguishable in the dusk.

Smith brought candles and set them at the foot of the bed. He took Halsey by the hand and lifted him to a sitting posture, telling him in clear strong tones what was required of him. Halsey understood. He became completely conscious under Smith's influence, and for the hour almost strong. He would know where he was and how he came there, who the minister was that had come. He even required that this stranger should show his license to marry.

The minister was a common-looking man, small, shaggy as to the beard, business-like. He knew nothing of Joseph Smith's prophetical claims, and cared only to know that Susannah was over eighteen years of age. Marriage was a thing easily accomplished in that day and region. A few minutes more and Susannah was a wife.

In after years, when she used to think of Angel Halsey as having gone before her into the unseen, Susannah held the belief that the part of him which she would meet there would be that which shone out in the rare half-playful smiles he gave, in the glance which, at the moment of smiling, he bent on her. He was a very grave man, shrewd, in many ways, in others as simple as a child, but above all greatly religious. His religion, however deep might be its root, was also always upon the surface. Only now and then, when, as at their first meeting, he recognised in his serious way that something else was required if he would truly hold communion with Susannah, the smile would come as from some inward part of his spirit, like a dawning light slowly breaking through the surface, soon withdrawn again by the power of custom. When he thus smiled, Susannah in those days trusted him absolutely, avowed herself entirely to his service, and felt within her heart a large measure of affection.

Halsey's was the first case of illness in the newly-formed sect that called itself already "*The* Church of Christ." Joseph Smith and Cowdery and a man named Whitmer, with whom the Smiths were now housed, having consulted upon it, decided that they must begin at once to carry out the commands of Scripture. They came together, therefore, and anointed Halsey with oil, laying their hands upon him and praying fervently. Halsey, believing himself to be healed, got up from his sick-bed, and his recovery progressed rapidly.

Full of excitement, fervour, superstition, and faith, the apostles of the new doctrine were fully persuaded that they might expect a literal fulfilment of the promise that signs and wonders should follow them that believe. The fierce opposition and hatred which were roused by the reports of their doings are easily accounted for when we consider that their opinions had to encounter that curious distortion of reason which has caused religious warfare in all times and places to become the worst sort of warfare, and the fact which Smith himself had acknowledged when he first saw Susannah, that many evil reports about him had formerly been true; then also the new sect produced vehement psychical disturbance wherever it touched the surrounding population, and many things occurred which might, or might not, be termed miracles, according to the interpretation of the observer. It was no longer possible for Joseph Smith to ride, as he had done on the day of Susannah's marriage, with a minister of one of the older sects. He became very notorious, and to every one except those who were interested enough in his doctrine to give him a fair hearing, his name became a synonym for all evil.

Halsey remained with Susannah at John Biery's hotel. Halsey was one of the few converts who could afford to live in comparative comfort and to pay something for the entertainment of destitute disciples. For that reason the landlord, John Biery, held himself from the religious quarrel that was shaking the region.

Even before Halsey had regained his strength he drove Susannah to swell the congregation at the preachings which were daily taking place in different places within the township, for such converts as had already professed themselves were gathered now in the neighbourhood of Fayette.

Experiences came to Susannah in such quick succession that this was not a time of reflection. Such part of her husband's religion as she could appropriate she endeavoured very sincerely to embrace. After the manner of the thought, of the time she supposed that the sect was either right or wrong—if right, all right; if wrong, all wrong. Sometimes the ghastly fear that her growing belief was false would arise with hideous menace.

CHAPTER XI.

All the doings of the infant sect were directed by those utterances of Joseph Smith which he held to be revelations. These were confided sometimes to the elders, sometimes to the converts at large. Susannah frequently heard of them first through Emma Smith, whose pious heart was constantly filled with wonder and thankfulness at the thought of the great honour vouchsafed to her husband. These revelations, sometimes illimitable in their sweep, and sometimes having reference only to the most minute practical details, were at this time all in accordance either with the dictates of common sense or with the severely literal meaning of some Scripture text. They were therefore easily justified either to reason or to the eye of faith, but the results of their application were often startling, and it was facts, not theories, that chiefly caused Susannah to stagger.

At length the growing excitement among the congregation seemed to gather toward some climax. It was then that Joseph Smith was said for the first time to cast out devils.

Near to John Biery's hotel lived a family of the name of Knight. The worthy farmer became a convert, and so also, in appearance, did his son. Susannah first saw them at their baptism, which took place one cold bleak day in the margin of Seneca Lake. The horses which had brought the little company to the edge of the water, having been tied among the trees, made a constant rustling and trampling among the fallen leaves. The sharp rustle, the thud of the hoofs upon the ground, were sounds long connected in her mind with the crisis of her doubt, which then began. The maples stood above them, tall and leafless; the waters of the lake were leaden in hue and cold. Looking southward on either side of its long flood, the snores with their many points and headlands lay cold, almost hueless, near by, and in the distance blue as tarnished steel.

It was a bitter day for baptist and for the immersed. Joseph Smith went out alone into the water, commanding the other elders to remain upon the shore. Whatever else the man had or had not, he had splendid courage in facing physical ills. There were but few candidates. Susannah, standing apart near the shore, chanced to be in the path by which the younger Knight descended to the water. He was a young man with strong features and a thick, unhealthy skin. He was dressed in the wet garments which another candidate had taken off. Cold he might have been, but as he passed she heard his teeth chatter so loudly that it almost seemed to her that his very bones rattled. She drew back with the impression that some horrible thing had passed by. Before she had time to wonder that the chill should have had such an effect upon the hardy fellow, his feet were in the water, and he turned and caught her eye. The look he gave her became suddenly one of terrified entreaty.

Susannah did not move; she was spell-bound. He began to wade toward Smith, who stood in the deeper water. She wondered why he allowed himself to be immersed. She was certain that he did not desire it, was certain also that no motives of interest, no physical force, could have operated to compel, when suddenly she asked herself sharply, what force had taken her into the waters of this extraordinary baptism?

To her astonishment, when Newell Knight came up from the water he was shouting aloud. She thought that his accents were a horrible simulation of merriment, but by the others they were accepted as an evidence of holy joy.

Two days after, when Susannah and her husband were returning from Smith's preaching through the autumn night, they were met as they were approaching Biery's hotel by a messenger from Knight's house. The messenger had been sent to fetch Halsey. He reported that Newell Knight was in "an awful way." Susannah alighted at once and walked to the tavern, in order that her husband might drive with all speed to the afflicted man.

The lights as they shone from John Biery's windows reminded her vividly of the first time, a month since, when she had driven to that house at night. She had grown much older since then, stronger in many ways, weaker in some, but she was not conscious of this; it was not her way to give even so much as a passing glance at herself as one of the actors in life's drama. The road on which she trod was heavy with mud. The night-winds cried around and through the empty branches of two or three neglected trees in the clearing. The square wooden tavern stood at the cross-roads. The light from the door made a pathway through the darkness, up which Susannah walked.

When she entered, the heat and fumes from fire, candles, tobacco-pipes, and steaming mugs met her. She was accustomed to walking through John Biery's main room to gain the stair that led to her own; on the whole it was not disorderly, or Susannah had but to appear on the threshold to reduce it to order. Tonight the men did not let her pass with their usual civil "Good evening"; they assumed that she had an interest in their talk.

"Is Mr. Halsey stopping over to Farmer Knight's?" asked Biery. "My! and they'll be real glad to get him, ye know. Twiced they've been here fur him. They say that Newell Knight he's possessed with a devil."

Susannah wrapped her shawl tightly across her breast, a nervous movement caused not by cold but by the desire to withdraw her real self from the surrounding circumstance.

A tall thin man sitting by the table set down his mug with a clatter upon it. "Wall now, tain't my idea thet thet's exectly what's taken Newell. I saw a case of a man thet was taken under the preacher Finney. 'Twas over to Ithica. The hull town knew about it. A lot of folks went in. I jest looked in when I was passing, and seen the man meself. He was lyin' on the floor. His wife was aholdin' his head, but he didn't know her. He hedn't no knowledge of any of the folks. He jest lay there rollin', and his eyes was rollin'. And when Finney was fetched, Finney he said 'twas 'conviction.' I don't know what the man was convicted of, but 'twas 'conviction' Finney called it. He didn't say nothing about being possessed with devils."

The third speaker was a small fat man. His face was smooth and had the peculiar boylike appearance that chubbiness gives even to the middle-aged; he had bright black eyes, and before he spoke he glanced at Susannah critically.

"When they're taken that way under Finney," he said, as if meditating, "'conviction' commonly means conviction of sins—their own sins, ye know, not other folk's; and when they git up, if they've taken anything wrongfully they hev to restore it fourfold afore the conviction will leave off a-worrittin' them. I don't know how 'tis among the Mormons." The last words were said in an undertone and he had dropped his eyes. It would have required a brave man to treat Susannah to open sarcasm.

She stood looking from one to the other. She still wore her girlish cottage bonnet, and as its fashion was, it had slipped backwards upon the amber ringlets that hung upon her neck; but the girlish look was fast passing from the face, the hair parting fell on either side of pale cheeks.

"Oh, as to thet, 's fur as I know, one religion's as good as another," said the politic Biery.

Susannah looked at the fat, bright-eyed man who was no longer looking at her. "I know" (her voice fell with a strange gentleness through the thickened atmosphere of the room) "that there are many malicious stories abroad about the dishonesty of our people which are not true."

But as she went up the stair she remembered that she had heard of no case where reformation of character had been followed by the returning of the fourfold. Most of these saints of the new sect had before their conversion been, like her husband, already God-fearing and righteous, but in cases where, like their leader, they had been reclaimed from evil courses, had they not been satisfied with offering the present and future to God, leaving the past? She had heard of no case of restitution such as Finney insisted upon.

Susannah entered the low, wide room in which she lived. The chimney from the lower room passed up and was always warm. She went and laid her cold hands against the rough plaster that covered its bricks, and, being tired, she leaned, laying her cheek too against its warm surface. The one candle cast but a faint light upon the chairs, the bed, the table. The small panes of the window-glass were bare to the darkness without and the empty tree-branches. The heavy latch of the closed door was fastened crookedly for lack of good workmanship.

Her unsatisfied mind ached for counsel, and her thought, roving over the world, could fix only on Ephraim as she had at first learned to know him, wise and quiet and kind. The warm chimney seemed a poor thing to lean her head against while she felt that her faith was failing. Then the remembrance of the shot Ephraim had fired and his callousness choked back her tears.

She waited an hour, two hours; then, becoming anxious on Halsey's account, she borrowed a lantern and went across the fields to Knight's farmhouse.

Quite a number of people had gathered. Susannah met some of them coming from the house, but others were still there, standing about the fire in the kitchen. She heard that the later arrivals had all been disappointed of the sight of Newell Knight in his fit. Halsey had assumed authority, stating that it was indeed a case of possession, and that none but those who were strong in faith and in the power of prayer must come near the possessed. The craving of the visitors for excitement was only fed by the sound of the young man's voice, heard at short intervals.

He cried aloud, sometimes shrieking that he was being taken into "the pit" and that Joseph Smith could alone deliver him, sometimes exclaiming in a strange voice that he was no longer Newell Knight but a demon, and sometimes only moaning and gibbering words that no one could understand.

Halsey came out to Susannah. "Wouldst thou see him?" he asked tenderly. "The sight will distress thee, for it is truly terrible to see with the eye of flesh the power of hell, and yet I cannot forbid thee if thou wouldst come, for perchance the Lord may mean it for our edification."

Susannah went with him into the inner room, hardly knowing why she went, but probably impelled by the instinctive desire to relieve suffering which was part of her womanhood. The young man's father and mother, together with two or three Mormon converts, were kneeling upon the floor, saying prayers for the sufferer in more or less audible, more or less agonised tones.

The young man lay upon a pallet-bed, in what would have been called by the medical science of the time "convulsions." His eyeballs were rolled upwards in a manner most disfiguring to his face. His hands were clenched. Halsey no sooner entered the room than he, too, fell upon his knees, lifting his face upward as if in silent and fervent prayer.

For a moment Susannah felt impelled to follow his example. "But perhaps," she thought to herself, "cold water upon the patient's head, or a warm foot-bath—" Such suggestions caused her to resist the impulse to join the praying band, and, having resisted it, she suddenly experienced, as one feels a fresh breeze entering a close room, a strong, clear sense of knowledge that in this matter, at least, her husband was deluded, that the friends had better rise from their knees and betake themselves to ruder remedies.

Susannah had never learned to command; she had never even learned to advise. She had too much reverence to speak aloud, disturbing those who were at prayer. She stood hesitating, and then, in very low tones, whispered her belief in her husband's ear.

No doubt Halsey was shocked at his wife's unbelief; perhaps by the law of telepathy, for whose existence some psychical experts vouch, his thought penetrated the mind of the sensitive upon the bed. Whatever the cause, Newell Knight sat up and pointed at Susannah, crying aloud that he saw the devil about to seize upon her. So excited was the mental atmosphere, so vivid were the sufferer's words and the effect of his pointing finger, or, perhaps, so substantial was his vision, that more than one of the saints afterwards averred that they had seen the Evil One about to embrace Susannah. But they did not agree in the description of his form.

Halsey wrapped his arms about his wife, and led her like a child from the room and from the house. She hardly had time to speak before she saw the night again about her. He set her down upon an old log that chanced to lie against Knight's barn, kneeling beside her. There, when they were alone in the darkness, he invoked that name to which throughout all Christendom the devils are believed to be subject.

"Angel," she said gently, "stop praying and listen to me. If you can command the devil in the name of our Lord, why don't you do that to poor Newell Knight?" She felt strong sympathy for the young man; she was moved almost to tears to think they were taking the wrong way with him.

"I have tried and failed. We have sent for Joseph Smith. My faith is not strong enough," he added humbly. "This cometh not forth but by prayer and by fasting. Look! I am even now unfaithful to my charge because I love thee, friend, more, I fear, than the work of the Lord."

They were left alone because Halsey in passing out had left the door of the sick room open to the eager neighbours. Now reluctantly he went back to his task of guarding the patient, and Susannah, after assuring his anxious soul that she felt no ill effects whatever from the dire proximity, went home again across the dark frozen fields with her lantern. She sat half the night watching and waiting.

It was in the darkest hour before the dawn that she heard Halsey's step and crept down through the black house to unlock the door for him. When they had come again into the room she saw that he was greatly excited, filled with apparent calm of an exalted mood.

"We have beheld a most glorious victory, friend; and truly we have been shown signs and wonders, and a very great miracle has been wrought. I wish thou couldst have seen with thine own eyes, and yet—"

She thought that he had been going to say that her lack of faith had made it more expedient for her to be away, but that he had checked in himself even the thought that he was more worthy of privilege than she.

It seemed that Joseph Smith, having been preaching the evening before at a place some twenty miles away, had not been able to reach Knight's house until nearly two in the morning.

"He rode all night," said Halsey, "and lost not a moment in coming to the inner room; it was like him."

"Yes," said Susannah, "it was like him; he is very kind."

Halsey went on. "He spread his hands over Newell and commanded the devils to come out of him."

"And did they come?"

"They left him. Joseph said that it was given to him to see that there were three of them; but they departed, going out into the darkness."

The wind moaned against the window near which Susannah sat.

"They left Newell very weak, but at peace like an infant sleeping. But at first I feared that he was as one dead, for I could not see him breathe; but Joseph's faith was strong, for he lifted up his voice and began to give praise, and he took Newell by the hand and bade him rise, but his hand fell back as if there was no life in it. Then Joseph Smith knelt with us upon the floor, and Newell lay smiling, but his eyes were closed, and he seemed dead to this world, although the body was warm. Afterwards he told us that at the time he was seeing a vision of unspeakable light and glory. And then, as we watched him, I fearing because my faith was weak, a marvel happened as a sign and seal to our faith that Joseph is indeed called to be a great prophet. I wish that thou couldst have seen it, Susannah, for the miracle has given me a great uplifting in spirit, but I am come to bear witness to it, that thou, too, mayest rejoice in the marvel."

There was a few moments' pause. "What was it?" she asked.

"Newell began to rise from the bed. He did not sit up or move himself, but he was raised slowly into the air, still reclining as though upon his pillow. The invisible hands of angels bore him upwards."

Susannah knit her brows. "Did you see the angels? I don't understand." And then more vehemently she asked, "What was it that you did see?"

"Nay, friend, it was not vouchsafed to us to see the blessed spirits, but surely they must have lifted him, for he rose, soaring upwards, as thou hast seen the thistledown ascend gently, almost as high as the roof of the room. As we gazed in great astonishment, and the women fainted for fear, he sank again as slowly till he rested upon his bed, and he opened his eyes and spoke to us of the wonderful vision of light which he had seen, and then he arose in perfect health and walked."

Susannah sat silent for a minute or two. Her husband was also silent, wrapped in contemplation. Then Susannah said, "You are very tired, Angel. You were overwrought last night, even before you were called to the Knights'; you had better go to sleep now."

She darkened the window against the coming of the dawn that her husband might sleep in the day instead of the night. She herself went downstairs with the earliest stir of footsteps. Because of a whim that seized her, she helped to prepare the breakfast that was to be served to the household at sunrise, and then she partook of it heartily, looking out of a southern window as she ate, watching the red sun ascend behind the naked boles of the elms. She was glad that the new day had come. Her heart ached not so much with pure grief now as with mocking laughter. Her husband was mad, quite mad, or else—and this was the more bitter belief—he had seen that she was in danger of disaffection, and had told this lie to dupe her, thinking that because she was a woman she would be impressed by it. As the sincerity of Angel's look came before her she said to herself that if that were the case no doubt Joseph Smith had invented the story, and laid it upon Angel's conscience to tell it. That or madness was the only explanation.

CHAPTER XII.

It was long after the day of her departure before Ephraim again set out to find Susannah. An illness to which he was subject first came upon him, and then, when days were past and he was able to leave his bed, conflicting reports concerning Susannah had been brought to the house, and Ephraim's courage failed. Why should he go if by seeing her he could neither give her pleasure nor do her good? It was natural that report, dwelling on what it could understand rather than on what was incomprehensible, should magnify Susannah's love for Halsey. No man in New Manchester who in the past month had chanced to catch sight of any maid holding secret parlance with any lover but now swore stoutly that that maid had been Susannah.

It often happens that schemes least calculated to succeed attain success. Susannah and Halsey had not gone far, nor had they gone with great secrecy, yet it had happened that no one had observed them as they travelled, and as there was at that time of the year little communication between the towns to the east and west of Geneva Market, it was long before real news concerning them transpired.

At length, when many days had passed, it was told in Manchester where Susannah really was; and as if the mischief Rumour was ashamed of being caught telling the truth, she hastily added a lie, and one that had a fair show of evidence in its favour. She declared that Susannah had not been married except by some mystical Mormon ceremony which was void in law.

When Ephraim heard this circumstantial story, and with it many new tales concerning wicked mysteries practised by the Mormons in Fayette, he threw down his books, as long ago the fabled fruit that had turned to ashes was thrown down, and prepared for the road.

In the first day's journey he reached Geneva, and setting out again before it was light, he came to John Biery's hotel when the sun was rising red beyond the gray elm boughs on the morning on which Susannah breakfasted alone.

Susannah looked up from her breakfast and saw Ephraim standing beside her. It was his way to look calm outwardly, but she could see that he was struggling with the nervous untoward beating of his heart, so that he could not speak. Susannah did not understand why she could not immediately rise and speak. She was conscious of a red flush that rose and mantled her face, but she did not understand the emotion from which it arose. She only knew that she was glad to see Ephraim, more glad than she could have thought to be of anything upon a day when her heart had been set mocking.

"You have come at last," she whispered, and only knew when the words were said that she had hoped to see him before. Her whisper was broken by rising tears, which she checked in very shame.

"I want to speak to you," said Ephraim briefly.

So she rose and went out with him. She put her shawl over her head and walked upon the roadside. The day was mild, the first of the Indian summer. Ephraim had not put up his horse; he led it by the bridle as he walked.

"Sure as I'm alive, it's her uncle as has come after her at last," said the wife of John Biery, gazing through the small panes of the kitchen window. And, in truth, Ephraim did look many years older than Susannah, for his figure was bowed somewhat for lack of strength.

Susannah did not now think of Ephraim as old, neither did she think of him as young. To her he was just Ephraim, bearing no more relation of comparison to any other mortal than if his had been the only soul in the world beside her own. She was not aware of this; she was only thinking that if he had not shot Halsey she would have been able to speak freely to him now. It was so wicked of Ephraim, above all others, to do such a thing. It was, in fact, unforgivable because of the stain upon Ephraim's own character more than because of Halsey's blood. But that again she did not analyse. She only knew that her feeling kept her silent.

"I am here, Susannah"—in his battle to speak Ephraim economised words—"to ask you to come back with me."

Susannah considered. It would be perhaps the best thing that she could do after she had spoken her mind to Angel. He would not ask her to remain to join in a service she loathed. But when she thought of her aunt, and of the voice of an outraged Puritan neighbourhood, her heart naturally failed her.

"I cannot."

"Is this man more to you—I do not say than the ties of kindred, for that is natural—but more to you than the obligation to live a life of reason and duty?"

"No." Susannah spoke the answer aloud because it arose so simply and strongly within her. Had she not just come to a crisis in which her desire to abide by reason proved far stronger than the feeling which bound her to Halsey? And yet, as she thought of his love and his tenderness for her, she felt only pity for him, even if he had told a lie.

Ephraim had grown calmer, but at the clear denial his heart again beat against the breath he was trying to draw. She did not love Halsey then! she was not married to him! He could conceive of nothing that could have brought that word and tone to Susannah's lips if she were bound.

"Does not duty and reason, does not even mere sanity, call upon you to come back with me, Susannah, and spend your life where you can exercise the gifts God has given you among those who abide by law and order?"

"Perhaps, Ephraim, it is so; but I am too great a coward. Think of the shame that I should have to endure from my aunt, and all the world would taunt me with my folly and madness. I think it would kill what little good there is in me. For although I should be willing to suffer if I have done wrong, yet there would be no use in going where my punishment would be greater than I could bear."

He was shocked to think of the days that had elapsed before he had come to her. She had suffered much before she could speak in this way, and when he saw how mild and sad she was, and, above all, rational, he longed to comfort her as he would comfort a child with caresses and the promise of future joys. He could give her neither, because he believed that she cared for neither caress nor joy from his hand. There was something he could offer—all that he had to give that she could take, but the offer was so hard to make that he prefaced it.

"A way might be found by which you could return to our house, Susannah, and be troubled by no spoken reproach, and you could live down that which was unspoken." He paused a minute, and then said, "But I would know first that you leave all that pertains to your life here freely. You have found it true, what is so much reported, that the Mormons follow wicked practices?"

"No, oh no, Ephraim; that is not true—mad, deluded perhaps, but not wicked. The stories of wickedness told are malicious even where there is a colour of truth, and for the most part there is none. In the matter of daily life they abide by the laws of God and man, and nothing else is taught."

It was the thought of the sacerdotal deception that she felt had been so lately practised upon herself that caused her to put in the reserving words "in the matter of daily life"; but when she remembered the malice that had instigated report, the unlovely lives of the malicious fault-finders, the evil stains that lie even upon the best lives, she burst out, "There is not one in our community, Ephraim, who would stoop to a cruel act either in word or deed. There is not one of us, even among those who have recently repented from very wicked lives, who would try to take the life of a defenceless man when he was, at a great cost to himself, pursuing what he thought to be the path of duty—as you did, Ephraim."

Before this he had kept his eyes upon the ground; standing still now, he looked straight into hers. So for a minute they stood, the horse's head drooping beside his shoulder, the woman upon the roadside erect, passionate; around them the leafless wood through which the long straight road was cut. The long level red beams of the sun struck through between the gray trunks, burnishing the wet carpet of the fallen leaf.

"Did you think it was I who fired?" he asked.

Then he went on with the horse, and she at the side.

She was utterly astonished. "Who, Ephraim—who fired?"

He looked straight in front of him again. "It was my mother. She brandished the gun in his face. She couldn't have intended to shoot."

From Susannah's heart a great cloud was lifted. She felt no confused need to readjust her thoughts; rather it was that in a moment her apprehension of Ephraim's character slipped easily from some abnormal strain into normal pleasure.

She pressed her hands to her breast as if fondling some delight. "Forgive me," she said, "but I am so glad, oh, so very glad." She drew a long breath as if inhaling not the autumn but the new sweetness of spring.

So they went on a little way, he somewhat shy because of her emotion, she meditating again, and this question pressed.

"And you think," she asked, "that your mother would receive me if I went back with you? that I could live at peace with her?"

"Do you think that whatever I might do she would ever try to shoot *me*?" he asked with half a smile. "Do you think that she would ever, by word or deed, do anything that would hurt *me*?"

"Never." Susannah said the word as a matter of course.

"Or that my father would ever deny me anything that I seriously asked for, or that he knew my happiness depended upon?"

"No, surely not; but, Ephraim—"

"Oh," he continued, growing distress in his voice, "Susannah, is there any place else in the whole world that you can go for shelter and comfort but to our house? You have spoken of this madness and delusion; you are satisfied that you must leave—" He had meant to say "this man," but he was too shy, and he faltered—"that you must leave these people?"

She cast her eyes far in among the trunks of the close-growing trees, upon one side and then upon another, as if looking for a way of escape. Yes, surely her faith in Angel's creed had been hurt beyond recovery, and she must free herself, but how? She dallied with Ephraim's offer of asylum because she could think of no other.

"Yes," she said mechanically; "yes, but how can I?"

"Oh, my dear cousin, don't you see that it is wrong for you to stay one day longer here? If you believed at first that the bond that united you to this man was binding, you do not believe it now. You were so young when you went, yet the thing cannot be undone on that account. You were so beautiful that I had hoped a great and prosperous life lay before you. Now, of course, that cannot be, but—but—at least you can live a life of peace, live truly and nobly, using your faculties to glorify God."

She began to see that he was trying to work up to something else that he had to say. She followed him heedfully, knowing that with Ephraim the steps in an argument were important. He saw some way out which she did not see, and her whole mind paused in eager listening.

He turned and faced her again, lifting his eyes, holding out his hand; his voice, usually weak, was strong. She knew that it was a strong man who spoke to her.

"Susannah, will you take my name and protection?"

She gazed at him incredulous, and then, beginning to understand what it was that he thought, and all that he meant, she leaned against one of the cold gray tree trunks, weeping weakly like a child.

"But I am married," the words came with a long sobbing sigh.

"Not legally?" and then he added, "nor in God's sight."

"Yes, yes, oh! you are making a great mistake, Ephraim. Joseph Smith and my husband are not like that. A minister came and did it. He had his license, and we have the paper he signed."

Ephraim set his teeth hard together and kept silence. He said to himself that he might have known that the rascals would be clever enough to make the tie secure.

Susannah wept on, not loudly, but with long convulsive sighs that broke into the tears she was endeavouring to check.

"And, Ephraim, my husband is good—oh, very good, and very kind to me, and up to last night I thought that what he believed might be true. I was not sure, but I thought that Joseph Smith might be a prophet. I knew they were far, far better than the other people who despise them, and so I was glad to be with them; and up till last night" (she repeated the words, controlling herself to give them emphasis)—"up till last night I thought that they at least believed everything they said to be true."

Then, after an interval of unthinking pain, Ephraim perceived that if he had come under a mistaken belief, he had at least come at the right moment; if the bond of her marriage held, the bond of her delusion was broken; she had detected some fraud. His hope, dazed by one blow, now began to look through the circumstance more clearly. If he could lead her to renounce the religion in which she had apparently ceased to believe, and persuade her to return to his father's roof, the Mormon husband himself might seek the dissolution of the marriage. Therefore Ephraim made no comment on what had passed, but asked gently, "What of last night, Susy?"

With a great effort she stood up, brushing away her tears, brushing back with both hands the hair that had fallen about her face. In the shock which Ephraim's proposal had given, in the brief interval of her tears, she had realised as never before that she could not shake off her duty to Angel as she had thought to shake off his creed. She spoke tremblingly.

"Ephraim, you are so good that you are above us all. You live in some higher place. You would have made this great sacrifice to help me." (She never doubted that Ephraim's proposal had been born in self-abnegation.) "Surely you can tell me what to do, for I am in great distress; but I want you first to remember that my husband is good, and that he loves me more than all the world, more than everything except God, and if he has told me a lie now, it must have been because he thought to save my soul by it, but I think—I think that the lie could not have been his. I think it must have been Joseph Smith's." She spoke very wistfully.

"What was it?" he asked again, tender of the shock she had received, yet still confident that it would be his part to widen this breach.

Looking down with burning cheeks, she told him what Halsey's story about Newell Knight's levitation had been. She remembered it quite clearly and told it baldly.

Before she finished it she heard him mutter below his breath that it was very strange. She was surprised at his tone of perplexity.

"It is very strange to me," she cried, "because I know my husband, and up till now he has been so upright and, except that he believed in Joseph Smith, so sensible and wise."

"And is this all?" asked Ephraim. "If it were not for this, would you be content to go on as before?"

He had begun to walk slowly on with the horse, and she too walked. After she had answered him the long silence became oppressive, and she knew that Ephraim was suffering to a degree that she could not understand. At length when he did speak his words were most unexpected.

He was looking toward the rising sun, which was still dim and flushed with the autumn haze. "The Christ whom we all worship," he began abruptly, "each in our different way, called himself by the sacred name of Truth. Does he desire, do you think, that we must worship him by adhering to what we know to be fact, no matter what would seem to be gained by slighting facts? It is a great temptation to me to conceal from you, Susannah, a part of my book knowledge which I cannot help thinking has some bearing upon this case—how much or how little I do not know."

He walked on for a little way, and at length, with a great sigh, he began to speak again, answering her first appeal for advice.

"I think that your prophet is mad or false, that his Mormonism is utter folly, but you knew that I thought that long ago. As to this story your husband has told you, I am bound to say that it has happened before in the world's history many times that men have seen, or thought they saw, a man rise into the air. In my opinion it is not the indication of a sound mind when men see such things, and I feel sure that such a phenomenon, fact or delusion, whatever it may be, cannot bear any relation to the religious life. My advice to you is—ah, Susannah, I can say it truly in the sight of God and of my own conscience—my advice to you is to be quit of such men and such scenes, but I dare not keep back from you the truth that this one story, so far from lessening my confidence in your husband's probity or in Smith's, has rather increased it; for, being very ignorant men, they could not have heard of these stories that I have told you, for I have read them only in rare books; that they have reproduced the same incident seems rather to prove that they have by accident stumbled upon the same fact—whether a dizziness of the eyes, or an affection of the brain, or an actual counteraction of gravity, I cannot tell."

She listened, drinking in each slow word. After all, then, today was just like yesterday, and that which she had to decide was as to the reasonableness of the whole new doctrine, as to her willingness to live among such scenes and such men.

There had been no sudden madness or deceit to give her reason for sudden revolt (perhaps her heart said excuse instead of reason).

Ephraim had grown very pale. After he had watched her for a while, he said with a sad smile, "You will not come home with me today, Susannah?"

"I must think over all this again, Ephraim. I don't know how these things can be, but what you admit is very strange."

He knew from her tone that the die was cast; he had no heart to discuss the laws that govern marvels.

"If at any time, any hour of the day or night, you should wish to come to us, Susannah, the door is open."

"You have been very kind, Ephraim. There is not much use in my trying to say anything about how good you are, but—" She stopped, thinking of her recovered confidence in his character and her husband's; in this thought she experienced an elevation of the spirits, a new hopefulness, which, after the dreary blank of the morning's outlook, was like sunshine after rain. With this elevation the religious habit of thought which she had learned from Halsey intermingled. "O Ephraim," she cried, "I believe that God sent you to give me back my faith."

He had nothing more to say after that. He rode away leaving her standing upon the tawny carpet of the fallen leaf, standing in the pink sunshine under naked trees, and looking after him with tears of gratitude in her eyes. Ephraim looked back once, but not again.

CHAPTER XIII.

When Susannah was returning from her parting with Ephraim Croom, she found Joseph Smith was walking slowly upon the road not far from John Biery's hotel. He was holding a small book open before his eyes, conning a lesson, repeating the words aloud again and again as a schoolboy might.

"It has been given to me to see that the Lord hath need of the learning of this world, Mrs. Halsey. When I have got the Latin and the Greek, I shall try to find some man who can teach me the Egyptian language, that I may know how far the ancient Egyptian from which I translated the Book differs therefrom."

Susannah had expected to find him excited after the events of the past night, but instead he was intent only upon committing a portion of the Latin grammar to memory, learning by rote as children did in those days.

"My husband told me," she began. She stood in awe of Smith, hardly knowing how to express herself to him; then she went on, almost roughly, "I don't see how Newell Knight could have gone up in the air and come down again; it does not seem to me sensible."

He clasped his hands behind his back, his large thumb holding his place open in the lesson-book, and walked beside her, his head bent somewhat forward in reverie.

"I am often much taken aback at what happens to me now, Mrs. Halsey, but I do declare to ye that that was the greatest wonder I ever saw before my eyes; and it's given to me to see that ye've got the same sort of difficulty about him as it's natural for me to have." He began to lapse in his own dialect. "Ye want to see the reason why of things. Well, I tell ye, I've just got down to this point, that I've give up tryin' to see why. If ye come to that, why was I chosen to lead this people? I tell ye when the words of the interpretation of the Book began to pour through my mind, and I'd no power to stop them, and I just felt as if I could cry like a baby when I couldn't get any one to write 'em down—I tell ye, I used often to ask why. But it ain't no use. What I've got to do is jest to get hold of the guiding that comes to me as clear as I can, and jest walk straight along those lines."

She was returning with a heart bruised with the pain of the recent colloquy at parting, but full too of purpose, feeling that she owed it to Ephraim to reconsider the evidence for Smith's prophetical claim. She glanced shrewdly at him as he walked and spoke—young, blue-eyed, large, and mild. The man seemed to her harder to comprehend if his word was disbelieved than if it was believed. On either supposition her understanding faltered.

"It is very hard for me to believe these things, Mr. Smith. It is very hard for me to believe, for instance, about the gold plates. How could they appear only to you and vanish again? It doesn't seem to me reasonable."

"No more is it reasonable, but lots of things in the Bible is as lacking in reason, like the sheet that appeared to Peter with beasts. But about the plates, I'll tell you just how it was, even though it's not just the way other folks has got hold of it. This is the truth, and you can think how hard it was to put it much straighter to folks who didn't believe in me then as they do now. The night that the angel came down three times and stood at the foot of my bed, and told me to go and get the plates and where they were to be found, my brain just seemed to go on fire. I could see things I never saw any other time. Why, that night I saw through the wooden wall and into the next room, just as if there hadn't been any boards there, and I saw all the air about me full of motes, just as they are in that sunbeam, and it was dark to other people. I could hear, too, the cocks crowing and dogs barking for miles round; and when morning came I got up and looked out, and it was as if I had my eyes to a telescope. I could see the houses for miles and miles. I ran up the hill and worked into the hole, and there I saw the plates, just as the angel had said. I'll never forget to my dying day just what they looked like, and the sort of writing they had. I took them up and covered them up as the angel had said, and I carried them home and hid them, and told my folks. That night I was an awful sick man, and the sickness was on me for some days, and when I looked again at the plates they just looked like bricks, but the angel told me that they were really the gold plates with the writing I remembered on them, but were changed lest any one should see them and die. And I was to keep them hidden. I know that it was true they were the plates by these two signs; firstly, whenever I hid myself and took the bricks in my hand, the words of the Book of Mormon came pouring through my mind, so I was like to cry out if I couldn't get some one to write them down; and Cowdery he did it and believed, and Martin Harris he heard me at the dictation and he believed, and likewise the Whitmers. And the second proof is that after I had buried the bricks by command, and we was far away from the place where they lay, Martin Harris and Cowdery and David Whitmer saw the plates, the very same as I had told them; they were floating in the air at the time of prayer."

"But, Mr. Smith, St. Peter saw the sheet in a dream; there isn't anything in the Bible about things or people floating in the air when people are awake."

"Well, I don't know, sister, about that. There was Philip when he finished baptisin' the African. Ye see, in going to Azotus he must have gone up before he went along, or he'd have struck agen the trees; and our brother Newell, not being as good as Philip, and not having as much faith, ye see, he jest began to go and had to come back again. Mebbe when he's engaged in the work for a year or two he'll become an apostle too. Did ye never think, Sister Halsey, that Providence might take us up, intending to do great things with us, and jest have to set us down because we hadn't learned to have faith enough?"

This spiritual significance of the episode of Newell Knight had not occurred to Susannah before. It touched her own case.

He went on. "When I think of the future that is opening before us, Sister Halsey—why, when I think of how all the nations are to be gathered in—there's persecutions in store, and we must be tried by fire, but there's riches and honour and blessing for those as shall be steadfast; and it's borne in upon me that the Kingdom shall be set up in the west of this land." He turned and looked at her, becoming elevated in mind and rising again into finer language. "And the men that are like unto thy husband, and have the single eye to believe and obey the word of the Lord, shall become as princes, dispensing bread to the hungry, and the water of life to them that are athirst; and the beautiful women who fail not but continue faithful, shall be as princesses driving behind white horses and wearing silken robes, and comforting the sick in their sickness, and welcoming the women of the nations as they come from distant lands, teaching them that which is good—" He drew his breath, as if about to say more and yet larger words, but remained silent, looking upon the open space of the fields. Then his mien, which had become enlarged, contracted somewhat, as if the vision were past.

"Why, Mrs. Halsey, when I do think of it, it seems as if one day at a time were'nt enough, and as if I couldn't just set myself to get the Latin and the Greek, and preach just to a few folks and help a person that's needing a bit of help; but it's borne right in here upon me that what we need is the learning of the world, otherwise called the wisdom of the serpent. I never was a great hand to learn, and father he didn't make me, so it comes harder now; but I'll see to it that the young ones of our folks shall take to learning mighty early; and what we want is to be faithful in small things, and not stumble in our faith if now and then a man do rise into the air."

She felt his blue eyes, mild but shrewd, meeting hers as he came to this last item.

"Sister, 'twas given to me to know the first time as I saw you that there was a great work for you to do in comforting and establishing the elect, and it comes to me now that you'd better be getting some more education, for although I suffer not a woman to teach, yet she may establish that which is already taught."

Inclined to put some question that would bring out more definite instruction as to her own special function in the Church, she did not notice two men who were approaching from the other side in a gig until they were close upon them.

One of these was a well-to-do farmer, the brother of a woman who had recently been converted at one of Smith's meetings. Now he was breathing out revenge. He sprang to the ground, striking at Smith with a heavy whip. Susannah saw the mildness of the prophet's eye turn into a sharp glitter. She realised that he was not afraid, although when the other man also sprang upon him there was not the least doubt but that he must be worsted in such an assault.

In the minute that Smith was wrestling with the farmer for the possession of the whip, Susannah wrung her hands in an agony and ran forward toward the hotel, screaming aloud for help; then, afraid of what might befall in her absence, she ran back. By this time the two men had thrown Smith down. Even then he showed his strength, for they struggled hard to get the whip, which he had seized from them.

In her storm of feeling Susannah for the first time came out from the habits of girlish timidity. Hardly knowing what she said, what she was about to say, she heard the words of her own fierce indignation ring out on the air of the mild autumn morning. The scene—the bare road, the sere weeds and grasses, the prostrate prophet, the flushed faces of the two burly countrymen upturned to hers as they stooped, crushing him down—all was photographed on her mind by excitement.

By the intensity of her upbraiding she arrested the attention of Smith's enemies for a minute till, as if he revolted against his own weakness, one of them gave vent to a loud jest, at which the other laughed.

The words meant nothing to Susannah, nothing more than the Latin words of the lesson-book that lay torn and muddy at her feet, but Smith no sooner heard them than he hurled himself from the ground with almost superhuman strength.

Both men were forced in self-defence to close upon him. Smith shouted aloud, although a hand on his throat almost choked him, "Go to the hotel, Mrs. Halsey; go in to your husband." Susannah knew now that he was fighting for her, not for himself; the allegiance of his glance gave her a thrill of loyalty to him which was wholly new.

Two men ran out from the hotel, and behind them John Biery. When they neared the place the farmer and his accomplice got into their gig and called back fierce threats against Smith as they went. John Biery was a constable, yet, although he saw that Smith had been brutally assaulted, he made no attempt to pursue and capture the offenders. The other men contented themselves with picking up his hat and book and remarking that the men that had run away hadn't had no sort of right, and that Smith ought to have the law on them. Susannah was the more enraged by this refusal to interfere.

Smith wiped his face from dust and blood. It pleased Susannah's love of dignity to observe that when he spoke it was not in impotent wrath.

"Go in to your husband, Mrs. Halsey, and tell him to rejoice that we are accounted worthy to suffer."

That was not exactly the news that Susannah did bring when she went back to her husband's room. Her feelings were so upwrought that it was some time before, in pouring out to Halsey her indignation, she could find relief. Whatever might or might not be the truth of Smith's heart, it remained true that in this persecution the many were ranged against the few, and were lashing each other on by false reports to lawless brutality. Like the Psalmist, Halsey led her as it were into the house of the Lord, and pointed out the end of the wicked and the award of the righteous. He added to the then popular notion of external reward thoughts which had been working in his own mind under the influence of that time-spirit which leads such minds as his in the foremost paths. He spoke to her of the strength of character gained and lost by all that was done and suffered in the right way or in the wrong.

Susannah was soothed. She knew that the truth was being spoken to her, and her heart leaped forth to do reverence, not only to it, but to the man who could find it in the midst of such insults. Ephraim was good. If he could only know how good Angel was, he would not have asked her to return. All thought of deserting the new cause now was gone; the blood that had trickled from Smith's bruised head, the danger that menaced Halsey, sustained her. She wrote to Ephraim to that effect.

Some days after, when driving past Biery's hotel from a meeting he had been holding in the town of Geneva, Joseph Smith entered and laid before Susannah books for the cultivation of her mind—a Latin grammar and exercise book like his own, a Universal History, and a primer of Natural Philosophy. He told her that in two weeks, when she had mastered their contents, he would bring her others. He left hastily, the business of the Church pressing.

In his idea it seemed that the rudiments of a language would take no longer to acquire than the contents of an English book written in a popular style. The man was very ignorant of the things that most men know, but possibly no other man in the world would have known that writing Latin exercises would bring contentment to Susannah's heart. There was nothing in such a request to awake suspicion and antagonism, and there was much in the regular mental exercise to keep her mind from brooding on its scepticism or upon Ephraim's kindness. As a child sits down to an intricate game, she sat down, day after day, to her lesson. Soon the stimulus of knowing that the prophet had actually mastered his grammar in two weeks wrought the determination not to lag very far behind. Her husband, who had had fair schooling, helped her.

There began to be a strange race between the prophet and Susannah for the acquisition of knowledge. They learned out of all sorts of lesson-books, not on any sound principle of work, but with avidity.

Susannah was the only woman in the new sect to whom Joseph Smith gave the commandment to become learned. She was not impervious to this subtle flattery. Rude and poor as he was, Smith was now spiritual dictator to a large number of souls, and she saw that from herself he sometimes asked counsel. Parted from Ephraim, having grown accustomed to a husband with whom self-repression was one of life's first laws, it was not surprising that under Smith's suggestion a new phase of life began in which her understanding, not her heart, developed. "Why believe in Moses and the prophets if not in Smith—in the miracles of yesterday if not in those of today?" was the question with which Halsey prefaced the sermons he began to preach. The answer that his logic deduced carried conviction to many of his hearers, but in Susannah's mind the question alone made way.

BOOK II.

CHAPTER I.

In the next year, 1831, the new church was formally organised, and this was the "revelation" given for her direction by the mouth of Joseph Smith—"And now, behold, I speak unto the Church; thou shalt not kill; thou shalt not steal; thou shalt not lie; thou shalt love thy wife, cleaving unto her and to none else; thou shalt not commit adultery; thou shalt not speak evil of thy neighbour, nor do him any harm. Let him that goeth to the East tell them that shall be converted to flee to the West."

The reports of the first missionaries, who had travelled westward, preaching both to the Indians (called by the "Saints," Lamanites) and to white men, were received in the beginning of this year, and the point designated for the first station of the Church on its way westward was a place called Kirtland, on the banks of the Chagrin River, in northern Ohio. Thither Halsey was sent, having commands to preach by the way.

At Halsey's wayside meetings the old hymns and the old tunes were sung. The new doctrine embraced all that was supposed to be alive in the old; it repudiated only what was supposed to be dead. It offered that enlargement of human powers which the belief in wonders implies, a new form of church government, a new land to live in, a new hope of a visible and glorious church, and, above all, a living prophet. If the personality of the prophet seemed more attractive to those who believed, not having seen him, to Susannah, who knew the baseness of his origin so well, the sudden increase of his influence over hundreds of people seemed the greatest of marvels; and it was impossible but that even his person should gain some added grace from the reflected light of success. Halsey was only one of a dozen successful Mormon preachers who were converging with their train of followers upon the first station of the new church.

There is no spot in northern Ohio more lovely than the five hills or bluffs that rise from the banks of the Chagrin River and its tributary brooks twelve miles to the south-east of what is now the city of Cleveland. On the shores of the river and its streams lie green levels; from these the bluffs rise steeply for some one or two hundred feet to tablelands of great fertility.

The site for the first Mormon temple was on the highest of these hills overlooking the three valleys. Its foundations were quickly laid. Around it upon the slope and tableland, up and down the valleys, and upon the opposite hills, the wooden houses of the converts began to spring up, not unlike in colour to a crop of mushrooms, and very like in the suddenness of their growth.

Not long after Susannah and Halsey had reached Kirtland, Joseph Smith, with a convert named Rigdon, went on, with missionaries who were travelling farther west, in order to find in the wilderness the place that was appointed for the building of Zion or the New Jerusalem. At the same time all those men among the converts who were deemed fit were sent out in couples to preach the new Gospel, some back to the eastern States whence they had come, some to Canada, some to the south. To Joseph Smith it was given to know who was to go and who to stay. Halsey was directed to remain, to receive and establish the new converts who came, to tithe their property for the building of the temple, and to found, according to Smith's direction, a school of the prophets.

"And to thy wife, Susannah, it shall be given to teach the children such worldly learning as she has herself acquired, until it may be possible for us to appoint for them a more learned male instructor."

Joseph Smith spoke these words in the room which served him as business office and chapel. He was drawing on his gloves, ready to go forth upon the journey to Missouri.

Several of the elders and their wives were present, some busy on one errand and some on another. Susannah, being with Halsey, received the command in person, although it was not directly addressed to her. She had observed that since her arrival at Kirtland the prophet never addressed himself to her directly when in public. In many ways his manners were becoming gradually more formal, and his relapses into his native speech less frequent.

Susannah could not criticise keenly, so much she marvelled at the man. His activities before starting on this journey were almost incredible. Every hour he had made decisions, for the most part successful, concerning the adaptability of men whom he had only seen, for labours of which he knew as little. He had preached continually. He had baptised newcomers in the icy floods of the April stream. He had advised as to the choice of lands and their manner of cultivation, as to the size and form of houses. He had visited the sick and planned merry-makings for the young. In addition to all this, even while preparing for the long journey into an unknown region, he was busy learning three languages, and was laying plans, not only for missionary campaigns that were to spread over the whole earth, but for a new translation of the Old Testament. If the better clothes that he had begun to wear sat somewhat pompously upon him, if his manners now sometimes indicated an attempt not only to be, but to appear, a prophet, such small affectations sank out of sight in the light of such extraordinary ability.

After Smith and Sydney Rigdon had started westward, Susannah went over to console Emma. The prophet's wife was at that time living in a building of which the front part was the general store whence the material needs of the growing church were as far as possible provided. Susannah passed through between bales of cloths, boxes, and barrels of provisions. It was dusk; a young man who served in the store carried a candle before her, and the odd-shaped piles of merchandise threw strange moving shadows upon the low beams of the roof and walls. The young man held the candle to light the way up a straight staircase. "Mis' Smith," he shouted, "here's Mis' Halsey come to see you."

At the top of the staircase Susannah was met by a cooing, creeping baby, who beat with its little fist upon a wicket gate fencing off the stair.

"It was the last thing he did before setting out, to nail that gate together and fasten it up with his own hands, so as I wouldn't need always to be running after the young one, lest he should fall down the stair." It was Emma Smith who spoke; she emerged dishevelled and tearful from an upper room. "When he has so much to think about and all, and Elder Rigdon waiting for him at the office till he'd finished. Mr. Smith, he's always so kind, and he knew as that would be the thing as would give me the most help of anything."

Emma subsided again into tears—tears that were the more touching to Susannah because Emma was not like most women; she seldom wept.

"I don't mean to give way," Emma continued, "but if it was your husband as had gone, you'd know how it was, and it's the first time I've ever been separate from him so long."

Susannah sat down with the child in her arms. When the question was brought home to her she did not believe that temporary separation from Halsey would cause her tears.

Emma began again with an effort at self-control. "It's a long way to Jackson County, quite across Missouri. It's all Elder Rigdon's doing, his going just now."

Susannah found something that she could say here in agreement. "It may be wrong, but I—I don't like Elder Rigdon."

"Well, of course the way he believed, and all his congregation, when the word was first preached to them makes Joseph think that he must be full of grace. Ye know, to see Joseph when he's quite by himself, ye'd be surprised to see how desponding he is by nature. He's that desponding he was real surprised, real right down taken by surprise, when he heard that Mr. Rigdon, so clever a minister as he was, and of the Campbellites too, had been baptized and a hundred and twenty-seven of his congregation with him. (That was first off, and ye know how many he's brought in since.) He could hardly believe it; he says, 'It seems as if I hadn't any faith at all.' And that night he couldn't sleep, but just walked up and down, and two revelations came to him before morning, and one of them addressed to Rigdon, so Joseph knows of course he's got the right thing in him. Then his education, too; he's got a sight more education than Cowdery. Joseph thinks a deal of education."

"I don't like him." Susannah sat upright; her hands were busy with the baby upon her knee.

"Well, I dunno." Emma spoke meditatively. "It said in one of Joseph's revelations that we should dwell together in love."

Susannah laughed; it was a bright, trilling laugh, and filled the large, low room with its sudden music. It almost seemed like a light in the growing darkness.

"I guess I'll light up," said Emma, "it'll be more cheerful."

Susannah was still playing with the baby, and Emma looked at her critically. "Joseph thinks a great deal of you, Mrs. Halsey; he's told ye to teach school?"

"I have got more time than most of the women, and my husband can afford to hire a school-room."

"'Tain't that," said Emma decidedly, "it's the same thing as makes ye say that you don't talk to any of the other folks except in a civil way. Ye're a bit above all the rest of us ladies in the way ye hold yerself and the way ye speak. I guess it comes of yer father's folks having been somebody, and then being so clever at books—ye see, Joseph sees all that; there ain't anything that he doesn't see."

Susannah perceived that there was something behind this. "You're not vexed, are you?"

Emma continued with more hesitation in her tones. "No, I'm not vexed. Why should I be? And besides I like you and Mr. Halsey better than any of the folks, although I couldn't let it be known."

"There's something that you are thinking about."

Emma sighed deeply; her mien faltered; she subsided again into her seat by the wall and into tears. "It's only that I feel that Joseph's getting to be such a great man. Why, there's more than a thousand folks now looking to him all the time to be told what to do, and thousands more drawing in, and Joseph beginning to wear the kid gloves whenever he goes on the street."

There was an interval of sighs and suppressed sobs.

"Aren't you glad? I thought you were glad about it."

"I declare papa and mamma were just wild when I ran away and married Joseph, because they said that he was a low fellow, and poor, and not good enough for me, and now—and now—I begin to feel that I'm not good enough for him."

Susannah went over and sat beside her, chiding indignantly. "You know very well that nobody could be the same help to him that you are, and you know very well that there's nobody in the world that he thinks so much of as you." She did not say all she thought. She considered Emma to be Smith's superior, but that opinion would have given acute pain.

The young church worked upon Smith's principles of thrift, temperance, and co-operation, and Kirtland rapidly assumed the proportions of a town. Susannah became the mistress of the children's school. Smith was a good economist; although he helped the needy, nothing that his converts could pay for was given to them for nothing. Hence it was that Susannah's private purse was well filled with tuition fees.

She had already in mind what she would do with this money; she would write to the booksellers in Boston who fulfilled Ephraim's orders, and obtain from them some of the books whose names she remembered to have seen on his shelves. She knew nothing of their contents, she hardly knew whether she wanted them more for the sake of their contents or for their familiar appearance, but she thought that if she did not understand them when reading, she could write to Ephraim and ask for an explanation. She could not think of any other excuse for writing to him again. It had taken her a good many months to think of this one.

Halsey, who had learned to drop the Quaker forms of speech when speaking to others, still, moved by the remembrances of his early home, used them in speech to Susannah. He inquired somewhat anxiously concerning the proposed purchase.

"Dost think that they will contain what the prophet has called 'sound learning,' and that there will be nothing in them to distract thy soul?"

"How can I tell when I do not know what is in them?" She did not speak with impatience.

"Art wise, dear heart, in this longing?" he asked wistfully.

Then he carried away her order and despatched it.

In the meantime Smith had returned from Missouri, his mind filled and, as it were, enlarged by the new land which he said was appointed by revelation as the site of the New Jerusalem. Jackson County, on the south bank of the Missouri River, was the place. He had already gathered four or five hundred new converts there, and he was now possessed with the desire for money to build the new city, and for a million proselytes to dwell in it. In spite of this, after sending out new relays of missionaries in all directions, he settled down to the most sober routine of study. Hebrew was the new language he wished to acquire, and he felt the call to revise the Old Testament.

CHAPTER II.

Only one unusual incident occurred in Susannah's presently peaceful life. One day in the golden October she set out to walk some distance up the valley of the Chagrin River. The object of the walk was a visit to one of the outlying farmhouses occupied by a family of the Saints; but Susannah, as was her wont, found more joy in the walk than in the visit. When she had passed beyond the meeting of the waters, the valley lay long before her, about a mile in width and quite flat. The stream was scarcely seen; the ground was covered with flowery weeds, white asters with their myriad tiny stars, the pale seed feathers of the golden rod, high grasses, and wild things innumerable which had been turned brown and gray by the autumn sun, pink clumps of the rice weed, and small groves of the scarlet stalks of the wild buckwheat. This level sea of weeds stood so high that when she threaded the narrow path they reached above her waist. The bees in the white asters were humming as they hum in apple bloom. The blue jays were calling and flying in low horizontal flights. The valley stretched to the south-east, then curved; a little mountain barred the view, upon whose pine-trees the distant air began to tinge with blue. On the curving bluffs on either side the trees stood in stately crowds; hardly a leaf had fallen, except from the golden walnut-trees; the colour of the foliage was for the most part like the plumage of some green southern bird, iridescence of gold and red shot through. To her right, where a part of the long hill had been cleared of trees, the sun shone upon bare gullies in the soap-stone cliffs, making the colour of that particular brown bit of earth very vivid. Everywhere a soft autumn haze was lying, and above white clouds were swinging across the pale blue sky.

After threading the valley path for a mile Susannah was ascending the bluff to get to the level of the upper farms, when, much to her surprise, she came, as once before upon the hill Cumorah, upon Joseph Smith. He was lying under a group of giant walnut-trees, whose boles were sheltered from the road by a natural hedge of red dogwood and brambles. He had apparently been occupied at his devotions, but she only saw him arising hastily. This time there was no peep-stone; it had long since been discarded. The prophet had a Bible in his hand, and it was evident that he had been weeping. It was in those lands the habit of religious men of all sects to make oratories of the woods. Susannah's only desire was to pass and leave him undisturbed, but he spoke.

He began severely, "Sister Susannah Halsey, it is not meet that a woman should stray so far from home and without companions."

For a moment Susannah stood abashed. Unaccustomed to censure, she supposed that she must have done wrong. "I have walked this way before," she began meekly, "but if—" She stopped here, her own judgment in the matter beginning to assert itself.

The prophet had forgotten his reproof. At all times his conversation was apt to reveal that sudden changes of mental phase took place within him apparently without conscious volition. He now exclaimed with more modest mien, "It is, no doubt, by the will of the Lord that you are come, for I stood in sore need of comfort, for the revelation of the truth is a trial hard to endure, and at times very bitter."

"Is it?" asked Susannah intently. It was impossible but that her long curiosity should find some vent, and yet she shrank inwardly from her own prying.

The prophet leaned against a huge bole. The ground at his feet was covered with yellow walnut leaves and the olive-coloured nuts. The sunlight fell upon him in patches of yellow light. He opened the Bible, turning over the leaves of the Old Testament as if making a rapid survey of its history in his mind.

"Sister Halsey," he began, "when the favour of the Lord rested chiefly upon the Jewish nation, at the times of the patriarchs and David, and when Solomon, arrayed in all his glory and in the greatness of his wisdom, reigned from Dan to Beersheba, mustn't those have been the times when the people walked most closely with the Lord?"

"I suppose so, Mr. Smith."

"It is not enough to suppose, Sister Halsey, for it is clearly written that when the Jews went contrary to the will of the Lord they were given over into the hands of their enemies."

Susannah endeavoured to give a more unqualified assent.

"Sister Halsey, there has come to my soul in reading this book in these last days a word, and I know not if it be the word of the Lord or no."

She saw with astonishment that his whole frame was trembling now. She began to realise that he was truly in trouble, whether because of the greatness of the revelation or because of private distress she could not tell. She became more pitiful.

"I hope you are well, Mr. Smith, and that Emma is well. There is nothing to really distress you, is there?"

In hearing the increased gentleness of her tone he seemed to find a more easy expression for his pent-up feeling. "It's come upon me in a very cutting way, truly as the prophets said like a two-edged sword, and at the time too when I was inquiring of the Lord concerning—" He stopped here, and she felt that his manner grew more confidential, but he did not look at her, his eyes sought the ground—"concerning a matter which has given me no little heart searching." He stopped again, she listening with a good deal of interest.

"It's come to me to observe that among the chosen people—there ain't no gainsayin' it, Sister Halsey, though I trust you to be discreet and not mention the matter, but in the days when the divine favour rested on Israel each man had more than one wife; and the Lord Himself says He give them to Solomon, the only objection being to heathen partners."

"Do you mean, Mr. Smith, that I'm not to mention what everybody knows already, that in the Old Testament times polygamy was practised?"

The now entire lack of sympathy in her tone affected him as an intentional act of rudeness would affect an ordinary man. The tissue of his mind, which had relaxed into confidence, grew visibly firmer. He assumed the teaching tone.

"No, Mrs. Halsey, the only thing that I asked you not to mention was that I had any light of revelation on a point on which most of our minds is already made up."

"Mr. Smith, you can't possibly be in the slightest doubt but that it would be very wicked for any man now to have more than one wife."

"I've heard a great many of the ministers who in times past, in the time of our bondage we heard and believed, say as it would be very wicked for any one nowadays to take God at His word and expect Him to do a miracle or heal the sick; but I've come to the conclusion, Mrs. Halsey, that it isn't a question of what we in our ignorance and prejudice might think wicked, but it's a question of what's taught in this book, looked at without the eye of prejudice and tradition. What we call civilisation is too often devilisation—*devilisation*, Mrs. Halsey."

He tapped the book. He was becoming oratorical. "The idea of one wife came in with the Romans. 'Twas no institution of Jehovah, Mrs. Halsey."

Susannah, more accustomed to his oratorical vein than to private conference, became now more frank and at ease.

"You said you didn't know that the idea was from the Lord, Mr. Smith, and I don't think it is. I don't think you'll entertain it very long, and I don't think, if you did, many of the Saints would stay in your church."

She bade him good-day, and went on up the slope. When she was walking along the brink of the bluff in the open beyond the nut-trees she heard him call. He came after her with hastened gait, Bible still in hand. She was surprised to find that what he had to say was very simple, but not the less dignified for that.

"I sometimes think, Sister Halsey, that you look down on us all as if we weren't good enough for you, although you're too kindly to let it be seen. According to the ways of the world, of course, it's so. If I'm as rough and uneducated as most of our folks, at least I can think in my mind what it would be not to be rough, and I can think sometimes how it all seems to you."

His words appealed directly to strong private feeling which had no outlet. While she stood seeking a reply the natural power that he had of working upon the feelings of others, vulgarly called magnetism, so far worked in connection with his words that tears came to her eyes.

"I don't often think about my old life," she said with brief pathos.

Smith was looking at the ground, as a huge, shy boy might stand when anxious to express sympathy of which he was somewhat ashamed. "I know it must be a sort of abiding trial to you." After a moment he added, "I wouldn't like to make it worse by having you think that I was goin' to preach any strange doctrine. I'd sometimes give a good deal if the Lord would raise me up a friend that I could speak to concerning the lights that come to me that I know that it wouldn't do to speak of in the public congregations, because of their upsetting nature, and likewise because I doubt concerning their meaning. And of this matter there was no thought in my mind to speak in public, for it is for the future to declare whether it be of the darkness or of the light; but to you I spoke, almost unwittingly, and perhaps in disobedience to the dictates of wisdom."

He looked at her wistfully.

Susannah leaned her arm upon the topmost log of the snake fence and looked down the slope. His insight into her own trials caused her to sympathise with him in spite of his absurdity. She made an honest effort to assist him to self-analysis. She said, "A great many things come into our minds at times, Mr. Smith, that seem important, but, as you say, if we do not speak about them, afterwards we see that they are silly. Of course with you, if you think some of your thoughts are revelations, it must make you often fancy that the others may be very important too, but it does not follow that they are, and, as you say, time will weed them out if you are trying to do right." She wondered if he would resent her *ifs*. She stood looking down the bank in the short silence that followed, feeling some-what timorous. The steep ground was covered with the feathery sprays of asters, seen through a velvety host of gray teasles which grew to greater height. Through the teasles the white and purple flowers showed as colours reflected in rippled water—rich, soft, vague in outline. At one side, by an old stump, there was a splendid feather, yellow and green, of fading golden rod; yellow butterflies, that looked as if they had dyed their wings in the light reflected from this flower, repeated its gold in glint and gleam over all the gray hillside, shot with the white and the blue. At the foot of the bank lay the flat valley, and from this vantage ground the river could be seen. The soft musical chat of its waters ascended to her ears, and among the huge bronze-leafed nut-trees, whose shelter she had just left, the woodpeckers were tapping and whistling to one another.

At length Smith sighed deeply, but without affectation. "Yes, I reckon that's a good deal how it is. It ain't easy, Mrs. Halsey—I hope in your thoughts when judgin' of me you'll always remember that it ain't easy to be a prophet."

When he had gone, Susannah found herself laughing, but for Halsey's sake the laughter was akin to tears.

CHAPTER III.

Ohio was being quickly settled. Within a few miles of Kirtland, Cleveland and Paynesville were rising on the lake shore, and to the south there were numerous villages; but the society of the Saints at Kirtland was especially prosperous, and so sudden had been the increase of its numbers and its wealth that the wonder of the neighbouring settlers gave birth to envy, and envy intensified their religious hatred. Twice before Smith had left Fayette he had been arrested and brought before a magistrate, accused of committing crimes of which the courts were unable to convict him. Now the same spirit gave rise to the same accusations against his followers. About this time webs of cloth were taken from a woollen mill near Paynesville, and several horses were also stolen. The Mormons, whether guilty or not, were accused by common consent of the orthodox and irreligious part of the community. Hatred of the adherents of the new sect began to rise in all the neighbouring country, as a ripple rises on the sea when the wind begins to blow; the growing wave broke here and there in little ebullitions of wrath, and still gained strength until it bid fair to surge high.

About Christmas time there were a number of cases of illness in Kirtland. Joseph Smith healed one woman, who appeared to be dying, by merely taking her by the hand, after praying, and commanding her to get up. After that he went about with great confidence to others who were stricken, and in many cases health seemed to return with remarkable celerity. It is hard to understand why the report of this, going abroad with such addition as gossip gives, should have greatly added to the rage of the members of other religious sects. Perhaps they supposed that the prophet arrogated to himself powers that were even more than apostolic. They threatened violence to Kirtland on the prophet's account, so that before the new year he took Emma and the child and established himself with them in an obscure place called Hiram, some twenty miles to the south. Sydney Rigdon, who by this time was, under the prophet, the chief leader of the Saints, went also to Hiram to be beside him. Smith was toiling night and day to produce a new version of the Hebrew Scriptures, believing that he was taught by inspiration to correct errors in them. Rigdon was scribe and reviser. These two being absent from Kirtland, responsibility and work without limit rested again with Angel Halsey.

With unsatisfied affections and thoughts wholly perplexed, Susannah beheld the days of the new year lengthening. Then she fell into the weakness, to which humanity is prone, of hoping eagerly for some external circumstance that should lighten the inner darkness. A bit of stray news one day came to her with the shock of an apparent fulfilment of her vague expectation. Finney was passing through that part of the country preaching. Of all human beings she had ever met, this remarkable evangelist most impressed her as a man who had intimate dealing, awful, yet friendly, with an unseen power. She had no sooner heard that he was within reach than her mind leaped to the determination to hear him preach and speak with him again. She would lay her difficulties before him; she would hear from him more intelligence concerning the home which she had left than a thousand letters could convey.

It was March now. The winter's snow was gone. Finney, as it chanced, was to come as near to Kirtland as the village of Hiram. Susannah spoke to her husband.

"Did you hear that Mr. Finney was going to preach at Hiram?"

She stood turning from the white spread table in the centre of the room. The morning light was shining on the satin surface of the planed maple wood with which walls and ceiling were lined. Halsey was putting on his boots to go out to his day's round of business and pastoral work. He knew just as well as if she had explained it to him that a great deal lay behind what she said. He fell to wondering at once what she could want. Was it to send a message to the old home by the man whose very name must recall all its memories?

"I want to go and hear him preach," Susannah went on.

Halsey was disturbed. "Thou canst not really have such a desire," he said severely.

"Why not? A great deal that he preaches is just the same as what you preach, Angel."

He saw that she was in a turbulent mood, and that grieved him; but as for her request, he could not believe it to be serious.

"Thou art speaking idle words," he said with a sigh, and he rose to go out.

"You have not answered me. Why shouldn't I hear him when you agree that much that he says is true?"

"He is in the camp of those whom Satan has stirred up to do us injury. That which thou callest truth in his mouth is but the form of godliness, for it is clear that if God be with those who fight against us he cannot be with us."

Something in the expression of her face brought him now a more distinct feeling of alarm. His nature was singularly direct. He had scarcely finished his meditative argument ere he sought to clinch its purport, and, stepping near, he laid his hand gently upon her shoulder.

"Dost thou doubt, Susannah, that God is with us?"

The crimson colour mounted from her cheeks and spread over her white brow. It was as if Angel had asked what he never had asked, whether she loved him or not, whether all her thoughts and feelings were loyal. She knew that for him there was no line of separation between life and love, and love and religion. She was careful for him always, as a mother is for a delicate child, as a sick nurse is for a patient. She could not have endured to give him the pain of hearing her denial, even if such denial would have expressed her attitude truly.

"Indeed, Angel, I—I know that you—" she faltered.

The trouble in his face was growing. "Has not *God* made the signs of his presence clear to us, and even visible before our eyes? If thou shouldst deny the outward signs, is it not by his grace that we live? Susannah, dost thou think that it is in me by nature to bear with the infirmities and murmurings of our people as I bear with them daily—babes as they are, learning, but not yet having learned, to live at peace with one another? Or dost thou think that it is in me to forgive daily the outrageous acts and words of our enemies, trying as they do to injure our innocent brothers, or even our prophet himself? Yet, Susannah" (his voice was stirred with emotion), "I would bear witness to thee that every day, as I pray, the anger is taken out of my heart, and I can deal with these very men in the spirit of love."

Standing erect before him, confused and distressed, she made another effort to soothe, even taking his hand from her shoulder and trying to caress it between her own, but so tense was the question in his mind that his fingers were limp and unresponsive to her touch.

"I know all that you would say, Angel; I know that you are good; I know that our people, although they have many faults, are trying to do right, and I believe that the people in other sects around us are far more wicked, but—Mr. Finney is not like that."

"Dear heart, thou knowest well that there is no goodness but that which comes from above, and although this Mr. Finney may have a show of goodness, as thou or I might have in his place, yet what avail can his preaching be if God be not with him? So what show of goodness he has only aideth the devil; for how can it be possible, when two armies are encamped one against another, that God can fight upon both sides? Is Christ divided?"

A loud knock came to the outer door; Elder Halsey was late in getting to his work; men were waiting for him. He let the sound of the raps die away before he answered them; his searching look was upon her face, hungering for some assurance that his words had met and slain her doubts. Then he was forced to leave her.

It was easy for Susannah to obtain a horse to go to the village of Hiram. When the day of Finney's preaching came, after her husband had gone to his afternoon work, she rode out of Kirtland.

Since she had made up her mind to disobey she had said nothing further to Angel. Why inflict upon him the painful attempt to hinder her which his conscience would demand?

The last snow-wreath had faded, but there was not as yet a bud or blade of perfect green. The valley of the Chagrin lay almost hueless in the cold sunshine. A light wind was blowing over its levels of standing weeds, and whispering in the bare arms of the huge nut-trees upon its bluffs.

When the sun began to sink, Susannah had reached the low rolling ground that surrounds Hiram. The landscape here had a less distinctive character, and there was no vapour in the sky to make the sunset beautiful. She was weary of her horse's rough trot, and still more so of its slow plodding, but she felt excitement. She had conquered those forces, part of her womanhood, which urged compliance with her husband's desire and her own desire to abide by the homely routine whatever it might be. The thing that she had done seemed so large that her imagination told her that the event must justify it.

She had no thought of concealment. She knew only the two families in the village of Hiram. Her plan was to go first to the Rigdons and ask for refreshment, thence to the meeting, and after that to ask for the night's lodging which she knew that Emma Smith would not refuse.

In the village she saw that people were moving about and talking with an air of excitement. When she turned to a quiet corner and asked an elderly man for Mrs. Rigdon's house, he stared at her as if at an apparition.

"Is it Sydney Rigdon's wife that you're wanting?"

Susannah had raised her veil, and he looked at her face with the greatest curiosity. Flushed with exercise, braced by the sharp air, her colour was brilliant and her eyes sparkling. Her plain dress and heavy veil appeared to the man to be a disguise, so surprising to him was the brilliancy of her face and the modulation of her voice.

"Do you not know where the Rigdons live?" she asked.

He was chewing tobacco, and now he spat upon the ground, not rudely, but as performing an habitual action in a moment of abstracted thought. "Oh, I know well enough, but if ye won't mind my saying a word to ye, young lady, I'd advise ye to put up somewhere else. I've got darters of my own—in course I don't know who ye may be or what ye may be doing here." This last was added in an apparent attempt to attain to some suspicion that he felt to be reasonable.

"You think ill of them because you despise their sect," she said gently, "but I am the wife of one of the elders."

"Have ye got hold of some news that ye're carrying to them?" He evinced a sudden interest that appeared to her extraordinary.

"What news?"

"Oh, I don't know. I jest thought 'twas queer, if you'd got hold of anybody's secrets, that you should be asking where they lived, straight out and open in the street like this."

His words suggested to her only the idle fancies of prejudice. Some other people drew near, and, dropping her veil, she was starting in the direction in which he pointed when he spoke again in a more determined voice. "You jest tell me one thing, will you?" He even laid his hand upon her bridle with authority, "Are ye going to stop at Rigdons' all night?"

"No."

"Sartin?"

When he received her reply he let go the bridle, saying in warning tones, "Well, see that ye don't do it, that's all."

The incident left a disagreeable impression on Susannah's, mind, but she did not attach any distinct meaning to it.

Rigdon and his wife were both within. Rigdon locked the door when Susannah had entered. Then with crossed arms, standing where he could watch against intruders from the window, he began to tell her news of import. His mother, who was an old woman, his wife, and some younger members of the family, gathered round.

The light fell sideways upon his thickset form and large hairy face. His manner was the result of struggle between effort for heroic pose and an almost overmastering alarm. His matter was the evil conduct of the surrounding Gentiles toward the Saints. It seemed that in this and neighbouring places, evangelistic meetings had been held in which Presbyterians, Baptists, and Methodists had joined, and Rigdon averred that the preachers had used threatening and abusive language with regard to the Saints. A series of such meetings had begun in Hiram, small as it was; and Joseph Smith, like a war-horse scenting the battle, had set aside his arduous task of correcting the Old Testament and gone forth to preach in the open air. At first he had been greeted only with derision or pelted with mud, but in the last few days he had made and baptized converts, and now the fury of the other sects was at white heat.

Susannah's mind swiftly sifted out the improbabilities from Rigdon's wrathful tale.

"But the people that gather to such meetings as Mr. Finney holds are for the most part awaked, for the time at least, to a higher Christian life. It cannot be they who have used the vile language that you repeat."

She almost felt the disagreeable heat of Rigdon's breath as he threw out in answer stories of coarse and brutal insult which had been heaped upon himself and Smith. The large animal nature of this man always annoyed her. There was much of breath in his words, much of physical sensation always clinging to his thoughts. At present, however, she was not inclined to judge him too hardly; although visibly unstrung, unwise in his sweeping condemnation, coarse in his anger, and somewhat grandiloquent in his pose, there was still much of real heroism in his mental attitude. Braced by the fiercest party spirit, he stood staunch in his loyalty to Smith and the cause, with no thought of yielding an inch of ground to the oppressors.

"I do not believe," repeated Susannah sturdily, "that it is the more religious of the Gentiles who have said and done these things. I have come here tonight to hear and to speak with Mr. Finney, whom I know to be a very godly and patient man."

"Why has he come here?" demanded Rigdon. "He who by his preaching can gather thousands in populous places, why should he ride across this thinly settled parcel of land, preaching to mere handfuls, if it is not to denounce us? And he has not the courage to go nearer to the place where the Saints are gathered in numbers. He will teach his hearers first to ravage the few sheep that are scattered in the wilderness, that by that they may gain courage even to attack the fold."

Susannah drew upon herself their anger, and so strong was Rigdon's physical nature that even his transient anger seemed to embody itself in some sensible influence that went out from him and preyed upon her nervous force.

The night had fallen. A bell, the rare possession of the largest meeting-house, had already begun to ring for Finney's preaching. Susannah went out on foot. The Rigdons, as also the Smiths, were living some way from the village. She had now a mile of dark road to traverse.

Closely veiled, Susannah stepped onward eagerly. She felt like a child going home. The scene which she had left showed up vividly the elements of Mormon life that were most repulsive to her, the broad assumptions of ignorance, the fierce beliefs born of isolation, and the growth by indulgence of such animal characteristics as were not kept under by a literal morality or enforced by privations. She was going to see a man who could speak with the voice of the sober past, whose tones would bring back to her the intellectual delicacies of Ephraim's conversation, the broad, pure vision of life which he beheld, and the dignified religion of his people.

The meeting-house was of moderate size. It was already filled when Susannah entered, but she was able to press down one of the passageways between the pews and seat herself near the front, where temporary benches were being rapidly set up.

Many of the congregation had doubtless come as far as she. Men and women of all ages, and even children, were there. Some, who it seemed had followed Finney from his last place of preaching, were talking excitedly concerning the work of God which he had wrought there. On every face solemnity was written, and stories were being told of one and another who in his recent meetings had "fallen under the power of God."

When Finney ascended the pulpit Susannah forgot all else. The chapel was not well lighted, but the pulpit lamps shone upon him. He had a smooth, strong face; his complexion was healthy and weather-beaten; his dark eyes flashed brightly under bushy brows. His manner was calm; his style, even in prayer, was that of keen, terse argument; he spoke and behaved like a man who, having spent the emotional side of his nature in some private gust of passionate prayer, had come forth nerved to cool and determined action.

With her whole soul Susannah hung upon his every word, unreasonably expecting to find some new and unforeseen solution to the problems of her life. He had pointed out a straight path to multitudes; she hoped that he could now show it to her.

The power of Finney's preaching lay in its close logical reasoning, by which, accepting certain premises, he built up the conclusion that if a man would escape eternal punishment he must forsake his sin and accept salvation by faith in the doctrine of the substitution. He began always by speaking to the indifferent and the unconvinced; he led them step by step, until it appeared that there was but one step between them and destruction, and that faith must make one quick, long leap to gain the safety of the higher plane, whose joys he depicted in glowing terms.

For the most part there was intense silence in the congregation, although sometimes an audible whisper of prayer or a groan of suppressed emotion was heard. The infection of mental excitement was strong.

Susannah was experiencing disappointment. Accustomed as she was to excitement in the meetings of the Saints, her mind easily resisted the infectious influence. Finney's teaching had not differed in any respect from the doctrine which she heard from her husband daily, a doctrine which she knew by experience did not save men from delusion and rancour. She still listened eagerly to hear of some provision made in the scheme of salvation against injustice and folly. Surely Finney would say something more.

As it happened he did say something more. When for more than an hour he had explained the great plan of salvation he touched upon the responsibility that the hearing of such conclusive reasoning imposed. The sower had sown broadcast; it remained for him to speak with awful impressiveness of those forces which would be arrayed against the convicted soul. Under this head he referred at once and with deep emotion to the devil, who, in the guise of false teachers lying in wait, caught up the seed.

There could be no doubt that the Mormon leaders were in his mind, as they were in the mind of his congregation. It became swiftly evident to Susannah that Finney was stirred by what he believed to be righteous indignation, and that he was as content to be ignorant concerning the doctrines and morals of the people against whom he spoke as were the rudest members of the outside rabble who now pressed with excitement to the open doors and windows.

The righteous Finney had no thought of unrestrained violence. He spoke out of that deep well of hatred for evil that is, and ought to be, in every good man's heart, but he had not humbled himself to gain any real insight into the mingling of good and evil.

"They are liars, and they know that they are liars," said Finney, striking the pulpit cushion. "The hypocrisy of their religion is proved by the lawless habits of their daily lives. Having sold themselves to the great enemy of souls, they lie in wait for you and for your children, seeking to beguile the most tender and innocent, that they may rejoice in their destruction."

He used only such phrases as the thought of the time warranted with regard to those who had been proved to be workers of iniquity, but to Susannah it was clear, in one brief moment, what effect his words would have when heard by, or reported to, more brutal men. She knew now that Rigdon's words were true. The so-called Christian ministers, even the noblest of them, stirred up the low spirit of party persecution.

She rose suddenly, sweeping back her veil from her face. "I will go out." She said the words in a clear voice.

A way was made to a back door by the side of the pulpit. Every one looked at her. Finney, going on with his preaching, recognised her as she began to push forward, and he faltered, as if seeing the face of one who had arisen from the dead. The excited audience felt the tremor that passed over its leader; it was the first signal for such obvious nervous affections as frequently befell people under his preaching; before Susannah had reached the door a stalwart man fell as if dead in her path.

There was a groan and a whisper of awe all round. This was the "falling" which was taken by many as an indubitable sign of the divine power. Susannah had seen it often under Smith's preaching. She waited with indifference until he was lifted up.

Then the sea of faces around her, the powerful voice of the preacher resounding above, passed away like a dream, and were exchanged for a small room and a dim light, where two or three people were gathered round the form of the insensible man. She escaped unnoticed through a private door into the fields, where the March wind eddied in the black night.

CHAPTER IV.

The house in which the Smiths lived was small. Susannah crossed a field-path, led by a light in their window. In the living room a truckle bed had already been made up. By the fire Joseph and Emma were both occupied with two sick children. These children, twins of about a year, had been taken out of pity at their mother's death, and Susannah was told as she entered that they had been attacked by measles.

Susannah found that the fact that she had been to the meeting had not irritated the Smiths, although Mrs. Rigdon had called to make the most of the story. Emma, absorbed in manifold cares for the children, was only solicitous on Susannah's account lest a night's rest in that house should be impossible. Smith, pacing with a child in his arms, seemed to be head and shoulders above the level whose surface could be ruffled by life's minor affairs. With the eye of his inner mind he was gazing either at some lofty scheme of his own imagining, or at heaven or at vacancy. All of him that was looking at the smaller beings about him was composed and kind.

One of the twins, less ill than the other, had fallen asleep in Emma's arms. The other was wailing pitifully upon the prophet's breast.

"Do you and Mrs. Halsey go in and lie down with that young un, Emmar, and rest now for a bit while ye can."

"I can't leave ye, Joseph, with the child setting out to cry all night like that."

But he had his way. Long after they had lain down in the inner room Susannah heard him rocking the wailing babe, or trying to feed it, or pacing the floor. Emma, worn out, slept beside her. Upstairs the owners of the house, an old couple named Johnson, and Emma's own child, were at rest.

Susannah lay rigidly still in the small portion of the bed which fell to her share. Her mind was up, wandering through waste places, seeking rest in vain. The wail of the child in the next room at last had ceased. The prophet had lain down with it on the truckle bed. Long after midnight Susannah began to hear a low sound as of creeping footsteps in the field. Some people were passing very near, surely they would go past in a moment? She heard them brushing against the outer wall, and gleams of a light carried fell upon the window.

In a minute more the outer door of the house was broken open. Emma woke with a cry; instinct, even in sleep, made her spring toward the door that separated her from her husband.

The two women stood in the inner doorway, but the coarse arm of a masked man was already stretched across it, an impassable barrier. The prophet lay on the child's bed, so heavy with sleep tardily sought that he did not awake until four men had laid hold of him. All the light upon the scene came from a smoking torch which one of the housebreakers held. Some twenty men might have been there inside the room and out. The women could barely see that Smith was borne out in the midst of the band. He struggled fiercely when aroused, but was overpowered by numbers.

The owners of the house came down from above, huddling together and holding Emma, who would have thrown herself in the midst of the mob.

Susannah had not undressed. She threw her cloak over her head and ran out, determined to go to the village and demand help in the name of law and a common humanity. She was in a mood to be reckless in aiding the cause she had espoused.

By the glow of the torch which the felons held she saw the group close about the one struggling man as they carried him away. She fled in a different direction.

She had gone perhaps sixty rods in the darkness out of sight of Smith and his tormentors when she was stopped by three men and her name and purpose demanded. When she declared it in breathless voice they laughed aloud. In the darkness she was deprived of that weapon, her beauty, by which she habitually, although unconsciously, held men in awe.

"Now, see here, sister, you jest sit quietly on the fence here, and see which of them's going to get the best of it. Your man's a prophet, you know; let him call out his miracles now, and give us a good show of them for once. He's jest got a few ordinary men to deal with; if he and his miracles can't git the best of them he ain't no prophet. Here's a flattish log now on top. Git up and sit on the fence, sister."

While she struggled in custody another group of dark figures came suddenly at a swinging trot round the dark outline of one of the nearer houses. They brought with them the same kind of lurid torch and a smoking kettle or cauldron carried between two. The foremost among them were also carrying the body of a man, whether dead or alive she could not see. When he was thrown upon the ground he moved and spoke. It was Rigdon's voice. She perceived that he was helpless with terror. The prophet had certainly struggled more lustily.

"Now you jest keep still, sister," said the loudest of her three companions. "Kill him? not if ye don't make a mess of it by interferin'. It's only boilin' tar they've got in the pot."

Susannah covered her face with her hands; then, too frightened to abstract her mind, she gazed again, as if her watchfulness might hinder some outrage. The group was not near enough, the light was too uncertain, for her to see clearly. The shadows of the men were cast about upon field and wall as if horrible goblins surrounded and overshadowed the more material goblins who were at work. They were taking Rigdon's clothes from him. Their language did not come to her clearly, but it was of the vilest sort, and she heard enough to make her heart shiver and sicken. They held over him the constant threat that if he resisted they would kill him outright. If Smith, too, were exposed to such treatment she did not believe that he would submit, and perhaps he was now being done to death not far off.

When they began to beat Rigdon with rods and his screams rang out, Susannah could endure no longer. She broke madly away from her keepers, running back along the road towards Emma's house. They essayed to follow; then with a laugh and a shrug let her go, calling to her to run quick and see if the prophet had fetched down angels to protect him.

Susannah ran a long way, then, breathless and exhausted, found that she had missed a turning and gone much too far. Afraid lest she should lose herself by mistaking even the main direction in which she wanted to go, and that while out of reach of any respectable house she might again be assailed by members of the mob, she came back, walking with more caution. She had no hope now of being the means of bringing help. She had come farther from the village instead of nearing it, and what few neighbours there were, having failed to interfere, were evidently inimical.

When she found the right turning she again heard the shouts of some assaulting party, and, creeping within the shadow of trees, she waited.

At length they passed her, straggling along the road, shouting and singing, carrying with them some garments which, in rough horse-play, they were tearing into fragments. When the last had turned his back to where she stood she crept out, running again like a hunted thing, fearing what she might find as the result of their work. To increase her distress the thought came that it was more than possible that like work had been going on at Kirtland that night. Tears of unutterable indignation and pitiful love came to her eyes at the thought that Angel, too, might be suffering this shameful treatment. Across some acres of open ground she saw the Smiths' house, doors and windows lit by candles. Thither she was hastening when, in the black space of the nearer field, she almost fell upon a whitish form, grotesque and horrible, which was rising from the ground.

"Who is it?" asked Joseph Smith.

He stood up now, but not steadily; his voice was weak, as if he had been stunned, and his utterance indistinct because his mouth had apparently received some injury. She thought of nothing now but that he was Angel's master, and that Angel might be in like plight.

"What have they done? What is the matter?" she whispered tenderly, tears in her voice.

"Is it you?" he asked curiously. He said nothing for a minute and then, "They've covered me with the tar and emptied a feather-bed on me. If ye'd have the goodness to tell Brother Johnson to come out to me, Mrs. Halsey—"

"They have hurt you other ways," she said tremulously, "you are bruised."

"A man don't like to own up to having been flogged, ye see; but Peter and Paul and all of *them* had to stand it in their time, so I don't know why a fellow like me need be shamefaced over it. But if you'd be good enough, Mrs. Halsey, to go and tell Emmar that I ain't much hurt, and send Brother Johnson out with some clothes or a blanket—"

He stopped without adding that he would feel obliged. As she went she heard him say with another sort of unsteadiness in his tone, "It's real kind of you to care for me that much."

In her excitement she did not know that she was weeping bitterly until she found herself surrounded by other shuddering and weeping women in Emma's room; for other of the converts in Hiram, hearing of the violence abroad, had crept to this house for mutual safety and aid.

It is the low, small details of physical discomfort that make the bitterest part of the bread of sorrow. Now and afterwards, through all the persecutions in which she shared, Susannah often felt this. If she could have stood off and looked at the main issues of the battle she might have felt, even on the mere earthly plane, exaltation. Yet one truth her experience confirmed—that no human being who in his time and way has been hunted as the offscouring of the world—no, not the noblest—has ever had his martyrdom presented in a form that seemed to him majestic. It is only those who bear persecution, not in its reality but in imagination, who can conceive of it thus.

All night the women were crowded together in the small inner room with the two sick babes, while Emma and two of the brethren performed the painful operation of taking the tar from Smith's lacerated skin. The prophet bore himself well. Now and then, through the thin partition the watchers heard an involuntary groan, but he was firm in his determination to be clean of the pitch, and to preach as he had appointed the next day.

At dawn Susannah went to get her horse at Rigdon's house. The animal was safe. When she had saddled it she inquired after the welfare of those within the house. Rigdon was raving in delirium. He had, it seemed, been dragged for some distance by his heels, his head trailing over stony ground. They had not been able to remove the tar and feathers. He lay upon a small bed in horrible condition. His wife, with swollen eyes and pallid face, was sitting helpless upon the foot of the bed, worn out with vain efforts to soothe him. His mother, a thin and dark old woman, vibrating with anathemas against his tormentors, led Susannah in and out of the room silently, as though to say, "This is the work of those whose virtue you extolled."

The village, the low rolling hills about it, lay still in the glimmer of dawn. The men of violence were sleeping as soundly, it seemed, as innocence may sleep. The famous preacher, and all those souls that he had thrilled through and through for good and evil, were now wrapped in silence. Susannah rode fast, guiding her horse on the grass by the roadside lest the sound of his hoofs should arouse some vicious mind to renewed wrath. Her imagination, possessed by the scenes of the past night, presented to her lively fear for Halsey's safety. She gave her horse no peace; she thought nothing of her own fatigue until she had reached the Chagrin valley, and the walls of the Mormon temple which was being reared upon Kirtland Bluff were seen glistening in the sunlight, with the familiar outline of the wooden town surrounded by gray wreaths of the leafless nut woods. It was high day, and the people were gathering for morning service when Susannah rode her jaded horse through the street of the lower village and up the hill of the Bluff.

As she lifted the latch of her own door Angel was about to come out to preach. His face was very white and sad. Susannah's glad relief, fatigue, and excitement found vent in tears.

"You are safe!" she cried. "Oh, my dear, I will never leave you again while danger is near—never, never again!"

In the evening of that day further news came from Hiram. The prophet had preached long and gloriously in the open air. New converts had been made, and he himself, scarified and bruised as he was, had gone down into the icy river and baptized them in sight of all. The mob had shrieked and jeered, but had been withheld by God, as the messenger said, from further violence.

Susannah made no further effort to find new life in the old doctrines. All her sentiments of justice and mercy combined to make her espouse her husband's cause with renewed ardour.

CHAPTER V.

In the summer of that same year, while the wheat in the Manchester fields was still green, and the maize had attained but half its growth, while the ox-eyed daisies still stood a happy crowd in the unmown meadows, and pink and yellow orchids blazed in unfrequented dells, the preacher Finney, after long absence, chanced to be again travelling on the Palmyra road. As was his habit, he sought entertainment at the house of Deacon Croom in New Manchester.

The preacher remembered always that his citizenship was in heaven. From the thought he drew great nourishment of peace and hope, but as far as his earthly affairs were concerned the outlook was at present grievous.

He was returning from a long and dreary religious convention held in an eastern town, where one, Mr. Lyman Beecher, had stirred up against him the foremost divines of New York and Boston. They had asserted that Finney's doctrine, that the Spirit of God could suddenly turn men from following evil to pursuing good, was false and pernicious; that his method stirred up the people to unholy excitements which were productive of great evil. Now the accusations of these divines (who, thinking that a man's change of mind must needs be so slow a thing, some of them, gray-haired, had not as yet produced this change in a single sinner) were in many points wholly false, in many exaggerated, and where the article of truth remained in the accusation there was much to be said in defence of work that had resulted, if in some evil, certainly in much palpable good. To such groups of priests and soldiers and publicans as came forth to John's baptism of repentance, the godly Finney, travelling now east and now west, had appealed, and that the wide land was the better for the crying of his voice no candid person who knew the result of his labours could deny. He that had two coats had imparted to him that had none; the extortioner had returned his unfair gains, and some rough men had become gentle. But in the assembly from which Finney had just come the larger numbers and the greater power of rhetoric had been on that side which appeared to show least faith in God and least zeal for men, and Finney had come out from the combat bruised in spirit.

Some natural comfort the weary man experienced from the sweet charm of the summer afternoon, from anticipation of the welcome and sympathy which would soon be his. He heard, but could not see, the Canandaigua water as it ran under its canopy of willows, over whose foliage the light wind passed in silver waves. On the height of the hill above the mill-dam he turned his horse into the yard of the Croom homestead. The stalwart deacon in overalls, his excitable, slender wife, her cap-strings flying, came forth, the one from the barn, the other from her bake-house.

It was not to either of these worthy souls that Finney intended first to confide the story of his glimpse of Susannah. It said much for the sterling truth of this man's soul that, accustomed as he was to demand from himself and others public confession of those experiences most private to the individual soul, he had not lost delicacy of feeling or reverence for individual privacy in human relationships. He had not been at this house since the month after Susannah's departure, when excitement and wrath still raged concerning her. He judged that in the hearts of the older members the wound had healed, leaving only the healthy scar that such sorrows leave in busy lives. He knew, too, that in Ephraim's heart the blade of this grief had cut deeper.

The supper over, the full moon already gilding the last hour of the summer daylight, Ephraim donned his hat to take the solitary evening stroll to which he had become accustomed. He thought to leave the trio who were in complete accord of sentiment to talk longer over the persecution which Finney endured, but on the little brick path between the flower-beds the evangelist came up with him.

Ephraim was but half pleased. It was in this brief evening hour that he set his thoughts free, like children at playtime. Like other students forced to live in invalidish habits, he had established a rule of thought more strict than men of active callings need. At certain hours he would study his country's social, political needs; at others he would help in his father's farm management; at others he would study some exact science. But when the measured hours of his day were over, and before he lit his student's lamp, for a while he turned his fancies loose, and they ran all too surely to play about Susannah's charms, about the circumstances of her life. This was not his happiest hour. The eternal advantage of love was lost for the time in its present distress. Hateful thoughts were the results of this self-indulgence, yet he hated more anything that came as interruption. During these years the lover in him had not grown what the world calls wise.

For some minutes Finney, controlling the briskness of his ordinary pace, walked by Ephraim's side and contented himself with the gracious scene, passing remarks upon weather and crops. Soon, for the value of time always pressed upon him, his business-like voice took a softened tone, and he began preaching a heart-felt sermon to his one listener.

The subject of the sermon was "the fire God gave for other ends," and he ventured to point out to Ephraim, in his plain, logical way, that it was wrong to waste on a woman that devotion which God intends only himself.

Ephraim smiled; it was a good-tempered, buoyant smile. "Did it ever occur to you, Finney, to reflect that, with your opinions, had you been the Creator, you would never have made the world as it is made? What time would you ever have thought it worth while to spend in developing the iridescence on a beetle's wing, in adjusting man's soul till it responds with storm or calm, gloom or glory, to outer influence, as the surface of the ocean to weather?"

Finney was puzzled, as he always was, by Ephraim's *bonhomie* and his strange ideas. "But what have you to advance against what I have already said, Ephraim?"

"Advance? I advance nothing. I even withdraw my painted insects and the storms of emotion by which I had perhaps thought that God did his best teaching; I withdraw also my exaltation of that strait gate of use without abuse for the making of which I had almost said Heaven hands us the most dangerous things. I withdraw all that offends you, Finney, in order to thank you for having spoken her name. No one else has spoken it in my hearing since they knew of my last parting with her, and I—I am fool enough half the days to wish the clouds in their thunder-claps would name her."

The voice of the whip-poor-will complained over the tops of the woodland in near and far cadence through the warm moonlit air. Beside this and the throb of insect voices there was no sound. "I came out this evening," said Finney, "to tell you that last March in Ohio I saw *her*." His voice fell at the pronoun in sympathetic sorrow.

"Yes?"

"When I was about to return from Cincinnati I was advised to go northward to the Erie Canal, in order that I might pass through that part of the State which has been sorely infected by the cancer of that hypocrite's teaching."

There was no need in the district of Manchester for Finney to explain what hypocrite he meant. In his own country Smith was commonly held to be the arch-hypocrite.

"The devil has surely espoused that cause in earnest, for the number of deluded souls in that part of Ohio and in southern Missouri, and scattered as missionaries up and down the country, is, I hear, between three and four thousand."

"And always among those who worship the letter of the Scripture," remarked Ephraim, "for their missionaries give chapter and verse for all they teach."

"I was told that their customs were peculiarly evil. Even among themselves they lie and steal and are violent and licentious; and they teach openly that it is a merit to steal from the Gentiles, as they call those not of themselves; and, furthermore, they aim at nothing less than setting up a government of their own in the west."

"Who told you all this?"

"I am sorry to say that I had it on good authority. Some of the western brethren had it from a poor fellow who had been deluded into entering the Mormon community, and had barely escaped with his life when he desired to withdraw."

"Would you consider a pervert from your own sect the best witness of its tenets? But you say that you saw my cousin?"

Finney told what had led him to the village of Hiram, and said, "When I spoke of the sins of the Mormons, a young woman seated near the front of the congregation rose up. It was your cousin. I saw at once by the pallor of her face that the Lord was having direct dealing with her soul. The 'power' was indeed very great; a strong man fell as dead near her, who before the night was over gave testimony of sound conversion. After he and your cousin had been led out, many others in different parts of the building cried to God for mercy. When the sermon was over I sought for your cousin, but when I told who she was, the people of the place said that no doubt Mormon messengers had come while she was waiting, and forced her to depart. That night there was a disturbance in the place; some of the more hot-headed men had the leaders out, and tarred and feathered them—a dastardly deed! I have been threatened myself with being rid on a rail and tarred when the devil stirred up the people against my preaching, but the Lord mercifully preserved me. 'Tis a shameful practice, but I hear it was done to these men to intimidate them from the more violent crimes which they had conspired to commit. In the morning I was forced to go, as I was advertised to preach at many stations farther on, or I would have denounced the violence from the pulpit. I could not find out anything more concerning your cousin, but the Lord has never allowed me to doubt that the many prayers which we have offered on her behalf were answered that night, for I could see by the expression of her face that she, like those upon the day of Pentecost, was cut to the heart."

At the garden gate, under the boughs of the quince-tree, which had increased its branches since the day in which Susannah had last passed under them, Ephraim now stood in the moonlight, barring the entrance. At length with a sigh he said, "Alas! Finney, I believe that there are few souls under heaven more true and more worthy than your own; but as for the power of God, 'His way is in the sea and his path in the great waters, but his footsteps are not known.'"

Out of his breast Ephraim took a thin leather book, and from out of the book gave Finney a letter much worn with reading.

Finney took the letter reverently, and read it by the light of his bed-room candle. In those days letters were more formally written; this one from Susannah to Ephraim began with wishes concerning her aunt and uncle and the prosperity of the household. The fine flowing writing filled the large sheet.

"I write to you, my dear cousin, rather than to my aunt, to whom I fear my letter would not be acceptable, for although I can say that I regret my wilfulness and the manner of my disobedience, still I can never regret that, having been forced to choose, I threw in my lot with those who can suffer wrong rather than with those who have it in their hearts to inflict wrong, for if there be a God—ah, Ephraim, this is another reason why I address you, for I am in sore doubt concerning the knowledge of God, as to whether any knowledge is possible. My husband, who denies me nothing, has allowed me to send for some of your books whose names I remembered. I thought at first to write to you about them, but I distrust now my own understanding too much to venture. I would like you to know that they have helped me somewhat, for I do not now say to myself in hard, tearless fashion that I know there is no God, to which thought I was driven by the reflection that most of those who seek him most diligently sow the wind and reap the whirlwind.

"But the more immediate occasion of this letter is to tell you that a month since Mr. Finney held a meeting not far from us. I went, thinking to gain some help from him, and to hear news of you, but I was greatly disappointed, and made very angry. He preached as my husband and many of our elders preach, and there were among the crowd the same signs of excitement and peculiar manifestations that we have constantly among us. But toward the end of his sermon Mr. Finney spoke of my husband's Church, and he lent the weight of his influence to very evil slanders that are constantly repeated about us by those who have not sought to know the truth. He did us great injury by stirring up the roughest of the people to violence. Mr. Finney will, I suppose, visit you and repeat those lies, which no doubt he believes, but is most culpable in believing, because he has not investigated the scandal against us as he would have investigated scandal against any who are orthodox. I write now to tell you that that which he says is not true. For although there are a few criminals amongst us, as in every community, evil is not taught or condoned."

As Finney read this letter by his lonely candle he was so far stirred by what he deemed the merely human side of the incident as to say to himself, "Poor Ephraim! She has never even known that he loved her." But next day, in speaking to Ephraim, he pointed out that in the worst communities there were always pure-minded women who knew little or nothing of the evil around them, and said he believed that his message would still be the means of bringing home the truth to Susannah's heart.

CHAPTER VI.

In the meantime an interval of comparative peace had come to Kirtland. The Gentiles, because they discovered that the town was a good market for the produce of more fields than the Saints could till, allowed their religious zeal to slumber.

A female relative of Halsey, having lost her friends by death, came from the east to Kirtland upon his invitation.

Susannah went down the hill one summer day to meet the travelling company of new converts which brought Elvira Halsey. That young lady had seen about twenty-five years of life's vicissitudes, and had sharpened her wits thereon. Slight, pretty, and dressed with an effort at fashion that was quite astonishing in the Kirtland settlement, Elvira sprang from the waggon.

"I've come to be a Mormon. How do you begin?" With these words she presented to Susannah a new type of character, fresh, and in some ways delightful.

There was quite a crowd at the stopping place of the waggons. Halsey, with other elders and Smith, came to welcome the newcomer. Elvira stood on tip-toe, peeping about, pressing Susannah's arm with whispers. "Which is Joe Smith, do tell me? Do you go down on your knees to him, and does he pat your head?"

Guided by keen instinct, Elvira did not make remarks in Halsey's hearing which would have shocked him, but perhaps by the same instinct she at once claimed Susannah as a confidante in spite of some feeble remonstrance.

"Are you not wrong to speak so lightly of our religion?" asked Susannah, feeling that she was an elder's wife.

"First let me be sure that you have any religion to speak of." She looked up prettily in Susannah's face. "What a beautiful creature you are!" she cried. "And is it to please my cousin Angel that you wear a snuff-coloured dress and a white cap and a neckerchief like an old lady of seventy?"

As they proceeded together up the white curving road, over the crest of the verdant bluff, Elvira announced her further intentions.

"I am not going to live with you. I am going to board with the Smiths. I want to get to the bottom of this business, and see the apparitions myself."

"There are no apparitions," said Susannah gently.

"Gold books, you know, flying about in the air, and the angel Maroni and hosts of the slain Lamanites."

"You expect too much. Such visions as Mr. Smith had came but at the beginning to attest his mission and give him confidence."

"Tut! I should think he had sufficient of that commodity. It is I who require the confidence, and have I come too late?"

"I would question, if it did not appear unkind, why you have come at all?"

"Bless you, it's relations, not revelations, that I came after."

"I fear that Angel will not be satisfied with that attitude," Susannah sighed. She supposed that Elvira represented all too well the attitude of educated minds in that far-off world whose existence she tried to forget.

"Therefore," said Elvira, "I will board with the Smiths."

Elvira's whim to be received into the prophet's family could not be carried out, but by persistency she succeeded in establishing herself in the household of Hyrum Smith, where she distinguished herself by two peculiarities—a refusal to marry any of the saintly bachelors who were proposed to her, and a perpetual good-natured delight in all that she saw and heard. She resisted baptism, but to Susannah's surprise, remained on perfectly friendly terms with the leaders of the sect.

The next two years passed quietly in Kirtland. Susannah, imbued, as indeed were all Smith's friends, with his belief that the peace was but for a time, cherished her husband as though death were near, and grieved him by no outward nonconformity to pious practices. Many chance comments which she made were straws which might have shown him the way the current of her thought tended underneath her habitual silence, but they showed him nothing. It was mortifying to her to observe that Smith, rarely as he saw her, was always cognisant of her mental attitude, while her husband remained ignorant.

Susannah gave up the girlish habit of fencing with facts that it appeared modest to ignore. She was perfectly aware that she exercised a distinct influence over the prophet, of what sort or degree she could not determine. Little as she desired this influence, she could not withhold a puzzled admiration for Smith's conduct. He rarely spoke to her except in the most meagre and formal way, and all his decrees which tended for her elevation in the eyes of the community or for her personal comfort were so expressed that no personal bias could be detected.

She asked herself if Smith practised this self-restraint for conscience' sake, or from motives of policy, or whether it was that several distinct selves were living together within him, and that what appeared restraint was in reality the usual predominance of a part of him to which she bore little or no relation. There was much else in his character to admire and much to condemn. He had steadily improved himself in education, in mental discipline, and in personal appearance and address. He could hardly now be thought the same man as when he had first preached the new doctrine in Manchester. This bespoke an intense and unresting ambition, and yet the selfishness that is the natural result of such ambition was absent. As far as his arduous work would permit, he gave himself lavishly to wife and child, to all the brethren, rich and poor, when they asked for his ministrations. The motherless babies whom he had helped Emma to nurse through their infancy had gone back to their father's care, but there was never a time when some poor child or destitute woman was not a member of his household. On the other hand, many of the actions of his public life were questionable. He had established a bank in Kirtland, of which he was the president. Even Halsey admitted to Susannah that this was a great mistake, that the bank ought to have been under the control of some one who understood money matters; the prophet did not. He had also set up a cloth mill, and undertaken to farm a large tract of land in the public interest. The prophet showed to much better advantage when instituting new religious ceremonies, of which there were now many and curious, or when giving forth "revelations" which had to do with the principles of economy rather than its practical details. Susannah thought that the voice of the Gentiles all around them, shouting false accusations of greed and dishonesty, would sooner or later find much apparent confirmation if no financier could be found to lay a firm hand upon the prophet's sanguine tendency toward business speculation.

CHAPTER VII.

In the bleak December two elders came from Zion, the holy city in Missouri, bringing the history of dire tribulation.

It was a cold night; the first snow was falling upon the wings of a gale. Susannah was sitting alone quietly working out problems in algebra, in which study Smith had desired that her elder pupils should advance. The storm beat upon the window pane, and set the bright logs of the fireplace now flaming and now smoking, the varnished wooden walls dimly reflecting light and shadow.

Halsey had been out to see the newcomers, who were staying at the prophet's house. It was late when she heard his tread, muffled in the drifted snow. He hardly paused to shake it from his clothes before he came near. She saw that he was in a mood of strong grief and excitement.

"Angel," she spoke pityingly, "you have had a hard, hard day; you have stayed so very late at this evening's conference." She held out her hand to him. "Do not tell me tonight if you can rest before telling." Young as she was, her countenance, as she lifted it toward him, was motherly. She remembered what a mere boy he was, fair and hopeful, when she had first seen him three years before, and now strong lines of purpose and endurance were written upon the face that was thin and pale, the paler, it seemed, because of the transient colour that the storm had given a moment since to the clear skin.

"I would that thou didst not need to hear, but it is not for us to turn our eyes from that which the Lord hath written for our instruction in the suffering of our brethren." Then he added, "The elders from Zion have told us all. There was great joy and prosperity among them, and the more foolish boasted of their wealth to the Gentiles, saying also that the Lord had given the whole land to them for an inheritance."

"That, indeed, was very foolish," said Susannah.

"Nay, but it was small blame to them, for that which they said is true. But among the Gentiles the political demagogues began to be afraid that we should rule the country by the number of our votes. The Gentiles gathered together in the town of Independence, and three hundred of them signed a declaration demanding that every one in Zion should sell all that he possessed and leave the country within a certain time, and that none other of us should settle there."

"But forced sale would mean that no fair value would be given for the property; it would be simple robbery," she cried; "and they call this the land of freedom!"

"They appealed to the Governor of Missouri, but they found that the Lieutenant-Governor, a man called Boggs, was among the fiercest of the persecutors. As for the Governor himself, he advised them to resort to the courts for damages."

"What next?" She was impatient at a pause he made.

He knelt down upon the floor in front of her, laying a calming hand upon her shoulder. "Susannah, there is this one great cause for our deep gratitude to heaven, that this time all our elders with one voice called upon our people to bear with patience, to cry to God to cleanse their hearts from all anger and revenge."

"I suppose that was well," she said, but with hesitation.

By the gentle pressure of his hand he still expressed his sympathy for her pain in listening. "Lawyers were engaged to carry the matter through the courts. But no sooner was it known that the thing was to be publicly tried than the Gentiles rose in arms. For three nights they entered the houses of the Saints, beating the men, burning their barns, and in many cases unroofing the houses. Some of our brethren went to Lexington for a peace warrant, but the judge was frightened at the mob, and, moreover, if he had offended them he would have lost much money, so he told the Saints to arm and defend themselves."

Halsey had paused again. The moral question here involved was to him of deep importance.

"If it was only for self-defence, Angel—" she began.

He shook his head. "Nay, it was a fierce temptation, and our people are not yet sanctified, but God in his great mercy withheld them from sinning against him. For they had no sooner obtained arms than Lilburn Boggs, the Lieutenant-Governor, came and disarmed them."

"And then?"

"Our people were driven from their homes. In the cold storms of November, women and little children and wounded men were forced to flee out upon the open prairie, and up and down the banks of the Missouri River. At last they gathered together on the river-side, and many of them have now crossed it, remaining in the opposite county, and the others have dispersed, poor and homeless, into less unfriendly parts of the State. These elders have come here that the prophet may send back some revelation at their hand, and that we may all gather together what we can spare from our abundance for the relief of our fugitive brethren."

His eyes were shining with triumphant faith, even though the close of his narrative seemed to admit of so little hope.

"And will Mr. Smith still teach them that they must not strike a blow for their rights?" she asked.

This was fast becoming the critical question of the hour.

In February the snow lay deep on the land. Susannah, like all her neighbours, spent some days isolated by the drifts, the men only going abroad. On one of these afternoons the prophet tapped at her door. His visit in Halsey's absence was unprecedented.

Without preface he began to make a statement as to the affairs of the Church in Missouri.

"The greater part of our fugitive brethren have at my desire gathered together upon a large tract of uncleared land that lies just across the river from Zion. It is the desire of the Lord that they should there await until it is his will to open the gates of Zion once more."

"It is *your* desire that they should gather and wait there."

She spoke with no rude emphasis, but he understood. This man could read her thought before it was expressed. He pushed his thick hair from his forehead with a heavy hand.

"Understand, Mrs. Halsey, that I *believe* the voice of the Lord has spoken, but it is also my desire."

"Does the voice of the Lord ever speak but in accordance with your desire?"

The answer burst from him with almost hysterical force, "I would to heaven it did not."

"But in such cases are not your desires divided against themselves? and the word of the Lord comes perhaps in accordance with one desire and in contradiction of another?"

He sat for some time looking absently upon the floor.

"The things of the Lord," he said, "are of vast importance, and require time and experience, as well as deep and solemn thought, to find them out. And if we would bring the world to salvation it requires that our minds should rise to the highest, and also search into and contemplate the lowest abyss"—he paused for a moment, and then added in sad undertone—"that is within our own hearts."

Susannah was silent, wondering what was the true secret of his elusive thought.

He went on with an effort. "Accepting your own words, Mrs. Halsey, that it is at my desire that they are there instead of being scattered among friendly settlements where they could obtain support, it remains true that they are naked, hungry, and cold. When I sleep the vision of their sufferings comes before me." He went on again with more vehemence. "It is also by obeying my doctrine that they are cast out of their own lands and from their own hearths. Whether the Lord hath spoken or no, it is by obeying the doctrines that I have taught that they are in wretchedness." He rose, pacing the room, apparently unconscious of what he did.

"I know that this has been weighing upon you, as it has upon my husband."

He shook his head impatiently, striking his breast suddenly with one hand. "There is but one heart," he said, "in which the pains and sorrows of them all are gathered."

She began to see that he had a plan to unfold.

At length he stopped in his pacing, looking toward her. "We must go to their relief," he said. "We must gather an army and conduct our suffering brethren back to their homes in Zion."

"By force of arms?" she asked.

"If need be."

He left time for the significance of these words to be fully comprehended, and then went on speaking as he paced again. "It may be that we will not need to fight, that if we get ourselves in readiness we shall need but to stand still and see the salvation of the Lord; and in plain language to you, who expect no miracle, Mrs. Halsey, I would be understood to say that if a sufficient number of our strong men, armed for defence, join our brethren in Missouri, the Gentiles will be afraid to attack."

At last she asked, not without excited tremor in her voice, "Who? How many? When?"

These were important questions with regard to the organising of an army, but the prophet had in mind a point that must previously be determined.

"Your husband," he began abruptly, "he has still upon him the taint of his Quaker upbringing, for the Lord Christ indeed taught long-suffering, and he sent them out at first, as we also have sent our missionaries, with nothing in their hand save a staff only, but afterwards he said, 'Let him that hath a sword take it,' and they said unto him, 'Lord, here are two swords,' and he said, 'It is enough,' which I take to mean that where one sword is raised there must be another to ward off a blow or to strike in return. But your husband is teaching the people that to bear arms, even in self-defence, is wrong."

Susannah saw that already in Smith's indomitable will the era of armed defence had begun. Her hatred of the persecution caused her sentiments to chime with his. She only said in defence of Halsey's meekness, "My husband would have gone before now to give himself and all that he has to help these poor people if you had not interfered, Mr. Smith."

A change of expression came in a moment over Smith's hulking form, as if a different phase of him came forward to deal with a change of subject. He turned upon her almost sharply, "There is one man in Kirtland who shall not go to Zion till peace is there. If he went, would he not of his own accord rush into the forefront, into the hottest of the battle, not to fight but to receive the sword in his breast and be slain, even as Uriah the Hittite was slain? Wherefore, I say unto you, he shall not go."

Susannah, like all good women, had no keenness of scent for scandals, ancient or modern. She did not remember who Uriah was, and took no offence.

The prophet had tarried in his pacing by the window; with hands clasped behind him he was looking absently out upon the driven snow. Upon his face was an expression which Susannah only sometimes saw, and that in the moments which she felt to be his best. She believed this man to have true moments of humility and high resolve; it was only a question with her how far they permeated his life. In a minute more he turned again and spoke modestly and sadly enough.

"As I have said before, it is not in me to greatly love our brother Halsey's manner of thought, but I perceive his holiness and the Church shall not lack his counsel. I am here today to tell you how much it grieves me to set a constraint upon his conscience, yet I am here also to ask you to tell him from me that it is not the will of the Lord that he should continue to preach against the spirit of self-defence."

When he was gone Susannah realised how angry she would have been if she had heard that Smith had rebuked her husband on this subject, yet now that the fiat lay in her own hands to impart with all gentleness, the task, because of her own fierce attitude toward the oppression, was grateful to her.

When the roof had been set on the white walls of the first great Mormon temple upon Kirtland Bluff, a small army, well armed, well provisioned, went out from Kirtland for the deliverance of Zion amid the prayers and huzzahs of the little community. There were many who, like Halsey, bewailed in secret this taking of the sword, but the doctrine of non-resistance was never preached again.

CHAPTER VIII.

After this Susannah's attention was centred upon the coming of her first child.

"'Tain't lucky to have a child when the leaves are falling," said Elvira Halsey, a certain mist of far-off vision clouding her sparkling eyes.

Susannah had been greatly weighed down by depression, not fearing ill-luck, but regretting for the first time unfeignedly that she had ever joined herself to the sect in which her child must now be nurtured. For herself, feeling often that all religions were equally false, it had mattered little; with strange inconsistency she now perceived that she would greatly prefer another faith for her child. Susannah literally found no place for repentance; to confess her grief to Halsey would only have been to crush out all the domestic joy of his life; she was too courageous to do that when she saw no corresponding good to be gained. Yet when the baby at length lay on her lap, grew and smiled, kicked and crowed, Susannah forgot at times, for hours together, the superstitions of the Latter-Day Saints. The motherly solicitude which she had long exercised over Halsey changed into something more like friendship when she saw him hang over her and her child as they played together.

Susannah had given up her school. The winter was severe, and mother and child hibernated together by the sweet-scented pinewood fires till the stronger sun had melted the frost flowers on the panes. Spring had nearly come before Susannah divined that for the child's sake Halsey had been protecting her for months from the fear of a near disaster that was weighing upon his own heart.

This was the year of what was called in the early Mormon Church "the great apostasy." One evening Halsey came in looking so white and ill that Susannah drew back the baby, which she had held out for his evening kiss.

In a few minutes she understood what had occurred. Some four or five leaders in the Church, with their families and friends, had charged Smith with hypocrisy and fraud.

It was not Susannah's own opinion that such a charge could be maintained. Smith appeared to her to be like a child playing among awful forces—clever enough often to control them, to the amazement of himself and others, but never comprehending the force he used; often naughty; on the whole a well-intentioned child. But she could well see that childishness combined with power is a more difficult conception for the common mind than rank hypocrisy.

Angel had been assisting in a solemn excommunication of the apostates. He looked upon them as having been overcome by the devil.

After this Halsey instituted a series of unusual meetings for prayer and revival preaching, which he held after the ordinary evening classes in the School of the Prophets, which was now removed to the upper chambers of the finished temple. Now, as at other times, his preaching was successful. His power was with men rather than with women; they gathered in excited crowds, and their prayer and praise went up in the midnight hour.

Susannah was not in the habit of going to bed till her husband returned. One night, after twelve had struck, while she sat warming the dimpled feet of her restless babe at the rosy fire-light, she was greatly astonished to hear a tapping, low but distinct, on a window that opened to the back of the house. She lifted her head as mother animals prick their ears above their young at the faint sound of any danger.

After an interval the tap was repeated; it was no accidental noise. Susannah laid the child in its cradle and went nearer the window shutters, hesitating.

She knew only too well that this secrecy was the sign of some one's dire distress. She knew the habits of the people; a neighbour's aid was sought freely and with confidence; doors were open at all times to need or social intercourse.

To her intent listening the accents of a low and guarded tone came in reply to her challenge; the voice was Joseph Smith's.

Susannah looked with anguish toward her child's cradle. Had some army of mad persecutors invested Kirtland? Nothing less than fierce persecution could be thus heralded.

For years Susannah had known Smith as a near neighbour, and the stuff of which the man was at this time made is indicated by the fact that instinctively she opened the window with noiseless haste.

Smith climbed in. "Has Halsey returned?"

The fire gave the only light in the room. Smith did not shut the window, but remained sitting on the sill. A bake-house at the back hid the place from neighbouring eyes.

"It's all up with our bank," said Smith.

"I feared so," said Susannah.

"The apostates took such a lot of money out of it. No bank anywhere in this region could have stood it. You have always been down on our management of the bank, Mrs. Halsey, but if it was not good, why then have so many of the Gentiles put in their money, and why have they taken our notes all over the State?"

"You never had the capital you advertised."

"We have land that stands for it."

"It is not worth half what you value it at."

Then Susannah became sorry for her sharp recrimination. Punishment had befallen; it was a time for mutual help, not for reproach. She saw that although Smith kept himself calm he was greatly stirred.

"Why are you here?" she asked.

Smith's huge frame was poised awkwardly on the window sill. He moved restlessly and touched one thing and another with nervous hands. Then he said with a short laugh, "The size of it is, I'm running away, Mrs. Halsey. Ye may think I feel pretty mean, but ye'll do me the justice just to think how it is. If they'd shoot me in fair fight, I'd go and, if it were the Lord's will, be shot tomorrow, and be thankful too; but ye know the sort of vengeance they'll take. I have been beaten time and again before now, and covered with pitch, and I've been knocked down and kicked and ducked in ponds a good many times, as ye know, and I ain't ashamed to say that I'm afraid of that sort of thing and afraid of the results on Emmar and the children. If the Lord clearly told that 'twas his will to stay and stand it, why then I'd have no choice, but I haven't had no word from the Lord."

His face was livid; in the effort to make his explanation, whether shaken by the recollections he described or by fear of her contempt, she saw that his limbs were actually trembling as if with cold.

"There ain't many men, Mrs. Halsey, as would stay and face that sort of music when they could get away, but if it was to do good to mortal creature I'd think about staying, but it's t'other way. It's me and Rigdon as has been advertised as working the bank; it's my blood and his the Gentiles that have our notes are thirsting for. Suppose we stayed and they took to mauling us again, wouldn't the Saints here take to fighting to protect us? I've taught them to fight in self-defence and they'd fight to defend me. God knows there are better men than we are that would be killed right and left if we stayed, and 'twould be no use, for the Gentile numbers would overpower us. 'Tain't no use. When I found today that there wasn't a chance of staving off the bankruptcy I sent Emmar and the children and Rigdon's folks off in a close waggon after sundown. Rigdon's rid off by another road, and I've got my horse ready and ought to be gone. And there ain't a man in Kirtland as will know which way we've gone by tomorrow, so that no Saint will need to do any lying on my account."

"You are very sorry for the mistakes you have made about the bank," she said pityingly.

He gave another short laugh that, like the first, was less like a laugh than a sob.

"I guess I'm sorry enough, but I don't know whether it's repentance, for I thought I'd done all just what the Lord told me to do, but at times like these I'm not so sure of the revelations I hear in my soul, but I know I thought I was right at the time; but as for being sorry, if ye had the burden of all these children of Israel in the desert on your heart, knowing that ye had brought them into the desert, and brought the hunger and the thirst and the pestilence and the enemy upon them, and weren't quite sure at times whether the thing that ye saw leading was the Lord's pillar of cloud or the devil's, and if ye was now being cast out before the face of men and called a liar and a swindler, and without a dollar in the world, I guess ye'd know what it felt like to feel sorry."

The room was a long one; in the fore part the glow from the hearth made clear the baby's cradle, the table set for Halsey's supper, the close shutters of the front windows, but the red flame rays were fainter as they came into this back portion where Susannah stood in dull distress a few paces from the stricken intruder.

This man had always the power at close quarters of producing strange disturbance in the emotions of his friends. Susannah was trembling, her heart heaving, if not with pure compassion, at least with wild excitement on his account.

With an effort Smith held himself still, but gave again the heartbroken laugh that appealed more than all else to her woman's heart. "'Tain't all that neither, that makes me the most 'sorry,' as ye call it. I tried to go in and out before this people, Mrs. Halsey, loving and serving all alike as a prophet should, but I wouldn't be human man, no, nor fit to be chosen by God for the honour he's put upon me, if I didn't know who amongst us was most worth care and respect, and it's come to my soul this night, now that I can't no longer stand between you and all the dangers that beset our people in the wilderness, that I wasn't right, maybe, to egg on Halsey to take ye away from your happy home, or to make a point as I did, first off, of getting ye converted—for I was more set on it than I showed at the time. It's because 'twas my doing you married, that I've come to say this; and I see well enough that 'tain't love that is between you and Halsey, though you are too tender of him to let him see."

She made a movement of the head, an effort to show reproving dignity, while in fact taken by surprise, her nerves in distressful panic, she had scarce the power to control herself, none to control him.

He answered her impulse, although he had not looked up to see the gesture. "Ye haven't got any call tonight to be offended with me, for I'm worth no more, unless the Lord see fit to lift me up agen, than the paper our bank-notes is written on; and I have just got one more thing to say, then I'm gone. If there's any grit in Joseph Smith, and if it pleases God that he's not going now to his death, he'll not make another home for himself without providing as good a place for you and the young one. Ye may depend on it."

He rose up now. "'Tain't no use disguising facts; I'm running away, and I'm leaving ye to dangers and privations. Your money and Halsey's is gone the way of all the rest, and without me to stop him Halsey will fly in the face of the first persecution that's within his reach. If I hadn't known that there was no chance at all of your coming I'd have asked you and the child to git into Emmar's waggon; but there's just this to say, there ain't a tribulation that can come to you that won't hurt me, living or dead, more than it can hurt you." Then after a pause he added, "Emmar sent her dear love and good-bye to ye."

He stood still a moment before her in humble attitude, the words of Emma's tender farewell lingering, as it were, in the air between them.

"Have a care what you do." (He resumed a more dignified manner of speech.) "It's borne in upon my mind that great dangers will lie round you. Tell brother Halsey from me that it is the will of the Lord that he should seek first the safety of his wife and child, and to abide in a place of safety till the child be grown."

He climbed through the window. His last act was to close the casement behind him to save her trembling hands the exertion. His movements must have been very stealthy, for she did not hear the sound of his steps or the steps of his horse in the silent night.

CHAPTER IX.

After Smith left Kirtland there was a great exodus Missouri-ward of his more devout followers. The army which had gone out from Kirtland in '34 to the rescue of the fugitives from the city of Zion in Missouri had failed, through disease and exhaustion, to make warlike demonstration; but the principle then accepted by the children of Zion of opposing force to force in self-defence, had been bearing fruit ever since in a bloody warfare between the hunted Saints of Missouri and their more powerful neighbours.

Before the Saints took up arms the Missourians had, it would seem, no real ground of offence against them except the religious faith which led them to proclaim that the land was to be given to them by the Lord for an everlasting possession. Now this provocation was still in force, added to the greater one that the worm had turned.

So futile had been the mad persecutions, so fruitful the blood of the martyrs, that by this time there were some ten thousand Saints in Missouri, all heads of families, for although Zion in Jackson County still lay waste, and the colonies of Clay County had been swept away, the cities of Far West and Diahman, and numerous villages near them, had risen like magic, built by the thrift, the organisation, and the temperance of the Saints.

As for Kirtland, the hope of making it a prosperous city had died with the failure of the bank. Of the few who remained two distinct parties were formed—the orthodox, headed by Halsey, and the reformers, encouraged, if not headed, by the former leaders who were now apostate. In the camp of the reformers there were those who saw visions and had revelations. Before this, when Smith was at the helm, it had been counted unlawful for any but himself to have direct dealings with the Unseen; but the prophet was distant, directing the sect only through his published journal, and in this case it were hard indeed if no authoritative local word were spoken in the orthodox party. Angel Halsey's mystic soul fell easily into the region of voices and visions. In his adversity, fasting and praying more than ever before, he heard voices which gave practical directions not only for himself but for his neighbours. When the neighbours refused to accept these ghostly counsels, which all tended toward a more rigorous holiness, there was no room left for Halsey's work in Kirtland. He determined to fare forth to Missouri, there to comfort and edify the Saints scattered abroad in the rural districts.

It was now that Susannah expected the sprightly Elvira Halsey, still unbaptized, to return to the east. Instead of that she proposed to travel with them, helping to take care of the child.

"Why should I take the trouble to help you and the young un?" she asked, sitting on Susannah's doorstep, languid with the heat. "When I was going along the lane last night I met a spirit, so I held out my hand according to Joe's latest. You've not heard! My! it's in the Millenial Star that if any sort of a voice or dream comes to you, the way to know, whether it's an angel or devil is to shake hands, and if it is an angel you'll feel a good, firm, solid grip sort of coming out of nowhere, but if it isn't an angel you'll feel nothing. It's kind of Joe to put it in a nutshell, necessary nowadays that we're all hard at it having revelations of our own. He thought that nobody would feel the grip but himself. Quite mistaken. I shook hands with my angel, tho' I couldn't see a ghost of him, and when he said, 'You come along now to Missouri, and carry the child half way,' I had nothing to do but say 'Amen.'"

But Susannah was too much afraid of what the result of private revelations might be to laugh at them; she expressed her fears.

"Bless you, all the dreams and 'voices' in this hustling world wouldn't have put any guile into the soul of Nathaniel, and they won't into Angel Halsey's. Saints are saints, sinners are sinners, middling folks are middling, just the same whether they have three 'revelations' a day apiece, or one once a year, or none at all. You're fretting because you think a righteous man might do something wicked, thinking that the voice of the Lord had told him. Not a bit of it! The Lord will take care of his own when they're a little off their heads just as much as at any other time."

What few worldly goods Susannah chose to keep were packed in two single waggons, Halsey driving the one, and Elvira and Susannah by turns driving the other and holding the child. Their long journey through the month of June was the most perfect pleasure that Susannah and Angel ever enjoyed together, the long nightmare of the last months at Kirtland left behind for ever, the stage of the future veiled, and the lineaments of natural hope painted upon the drop-curtain. A loving fate sent fresh showers on their behoof during the nights, which laid the dust and dressed field and forest in their daintiest array. The child, who had been pining somewhat, affected by the anxiety in the Kirtland home, became lusty and merry.

"If it wasn't that we are shortly going to be robbed of all we possess by the Missourians," observed Elvira, "this sort of jog-trot comfort would become too monotonous, but it adds spice to be saying, so to speak, 'Hulloa there! we've come to be persecuted too.' Of course we'll all be killed to begin with, but that's a detail; after that we'll take our rural mission bespoken for us in the dream."

Susannah actually smiled and called "gee-up" to the horse.

"How very little people know," she observed, "who talk about a persecution as if it would be a means of grace. There is nothing that so hardens and degrades as the constant report of barbarities; the more nearly seen, the more closely inspected, the worse is the moral result."

"Speak for yourself," cooed Elvira, "there's one person out there that isn't hardened and degraded." She looked with reverent eyes at Angel, who was walking at the head of the foremost horse, crooning a psalm; "and, as for me, I still feel myself quite soft, almost pulpy, and on an elevated plane."

"You could never talk in your irreverent way if you weren't a good deal hardened and degraded," persisted Susannah affectionately, "and, as for me, I know that I am. Is there any instance in history of a people emerging from prolonged persecution with high ideals of love toward their enemies and candour?"

"'Tis commonly said that faith rises from this fire," said Elvira.

"Faith that gives its body to be burned and has not charity," said Susannah.

When they reached the vicinity of Diahman and Far West the State elections were about to be held. It was reported that over all Missouri the stronger party, that of Lilburn Boggs, was threatening to prevent by force the Mormon vote.

Before commencing his mission to the outlying Mormon districts, Halsey, hoping to avoid this contest, stopped in the Gentile town of Gallatin to rest and obtain a fresh outfit.

"But why don't we pay our respects to 'Joe' now we are within reach?" inquired Elvira with pensive inflection.

"The prophet is full of cares. A man whom I met at the tavern said that his activity on behalf of the Saints in Far West is amazing, and since his public appearance there the Lord has prospered the city exceedingly; but, as for me, I have been commanded to turn aside to those of our people who are not encompassed by a shepherd's care."

"If he would but confess it," said Susannah with a sigh, "my husband was so sorely hurt with the appearances of fraud in connection with the bank—"

"Suppose you put that appearance of a child down and come and eat this appearance of your breakfast, and then we'll put on what appear to be our bonnets, and go for what appears to be a walk." Elvira's sunny serenity never deserted her. "Say rather," she cried, "that the prophet did defraud, but has repented."

That day was the 6th of August. The voting for the State legislature had commenced. The travellers did not know that there was any number of Mormon landholders in this place, but now they could not extricate themselves from the very contest that they had hoped to avoid. When the two women strolled through the streets to see the town they became involved in a crowd at one of the polling places.

Penniston, a candidate of the Boggs party, standing on a barrel, was haranguing the crowd, and the two women quickly heard the name of their sect mentioned with contumely.

"Shall we," cried Penniston, "allow our State to come under the control of Mormon horse-thieves and robbers by allowing these outlaws the civil rights that are intended only for good citizens?"

There was a commotion in the crowd near him. Susannah, knowing that her husband was abroad, felt a sudden heart-sick prophecy of evil. The next moment she saw Halsey spring into sight upon a low wall at the side of the crowd.

"Look on this picture and on this," cried Elvira in a voice audible to many too illiterate to comprehend.

The two men, each standing erect above the heads of the crowd, could not have showed sharper contrast. Penniston was coarse of limb and feature; a low grade of moral disorder stamped his face as clearly as inferior articles are ever stamped; no inspector of goods so relentless as God's servant Time! Halsey had bared his head to the open sky, as though invoking the presence of God in his temple. Upon features too thin and haggard for beauty, patience and love and truth were written by every line.

Halsey's voice, accustomed to preaching, fell with clear modulations upon the summer air.

"'Blessed are ye, when men shall persecute you, and shall say all manner of evil against you falsely, for my name's sake and the gospel's.' Friends, this evil that is spoken against us whom ye call Mormons is falsely spoken, and I stand here before you, and before the great Father of Truth, who is calling his children everywhere to repent, to say that every Mormon who has a vote has a right to exercise it, for we have committed none of the crimes of which you accuse us, but you yourselves, as you well know, are many of you here to try to put into office men who are undoubted criminals."

In surprise Penniston and his hearers had listened, but now a man, half-drunk perhaps, sprang upon the low wall upon which Halsey stood, and struck him savagely.

"He is all alone," cried Susannah, "all alone among so many." She tried to struggle forward toward her husband through the crowd.

Halsey believed himself to be alone, and it was not in accordance with his principles to make any attempt to return the violence by which he had been assailed; but to his astonishment now a stout man leaped to his assistance, suddenly belabouring his assailant with blows, and from far and near in the crowd there were shouts of encouragement from burly Mormon farmers who had only needed the voice of a leader to declare themselves. Halsey had thrown a spark, unconscious that a mass of powder lay near. When the men of Penniston's party turned with savage fury upon the Mormon who was beating their companion, and the Mormons, no less fierce, rallied round Halsey and his defender, the fight became general.

Elvira set her quick wits to work to weave a cord that would be strong enough to draw Susannah back to their inn. "They may find out that baby is alone," she said; "they're wicked enough to injure him out of revenge."

Along the wooden pavements of Gallatin, past the gaily-painted wooden houses, through the doors of which whole families were now emerging to ask the cause of disturbance, Susannah fled miserably, her cheeks blanched beneath her veil, her heart within weeping.

The sun was shining brightly on just and unjust; the gardens of Gallatin were brilliant with such flowers as had bloomed in the August when she first met her husband. Susannah felt then that the reason why she desired to clasp and guard the sleeping child she had left was that he was Angel's son; the pity for injured innocence had been from the first until now her strongest passion, and at the thought of Halsey, innocent and gentle, in the midst of the brutal fight she had left, her soul wept as it were the scalding tears that her eyes refused to shed.

The boy lay in rosy sleep, a woman of the inn keeping a kindly eye upon him. Probably nothing but a mother's love could have fancied him of sufficient importance to attract public attention, but Susannah, locking her door, knelt by the bed, and spreading protecting arms above him, listened with strained senses for news of Halsey's injury or death. For years she had feared that the violence she had seen wreaked upon others would touch her husband; violence offered to herself would have seemed a trivial grief in comparison. The fear that has long harped upon sore nerves has a cumulative action upon the pain of its realisation.

Susannah found herself giving forth short ejaculatory whispers of prayer upon the close air of the plain, small room in which she knelt. It was such prayer only as we come at by inheritance, prayer that is one of the habits by which the fittest have survived.

Before two hours were past Halsey had returned. He was bruised and much shaken, but appeared unconscious of injury, and made light of it. The open fight had ended with no decisive victory for either party; the chief result appeared to be that malice on either side was for the hour exhausted. Whether because of this or because Halsey gave himself to prayer on behalf of his brethren, the polls were opened quietly at noon and the Mormons voted with the other citizens.

In the cool of the evening Susannah was sitting beside her husband holding the sleeping child. The window of their humble room was open, not to any broad, fair landscape such as their eyes were accustomed to feast upon, but upon the yard of the small tavern. There is, however, in new countries no crowding; space, like air and sunshine, is the common heritage. Grass grew round the edges of the large yard, and an old white horse was cropping it contentedly. A cool air was blowing, and over the wooden roofs of the town stars were beginning to gather themselves from out the pale dusk. An old negro and two mulatto boys were sitting upon a log at the side of one of the sheds, quarrelling and singing slave melodies by turns.

Angel took the hand of the sleeping child and Susannah's hand and folded them in his own. "Susannah, it has been given to me to see this afternoon more clearly than ever before the material triumph of our people. They will rear high cities; they will lead armies; they will command wealth; but it has also been shown me that Zion will not be, as I had heretofore believed, pure from sin, for evil has already entered into her. Because she has taken the sword her spiritual warfare will not be soon accomplished; the wheat and the tares shall grow together, and I do not yet see the end."

There was a pause. Susannah watched the slaves taking their evening ease so light-heartedly. She looked down at the three hands which Angel had gathered together. The dusk was beginning to make all things indistinct.

Angel went on. "I would have thee teach the child above all things the unspeakable wretchedness of sin, for the least sin closes the eye of the soul by which we see God and the things of God, clogs them with the dust and dirt of the world; and when there is no more any clear vision, selfishness is mistaken for love, malice for righteousness, and folly for truth. So I pray thee, dear heart, be wary, and slay within thyself the evil nature, for though I cannot see it, perchance God does; and teach the child above all things from the first to fear sin more than death."

"You shall teach him, Angel."

"Dear heart, I would not lay upon thee the burden of knowledge of coming sorrow if I dared to withhold it, but I believe, Susannah, that it will soon be given to me to die for the truth and for our people." After a moment's pause he went on, and his tone, which had dropped involuntarily, became again cheerful. "That is why I have today determined to change the plan that we have made and to send thee and the child tomorrow with the company who are about to travel to Far West, where the prophet is now dwelling with his wife, for I know he will never see thee want."

Susannah rose up. In the dusk of the low, small room her figure, the child still in her arms, seemed to tower like a misty goddess or Madonna, such as praying men have often seen appearing for their succour; her voice came clear and strong from a heaving breast.

"Angel, I will never leave you, never," and then she added in a voice that faltered, "Send the child if you will."

CHAPTER X.

They did not send the child to Far West, or even insist on Elvira seeking safety there, because that town also became swiftly involved in the flames of the war which had flashed into new life at the Gallatin fight. The whole land was full of threats and terrors, and many open fights at the polling-booths were soon reported. The Mormons and anti-Mormons in various localities entered into mutual bonds to keep the peace, but in many cases these bonds were soon broken.

To the Mormons everywhere had been issued a proclamation, signed by Smith and the elders, commanding that no official tyranny, however unjust, was to be resisted. "Let every soul be subject unto the higher powers." "Submit yourselves to every ordinance of man for the Lord's sake." But when private violence was offered the order was that the men should fight in defence of their families.

It seems to have been this order to fight, and the fact that the Mormons proved themselves sturdy fighters, which alone caused any of the Gentiles to enter into a compact of peace. So mad was their anger against a sect claiming the land as an inheritance from God and voting to a man in obedience to its leader, that the Missouri journals of the day openly taught that to kill a Mormon was no worse than to kill an Indian, and to kill an Indian was tacitly considered as meritorious as killing a wild beast.

"I am just about as safe jogging along in one of your waggons as anywhere in this part of the country," observed Elvira; "and if it was a craving for peace and safety we had, why did we come to Missouri at all? I feel exactly like a rabbit when the men are out trying to thin them; I notice they get very frisky."

There was psychological truth underlying this statement. Stimulated by the excitements of sudden alarms, Susannah also found herself enjoying intervals of temporary security with peculiar zest.

They set forth again upon the country roads. Halsey had the burden of his message upon his spirit; wherever they found a few Mormon households gathered together, he preached to them the high ideals of Christian living and the need of humility and constant prayer. Another theme he had which he considered of equal importance; this was the interpretation of prophecy. He gave long rapt discourses upon the most obscure passages in the books of the prophets, the Revelation of St. John, and the Book of Mormon. These passages were found chiefly to refer to the rise of the Mormon Church, the iniquity of her enemies, and her glorious future. Susannah, who saw the value of his practical teachings, bitterly regretted this use of half his opportunities.

Only once or twice in many weeks did they come upon a Mormon household whose management was not such as the moralist would approve, and in those cases before Halsey's passionate denunciation sins were confessed and repentance promised.

So they journeyed slowly out of the September heats and oppressive shades into the cooler and more open glories of autumn. In that part of the country wild flowers run riot at the approach of winter, painting the land in broad leagues of colour, white and gold and blue, and the trees of the forest hang in red curtains overhead. The air was so light and invigo-rating that they all felt its tonic properties. Halsey seemed eased of his burden; the child began to talk, babbling wise and wonderful speeches. Elvira was even more frivolous than was her wont, and Susannah almost forgot Halsey's dismal prophecy of martyrdom.

About the middle of October they reached the place called Haun's Mill, where a small Mormon community was settled. Here they thought well to pause, shocked by renewed rumours of warfare. A truce for the whole region, which had been signed by Smith and some of his elders on the one side, and by a magistrate, by name Adam Black, for the Gentiles, had been broken by Gentile mobs in several of the counties near Far West. A number of the saints had been brutally killed, their wives and children driven from their homes at the point of the bayonet. This renewed outrage roused at last the fires of revenge, long smouldering in the breasts of the refugees from the desolate city of Zion, who had them-selves known the bitterness of such unmerited wrong. These fires fused religious principle and natural wrath together, till a chain was forged which bound many strong men in a secret society, whose members swore to fight, not only in defence, but especially in vengeance.

It was at Haun's Mill that Halsey first heard of this society, and he was deeply concerned. A young Mormon who had lately come to the place belonged to it, and after one of Halsey's sermons, in which the posts of the Gate of Life were represented as meekness and forgiveness, this young man came to the preacher by night to confess, but also to vindicate his position.

The missionary's little party, with the exception of Elvira, who had accepted hospitality at a neighbouring farm, were camping in a meadow not far from a stream called Shoal Creek, which drove the mill. The logs of their evening fire were still alight. Susannah sat just within the dark opening of a low canvas-covered waggon; the unsteady flame light fell upon her, and sometimes showed a farther interior where the child lay sleeping. Halsey was sitting at the roots of a tree, the utensils of a simple supper at his side. The gentle horses tethered near were to be heard softly cropping the grass, and the sound of the creek came from a farther dis-tance. Above, the poplar boughs, whose yellow foliage had been thinned by the advancing season, let through the rays of the brilliant stars. These were the sights and sounds which met the young man's senses as he came brushing the fallen leaves with his feet.

He leaned against the pole of the farther waggon and looked across the low-glowing fire at the preacher and his wife.

"Look here! I'm a Danite. Do you mean to say that the Lord's not going to accept of me because I can't stand by and see weak men and women and children killed, or worse than killed, without punishing the murderers? Supposing that a hundred of Boggs' men were to come down now and put an end to you, your wife, and your child, would you have me go along with them peaceably afterwards and pray they might be for-given?"

"What is a Danite?" asked Susannah.

The stranger took off his hat and answered her very respectfully. "We are under an oath, ma'am, not to tell who belong to us, but we've bound ourselves to punish them as take the blood of the helpless and innocent."

He seemed, as far as the light would show, a well-made youth, and his voice was clear and honest.

Halsey had not spoken, and Susannah asked again, this time of her husband, "Can it be wrong to do as this gentleman says?"

The preacher spoke slowly. "Vengeance is mine; I will repay, saith the Lord."

"But," said the young man eagerly, "the Scripture also says 'There's a time for wrath,' and 'he that sheddeth man's blood, by man shall his blood be shed.'"

Halsey rose up. It was a strong moment for him, for he had long seen that the spirit of retaliation, following hard on the spirit of defence, was the coming curse of his beloved church, and had prayed that he might be the means of helping to ward it off. Here was one asking counsel who from the strength of his person and character might have influence among the avengers of blood, yet with his helpless wife and child beside him none felt more keenly than Halsey the force of the Danite's arguments, and none knew better the multitude of Scripture prophecies that could be brought up in support of them. In the strength of his need this man, who had been spending the precious time of many a hardly-won audience in dwelling on obscure poesies in books held sacred, now seemed to step forth into a sudden illumination of truth just as he stepped from the shadow of the poplar bole into the light of the fire.

"Friend, I did wrong to answer you in this matter from any part of Scripture save from the mouth of our most blessed Lord himself, for he alone is the gate by which we must enter into life, and I would have you to consider most carefully his life and words, and find out if there be any promise of blessedness to those who strike back when they are struck, or any command to punish the evil-doer, or any example for such punishment. But if you would be more manly and more gallant than the Saviour of the world, I tell you it must be at your own peril, for he alone is the gate of that road which leads to everlasting life."

There was a silence for some long moments. Embers in the fire broke and fell; the horses cropped the grass; a nut or twig dropped somewhere among the adjacent trees.

"Well," said the young Danite reflectively, "if that's it, I guess I'll have to take my fling first and seek salvation after; but Smith and Rigdon don't only preach that sort of Gospel now; they are all for the Old Testament kind of thing, and the destroying angels in the Revelations."

CHAPTER XI.

So near came the rumours of war that the Mormons of Haun's Mill entered into a renewed compact of mutual peace with the Gentiles around them. The place was about twenty miles below the town of Far West, on the same stream of Shoal Creek. Around Far West the roads presently became very dangerous, haunted, it was said, by armed parties of bloodthirsty Gentiles who lay in wait for trains of Mormon emigrants coming from the east to the prophet's city. All travellers became alarmed; Halsey remained where he was; the people of the place accepted his pastoral services gladly. A train of Gentile emigrants also waited at Haun's Mill for the cessation of hostilities.

These emigrants were quiet folk and had children with them. Susannah used to go out upon sunny days with her sturdy yearling, talking to all mothers, Gentile or Mormon, who carried little children. The beauty of the season, the cloudless sun, gilded these few peaceful days. Susannah compared her child with other children, marvelled at the baby intercourse he held with them, at the likes and dislikes displayed among these pigmy associates; and the other mothers had like sources of interest in these interviews.

One among the emigrants, a dark-eyed woman of about forty years of age, was of better position and education than the others. One morning she noticed Susannah's child very kindly, speaking of things that did not lie on the surface of life.

"There is a seeking look in his eyes," the lady said; "he smiles, he plays with us all, but he looks beyond for something. I have seen that look in the eyes of children who were in pain, but yours is at ease."

"He has his father's eyes," Susannah sighed. "My husband is always looking for a virtue that seems to me impossible."

Both women turned toward an open grassy space in the midst of the clustered houses where Halsey was now standing, Bible in hand, teaching a little group of children to repeat the beatitudes. Only four children, one sickly boy and three girls, were willing to stand and repeat the lesson; others had straggled away and were shouting at their play.

Not far from where Halsey stood some fifteen of the neighbours had gathered together to put up a new wooden house; piles of sweet-smelling deal lay about them as they worked.

Just then on the road from Far West a horse bearing an old man was seen straining itself to the swiftest gallop. The old man began to shout as he came within hearing. No one could understand what he said. He shouted more loudly, and many women ran out of their doors to see his arrival. Before his words were articulate a cloud of dust was seen rising round a turning of the same road, and a large company of horsemen came swiftly into view.

The old man's voice was raised in a cry, but only the accent of terror was intelligible. He threw himself off his horse, brandishing his arms. Afterwards it was known that he wanted the villagers to take refuge in their houses, but now they only stared the more at him and at the small army that was approaching.

Susannah heard a shot; then she was deafened by the sound of a volley of muskets. Paralysed, she stood staring down the road, unable to believe that the two or three hundred mounted men had deliberately levelled their muskets and fired. Then all around her she became aware of shrieks and sobs and prayers that went up to God. The brown-eyed Gentile lady who stood beside her had fallen in a curious attitude at her feet.

Susannah darted into the emigrants' tent and, putting down the child, dragged the lady within. She perceived to her horror that the lady was shot; the bullet had passed through her neck. Not knowing whether she was dead or dying, Susannah stretched her on the floor. Then she lifted her hands above her head, wrung them together in agony of nerve and thought. She remembered afterwards looking upward in the cave of the warm tent and saying aloud "O God! O God!" many times.

The first thing she saw was her child standing watching her; both his little brown fists were full of flowers. Hearing the sound of horses trampling near, loud voices, and occasional shots, she bethought her that the canvas of the tent was no protection for the child, and, snatching him in her arms, she ran madly out into the sunshine and into the open war.

A large number of the horsemen had already passed on down the road; the sounds that came from them seemed to be of oaths and laughter. A number were still galloping in and out among the houses; the ground was strewed with bodies of the dead and wounded; the able-bodied, it seemed, must have suddenly huddled within their doors.

Susannah remembered her husband now, remembered where he had been standing. She forgot all else; she rushed toward the middle of the green, drawing back only when some of the horsemen dashed across her path to follow their fellows. They stared at her and, as they went, called to some who were still behind them.

One of these came on, checked his horse, and looked in Susannah's face insultingly. No doubt her eyes were dazed, and she looked to him like a mad woman, but she remembered afterwards that the child showed anger and babbled that the horseman was a bad man. At this the rider took out his pistol and pointed it at the child and fired and rode off laughing.

Susannah saw the young Danite bending over her. His words were hoarse and so sorrowful that she gathered from their tone that she was in great distress before she understood their purport or memory awoke. "Ma'am," he said, "I'll take you down to your own waggon by the creek."

She found herself sitting on the ground, her child in her arms. The child was dead; she knew that as soon as she looked at him. There was a little trickle of blood upon the light frock over his heart, but not much.

As yet no women, only a few men, had ventured forth, and the sound of the enemy's horses and shouting were still in the air. Susannah rose up, folding in her arms the body of the child; the momentum of her first intention was upon her will and muscles; she moved straight on toward the place where she had last seen Halsey.

The young Danite took hold of her sleeve when he perceived whither she went.

"'Tisn't no use, ma'am. Some of the brothers have attended to him."

Susannah looked straight in the young man's face with perfect courage. "Is he dead?"

But the Danite had not courage for this; he turned away and put his arm over his eyes; she heard him grind his teeth in dumb passion.

Some of the men and women lying on the grass were moaning or screaming with the pain of their injuries. The thought that Halsey might be in like pain made Susannah imperative. "Is he dead?" she asked again in precise repetition of tone and accent. "Is he dead?"

The Danite lifted his head. "He is quite dead, and I marked the man that did it, and I marked the man that did this too." He touched reverently, not the child, but the wilting asters that were still grasped in the baby hand. "If I'd only had a gun—but"—he ground his teeth again and muttered, "God helping me, they shall both die."

Susannah understood nothing then but the first part of this speech.

By this time many of the women and children had again flocked out of the houses. It was reported that the horsemen had been a detachment of State militia, that one of them had taken the trouble to explain to a wounded man that they had received orders from Governor Boggs to exterminate the Mormons. Immediately by other frightened tongues it was stated that the armed company were halting round the turn of the road, intending to return and shoot again when the people had come out from shelter. At this the greater number made a stampede for a thicket of poplar and willow saplings that was near the creek. The Danite still held by Susannah's sleeve.

"Where is my husband?" she again asked. She had not moved since he last spoke to her.

Some men were busy laying the dead, of whom there were eighteen, on the floor of a shed which was not far off. Susannah and the Danite moved about together and found Halsey lying still on the green, his limbs decently composed, his eyes for ever shut. The bearers were about to lift him, but the Danite interposed. He had an excited fancy concerning Susannah's dead and what must be done for them. He lifted Halsey easily in both his arms and walked away, Susannah following with the dead child.

Without a word they went till they came to Halsey's camp. Nothing had been touched since Susannah left in the morning. The Danite, remembering the camp as he had seen it a few evenings before, looked about him now curiously, and laid Halsey down on the very spot where he had stood to plead for a divine righteousness.

It was not a time for words. Having deposited his burden, he looked to Susannah, but she had no directions to give. She sat down beside her husband, as though preparing to remain.

"I thought you'd like to lay them both out here, but I guess I ought to get you into the bush, ma'am."

"I will stay here," she said; "you had better go to help some one else."

The cries of the wounded were still heard from the vicinity of the houses. A crowd of the uninjured people were to be seen making their way through the first bushes of the thicket. They seemed to be carrying the wounded thither, for men bearing shutters, and doors upon which the sick were stretched now started in the direction of the bush. There was need for help, as the Danite well saw; then, too, inactivity was torture.

He left Susannah and ran back to bear his part in the common task.

When almost every other living soul was lost in the close thicket he came again, approaching the camp with soft footsteps, peering anxiously. Susannah had laid the child in his father's arms. Their enemies seemed to have taken aim for the heart, for Halsey's wound was also there. She had so laid the child within his arms, heart to heart, that no sign of injury appeared. She sat by them now, sobbing her tearless sobs, stroking gently, sometimes the hair of the child, more often the thick locks of light hair that lay above her husband's brow. She was talking to them between her sobs in rapid phrases exactly as if they were not dead. The young Danite was sure that she had lost her wits; he leant against a tree confounded.

Susannah was saying, "I wanted to keep baby, Angel, I wanted so much to keep him, but I could not have taught him your way; there was no use telling you that before, for you could not understand. When you told me that you would go you did not tell me you meant to take baby. You have the best right to him, dear, he is all yours, but oh! remember—remember that I will be very lonely—very lonely—O Angel." There were a few moments of wordless moans and sobs, but she went on clearly enough, "I want you to know, Angel, that I never was disappointed in you—never disappointed in you, dear; and about my lack of faith—it would have been no use to tell you before, would it?"

She took her hand from Halsey's hair and played a moment with the rings of gold on the baby's head lying on his breast. She laid her hand upon Halsey's hands that she had clasped together above the child. "It is better for you to have baby with you. I could not have taught him your thoughts. It is better, dear, isn't it?"

The earnest inflection of her voice in these interrogations brought so wild a sense of pathos to the Danite's heart that his eyes filled with tears and brimmed over, but Susannah's sobs were like a nervous gasping of which she was scarcely conscious, and no hint of tears.

She lightly touched the baby hand that was lying on its father's shoulder, still grasping the blue blossoms. "See," she sobbed, "he has brought his flowers to you; he always loved you best."

There had been a great silence in the air about them, but now there was again the sound of firing at the distance of about a mile. The Danite's pulses leaped, but he did not, because of that, allow himself to speak or move.

Susannah spoke again, resting her hand on Halsey's brow, "You know, dear, I don't know whether you and baby are anywhere—anywhere"; wildly, as if the appalling loneliness of its meaning had flashed upon her dulled brain, she repeated the word.

The Danite's sympathy rose within him; he staggered forward and bent over her. "Don't, ma'am," he said, "don't go on talking like that. I was with my own mother when she died, when I was a little chap, and I know how it is, and you'd much better try to shed tears, ma'am, indeed you had."

Susannah lifted to him a blank face, disturbed but uncomprehending.

He decided what to do; the thought of action restored him. He ran with all his might back to the houses, and, finding a pick and spade, came again. This time, more confident of himself, he had more control over Susannah.

"We must make the grave right here, ma'am, and do you go and gather some flowers to put on it, for we must just put them two away out of sight before the devils come back. It's what he would want, you know." He pointed to Halsey and repeated the words until she understood.

It even seemed a relief to her then to move about too, and find that there was something she could do, but she did not obey him blindly. While in a soft place close by he delved with might and main, displacing the earth with incredible speed, Susannah, sobbing all the time, but tearless, went into the waggon and brought out certain things which she chose with care—a locked box, the best garments belonging to herself, her husband, and child, and the baby's toys.

It was no neat gravedigger's work that the Danite accomplished; he had made a deep, large hole, but the cavity sloped at the sides so that they could step in and out. Susannah brought her little store and lined the earth first with the garments.

"You may want some of those things of your own, ma'am," said the Danite.

She paid no heed; when she had made the couch to her mind she signed to him to lay Halsey and the child in it, which he did. She herself stooped in the grave to clasp the dead man's hands more tightly over the little one's form, and her last touch was to stroke Halsey's hair from off the brow. She laid the baby playthings at Halsey's feet; she unlocked the box and took from it all the household treasures that so far she had sought to keep—some silver, a few small ornaments, a few books, and Halsey's Book of Mormon, in which was written their marriage and the baby's birth. She brought a silken shawl, the one bit of finery that remained from her girlish days. She covered her dead with it very carefully, tucking it in as though they slept; then she moved away, wringing her hands and heaving convulsive sighs. The Danite put back the earth.

All the grass was strewn pretty thickly with poplar leaves, gold, lined with white, and after leaning against a tree some minutes looking away from the grave, Susannah began gathering up these leaves hastily, so that when he levelled the earth she could strew the top, hiding the place from the curious eyes of strangers.

"I guess, ma'am, if there's anything you would like to take with you now, we'd better go into the bush."

"No, there is nothing, but," she cried, "I thank you very much, and if there is anything that would be of use to you—"

When the Danite had first laid Halsey under the tree he had taken a white cloth from the tent and wiped the blood from the coat, that Susannah might not be too much shocked at the sight. He took this cloth now and tore it till the stained fragment alone remained in his hand. He thrust it in his breast.

"This will stand for the blood of them both," he said. "I guess that's all I want." But when he had started towards the thicket he remembered Susannah's needs, and went back for a blanket.

The poplar saplings that bordered the creek were still holding a thin gold canopy overhead, and the dogwood was glinting with scarlet. The other members of the community had gone so far ahead that it was a long time before, making their toilsome way, they came upon their former neighbours.

The fugitives had called a halt where a brook which passed through the bush offered some relief to the pain and fever of those who were wounded. One of these, a little girl, had already died by the way, and her frantic mother began to reproach Susannah, wailing that if the child had not been saying her texts to the elder she would not have been a mark for the enemy.

The men were cutting down saplings to make place for a camp. It was their intention to remain, going back under the cover of night to get food and blankets from the houses, if they were not pillaged and burned, going back in any case to bury their dead at the first streak of dawn.

The Danite turned to Susannah. "I guess, ma'am, neither you nor I have got any business to take us back, and there's enough of the brothers here to do the work."

Susannah went on with the young man through hour after hour of the afternoon farther and farther into the unknown fastnesses of the wood. They left behind them the low thicket of second growth, and penetrated into an uncleared Missouri forest.

CHAPTER XII.

All the powers of the young Danite were strung by excitement into the fiercest vitality, and he thought that physical fatigue was the best medicine for Susannah's mind. Why he had accepted the work of saving her as part of his mission of Mormon defence he did not ask himself. In him, as in many athletes, thought and action seemed one. He acted because he acted; he knew no other reason.

In the middle of the night Susannah woke up. The stars glimmered above the trees; she was lying on a heap of autumn leaves wrapped in the blanket. Sitting up, she remembered slowly the events of the preceding day.

Her movement had caused another movement at some distance. The Danite, sleeping on the alert like soldier or huntsman, was roused by the first sound she made, and when she continued to sit up he came near in the glimmering light. She saw his dark form where he tarried a few paces away.

"You're all safe, ma'am. Can't you go on sleeping?"

A watch of the night often brings to recollection some duty forgotten during the day. "Do you know where Elvira Halsey is?"

"The young lady with the brown eyes that I have sometimes seen you with, ma'am?"

"Yes." Then Susannah added with the weak detail of a wretched mind, "She isn't very young."

"Was she any relation to you, ma'am? Were you very affectionate with her?"

Susannah explained the relationship.

The Danite thought, "If I tell her she's there she'll think it her duty to trapse back all the way to find her; she's that sort." Therefore, judging that a minor grief could not make much difference, he gave it as his opinion that Elvira was dead. At this Susannah shed tears for the first time, which eased his anxiety not a little.

Susannah did not know the Danite's name; it never occurred to her to ask him any question about himself.

At dawn they started again upon their tramp. The man knew the country, and when the sun was up he brought Susannah out of the forest to a settler's farm. She was faint now for want of food, walking again, as she had walked last night, with vacant eyes and dull mechanical tread.

The Danite made her sit down upon a stone near the house, and brought a woman to her who carried bread and milk. Susannah ate and drank without speaking.

"My! but she's tired," said the farmer's wife. "It's a cruel shame to make her walk so far; you're not a good husband to her, I'm thinking."

Having satisfied her need, Susannah turned away dully without a word. The settler's wife offered the remainder of the bread and milk to the Danite, who regarded it with famished eyes.

"Where's your husband?" he asked.

"We've enough men about the place."

"Where is your husband?"

"He's away with the militia under Lucas."

"Then I'll not touch his food," said the Danite. With an oath he flung the cup and plate upon the ground. "Do you see that woman there?" He pointed to Susannah. "I took the food for her, for she had died without it. Yesterday devils like your husband shot her child in her arms and her husband before her eyes, and to Almighty God I pray that when I've got her to some safe place I may have strength yet to shoot your husband and your children, shoot them down like dogs, and laugh at you because you don't like it." The restrained passion of all the long preceding hours broke out. His face was ashen, his eyes burning; there was foam about his lips as, with thick utterance, he hurled the words at her.

The woman stepped back in dismay, but she, too, was enraged now, and courage was the habit of the free life she led. "You are a bloody Mormon," she cried, "and if I'd known it I'd have let your woman die before I'd have fed her." She walked backwards, her voice rising higher with passion. Unable to think connectedly, she shrieked the phrases she had in mind. "Coming here to spread idolatry in a Christian country! Teaching superstition in a free Christian land!" She was still shrieking some jargon about the United States being founded on the Word of God, and the divine right to exterminate all Mormons, when he, walking fast, joined Susannah.

They had not gone much further before a large dog which the settler's wife had evidently let loose, came after them with fierce intent. The Danite turned, and as the dog sprang, slew it with one stab of his knife, and, leaving it bleeding upon the road, hurried Susannah into the forest.

It was a tradition upon that farm for years afterwards that these two Mormons, after receiving charity, had made an open display of that wanton wickedness which was habitual to them.

Susannah and the Danite travelled on for many hours. The way was not easy. Sometimes where the trees were thin their legs were tangled knee-deep in a plant covered with minute white feathery blossoms, looking like white swan's-down shot through with green light, that carpeted miles of the ground; sometimes the trees had fallen so thickly that they had to clamber from log to log rather than walk; sometimes their way was a bog, and they were in danger of sinking deeper than was safe.

Susannah asked no questions. She had heard and understood all the words that had passed in the incident of the morning. She felt cowed now, afraid to think what might come next; it was enough that the Danite had evidently some point in view.

About four in the afternoon they left the forest and came to another and much larger house. The Danite advanced here with more confidence and spoke with some men who gathered at their approach. Afterwards three men, a father and sons, came and one after the other shook hands respectfully with Susannah. Within the house she found a motherly woman, the wife of the elder son. When Susannah's misfortunes were related to her in undertones she cast her apron over her head and groaned as with pain.

Susannah thought that the concern of this household must arise from fear on their own account. "Are you Latter-Day Saints?" she asked mechanically.

The eldest man, with the air of a patriarch, replied, "No, madam, we are not Saints; the fact is we don't hold by religion of one sort or another; we just believe in being kind to our neighbours and living, good lives; so whatsoever your belief may be it is no affair of ours, and you shall rest here for the sake of our common humanity. We'll look after you, madam." He made a bow that was a queer mixture of uncouthness in keeping with his surroundings and a recollection of some more formal society.

The woman of the house, taking her apron from her head, suddenly bethought her of the best things that she had to offer. Gently forcing Susannah into an elbow chair, she ran, and lifting an infant a few weeks old from its cradle, put it in Susannah's arms.

The next night the young Danite went away.

CHAPTER XIII.

Only the outline of passing events was reported to Susannah in her haven of peace. The elder man took her into his courtly care, and made a point of explaining to her what he thought she needed to know. The newspapers were sedulously kept from her, and so reticent were the other members of the household on the subject of their contents that her heart constantly sickened at the thought of what she was not allowed to hear.

"You see, madam," the old man explained, "it was Major-General Atchison that called out the militia in first defence of your people against Gilliam's mob. Gilliam had about three hundred men, and they started in the north of the State. Well, Parks and Doniphan, commanding the militia called out by Atchison, seem to have set about fighting the mob sincerely enough." The old man pushed back his spectacles and rubbed his hair. "Then you see, madam, that didn't please Governor Boggs. Here was the militia of his State shooting down his own good, honest Christian voters who keep him in office, that's Gilliam's men, and all the mob; so Boggs gets a lot of his men in all parts of the country to write him letters saying what dreadful crimes the Mormons are committing. These letters will no doubt pass into history as a genuine account of your people's doings. Well! well! I wouldn't shock your prejudices, but I'd like just to point out by the way that it's all done in the name of religion. There's Boggs has got an old mother who spends a lot of her time praying that the purity of the American religion may not be corrupted by the awful doctrines of Joe Smith."

The old man shook his head and rubbed his thin gray curly hair again with a smile of constrained patience. "You see, although I do not wish to grieve you by saying it, if we could only get rid of religion there would be a lot of brotherly kindness in the world that so far has never had a chance to say 'peep' and peck its shell. Well, but here's Boggs reading his letters, and he turns pale with horror at the thought of the corruption that has come among his good and pious people, so he writes off to the commanders of the militia that they are to stop fighting the mob, to fight against the Mormons, and only against the Mormons. So then Atchison resigns. He points out, fairly enough, that there hasn't been a single conviction in any lawful court against the Mormons for the crimes they are accused of. But what of that if Boggs is Governor? So they have taken away the arms from the Mormon company of militia, and the other day they went up to Far West with three or four thousand men, and they got Smith and his brother Hyrum and three of the elders to come out to them, and they court-martialled them and ordered them all to be shot the next day.

"But it wasn't done, madam," he added hastily. "General Doniphan had the pluck to stand out against it and say he would withdraw his troops, so they put them in irons and sent them to the gaol in Richmond, and then at the point of the bayonet they have forced the other leaders to bind themselves to pay all the expenses of the war and to get every Mormon, man, woman, and child, out of the State, or else they are all to be shot. That is how the matter stands at present."

"Do you incur any risk by the hospitality you give to me?" asked Susannah. She had not as yet had energy, even if she had had inclination, to explain that the Book of Mormon was not sacred in her eyes, nor Smith a prophet. "Do you think," she asked the old man wistfully, "that the Mormons have ever been the aggressors, that they have committed any of the atrocities they are accused of?"

"In some cases they have pillaged, and burned, and murdered; they wouldn't be human if some of them hadn't got fierce under the treatment they have been receiving; but when a man like Atchison, who has been scouring the country and knows pretty well what has happened, prefers to resign his honourable office rather than fight against them, you may be sure they are not very far in the wrong. Injuries, you know, will always set a few men mad. There is your elder, Rigdon, for instance; when he got here and heard of some of the things your folks had suffered, he up and made a wild oration on the 4th of July, and said that if any more outrages were committed on the Mormons, the Mormons would up and extermi-nate all the Gentiles in the State. But it has been well enough seen by any one who had eyes to see that no such language was ever countenanced by the real rulers of your sect."

When Susannah thanked the old man for his candour he drove his moral once more. "You see, madam, I can look at things as they are because I am not bound by any religion to look at them in any particular way."

Susannah rose up when the old man's story was ended, and stood for some minutes looking wistfully out through the window panes upon the leafless and storm-swept fields. They two were together in the long, scantily furnished living-room at the end of the long table. Her figure was stronger, more true in its proportions, than when she had been a girl. Her hair, trained into smooth obedience, was fastened within the muslin cap she had fashioned for herself, tied Quaker fashion under her chin. Her face was very white, as if, having blanched with terror in the tragedy of Haun's Mill, the life-blood had not as yet returned to it.

At last she said simply, "I thank you, sir."

The old man looked most approvingly at her form and at the subtle witchery which the eagerness of imprisoned thought gave to reticent fea-tures, at the depth of her blue eye. "I wish, my dear, that you could see your way to give up your religion and remain with us."

"I thank you, sir," she said again, and went back to the household tasks she had fallen into the habit of performing.

She was not eating the bread of dependence. In such a place, where woman's work is at a premium, it was easy for her to do what was reck-oned of more value than what she received. The old man had two sons. The elder and his wife were in the prime of life, having a large family; the younger son was unmarried. The farm was large and prosperous. The one woman, even had she been less amiable, would have naturally desired to keep Susannah as a helper; being the kindly soul she was, she reserved the more attractive tasks for her, and bade the children call her endearing names. In her blindness, in her slow recovery from utter exhaustion of mind and nerve, Susannah never thought of connecting this long-con-tinued kindness with the fact that the old man's younger son had as yet no wife.

At first Susannah had fixed her thoughts upon an immediate return to the east, but weeks went by and she had not written to Ephraim Croom for the money that she needed. The whole civilised world contained for her but one friend to whom she would write.

The Canadian farm, the remote country village of Manchester, and the Mormon sect—these formed her whole experience. Her father, who had scolded and played with her; Ephraim, who had understood her and had been the authority to her heart that his parents could not be; her husband, who had wrapped about her such close protection that she had tottered when she thought to walk alone—these were her real world, and of them only Ephraim was left.

It was not in her nature at any time, above all not in these stricken months, to desire to go out into the world alone to make for herself a sphere of usefulness and a circle of companions. Hence she thought only of returning to Ephraim, and by his help obtaining some occupation by which she could live simply and within his reach. But when she thought more closely of throwing herself, as it were, penniless and desolate at the feet of this one prized friendship, doubts arose about her path.

One thing which she had lost in the broken camp by her husband's grave, one that if she had had greater power of recollection she would not have left behind in that complete breaking with the past, was a packet of the few letters which Ephraim had from time to time written to her. She did not know whether she had thrown them into the grave with her treasure, or whether they were left a prey to fire and theft, but in her heart she had carried them beyond the loss of their material existence.

The first had answered her insistent question concerning the vexed condition of the devotees of prayer. It contained no word of criticism of the Mormon creed, nothing that if read aloud could have disturbed Halsey's peace. "Perchance," he had said, "as a medical man applies a poultice or blister to a diseased body to draw out the evil, so to those who pray and are too ignorant, *i.e.* opinionated, to follow perfectly the greatest teacher of prayer, God may apply circumstances to bring all the evil of heart to the surface, that in this life and the future it may the more quickly work itself away." Susannah had so conned this passage that she could now close her eyes and read it as written upon the red dusk of their lids.

The next letter had been written a year later. He described a great change in his life. He had gone to spend the winter in Hartford, on the Connecticut River, to be under a new physician, and had there met with a preacher called Mr. Horace Bushnell. This acquaintance was evidently much to Ephraim. Susannah had made some complaint of the harshness of the divine counsel in which he asked her to believe; his answer was to send her Bushnell's sermons on the suffering of God. Ephraim had added: "When you went from us, Susy, would you ever have been satisfied if we had detained you by force? Yet that is what you ask of God. If you were right in going, let the circumstance prove it; if we were right, let it appear by time. So says God; and his friendship has eternity to work in; so also has every human friendship. Let us wait, but in faith." This ending, somewhat enigmatical to her, had yet recurred to her heart so often that she knew the words by heart.

The next letter had been written more recently, after a long interval. At the end of this letter Ephraim had said, "I am persuaded that what we need to help our faith is never more knowledge, but always more love. I cannot interpret this but by telling you of a fact which I feel to be the key to a great—the greatest—truth. I know a man who believed in God. He met a woman whom he loved, not as many love, but (I know not why) with all the loves of his heart, as father, as mother, as brother, friend, might love; as lover he loved her with all these loves. After that he knew God with a knowledge that passed belief. He could argue no more, but he *knew*. This I think is the sort of knowledge which guides unerringly." Susannah remembered, if not the words, all that this passage contained. She had wondered at it not a little.

Up to the time of Angel's death she had rejoiced in these letters, not doubting that Ephraim had remained the same self-sacrificing friend— ready out of mere but perfect kindness to befriend her to the uttermost. She had not doubted because she had not questioned. Now disquieting thoughts intervened, producing a new shyness. She remembered their last interview, and wondered if Ephraim would feel the same responsibility for her if she returned destitute. Perhaps the ardour of his friendship had cooled. Perhaps in the last letter he had intended to suggest to her that he thought of marriage, and this time for love, not kindness, the lady being one of his new Hartford friends.

But no doubt the principal reason of Susannah's dalliance with time in those first weeks of her moral freedom was the mental weakness that succeeds shock. Every day she thought that she would soon write that begging letter, until the day came when opportunity ceased.

When the Danite left he had promised the farmer to return as soon as it was possible to place Susannah in safety with her Mormon friends. When she began to speak of leaving, her host told her this for the first time.

"And what is the young man's name?" the old man asked of Susannah. They were in the long living-room at the mid-day meal. His sons, who were leaving the table, waited to hear the answer; the mother, the very children, looked at her with interest.

"I do not know," said Susannah.

There was a pause, and for the first time she was aware that there was some sentiment in the minds of her hearers which did not appear upon the surface.

She went on, "I don't know why he should trouble himself to come back for me except that—I think that he was much touched by some earnest words my husband said to him that he did not see his way to accept, and I think also that he is zealous for the Church."

Her surpassing wrongs had so far set her apart and made all that she said and did sacred. No one questioned her further.

In the beginning of February the Danite reappeared. He came under the cover of night, but showed himself only when the household was awake. He was much thinner, more gaunt than before, but in frankness and quietude the same. His first words to Susannah had an import she did not expect.

"That young lady you mentioned to me—I said she was dead because you were half crazy, and would have gone back to her, but I worked round till I found her; she got to the city of Far West right enough."

After a while he said, "That young lady and some other of our folks have got horses and they're going into Illinois now. Most of our folks are walking. It's about as bad as can be, but I guess you'll have to go. We'll be safe enough, for as long as we go straight on the Gentiles are bound to let us pass. I tried to get some better sort of a way for you and her, but there ain't no way unless we would have sworn we weren't Saints and gone pretending to be Gentiles, but even then we haven't got the money."

Susannah was thrilled with excited distress. She was not prepared to make an abrupt decision, and it appeared that if she desired to join this company she must go that evening or not at all.

During the hours of the morning her mind cowered, dismayed. Should she now renounce her husband's sect, refusing to suffer with them? She had not as yet fortitude to do this. Halsey's eyes, the touch of his hand, her baby's voice lisping the tenets of their faith in repetition of his father's solemn tones, these were sights and sounds as yet too near her. To her shocked fancy the child and his father were only gone out of sight, but near enough to be cruelly hurt by her public perversion. And, moreover, if she should take this course she must write to Ephraim at once, for she could not well remain where she was without definite purpose in view.

Susannah had sought seclusion in which to think, and the younger son of the house intruded himself. He was perhaps about thirty years of age, a burly man, resolute and passionate. He spoke fairly enough. The Danite himself had said that the journey to which she was haled by her friends was one of untold hardship, its end uncertain; he offered her all that an honest and prosperous man could offer, but went on to urge on his own behalf the strength of those sentiments which he had learned to entertain for her—his admiration (Susannah sickened at the word), his love (she shrank in fear).

She rose up with the moan of a hunted thing. She did not pause to make excuses for the hunter, to consider the pioneer life that wots little of sentiment in proportion to utility; she only saw again the grave at Haun's Mill and the white faces of her dead upturned to hers. It seemed that this man, with the consent of his people, was urging his suit as it were beside the very corpse of her husband. The Danite had shown Angel reverence, had shown by his every word and glance that he counted her as belonging to the dead man whose blood he carried at his heart.

Susannah rode out from that temporary home at nightfall upon the Danite's horse.

CHAPTER XIV.

It was the season of rain and sleet, of rude northerly winds. The roads, across a tract of flat fields and in among the low woods that fringed the rivers, were heavy with mud.

After riding half the night on a pillion behind the Danite, Susannah entered the Mormon camp. Up and down the sides of a dirty road, in waggons, in small tents, and in the open, men, women, and children were lying huddled in family groups. How far these crowds extended she could not see. Watch-fires were burning here and there, and in the fields on either side a patrol of Missouri militia were heard scoffing and shouting in the darkness. The Danite answered the challenge of one of these men with apparent meekness; Susannah perceived that he had gained in self-control. When they had entered the road, along the sides of which the forlorn multitude lay, they travelled for some way upon it, the Danite speaking in low tones now and then to the Mormon watchers. At length they came to a place where a few waggons of better description were standing and a number of horses were tied; here he lifted Susannah from the horse. Three of the Mormon leaders came up; they evidently knew her and her story. The eldest took her hand and spoke in broken tones of the crown which Halsey had won in the unseen city of God.

These were the first words that Susannah had heard in unison with Halsey's own thoughts, and for his sake they endeared the whole wretched Mormon encampment to her.

A woman, her head and shoulders wrapped in a shawl, sprang down from one of the waggons, and Elvira encountered Susannah.

"You expect me to say that I am sorry for you," she said hurriedly; "I will not. It is not a time for grief. We each of us have just so much power of being sorry and no more, and the well has gone dry. I am glad you have come. There are a great many things that one can yet be a little glad for; but you must make haste to lie down, for we shall soon enough be called to the march."

The beds shaken down on the floor of the waggon were covered with reclining women. Some of them squeezed themselves together to make the place Elvira had vacated large enough for two. Susannah stretched herself out, loathing with her senses the crowded bed, but with a tender heart for her fellow-sufferers. After the long dumb weeks of her stern sorrow, after that day's revolt of injured sentiment, she felt that it was worth while to have come here if only to have made some one else, as Elvira had said, "a little glad."

The dawn came sighing fitfully, long sighs that rose in the distant fields to the east meeting them in their pilgrimage and dying away westward; the dawn wept also, scattering her tears upon them in like transient showers.

Elvira found her own horse. The Danite had used yesterday the animal he had provided for Susannah.

"But what right have I to his horse?" Susannah began her question impetuously, but Elvira silenced her.

"Hush! Don't let the other women know that it isn't yours. Poor things, they will begin to ask why it isn't theirs. Do you think that we are living on bowing terms, curtseying to each other and saying, 'After you, madam, if you please'?"

Elvira was changed. Terror had at last done its work. Her pretty features were drawn with anxiety; her eye glittered.

"I have been baptized," she said to Susannah in hard tones. "When I saw the water red with blood I went down into it."

Eastward, facing the gusty sobs of the winter morning, they went. The road was soft, and hundreds of feet treading in front of them had kneaded water and earth together into a slippery mass. As far as could be seen in front and behind, the line of the pilgrimage stretched, women and children plodding with burdens on their backs, men pushing hand-carts before them, only here and there a waggon or a group of horses.

Elvira took up several children on her horse, and pointed out to Susannah a sickly woman to whom she could give a turn upon the pillion that she herself had ridden during the night. So they began one of many weary days.

To the good the necessities of compassion are as strong as are the necessities of selfishness to the wicked. Within a day or two both Susannah and Elvira had given up their horses entirely to women who had been taken ill by the way. At first they plodded arm in arm, thinking that merely to walk was all that their strength could endure; but there were other women who had children to carry, women even who must push hand-carts before them, and there were little children who sank one by one exhausted on the winter road, as lambs fall when their mothers are driven far.

After the march had continued for a few days there was much illness. All clothing and bedding was wet with the winter rain, chilled and stiff with the frosts. On the faces of many the unnatural flush and excitement of fever were seen, and other faces grew pallid, the lips blue or dark, and the eyes sunken. To all who retained the natural hue and pulses of health a heavier burden was added every day because of the help they must needs give if they would not bury too many of their comrades by the wayside. In that sad caravan souls were born into the world or freed from it by death almost every hour.

Susannah was greatly struck by the meek manner of the boldest and roughest of the Mormon leaders in their dealings with the parties of Missouri militia who, with the ostensible purpose of defending Missouri homesteads from Mormon violence, drove the stricken multitude as with goads. She had learned from her husband what the strength of true meekness could be, the lightness of heart which commits itself to God, who judgeth righteously, the glance of love that has no reserve of hatred, the infinite force that can afford to be gentle. Such a spirit had upheld Angel Halsey, but his widow looked in vain among the leaders of this band for a face that bespoke the same upholding. She soon perceived that there was among them a free-masonry of understanding, and that their mildness was assumed to serve the temporary purpose. By many a prayer she heard breathed, which was in truth, though not in form, a curse, she knew that in the souls of Halsey's successors there was no forgiveness, yet her heart went out in sympathy to men who were sacrificing their own sense of honour, holding in check their most delicious impulses of revenge, for the sake of being worthy shepherds to the weak.

"Do you love them the less because they are not angels?" asked Elvira. "Have you forgiven?"

Susannah shuddered at the intensity of the hard low tones, the passion in the word "love," the sneer in the word "forgive." Yet she knew that the rage against injustice which in youth had driven her forth upon this journey had, since the death of her child, changed into such fierce hatred of the persecutors that she could, except for very fear of herself, have taken upon her own soul the Danite's vow. In these days the pain of bodily suffering or heart-felt grief was as nothing compared with her agony when at times waves of this hatred passed over her heart.

The two friends were walking together, pushing before them a small cart in which, on the top of the bundles of household goods, a wretched woman and her newborn child were lying, covered under a scanty tarpauling from the driving sleet. The mud splashed beneath their feet; Susannah had little breath or strength for speech. Elvira, more slightly made, in every way more fragile, had seemed to develop, with every new phase of suffering, more strength of muscle and hatred and love.

They passed now two of the leaders. It was the custom for a certain number of these men to go forward and station themselves in pairs at intervals upon the road, cheering each group as it passed them, noting with careful eyes if any ill could be remedied by change of posture or exchange of burdens. One of them now, seeing the work to which Susannah had set herself, interfered. He was about sixty years of age, coarse in appearance, an elder whose wife and family Susannah knew by reputation. He and his fellows called a halt, looking for some man who might push the cart, but there was none within sight who was not already overburdened, nor was there a waggon that was not already overfilled with the sick and exhausted. The elder, whose name happened to be Darling, found in this particular instance reason to swerve from his position of guard. He left the post in charge of his fellow and pushed the cart. It was a habit with many of these leaders to seek to lighten the way by jocularities, and Susannah had before observed that, whether the jests arose with ease or effort from the heavy hearts of those who made them, a large proportion of the people were evidently cheered thereby. She could put aside her own tastes for the public good; she could even excuse when this rough comfort was offered to herself. Darling, labouring behind the cart, made light of the service he rendered.

He said first that the newborn babe must be called after him, and when he learned its sex he gave permission to the ladies to decide between them which should share this honour.

"Shall it be 'darling Susannah'?" he asked, making gentle his tone as he addressed the stately widow, "or shall it be 'Elvira darling'?" This time he turned his head with a broader smile toward Elvira's sharp little features.

Susannah felt that her hypersensitive nerves could almost have called his smile a leer; but she looked at the man's broad face, whose lines told of no resources of thought, no great natural capacity for heroism, and yet were furrowed by the sharpness of this persecution. The face would have been fat had it not been half-starved. It was pale now under the ill-kempt hair, and the set purpose of helpfulness was stamped upon it. She took back the word "leer" out of mere respect. Darling had given away his shoes; he was walking barefoot; he had given away coat and vest also, and the rotund lines of his figure were unpleasantly obvious under the wet shirt, and yet Susannah knew and bowed to the fact that some sick man or little child was wrapped in the garments that were gone.

But Elvira was expressing with hysterical warmth the same sentiments.

"I guess I'll feel it an honour to have my name joined with yours. I haven't got the length of taking off my shoes yet."

Darling began to sing one of the inspiriting Mormon hymns.

"When Joseph to Cumorah came."

"Poor Joe!" Elvira spoke to the elder in a confidential whisper, "when he cheated over the bank I thought some fiend had put a ring in his nose, and was leading him out to dance, and that I should be able to sit and laugh. Now he's lying upon straw in the gaol. What will they do to him if they lynch him?"

"Tear him limb from limb," whispered Darling, also under his breath. He was probably shrewd enough to know the force of Smith's suffering in stimulating the piety of the faithful, but truth, and grief concerning the truth, were in his words also. He sighed a big sincere sigh, and repeated sadly, "Tear him limb from limb, or burn him to death by a slow fire." Such atrocities, as practised upon criminal negroes, were not unknown in the locality, which gave the elder's words a graphic power, but Elvira's answer was wholly unexpected.

"How droll!" she returned.

The elder was annoyed. He had not refined susceptibilities which sought immediate relief from the dreadful pictures he had suggested, nor did he at all comprehend that her rippling smile was hysterical. "I don't see anything droll about it, sister," he said sulkily.

"Don't you? Now, it all seems to me very droll—you splashing along there barefoot, why" (she drew back a little to get the better view, laughing excitedly), "you've no idea how ridiculous you look; and Mrs. Halsey stalking along like a dignified ghost, afraid that you and I will kiss one another if we take to whispering, and this woman dying here with her head resting on a sack of potatoes, and the impudent little person you've just christened intruding herself upon the world only to go out of it again, and all these fine people in Missouri rubbing their hands and thinking they have done such a noble deed. I think," she added, laughing more loudly, "that they are the drollest part of it all."

"This nation will find that there's a sequel to it that they won't laugh at." These words of Darling came from some region underneath that of his ordinary conversation, as a man takes a dagger from under his cloak and lets it flash ere he hides it again. "The government of these United States that has laughed at our sufferings will rue the day."

"Even your saying that is very droll, but I love you for it." Elvira lifted both her hands as if testifying to her own sincerity. "I love you for it."

The elder thought it needful here to be again jocose. "Oh, come now, I am married."

Elvira did not feel herself insulted. "These United States," she cried, "they cackle over the word 'freedom' like so many hens that have each of them laid an egg and go strutting and boasting while the housewife empties their nests. The housewife represents the natural course of events, and in this case her name is 'Mrs. Mobocracy.'"

At other times, after a long period of silence, Elvira would burst forth in excited soliloquy audible to Susannah and others about her. On the last day when they were descending the hills to the Mississippi her increasing excitement culminated in a greater demonstration. The sun was shining, and a clear frost had hardened the roads. Elvira broke forth thus—

"It is Joe Smith who is conducting this march. We say that he is lying in gaol," she laughed. "In gaol is he? Have they got him safe? But it was he who taught all these men to work together, one under the other, and none of them kicking; and it was he who taught these women and children to do as they are bid—a wonderful thing that in the land of the free. It was he who taught one and all of us to be kind to each other, to the poor and the sick and the young, to the very beasts. Do you remember that when they caught our prophet at Hiram and dragged him out to be beaten and insulted, they had first to take from his arms a sick motherless baby that he was sitting up all night to nurse? Do you remember how he gave commandment about the animals? how he said that any man striking a beast in anger was thrown so far back on his road to heaven?" She paused when she had thrown out this question, and the men and women within hearing answered in broken chorus, "Yes, blessed be the Lord; we do remember."

"And who was it that taught us to give up the filthy Gentile habits of strong drink and tobacco?" (Again in the pause the chorus of thanksgiving to Heaven was heard.) "It was Joe Smith," Elvira cried more loudly. "And when the Gentiles thought that we would be scattered and separated and ruined, his spirit has gone like a banner before us. Twice they have taken our lands that we bought with our own money and cleared with our own hands, and the houses that we have built, and cast us out destitute, but we are not destroyed."

The enthusiasm of the crowd that now pressed upon her went like wine to her head; her cheeks flamed, her eyes brightened, and she lifted her small hands in fantastic gesture and danced, crying, "We are cast down, but not destroyed, because God Almighty has given to us a prophet, and a great prophet."

And the people around her answered again, "Blessed be the name of the Lord."

It was whispered about the camp that the spirit of prophecy had fallen upon Elvira Halsey.

On the afternoon of that day they saw the ice that floated in large cakes on the breast of the Mississippi flash back the sunbeams to their straining eyes. The sight of the limits of the hostile State from which they were flying was a great joy to every one of them. Susannah felt her heart leap; Elvira, with the growing tendency to cling to her which she had displayed since their last meeting, cast her arms around her and sobbed for joy.

After this blessed glimpse of the river they went down through the recesses of a low forest, the frost and the sunshine still inspiriting them. As they went, the melody of a hymn was taken up from one end of the caravan to the other by all those well enough to join in the song. It was a swinging triumphant air, and Susannah found herself uplifted for the first time since the days of her baptism upon the party spirit of the sect, and singing with them, although she could only catch the words of the refrain often repeated,

> "Missouri,
> In her lawless fury,
> Without judge or jury,
> Drove the Saints and spilt their blood."

Again the mind of Joseph Smith had overmastered Susannah's mind. As Elvira had said, he, lying in a gaol far away, enduring hardship, imminent danger of torturing death, was by his spirit animating this motley crowd, and now at last again his will broke down the barriers of reason that Susannah had raised and fortified even against the love of her child and the long reverence she had yielded to her husband. The true secret of human leadership is, perhaps, known only to the Divine mind, perhaps also to the Satanic. It would certainly seem that the men who chance upon the power and wield it, have often little understanding of the law by which they work, and their critics less.

CHAPTER XV.

The Mississippi was filled with large cakes of floating ice. Another company which had gone out from Far West some weeks before was still encamped on the Missouri banks of the river. Yet other companies from Far West came up before the main body of the Saints with which Susannah had travelled was able to cross. The surrounding woods were cut down to make shanties; the surrounding country was scoured for food. In the intervening weeks, while they lay encamped on the banks, the last enemy to be vanquished in that region, the malarial fever, grappled with the sect and dealt deadly wounds. Illinois, shocked by the cruelty of her sister State, held out kind hands and fed the fugitives to some extent, and when April came, helped them to cross the river.

Elvira had been ill in one of the women's sheds, now shrieking in hot delirium, now shaken with ague as if by a strong beast that worried its prey. When they at last crossed the river to the city of Quincy, Susannah was established with her charge, the one legacy of relationship Halsey had left her, in a meagre home with some of the Saints who already lived there.

Within a few days Susannah went to the tithing office, which had been swiftly established for the relief of the destitute Saints, and asked for paper on which she could write a letter. It was her first chance, since leaving her last asylum, of writing the proposed letter to Ephraim Croom. Elder Darling was officiating. She fancied that he looked at her with rude curiosity.

Until this moment she had presented so sad an exterior, had seemed so indifferent to all the ills of their common lot, that Darling and the other men who had dealings with her had stood not a little in awe. As outward physical details of suffering always appeal more largely to common sympathy than inward grief, the manner of her loss had set a temporary crown upon her head, to which the elders had knelt, refusing to admonish her because she took no part in their public services, or because, except for attention to the sick, she did not give much sign of social comradeship.

Now when she asked for the paper, Darling felt that the ice was beginning to break, and gave what seemed to him genial encouragement.

"First time that you've asked for anything but daily rations, Sister Halsey; glad to see you plucking up heart. The living God giveth us all things richly to enjoy." He repeated the last words in an unctuous drawl while he was looking for the paper, "richly to—enjoy. Well now, I was thinking we had some with a black border on it, but you're more than welcome to such as there is."

The stores indeed were scanty enough; food, cloth, household utensils, a little stationery, a large pile of devotional books, were arranged in meagre order in the shed used as a warehouse. Darling had as yet scarcely respectable clothes to wear, but Susannah was astonished only at the energy that had in a few days collected so much, at the order and patient kindliness which ruled in this poverty-stricken administration. Already those who could work paid into the common store, and those who had lost all had but to state their needs to have them supplied as well as might be.

"One, two, three—will three sheets be enough, Sister Halsey? You've been hearing, I suppose, that Mr. Smith is going to be moved to the town of Boome, and that he is going to be allowed to get his letters now? He'd be real cheered to hear from you, although"—he added this with decent haste—"it will be a great grief to him to hear of your loss!"

"Is he well?" she asked.

"The State authorities are in a fine to-do about him, I suppose you know, sister, for they can't find a single charge to bring him to trial on. You bet the trial would have been on long ago if they'd had a single leg to stand on. Anything else that I can serve you with today? We've got some new women's shawls and hats come in. Won't you just step here and have a look at them? No? Well, next time; but there ain't one of our women as doesn't want one of them new bonnets."

Susannah went out into the spring on the outskirts of the town. The birds were singing; everywhere the dandelions swelled out their happy tufted breasts to the sunshine; even a long worm that she noticed crawling lazily in the heat spoke to her of enjoyment of some sort. Her own heart leaped, and she thought it was in answer to the spring. She forgot the dire fates with which she had been grappling, forgot to hate and to grieve.

In the small wooden room that she shared with Elvira, while the invalid slept, she wrote to Ephraim, telling him all that had befallen her. She confessed to Ephraim the passion of hatred which had long tormented her, but she added, "Today I do not feel it; today, with the sweet voices of the birds everywhere in my ears, I feel that if I could be beside you again you could teach me to forgive as my husband forgave, for I do know today that in forgiveness alone is the true triumph, the only healing. I am more one with my husband's sect now than I ever was in heart and hope. I long to see it triumphant; I long to see its enemies abashed; but I will leave this people and come back to you, if you will have me, for with regard to their religious faith my life with them is a lie."

The writing took so long that when she carried the letter again to the tithing office to be stamped and sent, the post-bag of that day had already gone. Later, when the office was closed to the public and Elder Darling was alone, he took up the letter which Susannah had brought and looked at it curiously. His eyes had caught the address. He was not sure that he would have put it in the bag even if it had been in time, and now it was clearly his duty to consider. His was a mind in which there was no place for platonic friendship, and Susannah was obviously a most desirable piece of property to the struggling Church. The Church had provided the paper for this letter, must needs provide the stamp; he was officially responsible to the Church. The elder had been an honest man according to the average notions of honesty until within the last weeks, when stress of circumstance had made him reconsider, not for himself but for others, more than one rule of life, and obtain larger latitude. The building up of the Church in her present sore strait was surely an end to override small scruples. He acted now as an official, as a priest, when, after a good many painful qualms of conscience, he opened the letter. After having read its contents, he became convinced that it was for the good of Susannah's own soul that it should not go.

The ground about Quincy had been drained; the town was comparatively healthy; in a few days more some two thousand of the fugitives felt again the pulse of life in their veins. Then they looked abroad and clasped every man the hand of his neighbour, and said "Thanks be to God," and even embraced one another in the joy of relief. History often shows how exuberant is the joy of human nature at escape, and that the impulse of joy is almost one with the impulse of affection. At the abatement of the London plague we see Britons kiss each other in the streets, and at the relief of besieged towns, in our own day, staid persons have caressed one another, unmindful of what they did. So it was now with the members of this driven sect. The spirit of joy and a closer bond of affection went infectiously through the gathering Church. Upon the first Sunday they met together in the open air, and sang words that they verily believed had been written in particular prophecy for themselves at this very hour.

"If it had not been the Lord that was on our side."

The psalm rose from every throat with the swelling tide of joy.

"If it had not been the Lord that was on our side when men rose up against us."

Susannah, advancing, a little belated, to the rural preaching which was held in a dip of the plain, heard the lusty chant of irrepressible gladness rising to the blue heavens, and quickened her steps. In spite of herself she was carried into song by the enthusiasm which seemed to dart like a flame from the assembled multitude and enveloped her.

"Blessed be the Lord who hath not given us as a prey to their teeth. Our soul is escaped as a bird out of the snare of the fowler: the snare is broken, and we are escaped. Our help is in the name of the Lord, who made heaven and earth."

While she was exalted by the song she saw the face of her friend the Danite for the first time since the night on which they had ridden so far together. He was standing now upon the outskirts of the crowd as one who had newly come from a solitary journey. When he met Susannah's eye his solitary look passed into one of lofty and intense comradeship. He ran to her and embraced her, and emptied an inner pocket of a purse of money which he thrust eagerly into her possession.

"I have killed one of them," he said, speaking eagerly, as a child tells of some exploit. "His pockets were fat with money, and it is yours."

"See!" He took the fragment of linen upon which the stain of Halsey's blood had turned dark with time, and showed her a new and brighter stain upon its edges.

All around them were men and women, who now, for the first time since the hour of some terrible parting, spied kindred or comrades. By a common impulse these moved toward one another, and there was an interlude in the service for sobs of joy and frantic embracings, and many men and women clasped one another who could claim no kindred, and none forbade, for tears of mutual love were in all eyes.

After that, in the streets or in chance meetings in the houses, the remembrance of this festival of rapturous comradeship gave a new standard to the manners of private life. The Saints had, as it were, passed from death unto life; former things had passed away; the praises of God were ever upon their lips; they entered with joy into a kingdom of love which they doubted not God had ordained for his elect; many a command of Scripture became illumined with a new practical meaning. "Greet *all* the brethren with a holy kiss." "Greet ye one another with a kiss of charity."

Susannah was not much abroad, but she saw the new customs inaugurated. Believing that they must be transient, knowing, too, that the fierce undercurrent that they expressed must have outlet, and was not of that range of emotions which had to do with the common relationships of life, she felt no shock of offended sentiment. But in a short space of time, as Elvira grew better, Susannah perceived that the experimental nature of the new life was a dissipation to weaker minds. This grieved her because of the sacred memory of her husband's efforts for these people, and because, attuned by party spirit, she entertained a nervous personal desire that they should acquit themselves well. Just here she found occupation; she gathered the young girls about her in a temporary school, and set herself to soothe and calm the excitement of the women. The work was intended to last but a few weeks, until Ephraim's answer came.

To the unspeakable joy of his followers, Joseph Smith appeared suddenly in Quincy. It appeared to be true, as Darling said, that the Missouri authorities could in fact find no charge on which to try him.

Smith, with his brother Hyrum and their fellows, had suffered severely, but later their confinement had been more easy, and the news of the triumphant gathering of his people, together with the excitement of the escape, had induced in Smith a mood which spurned past failures with a foot that sped to a new goal. The acclamation, the sincere and touching joy, with which Smith was received by men and women and children, were enough to raise any man in his own esteem, and to set free the ambition which had been perhaps drooping in confinement.

Smith had not been in Quincy twenty-four hours before he mastered the situation there in all its details. He promptly sent out a decree against the new doctrine of what he called "lax manners." He preached a great sermon in the open air that night. "A man shall kiss his own wife and daughters and no other women," said Smith. The elders who had preached from St. Paul's texts on the subject were accused of error and called upon to recant. Smith commanded that the women should work and the children should study, and he publicly pronounced Susannah to be a fitting model for the women and a fitting teacher for the young. Susannah had not as yet met Smith face to face when she found herself made, as it were, an object of licensed admiration.

CHAPTER XVI.

It was that same evening, after Smith's commendation of Susannah, that Darling decided to lay the destruction of her letter before the prophet, hoping for approval.

Smith was looking over Darling's accounts in the tithing office, giving voluminous and minute directions. The May night had closed in. The men were in a corner of the large shed in which the stores were kept, a corner fenced off for an office by a low wooden partition. The candle flickered on the table between them.

The business side of Smith's soul was uppermost. He had power to keep in mind a huge number of details, and to classify them, and he estimated the relative importance of the classes as no other man would have estimated it.

Darling interrupted before Smith's interest in business began to wane. He prefaced his communication concerning Susannah by speaking of the much shepherding needed by the sheep. Some, he said, had done worse than be lax in manners; some had presumed to have revelations; some had doubted the faith.

Here Darling paused, feeling sure of rousing Smith to the mood he desired.

At the mention of revelations Smith's soul took a turn, like a ball on its axis; the plain speech that he had been using about business and stores and accounts changed into phraseology of a Scriptural cast, and the shrewd glance of his blue eye into a more distraught and distant look. Heretofore, as Darling well knew, heresy had been a greater evil in his eyes than any other; but Smith had come now out of long months of prison; days and nights in which a horrible death had faced him closely had not passed over this particular soul of his dreams without moulding it. It is noticed by all his historians that after this period he spoke little "by revelation," in comparison with his former full habit in this respect. At Darling's abrupt speech he sighed heavily. He looked, not at Darling as before, but at some vague object beyond him.

"There is one lawgiver who is able to save and to destroy," he said wearily, and then, gathering himself up with more pompous unction, he asked of the surprised Darling, "Who art thou that judgest another?"

Darling had grown fatter since he came to Quincy; the lines of haggard care were still upon his face, but were modified by dimples of good cheer. Much taken aback by the unexpected rebuff, he rubbed his head.

"But, Mr. Smith, if they are all going to be allowed to think whatever they like—"

The obvious difficulty of church government under these conditions confronted the nobler impulse of humility in the visionary's mind. "When have I said, Brother Darling, that they all should think what they like? But, behold, I say unto thee, it is not with the Lord to save with many or with few, but by whom he will send."

This was a little vague as to grammar and as to sense, but Darling had not the ability to criticise. He only perceived that to secure commendation he must be tactful in the setting forth of his act.

"It was in the case of Sister Susannah Halsey—" he began again apologetically.

A more eager look came into Smith's eyes; still a third phase of his character there was, the soul of his personal affections, and this began to merge now with his religious self. "Hath she prophesied? Hath any revelation been granted to her?"

If Darling had not understood the prophetical vein, he did understand a certain vibration in this tone. "Ha!" thought he, "if the prophet ain't a bit soft on her himself I'm out." He had lowered his eyes, and now he said evasively, "It is our sister Elvira on whom the spirit of prophecy has fallen; you will have heard how she gave praise concerning you before the Saints upon the road and was moved to dance before the Lord."

Smith saw through the evasion, but by shrewd reading of the sanctimonious face, saw also the inward suspicion as clearly as if Darling had spoken it. His tone and manner betrayed him no more.

"The head of our sister Elvira is not always set firmly on her shoulders," he remarked, "but I am glad if the Lord has given her grace."

"I've been hoping that he'd give grace to our sister Susannah, for she's been writing a letter to say as how she was without faith and wanting to leave us."

Smith answered him now only with a cool silence that puzzled his coarser understanding.

"'Twas in our first days here, when a good many of the women were flighty, and Elvira Halsey, she was ill enough to have worked the patience out of any one as they work the milk out of butter, and Sister Susannah came with a letter. She gave it to me unsealed."

"Was she without wax to seal it?" interrupted Smith in a casual tone. Darling could not know that the thought of such poverty wrung Smith's heart.

"Waal, I dunno" (which was a lie). "Mebbe she had no wax—I didn't think of that, but anyhow she gave me the letter. 'Twas too late for the mail; 'twas too heavy for one stamp. An' I didn't like to tell her, poor thing, that we'd mighty little to spend on stamps. So after she'd gone I just had a look to see who it was to."

"The address would be on the outside?" Smith rose, hat in hand, as if to depart, but fixed his eyes on the candle till Darling should have done.

"The name gave me very little hint as to whether the matter was worth the two stamps, so I just had a glance inside. Thought it might be but a line asking money of her friends, which, under the sad circumstances, of course I knew you'd rather the Church would supply."

This drew the first spark of the approval he was expecting. "Certainly, certainly, the widows and the orphans of those who have perished for the truth must ever be our most tender care."

"Exactly so, prophet; I knew that would be your opinion; so when I saw that our sister had felt drove to asking for money from some fellow—I guess there must have been some sweethearting between him and her before she married Halsey. She said in this letter that she'd go to him if he'd send her cash. She said as how she thought the religion of the Latter-Day Saints was a lie; but of course I could see it was not her right judgment, that she was awful lonesome."

"It was taking a great liberty, Mr. Darling." Smith tapped his stick upon the floor. He was far more angry than he showed, for policy had laid a soft hand of reminder on his shoulder. "Our sister, Mrs. Halsey, is not—" he coughed slightly, and sought by prophetical phrases to explain that Susannah was not upon the level of Darling and his kind—"is not, as it would be said in the Scriptures, among those who deck themselves with crisping pins or are busybodies, but she is as that lady to whom John wrote (and the letter is preserved unto the edification of the Church unto this day); for it was revealed unto me in the beginning that she was the elect sister, and to sit as one who judges—as one who judges Israel." He was just going to add in the flow of his phrases "upon twelve thrones," but the words died because even he perceived the lack of sense.

Darling grew testy. "Waal, I dunno, but it seems to me that if she'd gone off by now to be Mrs. Ephraim Croom somewheres in the East there wouldn't be much more elect sister about her."

"The gentleman whose name you have just been mentioning, Mr. Darling, is the lady's uncle. I was reared alongside them, and I know." He knew that he fibbed between uncle and cousin, but the slip was so slight and the end so worthy—to silence Darling.

"'Twas no uncle that she wrote that 'ere letter to," said Darling hotly. He stuck out his legs and leant back in his chair, the picture of offence.

"You are mistaken concerning the meaning of the letter, Brother Darling, and it appears to me that in casting your eyes upon it you have gone beyond what is written concerning the duty of an elder; but as to your duty in destroying it—considering that our sister asked for money, which it is our duty and privilege to supply—But I promised Emmar to be back soon. I will consult the Lord, Brother Darling, and have a word with you in the morning."

Smith tramped with dignity over the long wooden floor of the darkened shed and let himself out with decisive clatter of the latch.

To his right lay the wooden town with twinkling lights, to his left the black prairie, and above the crystal vast a moonless night, so clear that the upward glance almost saw the perspective between nearer and farther stars innumerable.

This man was at all times possessed with the sense of otherness, sense of a presence around and above. He was no sooner beneath the stars than he hung his head as if some one saw him. With shame and pain written in the attitude of his hulking figure, he skulked out into the black fields.

Later that night, a lad, not of the Mormon brotherhood, making his way home in the dark to the town of Quincy, a little afraid of the dark, as lads are apt to be, was terrified by hearing a voice in the darkness, by dimly descrying a man's figure prostrate upon the ground. The lad shrank back to a recess of the snake fence. There, trembling, he listened.

The voice in the hoarse whisper of intensity repeated, "Give me— this woman—give—give." The breathing, like command rather than prayer, set the words grating on the air again and again. "This woman— this woman—give! give! give!"

The cause of the lad's terror was a strange conviction that the writhing creature on the earth was certainly conversing with something not of earth, whether God, or angel, or devil he did not ask. He was encompassed by the dreadful belief that the other saw and heard what he could not.

The prostrate man clenched his fists and struck the black ground on which he lay. There was an intense silence, and then again the grating breath of a hoarse throat that lay among the grass blades babbled forth a multitude of confessions and fiercely-worded supplications which the little lad could neither understand nor remember.

There was a sudden change of attitude and voice. The lad saw that the man on the grass sat up, and as if he had received an answer, spoke in reply, not now in wailing supplication, but in quick whispered argument. The lad cowered with a fresh thrill of ghostly terror which burned the mad words into his memory.

"The loss would be to thee of the fairest of thine handmaids, and to her of her own soul, and to me—" but here the words of irritable contention failed in deep choking sobs. Then, to the lad's perfect dismay, the black figure bounded to its feet and the arms were flung about in the darkness as if wrestling with an unseen enemy. Now, being desperate, the lad darted forth from his nook; passing in tip-toe rush at the back of this struggling figure, he sped home in his gust of fear, and, with the fantastic secrecy of youth, did not tell what he had heard and seen till years had come and gone.

CHAPTER XVII.

The May morning was wreathing itself with opening flowers to meet the first hour of sunlight when Susannah was startled by hearing that the prophet inquired for her. There was in the house where she lived an empty chamber, unfurnished because of poverty; it was in this that the prophet, who demanded a private audience, awaited her.

So vexed was she at the public advertisement which he had made of her, that she forgot the bereavement she had suffered since she last saw him; but when she looked up she saw that Smith's face wore signs of emotion that he was not trying to conceal.

At first he made an attempt at some unctuous form of address, an effort at formality, a mechanical tribute to habit. Failing to finish his phrase, he stood before her, not as the lauded leader, not as the interesting martyr, but claiming recognition merely as a man, a large, coarse man feeling his own coarseness in her presence, a sinful man feeling his own sinfulness, but at the same time a man with a warm heart, which was now so beating with emotions of shame and pity and glad recognition that at first he could not speak, could not raise his eyes to hers until the warmth of his feeling rid him of self-consciousness.

Susannah had not expected to awake this emotion. She desired nothing less than condolence; and yet she was touched by seeing his huge strength broken down for the moment by her appearing. When he spoke his voice was hoarse.

"I—I told him—it was my earnest command to him not to go where there was danger."

Halsey's name was not spoken, but all through that interview Smith appeared to be haunted by his presence. "He was the best man amongst us," he said.

"My husband is gone." Susannah hoped by the reticence of her tone to ward off further excess of sympathy. "I am no longer bound to your Church, Mr. Smith. I should not be honest if I did not tell you that I hold myself free."

He faced her frankly, but with a glance of searching pain. "It must seem a rather poor trade I've chosen if there ain't no truth in it."

"But I did not accuse you of not believing it, Mr. Smith."

"Do you think I do?"

She remembered the day that he had first shown her his peep-stone with simple, childlike importance. How young they had both been! The sunshine on the hill, the voice of the golden woodpecker, the scent of the fallen beech leaves, came back to her. A decade of terrible years had passed over them both, and he stood seeking her faith just as simply.

"I have tried very hard to understand you, Mr. Smith, but I do not. I think you must believe most of what you claim for yourself, if not all. If you had made your story up for the love of power you wouldn't always be wanting the people to get a better education; you would, as they say of the Roman Catholic priests, want to keep the people ignorant."

"Go on," he said. She found that he was looking at her with intense sadness, but there was not a shadow of evasion in the eager look that met her steadily.

She went on, looking gravely into his face. "I do not believe that your story was false, Mr. Smith, but it seems to me that you must suspect now that your visions and the gold plates were hallucination, not reality." She paused, eager question in tone and look, but the question was of the head, not of the heart.

He knew that; he knew that it did not matter greatly to this thoughtful and beautiful woman whether he had sunk to the deepest degradation or not. Suddenly he answered her, but not as one who stood at her judgment bar.

"Where is your heart? Didn't you see how that man Angel—angel of purity if ever one walked in human form—kissed every day the ground you walked upon? And you did not love him. The child—you thought you cared for the child: I tell you if I had had a child like that, with eyes like the stars and a little mind so untainted, I had laid myself down on his grave and died there. There's Emmar and me, we'd be in more trouble if you lost one of your pretty fingers than you would have been in if they had taken and killed us over there in Missouri." He added, "If you were another woman, and had not the power to do more than just have a little shallow caring for one and another, where would be your sin?"

Something that she had dimly suspected of herself flashed into apparent truth. Ephraim, too, had perhaps intended to tell her this when he had said that love, not knowledge, was needed. She had not loved Halsey and his child as she might have loved.

Susannah had always recognised a certain bigness in Smith's character because of the power he had of giving himself to man, woman, and child; now she felt her own inferiority. Was she to stand babbling to him about hallucinations and gold plates? The man in him had flashed out at her, and because she was not without the heart whose whereabouts he had demanded, the flash awakened an answering fire. Her cheeks flushed, not with self-consciousness, but with the slow gathering of heart-stricken tears.

"And you," she said slowly, "you have poured out blood and soul for us all freely, but why?" The imperious need of truth awoke again. "Why have you let yourself be beaten and shot at and imprisoned and horribly threatened, to lead us all to this new Zion, wherever it may be?" She repeated the question. "If it was ambition, why did you hold to it when there did not seem to be the slightest chance that your sect could survive, or that you would escape death?"

She was asking with more heart in her tone now that she had been made to realise what she had of respect and friendship for this man.

"I hain't got the courage most people think I have," he replied sadly; "I am scared enough; I am scared sometimes of the very water I go into to baptize in, let alone men that want to murder me; but I am more afraid to go against my revelations, for I know if I went against them there would be nothing for me but the pit and eternal fire. I don't say that it would be the same for any of you. I used to preach that it would, but in prison, when I thought of my folks standing up to be killed, I thought perhaps I had gone beyond what was told me in preaching that way; but as for me, I've seen and I've heard."

He did not turn or take restless steps upon the floor. It would have been a relief to her if he had moved; but he remained just where he first stood, strong enough to have this colloquy over without restlessness.

"I am no saint," he said, "as you know very well, and there's a lot of things I've done, thinking that my revelations told me, which I don't know whether they told me or not, for in prison I saw that the things were bad things, like that mess of the bank, and running away as I did. I guess I could not have been living right, and the devil gulled me. But that hain't got nothing to do with the times I know that the Lord spoke. You don't believe it was the Lord at all. Well, then, who was it? For it's the same as has told me not to do the lots of wicked things I might have done and didn't. As to them plates, I told you before I didn't have them as much in my hands as I said I did. I got wrong a bit there too, maybe, but it isn't easy to keep quite straight between the thing you see and the words you say it in, when you are trying to talk to people about what they don't understand. It isn't easy to do just only what is perfectly right about anything at any time, at least, if it is to you, it isn't to me; but I often thought I was born worse than most people."

"The men who were your witnesses as to the reality of the plates are apostate," she said gently.

"They are apostate," he said gloomily, "and why? Because I would not let them live upon the Lord's tithes without labouring as we all laboured."

He spoke again after a moment. "The Gentiles have spread abroad a story about one Solomon Spalding, who they say wrote the Book of Mormon, which Rigdon stole, but you know—you who have been with us from the beginning—that neither I nor your husband nor any one of us saw Rigdon until we came to Kirtland, and if his word is to be believed he never saw this Spalding or his book."

She made an impatient movement of her head. "I know," she said, "that there is no truth in that story." She moved a little away from him; she was becoming oppressed by his still earnestness.

"Isn't it any proof to you that I hadn't the wits nor the education to make the book?" His words were wistful.

She sat down on the sill of the open window, the only seat in the room, and looked out on the moist earth.

"I guess you want to get rid of me," he said, "but I can't go till I know how it is with you, for I've been wrestling in prayer this night concerning you." Then after a minute he said, "Our brother gave you the money that he found on the person of your husband's murderer?"

"I paid it into the treasury."

"But if you don't believe, maybe you are thinking of going east?"

"Do you think I could use the price of my husband's blood for that? It is not for me to know whether the avengers of blood are right or wrong in a land where there is no law, but the money belonged to your Church."

He looked at her as one who has made a study of a certain class of objects looks at a fine specimen, as a jeweller looks at a gem of the first water. This man, with the genius for priesthood, was a connoisseur in souls. "Emmar wouldn't have thought it no harm to keep the money the Danites gave her," and he added more reflectively, "nor would I." There was admiration in his tones.

He came a step nearer now. "If you went east who have you to go to? Your uncle, he's dead."

Susannah started. "How do you know?"

His manner was pitying. "I saw it last night in the way I see things, in my visions, but Emmar she heard from some of the Saints that came from Palmyra that your uncle was sick unto death, and last night the Lord told me he was dead."

She rose up suddenly. She had known too many instances of this man's curious knowledge of distant events to think of doubting. Her first thought was that if Ephraim was in this trouble she must go to him at once.

"Your aunt will be awful jealous of your cousin now she's only got him."

Then under Smith's pitying glance Susannah shrank from the first impulse to go. She felt that there was something within her that merited his pity. She could not rush to Ephraim without invitation, because it was not for his sake but for her own she wanted to go. She believed that Smith knew it. She felt thankful, as he had dared to accuse her of not loving her husband, that he had the kindness not to accuse her of this. A certain awe of Smith came over her; he could be violent with those who were violent, coarse and jocular with his public who could be worked upon thus, but to her he spoke delicately, and he had shown her at times before this that he knew her better than she knew herself.

"Sister Susannah," said Smith humbly, "it's my fault that you've become the brainy woman that you are, for I encouraged you at book learning (knowing as how when you found your heart 'twould shine with the more lustre), but if you were to go and live along side of a man as is a bookworm you'd lose your chance of this life (let alone your soul's salvation by the apostasy which you think lightly of now). Anyhow I'd wait if I was you till his mother asks you, for she'd be in an awful taking if you and he were talk, talk, talking of what she didn't understand. And he is her only son, and she is a widow."

With this last phrase, which had a good and Scriptural sound, Smith had done.

Susannah gave him her hand in farewell, and listened gently while again he told her, as on the night of his flight from Kirtland, that his friendship and the friendship of his Church were always at her service.

The prophet walked down the street. A crowd of the Saints and a group of elders were waiting for him with impatience. Darling eyed his coming with looks gloomy and furtive, but the prophet was no longer, as on the previous night, wrathful and pompous. He spoke aside to Darling.

"I thought it right to tell our sister Susannah Halsey that her Gentile home had suffered bereavement. The uncle who has been as a father unto her is dead. I have been greatly exercised in grief for her," continued Smith, briefly and truly; and then he added, also with truth, but with subtle suggestion, "I cannot think that further dealing with that household could be of advantage to her, but having laid the matter before the Lord, I was made aware that we must seek the good of all our sisters not with regard to outward appearance or inclination of the eyes; therefore,

Brother Darling, let your motive be lowly, not having respect unto persons," and he added with the simplicity of a child, "as mine is."

Susannah was left with the bad picture in her mind which Smith had sketched there. She saw herself cold to her husband, lacking in passionate motherliness to his child, eager for the society of another man not out of love but intellectual vanity, and cavilling also at all religion because faith had no good soil to rest in. She sat long on the window-sill of the empty room, looking at an uncultivated patch of ground that even in May had no beauty save for here and there the stirring of a weed in the damp scented earth. She was stunned to see her life limned in such lines, and the truth in the drawing made it at first seem wholly true.

But Fate had another messenger that morning more potent than the prophet. A girl came by on the road, stopped, looked at her window, and by some impulse such as moved the buds and birds, tripped nearer in the sunshine and offered a flower. It was a sprig of quince blossom, and the girl stood laughing on the threshold of life just as Susannah had stood when Ephraim first showed her the flower of the quince. The false lines in the picture drawn by Smith faded at the touch of the pink winged flowers. Her heart sprang into the truth.

The girl looked up to see the face of the schoolmistress flushed and shining with sudden tears.

"My dear," said Susannah gently, "when I was your age flowers were given to me, but I did not love them half enough."

The maiden tripped away, resolving at heart to heed the admonition, although she understood it very vaguely.

Susannah knelt down upon the floor behind the sill, pressing both hands upon her breast lest she should cry aloud.

"No! No! No!" she whispered, "I loved Ephraim, and it was because I left him that my heart closed up—because in insufferable pride and impatience I left him. Oh, my love, now I know that you loved me too." She rocked herself in a passionate desire for Ephraim's presence. The scene in the cold autumn wood at Fayette came back to her eyes and ears. She felt the very touch of his hand when he went. "Fool! fool!" she said, "foolish and wicked. If I Had not been proud, if I had not thought myself better than you and yours, I should have understood." For some unexplained reason her mind reverted now to Halsey and the child, and she wept for them as she had never wept before.

After these tears she stood up and stretched out her arms as if embracing a new life. Alas! around her were only the ugly walls of the poor unfurnished room. Susannah, rousing herself from the warm scenes of quickened memory, felt the contrast.

The hope of Ephraim's reply to her letter came to her smiling each morning, and, as the days passed, retired from her heart with a sigh each night.

When six weeks had gone and no reply came Susannah wrote again. This time she addressed the letter to the care of Mr. Horace Bushnell in Hartford, thinking that perhaps by some extraordinary chance Ephraim's whereabouts might not be known in Manchester. This letter was, unlike all those that had preceded it, more brief, more reserved, and more gentle. It expressed interest only in his affairs, telling little of her own except the fact that she desired to return. Autumn came, and Susannah's faith in man was tested to the utmost by the dreariness of daily disappointment.

If Ephraim were dead surely his mother or his friend would return her letters. If Ephraim were not dead what could be the explanation of this silence? Many vicissitudes of life occurred to her as possibly producing a change in him, and only one explanation of his silence was possible—that he was changed. That was a terrible belief to face. Her faith took the bit in its teeth and refused to be guided by intelligence. The whole strength of her volition abetted the revolt of faith. Anything, everything, might be true rather than that the essentials of character which went to make up Ephraim's personality should be blurred or decomposed.

Susannah wrote again to Ephraim, to his mother and to Mr. Bushnell—three separate letters. She worked with the more zeal at her self-appointed task. So cheerful and energetic was she that she appeared to her pupils and acquaintance as a radiant being, and received the most genuine honour and affection from the Mormon settlement in Quincy.

CHAPTER XVIII.

With the jubilant Saints at Quincy the prophet could not remain long. He journeyed up the banks of the Mississippi. Here and there communities of his people welcomed him with touching joy; their numbers and their faithfulness must have raised his heart. He came at last to a poor, sickly locality, around which the great river took a majestic sweep, and here the prophet saw what no one else had seen—a site of great beauty and advantage. The inhabitants were dying of malarial fever. Smith bought their lands at a low price and drained them. Thus arose the beautiful city of Nauvoo.

In the Illinois State Legislature two parties were nearly equal in strength, and both coveted the Mormon vote. When Smith applied for the city charter, for charters also for a university and a force of militia to be called "The Nauvoo Legion," they were granted, and worded to his will.

White limestone, found in great abundance near the surface of the earth, served as material for the public buildings and the better houses. Wooden houses, and even log huts, were washed with white lime. On three sides of the town the air of the beautiful river blew fresh and cool from its rippling tide; the surrounding land was fertile. Fortune certainly smiled upon the sect that had borne itself so sturdily under persecution. The prophet's laws had much to do with the prosperity; neither strong drink nor tobacco were admitted within the city limit; cleanliness and thrift were enforced.

The Saints in settlement in the town of Quincy and other places remained while they could obtain lucrative employment and thus transmit the larger tithes for the building up of their future home; but from the poorer settlements artisans and farmers flocked to Nauvoo. Thither also the missionaries scattered in the eastern States, in England, and in further Europe sent the bands of converts who had been kept waiting till a city of refuge was founded. It was not long, not many months, before fifteen thousand people were hurrying up and down the broad streets of the new city.

During the rise of Nauvoo, Emma Smith was living at Quincy in a small house with her three children. She was Susannah's best neighbour. The prophet's enormous activity was fully occupied with the new city and the care of the scattered Church, so that he could not visit his wife often. Each time he came he sent for Susannah to listen with Emma to the triumphant accounts that he gave of his present successes. He was all aglow with the resurrection of his Church, tender towards its renewed enthusiasm for himself, compassionate more than ever for the pains it had endured; fixed in purpose to establish his suffering and loyal people in such a manner as might reward them for all that they had undergone. His spirit of revenge against the Gentiles, and especially against the perverts from his own sect who had sought to trample it down, was also increased; the prayers of the Hebrew Psalmist against the enemies of Israel were constantly upon his lips. More than once when at Quincy he preached to the little flock there with great effect from the blessings and cursings conditionally delivered to Israel in the Book of Deuteronomy, arguing that evils of a very material kind were to befall apostates, and blessings of a like kind were to be given to the faithful in the new city.

"It is not true," Susannah said to him defiantly. "There is no righteousness in desiring the downfall of your enemies, and earthly wealth can never have any fixed connection with spiritual blessing."

"Do I understand you, my sister, to say that the prophet Moses did not teach a true religion?" As he spoke he laid his hand upon a huge copy of the Bible, bound in velvet and gold, which lay as the only ornament upon Emma's centre table.

In these days Susannah began to have some fear of the word "apostate." Contrary to the freedom which had existed in the Kirtland community, the present Church, with its dogmas cast into iron moulds from the furnace of persecution, had begun to authorise a sentiment against perverts which differed not only in degree, but in kind, from the purely spiritual anathemas which had formerly fallen upon them. Personally she had no fear. The prophet knew of her unbelief, and his conduct was increasingly kind and deferential, but for others she disliked exceedingly the new symptoms of tyranny. Yet it was but natural, she admitted; men who had offered their own lives in sacrifice for a creed were likely to think it of more worth to the soul of another than his liberty. The sin, she thought, lay chiefly with the persecutors.

Sometimes during these visits Smith came and sat beside her in her own small room and talked to her about his plans, about new revelations which had come to him, about the future of the Church, just as if he were trying to persuade himself that she at last believed in the solemn importance of these things. He said to her that her judgment would always weigh greatly with him, that he was reserving a portion for her in the new city such as would have belonged to her husband and child if they had lived. He spoke of his pleasure in seeing the companionship between herself and Emma. He spoke also of Emma's worthiness, and of her devotion to himself.

His words about Emma were kind, but it was not thus that he had spoken of her in the first years. Susannah perceived a change analogous to that which she could not deny had taken place in Emma herself. In the beginning Emma had been slim, with a spiritual look in her eyes, giving herself to absorbed pondering over all Smith's words and ways. Now she was stout, and was given much to the practical care of her children, and, devoted as she was to her husband, she assumed often a tone of remonstrance, setting aside many of Smith's vagaries as unworthy of attention. She thought to please him and his Church by dressing well and appearing to be a person of some figure and consequence, but in private she grumbled at his personal extravagance. At both these changes Susannah smiled, but to her heart, ever weighing the chances in favour of Ephraim's constancy, they seemed an ill omen. It was because she was absorbed in the personal application of all things to her own secret case that she paid less attention to the prophet's remarks.

Once, passing through the street, when she saw him standing with Darling at the door of the tithing office, through which the mail for the Mormon settlement still went and came, she observed the two men were noticing and speaking of her; she received a disagreeable impression from their manner.

She supposed that she had found a complete explanation of this sinister parley when, the next time Smith came, he brought with him an elderly and foolish man, a new convert who had brought great wealth to the new city, whom he proposed as a suitor for Elvira's hand. Susannah was very angry.

Elvira had continued for many months in the lassitude that malarial fever leaves behind it. Susannah had need to support her, as well as herself, by the small fees which her day-scholars could afford. She had had the satisfaction of seeing Elvira restored in a great degree to health, but so capricious and fantastic were the bright little lady's words and actions that it was impossible to say whether or not she had slipped across the wavering line that separates the sane from the insane.

Susannah stood now in her small sitting-room fiercely facing Smith and his new satellite. She still adhered to the plain Quaker-like garb that her husband had liked, and the muslin kerchief crossed upon her breast was a quaint pearl-like frame to the beauty of feature which had slowly but surely, in spite of adverse circumstance, come to its prime. Smith's stalwart figure and the decrepit form of his friend were both clad in sleek broadcloth. They wore the high white collar and stock of the period. In Smith's light hair there was not a gray thread, nor were there many wrinkles in his smooth forceful face. The old man was gray and wrinkled; he cringed and leered as Susannah rated them for the proposition they had made.

But the answer to this proposition did not lie in her hands; before she could compel Smith to withdraw it, or know if his mind was tending towards that obedience, Elvira, curious to see the strangers, entered.

Elvira raised a coquettish finger and told Smith that he was a very naughty man. This was a new freak in her conduct toward the prophet. Light and frivolous as she had become, the title of prophetess, coveted among Mormon women, had been conferred upon her because some strange power of divination governed her freaks.

"A very naughty man." With her delicate prettiness, decked in what gewgaws she could afford, Elvira stood shaking her forefinger. "You don't know why? Oh, fie! you know very well, naughty, naughty creature."

Smith had the air of some unwieldy animal trying to adapt itself to the unexpected gambols of a light one. The first supposition was that Elvira had in some way learnt the object of his mission, so he began to declare it with a reproachful look at Susannah. "Our sister Halsey," he said, "does not wish you to wear jewels and beautiful clothes, and yet it is said in the Scripture that the clothing of ladies should be even of wrought gold."

"Naughty creature," she cried, "don't quote the Scriptures to me. I am not the lady you are thinking about. I am not the lady that you come here to see."

So intent they all were upon her and her affairs that this statement was somewhat puzzling. The only sign that Smith gave that he gathered any sense out of the vivacious nonsense she was pleased to talk was that he precipitated his explanation.

The brother by his side was very rich; it had been foretold him in a vision of the night that when he had professed the Mormon faith a pretty wife would be his reward. Smith had had it borne in upon his mind that Elvira was the lady designed by the vision. "For," said he unctuously; "the Holy Scripture saith that the solitary shall be set in families."

Elvira laughed. "How very amusing," she cried. "And into what family shall our sister Susannah be set?"

Smith frowned. "Our sister Susannah," he said, "is not solitary, but is surrounded by her spiritual children, to whom she imparts her own learning and goodness, to the great benefit of the Church; and I cannot but think, Sister Elvira"—the severity in his voice was growing—"that you are a great care to her, for she toils hard to give you even such poor raiment as you are now wearing, not wishing to accept of the bounty of the Church, while she would be an example of industry to others."

The hard truth of this statement, combined with the commanding voice and manner he now assumed, controlled Elvira. She stood for some minutes meekly contemplating her senile and smirking suitor. Susannah protested and warned her, but in caprice, as sudden as it was unexpected, Elvira decided to comply with the prophet's request without further persuasion or command.

When left alone with Susannah she only shrugged her shoulders and said, "I saw that I should lose my soul if I didn't; the prophet was so determined. Why should we bicker and consider, and why should I fly round and round, like a bird round the green eyes of a cat, or try to escape half a dozen times like a mouse when it is once caught, when I know from the beginning that Joe Smith will curse me if I don't do his will?"

"You are quite mistaken. He was not determined; he told me that he only wished to lay the matter before you and let you decide for yourself."

Elvira let her white eyelids droop until but a narrow slit of the dark eye was visible. "La! child," she said.

"And you cannot seriously think that Smith's curse, even if he were barbarous enough to denounce you, could make the slightest difference to your soul's salvation. You often talk that way, but you cannot seriously think it, Elvira."

But here Susannah struck against a vein of darkness in her companion's mind which it seemed to her had lain there like a black incomprehensible streak since the awful day of anguish and massacre at Haun's Mill.

"Don't speak of it," cried Elvira with a shudder. "Don't you know that Joe Smith is our prophet, and that he holds the keys of life and death? Didn't Angel Halsey die to teach us that? Weren't we baptized into it by being dipped in blood?"

She sat shuddering in the dusk and repeating at intervals "dipped in blood," "dipped in blood."

Whether Elvira was mad or not, Susannah had no power to stop this nefarious marriage. The prophet had departed hastily out of reach of her indignant appeals, and there was no one whose interference she could seek. In vain she besought Elvira, using both argument and passionate entreaty. With precipitate waywardness the strange girl was married by

Elder Darling, in the shed of the tithing house.

No letter came from Ephraim Croom or from his friends.

After Elvira's departure Susannah began to save out of her little income, trying to put by enough dollars not only for the eastern journey, but to give her respectable support afterwards until she could obtain employment. She had little heart for the object of her saving; she might, she knew, be going to ignominy and starvation, for with the stigma of Mormonism upon her, she felt that it was unlikely that she would be received with credit in any town where she was friendless and unknown.

Although the community prospered greatly, Smith did not again interfere to increase Susannah's school fees. Emma began to talk largely of the splendour of Nauvoo, reading from her husband's letters of the Nauvoo House, a huge hotel, which was being rapidly and grandly built for the perpetual occupation of himself and family and the entertainment of all such as the Church of the Saints should delight to honour.

Susannah found it hard to understand why Emma was not taken to Nauvoo even before the great house was built for her reception. It was indeed commonly reported among the Gentiles at this time that the prophet had secretly espoused other wives; but a malignant report of this nature, together with accusations of drunkenness and rank dishonesty, had persistently followed the sect from its beginning, and, as far as Susannah knew, were now, as before, totally untrue. This special report, however, reached Emma in an hour of depression, and she came to Susannah for sympathy, shaken with grief and indignation.

"What does it mean that they always say that of him when the one thing that he's done has been to excommunicate any of the brethren that taught any such thing? And there's just been an awful row on in the Council of Nauvoo against Sydney Rigdon and some pamphlet he's written on a doctrine he calls 'Spiritual Wives,' and Joseph has risen up and cast him out, even though he was his best friend."

The reason of the calumny seemed to Susannah clear enough; it was a natural one for low-minded politicians who hated Smith to formulate, and the religious world outside thought they were doing God service by believing any ill of a blasphemer; but this charge was an old one, and she probed further today for the real cause of Emma's excitement. She was first given a letter in which Smith told of Rigdon's excommunication.

"Rigdon's doctrine," wrote Smith, "is a vile one because it is held by the whole sect of Perfectionists which are now scattered through the Churches of the eastern States, and is a proof that the glory of the Lord is departed from them, for they say that a man may be married to one wife in an earthly manner, and she who is to be his in a spiritual and eternal manner may be another woman, and this is vile; therefore I've cast out Sydney Rigdon and called him apostate. But it seems to me in this matter and in the perpetual slander of the Gentiles it may be that it is being shown to us, even as things were shown by outward signs at times to the ancient prophets, that there is somewhat concerning the existing form of marriage that it would be well to reconsider, for I perceive that the more my revelations cause a difference to be set between our people and the Gentiles, the more shall we be bound closely together, which unity is undoubtedly of the Lord."

Susannah always found it difficult to gather much information from the prophet's vague and incoherent style. "Has he ever written anything else about this affair of Rigdon's?" she asked.

Then it transpired that another letter had that day arrived, giving another and more graphic account of Rigdon's rebellion and overthrow, after which Joseph inconsistently wrote:

"Yet with regard to the matter of his heresy it remains undoubtedly true for men who are called to some great and special work one woman may be needed as a bride upon earth and another woman may be called as a spiritual bride" (this word "bride" was crossed out, though left legible enough, and "guide" written above it) "to lead him into higher and heavenly places prepared of the Lord for this purpose."

After perusing this passage carefully, and with inward laughter at its inconsistency, she gave the letter back, endeavouring to render some help.

"Have you not observed that your husband's mind is very peculiar? When any idea is forcibly suggested to him, all his thoughts seem to eddy round it until he thinks that the whole world is to be revolutionised by it, and then when diverted to something else he forgets all about it like a child, and never thinks of it again perhaps for years."

Emma, unable to comprehend the analysis, drew back offended.

"Joseph has a great deal finer mind than any person I know." The last words were levelled with a nettled glance at Susannah.

On Emma's behalf Susannah confidently hoped that the prophet would forget this theory, as he had apparently forgotten the many theories which had ere now proposed themselves to his excitable brain, and which he had found unworkable. His practical shrewdness acted as a critic on his visionary notions—never in thought, for he did not seem able to exercise the two phases of his mind at once, but always in practice—and Susannah could not conceive that a new order of marriage would appear feasible, even though it would certainly raise a new barrier around the fold, and in consequence draw its votaries closer together.

Soon after this Emma was greatly comforted by a summons to Nauvoo. She could now enter in triumph upon the more glorious stage of her chequered career.

For a few days Susannah worked on still with a sense of mission towards her pupils, but of necessity also, for her work meant daily bread. It produced little more than that.

But at Nauvoo new schools in emulation of the State schools of other towns had been set up, and now a teacher with certificates of the latest style of education arrived in the Mormon settlement at Quincy, commissioned by the prophet to gather all the Mormon youth there into a new school under the direction of the Church. Susannah's mission and her means of livelihood were alike gone.

The change was made. It was not until Susannah had passed the first desolate day of her dethronement that Darling came to her, sent with profuse apologies from the prophet and the explanation that the chief motive of the change had been to relieve her from labour now that the Church was in a position to offer her adequate support. The message was accompanied by many compliments upon her work and her fidelity, and a document officially signed, in which it was set forth that the part and lot which would have pertained to Halsey in the Holy City was considered as hers; rooms and entertainment at the Nauvoo House were offered. It was handsomely done. Smith in his poverty had been no niggard, and of his wealth he was lavish. The documents explained what rooms, size and position given, should be hers, what furniture at her disposal, what ailment, what allowance from the Treasury for clothing and charity. The scale was magnificent. Darling was also commissioned to offer her a ticket on one of the river boats to Nauvoo, and his own escort. He urged her instant acceptance. Darling had been promoted from his post at Quincy to that of postmaster at Nauvoo, and he could not delay his journey.

Susannah sat long into the night and counted her little hoard, and figured to herself what the long-eastward journey, then a matter of great expense, would cost. Since Elvira left her she had with all her efforts saved hardly fifty dollars. No course lay open to her but to go first to Nauvoo, and there compound with Smith for a sum of money to be given in return for the relinquishment of all further claim upon the Church.

Book III.

CHAPTER I.

In a suite in the pretentious Nauvoo House Susannah found herself established.

She stood at her windows and looked east and west upon the fair white city, and more immediately upon the broad public square in which well-dressed people and handsome equipages were constantly seen. In this square a man called Bennet drilled the Nauvoo Legion in the cool of the evenings. This man had served in the regular army and had a native genius for soldiery. Smith, alive always to the educational importance of shows, now provided money lavishly for uniforms, horses, and accoutrements, and the Nauvoo Legion formed a much grander spectacle than any body of State militia.

Twice a day under Susannah's windows Smith's carriage drew up, a pair of fine gray horses carrying the prophet to and fro upon the affairs of Church and State. When he took Emma with him Susannah observed that she was always richly attired, and the other members of the Mormon hierarchy resident in Nauvoo, "bishops," "elders," "apostles," "prophets," passed constantly in and out of the house, positively shining in broadcloth and silken hats, their wives and daughters also in brilliant array.

Externally the success appeared to be complete, and beyond even the visionary's most glorious dreams. In the whole of the city no one was poor, no one ignorant of such knowledge as school-books could afford, no one drunken. Every one was uplifted and animated beyond their ordinary capacity for effort and enjoyment by this material fulfilment of prophecy and the more glorious future hope which it involved. Susannah was not well rested after her journey when Emma descended upon her with lavish gifts of silks and fine feathers. Emma, grown patronising with prosperity, always plain and maternal, displayed her gifts and argued for their acceptance with broad satisfaction.

"Joseph says now that the Lord has given us freedom as touching wealth and plenty, it looks real mean, when your husband gave all he had to the Church in her tribulation, for you to be wearing plain clothes when you're riding out with us. What will the folks say? Joseph says it looks to him as if you were real offended at being left so long up to Quincy when he was only waiting to get your rooms finished."

Carried away, as was only natural, by her husband's doctrine that the era of indulgence was ordained and not to be rejected, there was temporary deterioration in the fibre of Emma's character.

Susannah would gladly have walked out and seen the beauty of the city and its surroundings alone, but she did not think it kind or polite to resist the good-natured importunity of her friends. She was invited to drive with Smith to a grand review of the Nauvoo Legion which was to take place outside the town; then, finding that Emma and the children were to occupy another carriage, she made objection. It ended in Susannah being driven alone in a very fine carriage. Smith, resplendent in uniform and seated upon a very fine charger, rode in his capacity of Commander-in-Chief. Several other men whom she had known first in homespun, and latterly in cloth, were also riding in bedizened uniforms. The scene was very perplexing to Susannah. Elvira, with great display of dress and equipage, was not far from her, and waved her hand with patronising encouragement. The coach in which were Emma and her children presented also a very smart appearance. All the town drove to the scene of the review in what splendour they could afford.

Susannah was greatly occupied in looking from face to face, striving, to recognise some of her husband's friends of earlier days. She fully expected to see Smith or some of his friends fall from their saddles, as they could be little accustomed to manœuvring such light-footed steeds, but she was forced to admit that Smith rode well and his officers kept their seats. She had so much to observe, so much to think about, she hardly noticed that Smith rode constantly by her carriage, pointing out the beauties of the road.

When they stopped at the place of parade, many of the gentlemen in uniform approached her, and as this was her first appearance in public, Smith performed the introductions. Among them was the Rev. General John Bennet, a man who had "knave" written on his countenance, but who appeared to have duped Smith, for, as Lieutenant-General of the forces, he was actually in command. Her old friend the Danite also came, older than when she had seen him last by the hardships of an arduous missionary journey. He passed now by the name of "Apostle Heber." Susannah was so glad to be able to inquire concerning his welfare, so curious to speak with him again and judge of his development, that her manner gained the appearance of animation.

After some time Susannah perceived that she was, as it were, holding court. In their carriages the other women sat comparatively neglected. It was in vain that she tried to put a quick end to this curious and undesirable state of things. Smith continued to bring to her side all those whom he delighted to honour.

And this was only one of several fêtes which took place in rapid succession, to all of which Susannah was by some persuasion taken. At each she found herself an object of public attention. She was told that this occurred because she was a stranger, or out of respect to her husband's memory, and she placed more trust at first in these statements than a less modest or more worldly-wise woman would have done.

Soon her credulity ceased. She despised her own beauty because it was made a gazing stock. An article in the Nauvoo newspaper, officially inspired, spoke of her as a "Venus in appearance and an angel at heart." She was elsewhere publicly mentioned as the "Venus of Nauvoo."

It was indeed a strange experience, a strange time and place for the social *début* of this beautiful woman. Smith had calculated well when in her youth he had told her that her beauty would not diminish but increase until her prime was past, but she very modestly inferred that she might have passed, as heretofore, without much notice, if an agitation concerning her had not urged to admiration a band of men who were fast growing luxurious and pleasure-loving, and she knew that Smith was the author of that agitation.

It appeared to Susannah more dignified to ignore than to upbraid. She secretly laughed, she secretly cried with vexation, but she desired to leave the place without betraying her recognition of the homage offered.

She sought to discuss her plan for departure with Emma, but Emma's manner had changed to her. It was not jealousy so much as constraint that she showed, as if secretly persuaded into unusual reticence. Susannah then asked Smith for such a sum of money as he should consider to be a right acknowledgment of the property Halsey had given to the Church. At this Smith looked greatly aggrieved, and withdrew muttering that he would consider her request.

The only sign of this consideration which she immediately received was a gift of showily-bound books, and a rich shawl which he had fetched from New York.

Susannah's career as the queen of Nauvoo society came to a swift end, for she determinedly retired into seclusion. This was not because the men who paid court to her were all ignoble. Among the officers of the Church or of the Legion there were not few who were wholesome and friendly companions, or who, like her early Danite friend, the Apostle Heber, had frank modest eyes, incapable of any enthusiasms that were not religious. But in her long companionship with Angel Halsey Susannah had had her soul deep dyed in a delicate hue of Quaker sentiment. She could not admit for a moment that conscious display of personal charm was consonant with dignity.

She again sought friendly intercourse with Emma.

"There ain't no use in opposing the Lord," said Emma excitedly. "If the Lord, as Joseph says, has given you beauty and wants to set you to be a star, or a Venus; or whatever he calls it, in Nauvoo, I don't see that there's any good your talking of going away. I guess the Lord'll have his own way."

Susannah remembered how before her marriage the bigness of the authority quoted had confused her as to the truth of the message. "Ah! Emma, Emma," she cried, taking the fat, comfortable hand in her own, "if in the first days I had offered a little more humility, a little more love, to those to whom I owed duty, I should never have believed what you told me about the 'Lord's way,' but I have learned by hard experience, and I do not believe you now, Emma." She spoke the name in quicker tone, as if recalling her companion to common sense. "Emma," she repeated the name with all the tenderness she could muster, "don't you know that it is better for me to go away—better for you, better for *us all*?"

But Emma was obstinately evasive. She seemed almost like one possessed by a hardened spirit, not her own. On the afternoon of that same day she bustled cheerfully into Susannah's room asking the loan of what money she had to meet a temporary call.

Susannah never had the slightest reason to suspect Emma's good faith and good nature. She gave her money without a thought.

CHAPTER II.

The parlour which Joseph Smith had provided for Susannah was large and high. On its Brussels carpet immense vases of flowers and peacock's feathers sprawled; stiff and gaudy furniture was ranged round the painted walls; stiff window curtains fell from stiff borders of tasteless upholstery. Susannah, long ignorant of anything but deal and rag carpets, knew hardly more than Smith how to criticise, and her taste was only above his in the fact that she did not admire.

Smith came to reason with the rebellious woman.

Susannah no sooner saw him than she knew that he had come braced to try the conclusion with her. He sat himself before her in silence. His waistcoat was white, his neck-cloth white, his collar starched and high; his thick light hair was carefully oiled according to the fashion of the day, and brushed with curling locks upon the sides of the brow. At this critical hour Susannah observed him more narrowly than ever before. His smooth-shaven face, in spite of all his prosperity, was not so stout now as she had seen it in more troublous years; the accentuated arch of the eyebrows was more distinct, the beak line of the nose cut more finely. She noted certain lines of thickness about the nape of the neck and the jaw which in former years had always spoken to her of the self-indulgence of which she now accused him; yet she could not see that they were more accentuated. She had been schooling her heart to remember that Smith had been her husband's friend; Angel Halsey had loved him, had daily prayed for his faults and failings, and thanked God for his every virtue and success. Through the medium of these memories now Susannah looked upon him with the clearness of insight which the more divine attitude of mind will always give, the insight which penetrates through the evil and is focussed only on the good.

The prophet's breath came quickly, making his words a little thick. "Emmar tells me that you have some thoughts of wanting to leave us."

"You know that very well, for I have told you so myself. I want you to give me money for my journey. If I can I will repay it, as you well know; if not, I will take it instead of all this finery you offer."

He had folded a newspaper in his hand, and now he unfolded it. She was surprised to see that his hands trembled slightly as he did so, for she had seen him act in many a tragic scene with iron nerve.

"'Tain't often that the Gentile newspapers have a word of justice to say about us," he observed. "This is a number of the St. Louis Atlas. It seems there's one man on it can speak the truth." He gave forth the name of the newspaper as if expecting her to be duly impressed by its importance, and she looked at the outspread sheet amazed.

He went on, "There's an article here entitled, 'The City of Nauvoo. The Holy City. The City of Joseph.' I'd like to read it to you if you don't object, Sister Halsey."

The pronunciation of the last title seemed to inflate him; his hands ceased to tremble. A flicker of amusement lighted the gravity of Susannah's mind.

Joseph read, "'The city is laid out in streets of convenient width, along which are built good houses, and around every good-sized house are grounds and gardens. It is incorporated by charter, and contains the best institutions of the latest civilisation.'" He gave this the emphasis of pause. "Is that true. Sister Halsey, or is it not?"

She smiled as upon a child. "Yes, Mr. Smith, it is true."

"'Most conspicuous among the buildings of the Holy City is the temple built of white stone upon the hill-top. It is intended as a shrine in the western wilderness whereat all nations of the earth may worship, for on March 1, 1841, the prophet gave it as an ordinance that people of all sects and religions should live and worship in the City if they would, and that any person guilty of ridiculing or otherwise deprecating another in consequence of his religion should be imprisoned.' Is that true?" Smith inquired again. His questions came in the tone of a pompous refrain.

"Except in the case of those who have joined you and gone back from your doctrine," she said, but not thinking of herself.

He read on: "'Here, as elsewhere, Mr. Smith has attended first to the education of his people. The president of the Nauvoo University is Professor James Kelly, a graduate of Trinity College, Dublin, and a ripe scholar; the professor of English literature is Professor Orson Pratte, a man of pure mind and high order of ability, who without early advantages has had to educate himself amid great difficulties and has achieved learning. The professor of languages is Professor Orson Spencer, graduate of Union College, New York, and of the Baptist theological seminary of that city. No expense has been spared upon school buildings for the youth of both sexes, and the curriculum is good.' Is that true?"

"Yes," she replied.

He read on: "'The population is made up chiefly from the labouring classes of the United States and the manufacturing districts of England. They have been grossly misunderstood and shamefully libelled. They are at least quite as honest as the rest of us, in this part of the world or any other. Ardent spirits as a drink; are not in use among them; tobacco is a weed which they almost universally despise. There is not an oath to be heard in the city; everywhere the people are cheerful and polite; there is not a lounger in the streets. Industry is insisted upon, and with the hum of industry the voice of innocent merriment is everywhere heard. Now, as to their morality, if you should throw cold water upon melted iron, the scene would be terrific because the contrast would be so great; so it is with the Saints; if a small portion of wickedness happens among them, the contrast between the spirit of holiness, and the spirit of darkness is so great that it makes a great up-stir and excitement. In other communities the same amount of crime would hardly be noticed.'" Again he asked, "Sister Halsey, does this evidence of an impartial witness coincide with your observation?"

"Of the people it is undoubtedly true," she said. There was a reservation in her mind concerning certain leaders in the Church, but she did not make it in words.

He read on: "'With a shrewd head like that of the prophet to direct, with a spiritual power like his to say 'do' and it is done, what wonder that this thrifty and virtuous people should have made Nauvoo that which its name denotes—the Beautiful City, the home of peace and joy.'"

He laid down the newspaper upon the marble-topped table, his large hand outspread upon it. "My sister, why do you wish to leave this beautiful city? It is a place where each may have home and part and lot in its delights, but to you *all* its wealth and power and beauty is offered. Did I not say unto you, when as a beautiful damsel you gave up home and kindred for the sake of the Church, that you should be as a queen among its elect women, riding as in a carriage drawn by white horses and receiving the elect from among the nations?"

The recollection of the prophecy which he had delivered concerning her upon the desolate autumn road at Fayette brought with it another recollection—that of her parting with Ephraim the same morning—so vividly that her eyes filled with tears. Yet she marvelled too, with inquisitive recognition of the miracle, that the words of the visionary, then a beggar, should have been so nearly fulfilled.

"It is quite true, Mr. Smith, and very marvellous that what you promised me should almost be literally fulfilled. We have come to it, as you also foretold, by a path most terrible, and now we arrive at the consummation. We live in a palace, and at its doors pilgrims from England and all parts of Europe are arriving every day, and the richest of gowns, the grandest of carriages, and the whitest of horses are truly at my disposal. But there is one discrepancy between your vision and the fact—I will not wear the silk robes, nor welcome the pilgrims with the assurance that they have here reached the City of God. I will not because I cannot. I refuse to accept from the hand of God such paltry things as money and display, or even the honest affluence of our people, as compensation for the fire and blood through which we have waded. If there be a God who is the shepherd of those who seek him, this is not the sort of table that he spreads, this is not the cup which he causes to run over"—she had begun lightly, but her voice became more earnest. "Mr. Smith, we have walked through the shadow of death together; if you would be exalted in the presence of your enemies, have done with your childish delight in such toys."

Smith moved uneasily on his velvet-covered chair, and it, being of a rather cheap sort, creaked under his bulk.

"What says it in the end of the Book of Job, Sister Halsey? and what compensation did the Lord give for the sore temptations with which he had allowed the devil to tempt his servant? As I read, it was fourteen thousand sheep and six thousand camels, and—"

She gave him credit for knowing the passage by heart; she had the rudeness to interrupt. She rose and stood before him. All the long latent defiance which her heart had treasured against him found vent in her tone, "Very well, Mr. Smith, if that satisfied Job, it will not satisfy me."

Smith, cast out of all his shrewd calculations as to what would win this woman, fell back upon the inner genius of that priestcraft which so often surpassed his conscious intelligence.

"*What would satisfy you?*" It was a simple question, and he asked it with overwhelming force. "By the hand of trust and affection which your husband gave me; by the memory of the beautiful babe that he brought first to me for my blessing (and I laid my hand on its little warm head and blessed it); by these I claim the right to ask, Sister Halsey, what is it that in Nauvoo or in any other city would satisfy you?"

She was humiliated in her own eyes. Alas! she had strong evidence that Ephraim's affection, on which she had staked all earthly hope of happiness, had in some way failed. Now under Smith's eye all courage to hold the unrealised ideal was lost; as the fixed stars twinkle, so her faith went out for the moment of his interrogation. Her head sank in a shame she could not confess.

While she hesitated he was looking at her shrewdly. "You know not what. Shall I tell you? There is but one thing, and that is love—the love that works, for those who are in need. Work for the needy is love to God and man, my sister."

He paused, looking at her with a glow of enthusiasm. Whatever he might be to others, this man, coarse in his outer nature, but liable always to eruptions of the sensitive inward soul of the visionary, was in this woman's presence often merely what she compelled him to be. If she had known that this was the secret of his power over her, the spell might have been less.

"Is it not true, Sister Susannah?" he asked.

She gave the admission mechanically.

He went on, "I don't take it at all hard that you should feel that we are none of us up to you, but feel as you do that we are beneath you, for there isn't a lady in the place that's equal to you in delicate ways and sense and a mind to study books; but it seems to me that that's a reason why you should love us, Sister Halsey. There is work for you to do; we need your guiding hand. You say to me that I am content with horses and sumptuous living and fine raiment; and knowest thou not that there is upon my soul a great burden, even the burden of this great people, to go in and out before them and guide them aright? I have need of thy counsel, my sister; there's that which at this time is greatly agitating my own mind and the minds of our bishops and apostles, Sister Halsey, and it is of such nature that we cannot proclaim it openly until we know the mind of the Lord. On all other matters we have accepted the teaching of the Scriptures. For, behold, we have now the priesthood of Aaron in our midst, and the priesthood of Melchizedek, and the rites of the temple, save only the spilling of the blood of bulls and goats, which has been done away with by the Gospel. We have gone back to the first things, as is well known to you, Sister Susannah, and even here in the wilderness we have set up our theocracy, and for its civil law we have sought where alone such law can be found, in the command given unto the children of Israel before they desired a king, just as for all spiritual law we have accepted the commands given to the apostles in the new dispensation, taking them as they were, without whittling them away as a boy whittles a stick with a knife, as all those sects which will not hear our voice have done. Now, Sister Susannah, is this true?" He put his head a little on one side and looked at her with his eyes partially closed.

"You need not take very long to explain that you worship the letter of the Scriptures, for I know it already, Mr. Smith."

But he was in full tide, and went on, "When the Book says, 'Heal the sick,' we don't say that that means something else, but we set about and heal 'em." He slapped his knee with the palm of his hand. "When it says, 'Cast out devils,' we don't stare round like the other sects and say, 'There ain't no devils,' but we cast 'em out; and in the same way, when the Book says that the priesthood of Aaron and the priesthood after the order of Melchizedek shall be serving always in the church and in the temple, then we say, 'Amen, so shall it be'; and the same way with regard to tithing, for the Lord's tithes are recognised among us, and the first-fruits, and the Sabbath day, and all such ordinances, no picking and choosing as others."

Then he explained to her again, as in Kirtland, that he was in doubt concerning the marriage laws of the State. He said that, having searched the Scriptures, and learned what he could from other books, he was fully convinced that it was the modern so-called "orthodox" Christian Church (in which little else but signs of deadness and lack of faith appeared) that alone condemned the ancient usage of the patriarchs, which in the Bible was nowhere condemned. He had read in a book that many of the Jews and most of the Asiatics had more than one wife at the time of the apostles, and yet they had not preached against this as an evil.

"They did not preach against slavery," said Susannah.

"They did not," he said, "and I would say parenthetically, my sister, that it may be that our views on that subject, coming from the northern States as you and I have done, have not been according to the mind of the Lord. I would have no man a slave because of misfortune, but if a man proved himself unfit to rule himself, I'm not sure about his being free."

"Do you intend to revive slavery in our own race? Will your own people when they fail in business be sold, with their wives and children, as in the Old Testament?"

"I can't see but that it would be a deal less mean to arrange it that way than to bring a race of free blacks from their own country and make every child they have a slave because he happens to be a nigger." She remarked that his mild blue eye lit up with the true flash of the indignation of contemplative justice. "There's one thing certain," continued he, "in my Church of the Latter-Day Saints no man shall be a slave to his brother because he happens to have a black skin, for, as the Scripture says, 'Can the Ethiopian change his skin?'"

Surrounded as they were by the atmosphere of slavery, there was the resonance of true heroism, of true insight into the right, in his tone, but the reason he gave—could it be possible that he thought that the text he quoted was an authority for his instinctive justice? It was obvious to her that he was only a fool who walked by the light of sundry flashes of genius, but there was still the chance that the sum of idiocy and the genius might prove greater than the intelligence of common men.

He went on, "But, anyhow, it isn't the institootion of slavery that's come up for me to decide just here and now. Since we have been blessed with peace and prosperity, the female converts that our missionaries have been making all over the world (whom they have kept back from coming to us, letting no unmarried female come whilst the fires of persecution were passing over us) have arrived in great numbers, and the question is, Sister Susannah, how are we to steady 'em?"

What seemed so impossible to achieve in a pioneer State had in Nauvoo actually been achieved—the women were in excess of the men. He had, in sober truth, a social problem to solve, and the responsibility rested alone upon him. Brotherly love having been inculcated, the manners of the Saints were cheerful and familiar, more familiar, he said, than he desired; but after all that they had endured he was fain to lay upon them no greater burden than need be. He appealed to her, asking if on his first release from imprisonment he had not been strict in his injunctions.

"But now," he said, "who am I that I should be able to take care of all the young women that the Lord is sending to us from all parts of the world? or am I to deny to them the privilege of coming to live among the Lord's people? Am I to say to them that unless they have learning and wisdom and are perfect they shall not come? I guess that if it had been required of me to be perfect before I came to seek salvation, I wouldn't have come at all. But it's just like this—here they are! and they are nothing but poor ignorant working girls from England and Ireland and all parts of Europe. And am I to make nunneries to put them into?"

He confessed with some delicacy of language and words of bitter regret that there had been of late some cases in Nauvoo such as were common enough, alas! in Gentile society, but whose occurrence among the Saints had caused excitement. Joseph Smith paced Susannah's room; his harassment and distress on behalf of his people were either deeply felt or well feigned, and Susannah had no doubt that his feeling was true, that phase of him being for the time uppermost. When he came to sit down beside her again, it was to sketch the misery to men and women and children which existed in Gentile society from this evil, which he affirmed to run riot through the warp and woof of so-called orthodox communities.

Her ignorance of the world was so great that she assumed this accusation to be of the same stuff as the anathemas he constantly cast against the integrity of the orthodox clergy. The point that she grasped was that he believed the thing that he said. She had at first assumed that should he propose to institute polygamy she would know then, once for all, that he was a villain; but now this test deserted her. He was meditating this step, and it seemed that his arguments, if the facts on which he based them were admitted, had some value.

"There's that for one thing, Sister Susannah," Smith went on in a broken voice; "it has been a mean sort of thing to have to tell you, but it had to be said, and now there's another thing to be considered. Among the Gentiles who is it that has the most children? Is it your man that's high up in the ranks of society, who has money enough to give them a good education, to feed and clothe 'em? or is it your poor man, whose children run over one another like little pigs in a sty, and he caring nothing for them, and they have rickety bones and are half starved and grow up to be idle and steal? I have noticed that a good man is apt to have good children, and a clever man is apt to have clever children, and a worthless man is apt to have worthless children. Ain't that so? And what sort of children do we want the most of? Well, in this way we wouldn't let your worthless fellow have any wife at all until he had brought forth fruit meet for repentance, and your common man only one; but I don't see but that it would be a real benefit to the State if your good, all-round man, as would be apt to have pious and clever children, had two or three or four families agrowing up to be an honour to him and to the Church, if it ain't against the command of the Lord; and in Holy Writ the Lord himself says to Solomon that he would have given him as many wives as he wanted, barring them being

Gentiles."

"I will not argue about the Bible; you and I interpret it very differently," she cried. "Your social argument might be well enough if it were not that your good man when he had more than one wife *would cease to be a good man*"—her voice was vibrating with faith—"and his children would therefore have the poorest chance from inheritance or training."

He was again pacing, but paused in his ponderous walk, struck by a flaw in his argument which he had not before seen. "But if it were commanded by the Lord, Sister Susannah?"

"God does not command this wickedness. What you command in his name is at your own peril, Mr. Smith."

He paused before her, asking with reflective curiosity, "Why are you so sure that it would be wickedness, sister?"

She had not arguments at command; she held fast to her assurance with the same dogged unreasoning faith with which Ephraim's mother had of old held her belief that this Smith must be an arch-villain; she had put the whole power of her volitionary nature upon the side of faith in the ideal marriage, although she was painfully conscious that she had come across no particle of evidence for the existence of such a state. Out of faith, out of mere instinct of heart, which had not worked itself out in intelligent thought, she gave her unhesitating judgment. "I say that it would be wicked because I *feel* that it would be wicked; and any good woman," she paused and looked him straight in the eyes, "and any good man, would know its wickedness without arguments, and without weighing all possible considerations."

His eyes fell before hers. He looked not angry, but grieved. As for Susannah, in the heat of her indignation she did not know that her own long effort to resist the unreasoning acceptance of cut-and-dried doctrines and any dogmatic insistance upon opinion had here failed.

Smith stood for some moments before her, and her fire cooled. He sighed at her dictum. Then he said gently, "But your judgment in this matter has great weight with me, sister, and if I accept it you will perceive that you are indeed the elect lady, and that by living in the light of your countenance I shall obtain peace."

It was difficult for her not to suppose that her influence was beneficial. She thought at the moment that when she had left this place she might still correspond with Smith if he desired it. If it was part of his eccentricity to be willing to listen to her, why should she not be willing to speak, and thus keep his madness under control?

Smith, regarding her, caught the gracious look upon her face which had opposed to him so often only a mask of reserve. His imaginative hopes were always ready to magnify by many dimensions the smallest fact which favoured them. His unsteady mind was fired by the presumption of some triumph.

"Have not I, even the prophet of this great people, waited with great patience? As the apostle saith, 'Let patience have her perfect work.'"

Susannah started and wondered.

"For behold I did not desire that our dear brother, Angel Halsey, should go into the forefront of the battle, nor would I trouble the first grief of thy widowhood, but behold I have waited."

"For what?" Her question came sharply. His tone had changed her mood suddenly; a memory flashed on her of the ill-written letter which Emma had shown her of the phrases concerning the spiritual "bride" or "guide" who, even if all licence were denied to humbler folk, was to be a prophet's special perquisite. "What have you been waiting for, Mr. Smith?

"Nay, but I have waited, sister, until, having eyes, you should see, and ears, you should hear, till you should understand that, going in and out before this great people, it is necessary for me to seek wisdom in counsel, and, above all, of a woman who hath a finer sense than man. And it has been revealed to me, sister, that this may only be if thou shouldst give the counsels of thy mind and the smile of thy beauty to me alone and to none other, for that which is divided is not to be accepted for the building up of the Church."

"You would have me believe that you have waited many years with the virtue of patience before you say this? Understand yourself better. It was not patience; it was fear. You have known perfectly well always that I would never have listened to such a proposal for a moment. It has been fear and prudence that have hitherto kept you silent. What is it that has made you speak now?"

With sharp decisive tones she chid him as children are chidden in anger, but childish as he often was, he had yet other elements in his character; his blue eyes gave an answering flash that was ominous; the droop of his attitude stiffened.

"That which is ordained by the Lord is ordained, sister, and it causeth me grief to know that this revelation, which I told thee many years since, is yet to be received of thee as a grievous thing, nevertheless—"

"Nevertheless," she repeated in a mocking tone, as one weary of foolishness, "what nevertheless? Let us talk on some better subject, Mr. Smith, and after this be kind enough to have no dreams or revelations about me. Dream of your Church, if you like. I cannot hinder your people's credulity, and I hope that you will continue, as you have begun, to lead them in the main by righteous paths. And have your dreams and visions about yourself, if you must, for I sometimes think that you cannot be much madder than you are now, but be kind enough to leave me out of them, for I am going away."

She had now made him very angry. He was standing with flushed face, quivering with uncertain impulses of rising wrath, yet he still struggled for self-control.

"Sister Susannah Halsey, it is not meet that you should make a mock of that which is sacred"—he gave a gasp here of stifled anger, and there was a perceptible note of wounded affection beside the louder one of offended vanity—"of that which is above all sacred," he stuttered, "it is not meet—meet—to mock—to mock." The veins on his forehead were standing out and growing purple.

She had often heard of Joseph Smith's power of rage, before which all the Saints quailed. She saw it now for the first time.

She rose up, trying now a tone of gentle severity. "I spoke lightly because your words appeared to me childish and silly, but the more in earnest you were, Mr. Smith, the more need there is you should have done with a thought that could lead to no good. I am no elect lady. Why do you deceive yourself? I have told you before that I do not even believe in your religion."

As she spoke she became more and more amazed at the thought of what his self-deception must have been, for in his ever-shifting mind he knew her infidelity perfectly, and yet had persuaded himself that she would accept some fantastic position as prophetess-in-chief.

"How mad you are," she said pityingly, "to know a thing and yet to pretend to yourself you do not know it. Go and get your supper, Mr. Smith. Emma will be waiting to give it to you. And when you have thought quietly over what I have said, you are quite clever enough to see that my way of looking at it is more sensible than yours."

She had perhaps supposed that the mention of the domestic supper would be punitive rather than soothing, but she was not prepared to find that she had displayed scarlet to the blood-shot eyes of a bull.

"Woman," his voice, deep and hoarse, was like thunder about her ears, "woman, is it not enough that the Lord has spoken?"

She saw by his purple face and parched lip, by the hard shudder that went through his frame, that his fury was stronger than he. She quailed inwardly.

"It is not enough for me that you say the Lord has spoken."

His lips worked as if in the effort to form anathemas his dry throat refused to utter. Then, regaining his loud hoarse speech, with a choking noise he lifted his hand in a gesture of sacerdotal menace.

"Woman, it is the last time. Choose ye this day between blessing and cursing, for the Lord shall send the cursing until thou be destroyed and perish quickly, because of the wickedness of thy doings whereby thou hast forsaken me."

She cried in answering excitement, "I choose your curse rather than your blessing under the conditions you propose. You are mad; go and calm yourself."

Then, having exhausted her physical courage in this last defiance, she went into her inner room, locking the door, leaving him in the manifest suffering of an almost unendurable rage.

CHAPTER III.

That night Susannah packed her possessions in the smallest possible compass. The money she had lent to Emma would be sufficient for the journey to Carthage, which was the nearest Gentile town, and thither she was determined to go without an hour's delay, ready now to work or beg her way on the journey farther eastward.

As soon as the business of the next day was fairly started she went to the suite of rooms inhabited by the Smiths, confident that Joseph's excess of fury had been transient. Emma was surrounded by her children, to whom she had just given breakfast. The prophet was about to descend to his business office. They both received Susannah with moderate kindness.

The March sun shone in through the large windows upon the garish furniture of the apartment, upon Emma's gay attire, and upon the shining faces of the three children, who stood gazing upward at Susannah, quick, as children always are, to perceive signs of suppressed excitement.

Susannah explained that she had determined to go to Carthage that day, where she hoped soon to find some party of travellers in whose escort she could travel farther; she hoped that it would be quite convenient for Emma to return the money that morning.

Smith gazed at Susannah intently, but only for a few moments. It seemed that his mood had changed entirely, that he was now too much absorbed in the business of the day, whatever it might be, to care whether she went or stayed. He left them, saying that he would send money to Emma as soon as he could, that the trifling debt might be paid.

Money flowed in such easy streams through the hands of the leading men of Nauvoo, that Susannah supposed that a messenger with the required amount would come up the stairs in a few minutes. She sat with Emma in this expectation.

"You are offended with me for going?" she asked, for Emma's mask of indifference was worn obviously.

"You wish to destroy your soul," said Emma.

"Ah, but you know, you have long known, that I do not believe that salvation in this world or the next depends on the rites of Mr. Smith's Church."

"If I told this child that he would be dashed to pieces if he walked out of the window, and he did not believe me, would that save him?"

Emma made this inquiry with triumphant scorn; then she rose and began to attend to the wants of her children in a bustling manner.

Susannah sighed and smiled. "I have at least the right to reject your faith at my own peril, for there is not in the wide world, as far as I know, man or woman who cares whether I save my soul or not."

"And whose fault?" cried Emma, coarse now in her discomposure. "If you are so stuck-up that you think you can read your books and look down on us all, just because you are a beauty and the gentlemen bow down to you, 'tisn't likely that you'd have any friends acting that way. You can't even behave civil to the gentlemen when they offer you the best that's going."

It was evident that some version of Smith's interviews with her had been given to his wife. Susannah wondered how much truth, how much fiction, had been in the relation. It did not matter much to her now, since she had resolved to go at once. The whole of her life with that troublous sect seemed to be dropping from her like a dream.

Leaving word that she would receive the money on her return or else call at Smith's office for it when she was ready, she went down into the cheerful noise of the street and bargained with a man who had horses and vehicles for hire. Having arranged that he should come for her at noon, she went about to make the few farewells she felt to be desirable.

Darling was now postmaster of Nauvoo and one of the first presidency. To him she went first. She shrank from him because of his coarseness and the jocular admiration which he sometimes had the audacity to express for her, but she could not forget how assiduous his kindness had been in the days of Elvira's illness. She found him sitting, his heels on the upper part of a chimney-piece with a fireless grate, reading the Millenial Star. The hot April sun, streaming through the windows of his office, had caused him to take off his coat, which was no longer thread-bare. His shirt sleeves were fine enough and white; the high hat that was pushed far on the back of his head was highly polished. Opulence, self-indulgence, good-nature, and a certain element of fanatical fire mingled in the atmosphere of the postmaster's office, and made it somewhat turgid.

When Darling heard Susannah's errand he became serious enough. An apoplectic sort of breathlessness came over him, expressing a degree of interest which she could not understand. He settled his hat more firmly upon his head. "Does the prophet know?"

"He knows. I have said good-bye to him and to Mrs. Smith. It is sad to part with friends that I have known for so many years."

"And the prophet's going to let you go, is he?"

Darling, clumsy at all times, in this speech conveyed to Susannah the first faint suspicion that Smith might dream of detaining her by force.

Darling's youngest daughter, who had been an affectionate pupil to Susannah at Quincy, waylaid her as she came out, and clasped her about the waist with the ardour of an indulged child. She was a blithesome girl of about fourteen.

"I heard you tell father that you are going away. Is it true?" she asked impetuously.

Susannah tried to release herself from the embrace. "Yes, it is true. Never mind, you like your new teacher, you know, just as well as you used to like me."

"I just guess I don't," cried the child defiantly. "But anyhow, if you are going away, I'm going to tell you something."

Whether the childish love of telling a secret, the girlish love of mischief, or a dawning sense of womanly responsibility was uppermost, it would be hard to tell. There, in the open square, while worthy Saints hurried to and fro on the pavement beside them, while horses jangled their harness and drivers shouted and exchanged their morning greetings, Darling's youngest daughter drew Susannah's head downward and hastily whispered to her the fate of her letters to Ephraim Croom.

"I know, for one day since we came here I heard father talking to the prophet. He said you'd written lately while you were at Quincy, and all your letters had been burned. Now that's the truth; and I said to myself 'twas a sin and a shame, and that you ought to know. Now don't go and tell tales of me, or father will be mad—at least, as mad as he ever can be with *me*." A toss of the pretty head accompanied these words, a flash of conscious power in the bright eyes, the spoilt child knowing that her father was in her toils now, as truly as any future lover would ever be. The school bell was ringing. The girl, her bag of books hanging from her arm, ran with the crowd of belated children.

Susannah walked on, almost stunned at first by the throb of intense anger that came with this surprise. Then the anger was suddenly superseded, hidden and crushed down by a rush of joy. Ephraim had not neglected her; Ephraim had given her up for dead; but she had no reason to suppose that he was dead, no reason to doubt his faithfulness. Susannah trod the common street in love with motion as some happy woodland creature treads the dells in the hour of dawn and spring.

When Elvira looked up to see Susannah enter her gate she saw her friend transfigured in a glow of returning youth and hope. Elvira looked at her timidly; this Susannah she had never seen before. Elvira's husband was not present. The interior of the house was fantastic almost as its mistress, but sultry with luxury.

"Well now, you think you are going," said Elvira. "Who'd have thought it? And only last week General Bennet said to the prophet that if he'd marry you to him he'd send to New York for diamonds both for you and Emma Smith. He said he'd get a thousand dollars' worth of diamonds apiece for each of you; but Mr. Darling said that you ought to be married to Mr. Heber, who has just been elected an apostle, because—" She stopped suddenly, nodding her head. "You know why—blood is blood, and we have seen it run in rivers, but we don't mention it here in Nauvoo."

Elvira set the French heel of her slipper in the centre of a rose upon her carpet and spun round upon it till her flounces stood out.

"We don't mention it here in Nauvoo."

She sang as if it were the refrain to a song.

Susannah felt from within her shield of new delight an immense pity. Here again was a revelation of the coarse and frivolous talk that went on at the church meetings, and Elvira was privy to it through that old fool, her husband. How could she endure him!

"O Elvira, in the last few days I have realised as I did not before that riches are making fools of these men. How glad I am that my husband died before he knew that this was to be the reward of his lifework and his prayers!"

Elvira stopped dancing. The mystical side of her character now, as ever, came forward suddenly in the midst of her other interests. The sunshine was bright in the gaudy room. A tiny spaniel, which Elvira's senile slave had procured for her, lay on a red cushion in its full beam, looking more like a toy than a living thing. When Elvira stopped dancing her flounces settled themselves with an audible rustle, and her thin delicately-cut face looked at Susannah from out its frame of curled hair and gold ornaments like the face of a spirit imprisoned in some unseemly place.

"Heaven help us, Susannah," she cried shrilly, "if you call Nauvoo the reward of Angel's prayers. Look!" she cried, pointing out of the window, "see how the new temple rises; how its white walls shine in the sun! We are putting thousands upon thousands of dollars into it. It will be the grandest building this side of the Alleghany mountains." She let her small jewelled hand, with its pointing finger, fall suddenly, "and there shall not be left one stone of it upon another, for the House of God is not made with hands."

"I see little signs of its foundations here." Susannah spoke with fire. "Treachery and tyranny are poor bricks."

"Child, its foundations are in the whole earth, here and everywhere, in every nation and kindred. Men like Angel Halsey sow wheat; other people have sown tares. The tares happen to be in blossom just now here in Nauvoo." She seemed to forget her seriousness as suddenly, for again she spun round upon the centre of her rose, singing her little musical refrain.

Susannah made one more appeal of the sort that she had made so often before Elvira's marriage.

"You will not come away with me, Elvira? I do not like to leave you here; you have not been yourself since Angel died. You are not bound to this man because you were not sane enough to make a valid choice."

It was plain speaking, but it did not ruffle Elvira's composure in the slightest. She laughed and began to caress her spaniel. "Mad. Oh yes, we are all mad, and growing madder, but it is because they have huddled us together at the point of the sword, until now to be a Mormon means to be shut out from the world and shut in to—to what? To the prophet's dreams; and some of them are good, and some of them are bad, and some of them are mad; and let us thank Heaven that they are as good as they are, for to go back to the Gentiles who shot down Angel and the children he was teaching to pray, and your child in your arms, that would be the baddest and maddest act of life." She rose up suddenly again. "Go!" she cried. There was a flame of real anger in her eyes. "Since the wish is in your heart, go! We believe now in strange doctrines. Two new doctrines we have learned at Nauvoo. Do you know what they are? One is 'baptism of the dead.' If you get off safely, Susannah, and die in your sins, one of us must be baptized again for you, so that you will be saved in spite of yourself. But the *other* doctrine is *'salvation by the shedding of blood.'* Do you understand *that* doctrine?"

"Indeed I do not."

"And you speak with a tone that says that you neither know nor care what new things we have been learning. But you may have reason to care before many hours are over."

She came near and whispered, "They teach us now that if a *man* sin wilfully and will not repent, it is better that a minister of the church should slay him, for then his blood will make atonement for his soul." She ceased to speak until she had thrust Susannah out of her door, and her last words were in a whisper of awesome import. "Perhaps *a woman's soul can be saved in the same way.*"

Susannah was out again in the cheerful busy street. She made haste to fulfil the one remaining call before she met her chaise at the hotel. She felt that her last word was due to the member of the Danite band who had saved her in her hour of need and who had avenged her husband's blood.

To each of those who had made sacrifice for the sect, a lot of land in the best part of the city had been awarded. Heber, Danite and apostle, had built upon his lot, and there she found him at the back of the cottage feeding a mare and foal which were tied in a small plot of ragged grass. He was much older now than when she had first seen him; daring and danger can lengthen time. He had the same indomitable frankness in his dark eyes, but his face was hardened and fanaticism was stamped thereon. It was a homely precinct, with utensils of house and stable-work lying about. The mare was drinking from a bucket, her gentle head so near his shoulder that her love for him was easily seen.

"I am going away," Susannah said. "I have come to thank you for the last time for all your kindness to me and to say good-bye."

"You shall not go," he said harshly.

It was the echo of something which she had heard twice before this morning. This time it began to enter her mind with some sharpness.

"Why not?"

"If you saw a friend hastening to destruction would you not stop her? It is well known amongst us that you desire to go, and at the meeting of the presidency last night the prophet told us that you sought to apostatise. Go home, Sister Halsey, and repent, and obtain forgiveness from the Lord and from his prophet for your unbelief."

She was able to stand for a moment quietly and watch him still busy watering the mare, admiring the skill and gentleness with which he did it, thinking sadly enough that she would never see this remarkable man again, nor know to what the mingled fierceness and gentleness of his nature would grow. Then she offered him her hand in farewell without further argument.

He shook the mare's head from his shoulder and, taking her hand, held it in an iron grasp. "As your friend, and for the sake of that good man, your husband, I beseech you to repent; but if you will not repent, for his sake and for our sakes, because we have prayed for you, you shall still be saved."

Although beginning to be apprehensive of some coming evil, she smiled; and even rallied him upon one of the new doctrines to which Elvira had alluded.

"Do you believe that if I go away some one else will have to be baptized over again for me?"

He looked at her with the same steadfast glance. "It could do no good. Such salvation is for those who die in ignorance of the truth. But for you, who have been baptized into the truth and have fallen away, there is no hope except repentance or the shedding of blood."

Over the low paling she heard the neighbours' children at their play. Upon the other side was an open lot across which she saw the passers in the street. She withdrew her hand from his now, but with a sinking at heart which did not appear to her reasonable because the surroundings were so tranquil.

He let her go, accompanying her, as any gentleman might, to the gate of his ground. As he opened it he had taken something from his coat, and he showed it to her. It was a knife, very bright and sharp. Its blade when drawn out had a double edge. "It will be better for you," he said mournfully, "to die than to go"; and then he hid the thing again and went back.

This time the idea that had been forcing itself into her mind took possession. For a moment all her strength forsook her; she held to the post of the gate, looking after him as he disappeared up the narrow passage between the paling and the house, and then, hurrying onward, she found that it was only by the greatest effort she could walk with outward composure.

CHAPTER IV.

Susannah found her rooms as she had left them. Emma was not there to bid her good-bye, nor did any messenger wait with the money. She set her parcels ready for the driver to lift and waited until after the hour, but the chaise did not come.

At last she went down again to the livery stable, hoping, as against vague but almost overpowering fears, that mere delay was the cause. The man told her that he understood that she had countermanded her order. She gave the order again, but now he said that he could not go for the price named, and when she offered a larger sum, he assured her that his horses were all out. She knew now that her order had indeed been countermanded, and by an authority higher than hers. She went back and boldly entered the prophet's public office.

There were five men in the office. Joseph Smith sat in an elbow-chair before a central table. His secretary, a middle-aged man, sat at a small table beside him. Two of the leaders of the Church happened to be waiting upon some business, and a fresh convert was standing with them, a well-dressed English artisan but newly arrived. Susannah walked up to the table and addressed Smith.

"Will you go down to the stable and bring me up a travelling-chaise?"

Smith rose with mechanical politeness, or perhaps with a feint of politeness. "My dear madam," he expostulated, "I must say—"

"I am sorry," she replied, "that I have not time to hear what you would like to say. I must ask you to be quick and get me the chaise."

By this time she perceived that his companions were looking at her with ill-concealed curiosity and excitement, which proved to her that she was a marked woman. Her bosom dilated with a wilder anger as she looked at Smith expectantly; he returned the gaze sheepishly, as if dazzled by the audacity of her command. His face after last night's passion had an exhausted look like that of a man recovering from an illness.

"You also owe me money," she proclaimed clearly. "Your wife borrowed all that I had of the money I earned by my school. When you have brought the chaise you can give me the money."

One of the elders, a sleek man, thinking the prophet at a loss, now made a wily comment. "Has Sister Halsey paid anything for living in the House this month back?"

At the insinuation that her money might be justly kept in payment of this debt if she spurned the Church's hospitality, Susannah's heart sank. She admitted its justice. It was part of her character to admit all possible claim against her.

The sleek elder, following his advantage, spoke again. "The money given for tuition was given because of the ordinance of the prophet, and should in any case hardly belong to this lady if she is apostate."

Smith had the tact to see his opportunity, and, moreover, it hurt him sharply, hurt him far more than it hurt Susannah, to hear her right to the privileges of the place called in question, to hear the opprobrious term "apostate" cast at her. There were unbelievers in his community with whose hypocrisy or apostasy he could trifle, but he still had his faith and his inner circle of affections. Susannah, standing friendless and penniless, appealed to all that was sacred in the memory of early days, while her beauty, her courage, her unbounded wrath, stimulated his love of power. He spoke to the sleek elder in what was commonly called the prophet's "awful voice," rising, his blue eyes becoming black in their authoritative flash.

"Our sister Susannah Halsey, because of faithfulness when the Church was yet poor and unknown, and because of the faithfulness of her husband, who wears the martyr's crown—our sister Susannah Halsey, I say, is welcome to the hospitality of the Nauvoo House as long as she has remained and shall remain; and the money which has been given to her for the school shall be returned to her, and more shall be added to it, for she laboured faithfully."

He had left behind his moment of sheepish distress; with the return of his formal phrases he assumed full prophetical state and escorted Susannah out of the office with a manner of pompous deference. When they two stood alone together Susannah was aware that, although circumstances had not altered in the slightest, although she had just as much reason for extreme anger as a minute before, yet she could not summon the same haughty air of command.

"Will you get me the chaise and the money and let me go?"

"But in Carthage," he asked kindly, "who will attend to your wants there and protect you? I guess, sister, you haven't much notion how difficult a lady like yourself travelling alone might find it to get along. It isn't among the Gentiles as with the Saints, where brotherly-kindness is the rule. I guess you'd better go back to your room and think it over a day or two longer," he said soothingly. "I'd be very glad to take you and Emma out for a ride this afternoon if you'd be willing to go—"

"Be quiet." Her words fell sharp and quick in the midst of his gentle tones. "Make arrangements at once for me to go peaceably, or I will go out, if need be, to the middle of the Square and proclaim my wrongs, so that every woman and child in Nauvoo shall know what comes of trusting to you."

She had chosen her threat carefully. She knew well that he understood the force of object lessons, and that to have even a suspicion against his kindness, bred in the minds of the children would be exquisite pain to him.

"You know that I wouldn't like that, Sister Halsey; but when you come to think of it you'll see that it wouldn't serve your turn neither. It would only need for a few of us to say you was crazy and the whole town 'ud see the more reason for not letting you go. Moreover, it would be a monstrous injustice to me. When have I failed to do anything that I ever promised you? Did I ever promise to let you apostatise? I guess, Sister Halsey, that you're excited, and if you just think over things for a day or two you would see that we're not so bad as you think. But, anyway, this ain't just the place for us to have a talk together."

When Smith moved on to lead her back to her own rooms, she followed quietly until they stood together in her parlour, the scene of their last quarrel.

"And now," said Susannah, "you understand very well that it is no sudden intention of mine to go, that it is my irrevocable decision. I have this morning had my very life threatened; and I see now that unless you command that it should be respected I should very possibly be in danger if I went away alone. You have offered again and again to drive me in your carriage; I will accept the offer now. Get out your own horses, and drive me yourself to Carthage."

She saw a look of faint pleasure steal over his face. He liked to stand there in the quiet room listening while she spoke with some evidence of trust. The pleasure faded into embarrassment, but she had seen it.

"You have a good and a bad nature struggling within you, Mr. Smith. By all that we have suffered, you and I, since the day that by some mysterious power you forced me to come to your baptism" (she stammered in her eagerness), "by all that we have suffered, by that sympathy which we have at times felt for one another, assert yourself now. Do this one right thing for me, and in all the future I will try to remember only the good in your life and not the bad."

But he stood so long still looking steadfastly before him that she began to fear that, unnerved by his last night's fit of fury, he was ready to pass into one of those visionary trances which had been common in his younger days.

She touched the sleeve of his coat. "I do not know if Mr. Heber's threat could be serious, but it frightened me, and I know that I shall be safe on the road to Carthage if you take me. Go, get your horses and take me away yourself."

He looked at her pitifully, slipping into the style of his religious moods. "Thou sayest truly, sister, that there is none but I who could do this thing, for since in mine anger last night, fearing that I had no strength of my own to keep thee by me, I denounced thee to the council, there is no safety for thy life beyond the boundary of Nauvoo." He winced here, as if seeing what he suggested.

Noting how the idea of her violent death wrung his heart, she went on pleading with him. She quoted the exalted character of his early visions, reminding him of the hour when the angel had shown him the dark furnace of temptations through which he must pass. At this he was visibly stirred; the angelic vision of warning seemed to be again before his eyes. He roused himself, speaking in that tone of voice in which, when he rarely used it, she recognised his best spirit. "Sister, thou hast always been to me as Isaac to Abraham; for in the beginning when I was poor and alone and had nought in the world save the revelation which the Lord had given, and was tempted to doubt, then I saw thee and prayed that thou shouldst be given me for a sign; and behold when I put forth my whole strength to desire thee, thou didst come as a moth to the light, burning thy beautiful wings of youth and joy. But I said, 'It is well, for that which she has lost shall be restored to her with usury,' and I knew in my heart that our brother Angel Halsey would not live long, and that thou wouldst forget thy sorrow for him. But I swear unto thee that thou hast never been to me as other women, but, as I said unto thee just now, like the voice of the angel."

She never knew how far he was entirely under his own control when the tendency to a state of trance was upon him, but she was anxious to take advantage of the better mood.

She said, "And now what is required of you is that you should give me up. No blessing" (she spoke strongly), "no blessing can come to you or to your people until you do this one right thing."

He was again looking not at her but at the blank space of the shadowed wall, and as if the wall was not there and his look went far beyond it.

"You have loosened the bloodhounds and set them on my track," she cried.

He did not speak.

"You—you alone will be guilty of my murder, for, I tell you, if you do not take me, I will go alone and meet my death."

His head sank upon his breast with a groan such as a dumb creature in the utmost pain might give. Almost immediately, to her surprise, he went out.

She was left alone. She was under the impression that Smith had gone to do her bidding, but she could not be sure. No faith in angelic vision, no spell of psychic warfare, relieved the situation for her. The external evidences of some crisis which he had undergone only produced in her repulsion. Now, as ever since the temporary delusion that accompanied her baptism, Susannah endeavoured to possess her soul free from that sense of touch with mysterious powers which had worked such havoc with the sanity of the members of this sect.

From the window she saw the prophet crossing the road in the direction of his stables. He went, it was true, with slow, dreamy gait, but steadily. Strange mixture that he was of sanity and shrewdness, mysticism and grosser evil, he was at that moment her only star of hope. She paced the room unable to forecast the happenings of the next hour, yet supposing that her very life depended upon its content. The sudden joy that had come to her this morning joined with her fear, and produced panic of heart.

She computed the time it might take to harness the gay steeds, and tried to give the rein of her expectation the utmost length. To her delight she saw the prophet's horses and the light vehicle he drove upon long journeys emerge into the square. A servant led them up and down. At length she saw Smith returning, not with hasty steps, but as if against his will, walking again through the crowded place like a man in a dream. Men greeted him, but for once he gave no sign of seeing them. She heard his footstep on the stair. When he reached her door he almost fell against it in the opening, and staggered as he entered the room as if his self-control had just lasted so far. He knelt down by one of the fashionable marble-topped tables with which he had graced her room, and, like an ill-conditioned soul, burst into tears and broken complaints.

"But I cannot do it," he gasped. "I cannot."

In her hour of miserable waiting Susannah had thought of many things that might occur, and nerved herself to meet them, but this distemper of soul, this failure of will in the man who had been undaunted through years of persecuting torture, was so wholly unexpected that she stood aghast.

He clenched his hands as they lay helpless on the white table. "O Lord!" he cried, and she could not tell from the tone whether the words were oath or prayer. "O Lord, I cannot let her go." His thick tears muffled his voice, and still again and again during the paroxysm she caught the words as if reiterated in choking anger, "O Lord, I cannot."

His tears, however evil their source, laid hold of her woman's sensibility; she was no longer a critical observer. She no longer set aside his strange inward conflict as a delusion of madness. She participated in his consciousness so far as to think that she was actually witnessing the despair of a soul repulsing an opportunity of righteousness, and yet not so far dead as not to know its worth. She tried to speak, but found herself, as at other times, so affected by his overlapping emotion that she was trembling and had neither courage nor voice.

Smith lifted his head, looking with terror into vacant spaces of the dim room, as if following with his eyes some menacing form. He whined piteously. "I have purposed to be faithful"; he put up his hand as if to ward off a blow. "Thou knowest! thou knowest!" His voice was like a whispering shriek. The terror of his face and gestures was appalling to see.

Susannah was infected with fear of an apparition so evidently visible to him. Her mind swung, as it were, out of material limitations. She was overcome with the belief that a third person was with them, and her heart went out in gratitude to that mysterious other for taking her part.

But the gilt clock on the marble mantelshelf ticked on; Susannah felt herself aware that the person of Smith's vision was withdrawing, repulsed. She almost cried aloud to the invisible, but checked the prayer, holding on, as it were, to her own sanity with both hands. Smith writhed continually, moaning.

When at length she succeeded in telling him faintly that if he refused this opportunity he must fall lower and lower and lose even the desire for good, she found that her words had no longer any power to influence. He had passed beyond into some region of outer darkness, where the things of sense did not seem to penetrate, and where, if the actions of his body were the expression of his soul, there was literally "wailing and gnashing of teeth."

But Susannah hovered over him, not so much angry as pitiful, her own agony of mere physical sympathy increasing. Terrified to be near him, too compassionate to withdraw, she watched till at last the veins in his hands and his face became swollen and knotted. She was unwilling to lose the hope of her sole influence over him, and yet was about to call for help, when almost suddenly he seemed to become conscious of his surroundings again and shake himself free from the distress.

In a little while he was sitting on one of the chairs, wiping his purple face and swollen eyes with the large silken pocket-handkerchief that was one of the signs of his recent opulence. She saw the large ring on his swollen finger gradually loosen, and the hand return to its normal shape and colour. She felt convinced that his pulses had gone back to their common flow, because his whole volition had returned peacefully to its low ambitions and self-indulgence. She knew instinctively that it was not thus opulent and fierce that he would have looked had he come out on the other side of his temptation. She stood, outwardly patient, waiting helpless till he should speak.

"Sit down, sister," he panted condescendingly. He was fanning himself with the handkerchief now, as a man might who felt injured by undue heat in the atmosphere.

Her refusal was concise and severe.

He looked at her boldly, with no apprehension now in his eyes, not even the former conciliatory desire to receive her with fair words. She felt appalled. Could it be that his angel in deserting him had deserted her? Was there a devil strong enough to give her to him? It was perhaps only his belief which overshadowed hers, it was perhaps only, as she thought, a sickness of nerve but the impression that unseen personalities had been contending here was stronger upon her even than her anger and fear.

Smith got up and went to the window. His horses and buggy were still parading.

"I guess I've changed my mind," he said. He did not care, it seemed, to delude her, but he must still deceive himself. "I couldn't go against the voice of the church council to that extent; it wouldn't be safe for you or me; and besides, 'tisn't the Lord's will that you should go."

She recoiled, looking at him in steady reproach.

"Well, as I said before, I guess you can think it over for a few days." This was his easy answer to her look, and he went out, slamming the door.

CHAPTER V.

When that day began to wane Susannah was still sitting in the empty curtained room. No plan which offered even a fair hope of escape had occurred to her mind. Although in pictures of adventure her imagination had been fertile, throwing out suggestions unbidden, her judgment would have none of them. No one disturbed her. She was left in isolation, a prey to dismal thoughts.

She saw the happy crowds dispersing in the Square from evening recreation. There was nothing to hinder her from joining them. Sometimes her sense of imprisonment seemed only a morbid dream, for on all sides of the fair white city there was open ingress and egress for the faithful and the stranger. It was hard to believe that at wharfs and on the high roads fanatics watched for her, and yet after Smith's reluctant avowal she dare not doubt it.

She saw evening fade over the broad semi-circle of the river, over the multitude of cheerful homes that sloped to its edge. When darkness came she found herself more than ever pressed and tormented by the grim shapes of fear and remorse and despair. She had terrible reason to fear, and felt as never before that she had brought this horrid situation upon herself by joining and rejoining the prophet's following. She had no hope now that Smith would relent.

Beyond the city, eastward toward the sun-rising, lay the home of Ephraim's friendship, whither in the morning she had thought to bend her steps. She saw it through the glad glamour of her recent knowledge that he had not neglected her letters. All her desires fled to this thought of his friendship, like birds flying home. All her fancies clustered round it, like climbing flowers that caress and kiss the object they enfold when some rude wind disturbs. Whenever she withdrew her mind from its contemplation, the circumstances on which she looked were the more revolting.

Ever since Smith left she had been more or less under the impression that an unseen person there in that very room had contended with him. Again and again she had swept it aside as an infectious madness that she was catching from the fanatics about her, but it had recurred; and now as, not caring to light her lamps, she sat alone in the darkness by the very table against which Smith had writhed and wailed, she felt pressed upon by a spiritual life external to her own.

Within her soul from some unknown depth the word arose distinctly as if spoken, "Pray. You cannot save yourself. Pray."

"I am going mad." Susannah whispered the words audibly. It was a comfort to her even to hear her own voice. But when her whisper was past she again listened involuntarily.

The words within her rose again. "Even so. Pray. If you are going mad, you have the more need."

Susannah had come to class all search for definite and material answer to prayer as one of the superstitions of false religion. In this category stood also the hearing of voices and obedience to monitions from the unseen. Now she reproached herself because she could not immediately silence this fancy of disturbed nerves.

Long sad thoughts of all her reasons against prayer, strongest among them the futility of her husband's prayers, passed through her mind with their train of haunting memories, but in the cessation from argument which these pictures of the past produced, the words arose again dearly within her soul, like airdrops rising from the depths of a well and expanding into momentary iridescence on the surface, "Pray for help. If you have no faith in God's arm, you have the more need to seek it."

Stung by the fear that she was losing her mind, she rose as she would have faced a human antagonist.

"God's arm!" she said aloud, "my husband prayed such prayers, but I will ask nothing till I see his request fulfilled."

She spoke the quick words with an almost reckless sense of experiment. Her thought was that before she could honestly think of such prayer she must see some fruit of Angel's petitions for this man Smith and for her own safety.

"Save Smith from further degradation," she said, her breath coming sharply. "Save me now, if that sort of prayer is right. Do this in answer to my husband's prayers. Remember his prayers."

She had begun recklessly, supposing that she was contending only with her own sick fancy; she was astonished that a few swift moments had involved her in an increasing sense of personal contact, and she became awed by the strength of the encounter.

"My husband prayed for my safety," she repeated with softened attitude; then, as if seeking for the protection which had died with him, she repeated again and again, "Remember his prayers."

She left the challenge at last apparently to die where she had breathed it in the dark cold air of her lonely room. The tension of her mind relaxed.

She sat down again, not knowing whether anything had occurred, but a crisis in the morbid working of her strained nerves had in some way relieved her.

She was curiously unable to go back to her former agonised anxieties. Natural fatigue, even sleepiness, came over her, but not her fears, even though she wooed them.

"Ah, well," she said within herself, "it is quite true that it is useless to consider when I can give myself no help."

The habits of the Saints were early. When she heard silence fall upon the great house she went into her sleeping-room and lay down upon the bed. Sleep came quickly.

With the early dawn she opened her eyes. In the first moments of half-awaked consciousness she was aware that one thought lay alone in the empty horizon of her mind, like a trace left by a dream that had passed, as a wisp of cloud may be left in an empty sky.

This thought was that she would at once go down to the river bank upon the southwest of the town.

When other thoughts awoke and crowded within her ken this thought appeared foolish, and still more so the strong influence it had left upon her will, for in the momentum of this influence she had risen without debating the point.

She was not aware that she had moved in her sleep or dreamed. She was greatly refreshed and again unreasonably light-hearted. She opened her shutters and saw that the dawn was calm and fair. As yet the sleeping town had scarcely stirred.

"It is better to go out than to stay in," she said to herself as she remembered that this hour would be her one chance of taking air and exercise unobserved. She heard the main door of the house open and, looking over the banister, saw a slattern with bucket and mop passing into some back passage. She went lightly down and out into the fresh frosty air.

What had that dream been concerning the river bank on the south-western side? She could not recall it, nor had she ever explored the streets of white wooden villas and cottages that lay upon that side. She went thither now. There was no reason why she should not go, no reason to go elsewhere. It was a pleasant walk. When she had passed the last house, the bank sloped in open uncared-for grass where cows were grazing. Only here and there she had seen a house-door open, and as yet in this place no one was abroad except a boy who was playing idly in a boat, which was drawn half up on the muddy bank.

The broad river, milk-white under a dappled sky, stretched south and west. The other side was dim and blue in the faint vapour of the relaxing frost. The air was sweet and still. The sunbeams, imprisoned in eastern vapour, shone through the white veil with soft glow that cast no shadow but comforted the earth with hope.

Susannah had a further thought in her mind now, but she felt no haste or impatience of excitement.

The boy was of an active, restless disposition or he would hardly have been out so early. Lithe and idle, he sat see-sawing in the floating end of the boat, uncertain how to amuse himself. He returned Susannah's greeting with a lively flow of talk.

"You don't know how to row," said Susannah.

She showed no eagerness, for she felt none. The hope she had just formed was most uncertain, for it appeared not at all likely that she could escape in this way without being molested.

"I bet I can row," said the boy, "as well as any man in town."

"That isn't saying much," said Susannah. "The men about here have very few boats, and they are most of them afraid to go on anything smaller than the steamer."

"I could row t'other side and back," bragged the boy. "I could row t'other side and back three times in the day."

"You couldn't."

"I couldn't! What will you bet?"

"I suppose your father wouldn't allow you to go, anyway."

He was a fresh-faced, mischievous, eager young rascal, and he found Susannah's manner pleasant and provoking.

"Will you lay five dollars on it?" he cried. "Pap is away down to Quincy. If you'll lay five dollars on it I'll do it."

"But I won't."

The gambling spirit of the young pioneer was aroused.

"What will you lay on it, then?"

"I don't believe you could row once to the other side."

He bragged loudly and with much exaggeration of what he had done and what he could do, and began pushing off the boat to show her his speed.

The boat was a rude craft, unpainted, flat-bottomed, but light enough, and not badly formed for speed. Susannah stepped into it without much hope, scarcely caring what she did, but still provoking the young boatman to attempt the crossing.

"I shan't give you any money," she said, "but you can row me a bit if you like till I see how fast you can go. You don't understand the currents, I am sure."

"Currents!" said the boy, "I guess I understand all there is to know about them."

Talking thus in light banter, they actually proceeded out onto the bosom of the milky flood without hearing any cry from the shore or seeing any one who took note of their departure. The pellucid and comforting light of the blinded sun grew warmer; the hum of industry in the town behind rose cheerfully upon the quiet air, and as the calling of the April bluebird in the fields grew more faint, the splash of the oars and the whirr of the gray water-fowl began to be accompanied by a low distant sound as of a watermill.

"It's the excursion steamer," said the boy. "We'll get in her waves and you'll be scared. Ladies is always scared of waves."

She asked if the steam-boat would stop at the Nauvoo wharf, but he explained, with the knowledge that boys are apt to have of such details, that this steamer was coming from Fort Madison, and would keep to the Missouri side, that he had heard that there were some State officials on board her, escorting the Governor of Kentucky, who was prospecting for a Land Company.

They saw the white hulk of the steam-boat looming upon the water to the north. Her side paddle-wheels churned the flood. A strong purpose took possession of Susannah; she knew what she was going to do.

She said to the boy, "No one could stop a steamer when she once starts until she gets to her next port."

"I bet the engineman could stop her just as easy as that." The boy backed water with his oars suddenly.

"But no one on the river could make him stop and get aboard."

"Yes, they could. My pap stopped one once. We was living down near Cairo, but not near a wharf."

"How did he do it?" she asked, and her interest was intense.

"Why, you just put up your hands like a trumpet and yell through them as loud as you can, and you go on waving and hollering. My pap said the best plan was to call out 'Runaway nigger! Large reward!' They'd be sure to stop then to know all about it, and when they'd once stopped they don't mind your clambering up, if you can pay the fare."

Susannah felt herself wholly unequal to the loud task described.

"They would never stop for you," she, said. "You are only a boy, and they would know 'twas only mischief."

His reply was as before. He would lay five dollars on it that he could stop the boat.

She incited him to do this thing also. What faculty of caution the boy possessed was not as yet developed; he left the care for consequences to the sedate lady in the stern, and forgetting his quest of the Missouri shore, lay in the path of the steam-boat and howled unmusically, and marred the peace of the placid morning by shouting concerning a runaway slave and a fabulous reward that was offered for him taken alive or dead.

It is probable that what he said never rightly reached the ears of the men on the deck, but that they regarded the lady as a possible passenger; the engine was stopped.

"We'd better cut now as fast as we can," said the boy, somewhat frightened. He seized his oars excitedly. "Or shall I tell them a big yarn about the nigger?"

They were but slightly to one side. The prow of the steam-boat, which drew but little water, had already passed below them. A small crowd on the vessel's deck leaned over the paddle-box. Standing up in the boat, Susannah searched the faces of the men looking down. They all looked at her.

She singled out the captain by some sign in his dress, and pleaded urgent necessity for travelling with him.

"Look here," said the boy, looking up at her from beneath, "I call that a low-down, mean sort of thing to do. Why didn't you tell me square? I'd have brought you if you wanted do come."

She pleaded with the boy too. "It was better for you not to know my secrets. If they ask you in the city you can say that you didn't know."

A dozen hands were held out to help her to climb the ladder on the shelving paddle-box. "Keep off," they cried to the boy, and he swung away from the churning wheel.

Susannah stood upon the deck pale and trembling. The magnitude of the step came upon her, and she was beset by natural timidity and the painfulness of her dependence. The men who stood around her with the right to question were not of a low class. The captain, brawny and respectable, spoke for the group. Behind him was a short but dignified gray-haired gentleman whom she took to be the present or former Governor of the State of Kentucky, of whom the boy had spoken. With him were several men who appeared to have some fair title to gentility. Other passengers pressed in an outer circle.

She would fain have explained herself more privately, but she could not endure to accept the privileges of the boat without explaining first that she was not able to pay for them. "Gentlemen, I have no money. I am entirely unprotected. I have escaped in fear of my life from Nauvoo."

She spoke instinctively, only desiring to set herself right, but when the words were said she knew that she had helped to heap opprobrium on the sect in whose cause so short a time ago she would have died. The passengers were Missourians, as was the captain. Among them went a whisper of chivalrous pity for her and of execration for the prophet and his followers.

"Madam," said the captain, "any lady as is escaping from those devils has the freedom of this boat, and no ticket required, as long as I'm in command. Isn't that so?" he asked of the crowd.

The murmur broke into an open chorus of enthusiastic speech.

Wild and deep as was her panting anger against Smith's oppression,

Susannah shrank. The thought of profiting by this spirit of partisan hatred scorched her heart.

The Kentucky Governor, a dapper man, who had been regarding her with a temperate and critical eye, now, urged by her obvious distressed timidity, came forward.

"How did you get among the Mormons, may I ask?"

"My husband," faltered Susannah, "but he is dead."

It would appear that her words tallied with some conclusion he had been drawing concerning her, for without further parley Susannah found herself being led in a formal manner down the companion-way. The brief report which she had given of herself had preceded her through the boat. She heard the passengers whom she left on the deck making sentimental remarks. Two coloured girls who were washing dishes in a pantry came to its door and gasped with emotion as they stared at her. In the saloon the coloured waiters gaped.

At the farther end of the saloon a stout and magnificent lady in silk and diamonds was seated before innumerable viands which were spread in circles around her plate. She stopped eating while her husband presented Susannah. She alone of all upon the boat seemed to be overburdened by no surge of sentiment or curiosity. She was a most comfortable person.

Seated in safety beside her, Susannah could indulge the pent-up indignation of her outraged spirit in silent musings upon Smith's degradation and, the certain downfall of all righteousness under the new tyranny. And yet—and yet—the shock of the last few days, forcibly as it vibrated through all her nature, could not eradicate the sympathy of years—the memories of Hiram and Kirtland, Haun's Mill and the desperate winter's march. Justice, her old friend, now her inquisitor, said sternly, "It was in these scenes in which some lost life and some reason that these men lost their moral standards." But her heart cried, "Now that *I* am insulted, I cannot forgive."

The words of the Governor's wife, cheerful, continuous, and not without diverting sparkle, were an unspeakable rest to Susannah, weary above all things of herself. Whether because of a strong undercurrent of tactful kindness, or in mere garrulity, the good lady's talk for some time flowed on concerning all things small, and nothing great, like the lapping of the river against the vessel's bows.

But at last her companion's situation grew upon her; she enlarged more than once upon her surprise at Susannah's advent, and her feelings of extreme relief that she was safely there.

"What a mercy!" she sighed comfortably. "Such awful people! Why, I hear that when any child among them is weak or deformed they just murder it."

Like one who is enraged with his own kin but cannot hear them falsely accused, Susannah contradicted this statement.

"It is perfectly true," the Governor's wife declared. "I have heard it several times. How long have you been at Nauvoo?"

"Three weeks."

"And in that time they offered to kill you! Well, I assure you if you had been a sickly child they wouldn't have let you live three days. And they say that that monster they call the prophet has at least a dozen wives."

"Oh, no."

"Ten or eleven, at any rate."

"He has only one, and he has always been very kind to her."

"How they have imposed upon you! Where have you been living that you have not heard more of their iniquitous doings than that?"

Susannah was faint and ill with the conflict within her own breast when the dapper Kentucky Governor, on business intent, came to them from a group of the smoking men.

"James," cried his wife, with an edge of sharpness in her low voice, "this lady doesn't even know a tithe of the enormities that are practised in Nauvoo."

He shook his head, and said that it was a compliment to Susannah's heart and mind that the tenth part had been sufficient to alarm.

His manner was stiff and formal, but his disposition seemed very kind.

He asked Susannah if the Mormons had retained all her property, and what destination she now proposed for herself; and then with great delicacy informed her that there was a proposition among the passengers to make a collection, to defray the expenses of her whole journey.

Susannah's cheek paled again.

"How could I return it if it came from so many?" she asked. Her white hands were clasping and unclasping themselves. Must it indeed be by means of such humiliation that she saved herself from Angel's Church?

The Governor determined upon further generosity. "If you would prefer, take it from me as a loan," he said.

She gave him Ephraim's address. It was so long since she had spoken her cousin's name to any one that tears came when she felt herself bound to explain that she was not certain that he was alive.

"He is probably alive. Ill news travels fast."

She blessed the dapper gentleman for this unfounded opinion, for the kindness that prompted it, more than for all else that he had done.

His advice was that Susannah should continue upon that boat with them as far south as Cairo, in order to take advantage of the steam-boats now plying on the Ohio River, so that the expense and weariness of the land journey would be diminished to the small space between the upper-most point on the Ohio and the western entrance of the Erie Canal. There were several men upon the boat, he said, who could commend her to the care of every captain on the Ohio.

Susannah felt too weak and weary to say more in defence of the morals of Nauvoo. She could not struggle against the fact that her claim to the generosity of which she stood in such helpless need was recognised and satisfied by the hatred of these Gentiles.

When in the succeeding days she had time to meditate, while she spent many a long hour on the decks of river-boats watching the shimmering lights and shades that pass upon open river surfaces, the perplexing and contrasting aspects of her situation played in like manner upon her heart.

She had suffered so much, such long and deadly ill, as a member of this almost innocent sect, suffered bravely in protest against the vile injustice of the persecution, and now that she was escaping from miseries inflicted by this same sect, she was wrapped in the kindly reverse side of the persecuting spirit, and carried home in it, with all the deference that would be accorded to a lost child. She was too tired and helpless now to defy the good thus given. Did all her former suffering go for nothing as a protest against the wrong?

With more curious feelings, more involved sentiments, she regarded the history of her more inward life. With what strong protest against the obvious evils attendant upon unreasoning faith had she resisted through many years the infectious influences of belief in an interfering spiritual world. Now she had defied Smith with a faith in the ideal marriage unsupported by any conscious reason, and when she had looked to the interference of Providence, not even in meekness, but in desperate challenge, she had strong impression of being encompassed by invisible power and protection. In vain she said to herself that the simple and unlooked-for method of her escape was one of those coincidences which only appear to support faith, that her deliverance had been of no unearthly sort, but brought about by means doubtfully righteous—consent to trick the boy and to say little on hearing the Mormons falsely accused. When she had told herself this, the impression that underneath her folly a guiding hand had impelled and saved her, in spite of her small marring of the work, remained. Even while her bosom was swelling with shame at hearing her husband's sect derided, and eating the bread of that derision, and still greater shame at knowing that condemnation was merited, she would find herself resting in the assurance that beyond and beneath all this confusion of pain there was for her and for all men an eternal and beneficent purpose.

CHAPTER VI.

Susannah left the canal boat at Rochester. She had borrowed as small a sum as might be, and was now penniless, possessing only her travel-worn garments; she had no choice but to start toward Manchester on foot. Food was easily to be had; such a woman as Susannah had but to enter any house and state her need. She got a long lift on her way from a farmer driving to Canandaigua. Of the farmer she asked, while her pulses almost stopped, some information about Ephraim.

"He's kep up the place to a wonderful degree like his father," said the farmer.

From this she gathered that Ephraim was alive and in better health. She asked no more; her lips refused to form his name again.

"The old lady, she was took off with a stroke; she and the old gentleman is laying together in the graveyard." The farmer volunteered this information, and Susannah, who had nerved herself to meet Ephraim's mother with humility, now wept for her loss.

From the town of Canandaigua she walked beside the winding river and entered Manchester from the west at the hour when the May dusk was melting into moonlight.

The public road, then as now, was lined with elms and many an apple-tree. The dusk of the elm branches was flecked with half-grown fluttering leaves, and the outline of the apple branches was heavy with blossom. The air was sweet in the shade of the night-folded petals, the perfume bringing involuntarily the thought of the hum of bees which had gone to rest. There were some new houses on the road, but the tide of progress had here ebbed, leaving the once ambitious village like a rock pool, beautified only by those ornaments of nature which thrive in still-ness. There was more on the road of gable and shrub and tree which was familiar than of objects strange to her eye. The few people who were abroad gave her scarcely a glance, the half light veiling all that was foreign in her garb. The round moon hung above the willows of the river.

When she came in sight of the white Baptist meeting-house she scanned its homely appearance as one looks at the face of an old friend. The yellow light within was put out as she approached. Out of the door a group of men were issuing as if from some evening service.

What vivid memories the scene brought her!—memories of her uncle singing psalms with slow and solemn demeanour, of her aunt's high and more emotional voice, of the pew in which as a girl she had sat between them, listless and impatient, wondering at times why Ephraim remained at home.

Her uncle and aunt were now lying in the graveyard. She paused a moment at the thought, looking at the small host of modest headstones surrounded by wild-flowers and half-fledged shrubs. It has never been the custom in Manchester to cultivate God's acre. Above, the branches of the nut-trees stretched themselves in the sweet spring air—they too were just leafing.

Standing by the low, unpainted rail, Susannah wondered in what part of the yard her aunt and uncle lay.

She observed that the small coterie of deacons had passed on to the road and dispersed, leaving only one of their number, who was locking the main door with an air of responsibility. Susannah did not look twice; she knew that this man was Ephraim. He stooped slightly to fit the key in the lock; then, evidently having forgotten something, pushed the door again and went inside.

Susannah did not wait; she went up the graveyard path and in where the great square windows cast each a strip of light athwart the dark pews. Ephraim turned from his errand and met her in the aisle.

"Ephraim."

Ephraim Croom fell back a step or two, as if his breath was set too quick by joy or fear.

Susannah could not speak again.

At length Ephraim stretched out his hands and grasped her arms gently, then more strongly, making sure that she was not a trick of light and shade. Then, not knowing at all what he did, he clasped her in sudden haste to his breast.

Susannah felt his arms wrap about her as if she had been a little child. She had never felt, never conceived, of closeness and tenderness like this. Ephraim, his breast heaving and his arms folding closer and closer, was out of himself. There was no conscious meaning expressed by him, but she knew, knew at once without shadow of doubt that he himself had been the dreamer of whom he wrote to her, who had learned so much by yielding all the loves of his heart to one, and that she was that woman.

It was a long moment; at last, as if waking from a dream, Ephraim relinquished his hold. He leaned against the side of a pew, and his eager look seemed to hold and fold her still. In the dim light she could not see his eye, but she felt the delight of his glance falling upon her, a brighter, softer influence than the mantle of the moonlight.

She laid a hand lightly on his shoulder with a motherly touch.

"I have startled you, dear Ephraim; I hope I have done you no harm."

He made as yet no answer but to take her hand, grasping it with rough heartiness as if this was the first moment of their meeting.

Susannah laughed as women sometimes laugh over their cherished ones for very joy, not amusement. "Speak to me," she coaxed. "I have come back to you. Do you think we are in a dream?" She let herself kneel on the old floor of the old aisle, and, clasping both his hands, laid them against her cheek.

With his returning self, something of his habitual formality of manner would have returned had she remained in any common attitude, but to this coaxing, kneeling queen Ephraim (although his whole life had passed without caresses) could not behave with reticence.

One thing he did not do. He did not hint that it was unseemly that she should kneel at his feet. Chivalry was the very substance of the soul of this son of New England, and no outward seeming could disturb his serene reverence for the woman he loved. He stooped over her, now stroking her hair, how holding her hands close against his heart, now whispering words that in their audible passion were new and strange to his unaccustomed lips.

"I am all alone, Ephraim. I have no money, no clothes. I have walked most of the way from Rochester today."

"Are you very tired?"—as if the fact that she had been walking that day was all that needed his immediate attention.

"I was forced to come suddenly. I only escaped with my life. But I have long been wearying to come to you, for since my husband and the child died I have been quite alone."

"We heard that they were dead, but that was long ago." There was no tone of reproach in his voice, only curiosity. "You never wrote, and I—I supposed that if you were alive you—you preferred to remain, Susy."

She did not enter into explanation then. After a while, when he had raised her to her feet and embraced her again, she whispered, "Why are you in the meeting-house, Ephraim?"

"We have been having a prayer meeting," he answered. "And I keep the key because—because my father used to." He gave the reason with an intonation half playful. "I do many a thing now because he did."

"I thought that you at least would never become like the others. Are they less foolish" (she made a gesture toward the pews to denote their late inmates), "less unjust than they used to be?"

As they went toward the Croom homestead he answered her words in his manner of meditative good-humour which she knew so well. "I don't know that they are less unjust and less foolish than they used to be, or that I am either, Susy, but—it is not good to worship God alone."

She pressed close to his side and looked up through the honied blossom of the apple-boughs; the violet gulfs of heaven seemed to be made more homelike by his tones.

"The sun, they say, is ninety-three millions of miles away from the earth's surface, Susy; and think you that if some of us climb the mountains we are much nearer light than those in the vales?"

She remembered sentences which she had conned from his letters which ran like this, and her thought on its way was arrested for a moment by the memory of the spot where she had lost those letters, the thought of the grave by the creek at Haun's Mill and of her husband's steadfast faith. So they walked in silence, but as they stood by the garden gate under the quince tree, she detained him a moment with a child's desire to hear a story that she knew by heart.

"Ephraim, you wrote once that you knew a man who loved—"

When he had given the answer she wanted, they went up the little brick path, and Susannah noticed that the folded tulips and waxen hyacinths flanked it in orderly ranks. Their light forms glimmered in the branch shadows of the budding quince. It was true, what people said, that Ephraim had not let his father's home decay. The door stood open, as country doors are apt to do.

There was a lack of something in the dark appointments of the sitting-room. The traces of busy domestic life were not there, and sadness filled the place of the parents whom she had unfeignedly longed to see again. Through a door ajar she saw light in the large kitchens. A candle was upon a table, and an old woman, unknown to her, sat sewing beside it. Ephraim, holding a burning match in clumsy fingers, lit a student lamp—the fire of a new hearth.

CHAPTER VII.

Two years after that, Ephraim, returning one day from the field, brought with him a poor wayfarer whom he had met upon the road.

The stranger was of middle age, with hair already gray and face deeply furrowed. In ragged garments, resting his bandaged feet, he sat propped in the sitting-room. The warm air blowing from rich harvest fields came in at open door and windows. Attentive before him, Ephraim and Susannah sat.

"You are one of the Latter-Day Saints?" Susannah asked.

"I am, ma'am, and it's real strange to hear you say them words, for it's 'Mormons' the Gentiles calls us."

Then to her questioning he told the story of the downfall of Nauvoo.

"There was two causes for the persecution; we had got too powerful and too great for the folks in Illinois, just as we had done in Missouri; but there was another thing, and that was that wickedness crept in amongst us. 'Twasn't as bad as was reported, though, but 'twas there—I'm afraid 'twas there."

The man sighed.

"It's twelve years now since I joined the Saints in Missouri and when we were driven out there I went with them to Illinois; and I can never believe other but that the Latter-Day Saints has the truth, for the power of it is always to be seen among them; and now that I've lost everything a second time, and know that I have a sickness that I'll never get the better of, I have come east to see my folks once more and to testify to them of the truth."

He was going on into Vermont, passing by that way that he might refresh his eyes with a view of the sacred hill, and had only remained at Ephraim's request to relate his tidings to Susannah.

"After coming out of Missouri I never lived at Nauvoo. I had a farm midways, between Nauvoo and Quincy. As near as I can make out, the scandal they've got agen us, which they've always had agen us because of the wickedness of the Gentile mind, began to have some truth in it when Rigdon came out with his teaching concerning the nonsense of spiritual wives, which wasn't new with him, for I hear that it's held among all the folks as call themselves 'Perfectionists.' Well, our prophet made pretty quick work of that doctrine, and he rebuked Rigdon in public and private, and packed him out of the place, and no one can say that our prophet has ever done otherwise with any one as has had notions about marriage."

Susannah sighed. "I have heard that he has acted the same way in several other instances."

"You have, ma'am? Well, it's strange, too, to hear a Gentile say a good word for our prophet, but perhaps, as he came from here, ma'am, you may be some relation of his; and I ask you, is it likely, as he's always acted so severe in that matter, that he should have taught a false doctrine himself? But even some of the Saints do say nowadays that he was led away by some strange doctrines before he died; but, for my own part, I believe that the tales have arisen from the sinful natures of many of the men that he trusted; for he was too trustful, and there's apostles and bishops and elders amongst us that are servants of hell. There's been evil work since our prophet's martyrdom, for there's thousands of our people now deluded by them and going out after Mr. Brigham Young and his crew.

"You want to know how the prophet's death came about, and I can tell you; for when my disease came on, and the doctor told me 'twas fatal, I started to go up to Nauvoo to ask the prophet to lay his hands upon me and heal me. But when I got there the city was all in a buzz, for the cause that some of the elders had got out a paper accusing the prophet of having a lot of ladies for wives. Well now, I can tell you how that came about. When our prophet first got the charter for the Nauvoo Legion there was a man called Bennet, who had been general in the American army, and who was steeped in unbelief and ambition, and who came and offered his services to the prophet, and was allowed to build up the Nauvoo Legion. He was a most sinful man, and the prophet, he knew his sinfulness, but thought that he ought to take any help to build up an army to preserve his people from the fearful persecutions. Bennet got hold of the worst side of the worst men we had in the Church, among which was the new usurper." He paused here with ire in his eye. "I would be understood to mean Mr. Brigham Young, who has falsely usurped the prophet's place; but there are many of us who will not follow him, no, not one step. The Lord will requite him and his confederates, and will establish his true servants."

"I fear, my good friend," said Ephraim, "that although it is true that the Lord will establish his true servants, it is also true that their kingdom is not of this world."

"Well, sir, tramping along as I've done many a day, with no companion but the disease that's prevailing against me, I've thought that that may be true; but, whichever way it is, Bennet set himself to work iniquity, and they say that when the prophet could endure him no longer and gave him the sack, he had the vileness to dress himself up in the prophet's clothes and go about in disguise, talking Sydney Rigdon's rank spiritual-wife doctrine to the ladies and some of them were such fools that they thought it was the prophet, and that he disguised his voice and kept something over his face in order to work the iniquity in secret. That's what a gentleman who knew very well about it told me. But anyway, when Bennet was gone out he wrote awful things to the Gentile newspapers concerning the domestic iniquities of Nauvoo; and he had his own party in the sacred city, and they up and put their scandals in the public print in the prophet's own city.

"But the prophet he rose up and shook himself, like Samson when his arms were tied with the withes, and he denounced the wickedness, and went to the house where the paper was published, and kicked the printing press down himself, and burned the paper. And that day he preached most powerful in the Nauvoo Temple."

"We heard that it was on account of the illegality of his action in the printing office that the people of Illinois arrested him."

The stranger did not answer directly. His mind had passed on to scenes which had stirred him more personally.

"I was in the city all the time. The Government of Illinois sent to arrest Mr. Smith, but his people rallied round him, and said that in consequence of the lawless persecutions that had passed in Missouri they had a right to mistrust the justice of the State. They called out the Nauvoo Legion, and sent back the constables that had come from Carthage. That made the Gentiles terribly angry. The Illinois militiamen went about saying openly that they would burn down the town and kill every man, woman, and child in it. So then Governor Ford himself advised our prophet to keep the Legion under arms, for he said the Gentiles were so furious; but he asked the prophet to go to Carthage and pledge himself to appear for the trial when it came on, for it was a civil suit, and no harm could come to him and his. Governor Ford pledged his honour as the Governor of the State.

"I had been waiting about the town until the prophet should be less bothered before asking him to heal my sickness, but when I heard that he was going away, then I misdoubted that it would be long before he came back. I thought I'd make a push for it, so I went and hung round the door of the prophet's house. I was only a poor man and I did not like to go in, for the bishops and elders and all the grand folks were going in and out all that day. I heard the things they said, and most of them were saying that the prophet had had a vision, and that if he went to Carthage he would never come back alive. They said too that if he stayed, the town would be sacked, and I understood that they were asking him to run away. Towards evening I saw a buggy draw up at the back door of the hotel, and all the elders seemed to be holding a meeting, for they were singing hymns; so then it just come to me that they were going to get the prophet off, and I ran down the road to the ferry, for I knew he would have to go that way. I waited in the boat, and the same buggy came down to it, and a man with a cloak on and his hat over his eyes came out and sat in the corner of the boat, and we all knew that it was the prophet, and none of us durst speak to him. But I went over in the boat, for I hoped I'd get up courage to ask him when we came to the other side. When he stood on the shore he seemed like a man that didn't know what to do, although there was horses there for him to take, and he turned round and went off the road up on to a little hill; and I went after him a bit of the way behind, and I came and found him just standing looking at the city, for the river swept round two sides of it so noble like, and blue as the sky above, and the city stood all white, and the temple stood high in the middle, and all of it glistened in the sun. The prophet had taken off his hat, and he stood with his hands folded on the stick he carried, and he just looked and looked at the city. I had never seen a man look like that but once before, and then it was a man I knew whose wife died, and he looked at her face just steadfast like that. I couldn't think to speak to him about myself just then, although I'd got him alone, for my heart was just broke to see how sad he looked, and him just in the prime of life; for it was his own city, and the sound of all its work came over to us as we stood there, and the thousands and thousands of happy homes in it belonged to his own people.

"But when I moved a bit he saw me, and he started at first as if I'd been going to shoot him, thinking no doubt that I was an enemy spying on him. At that, because my disease had weakened me, and because I seemed to feel nothing all through me but the grief that he was bearing, I began to cry like a child.

"Then he stretched out his hands towards the city and I heard him say, 'My Lord, thou hast given me this people, and if I leave them without a shepherd they will be stricken and scattered and robbed by the destroyer.'

"So then in a few minutes he held out his hand to me, so gentlemanlike, as if I was as good as him, and he said, 'Come, my friend, let us go back, and let God determine what we shall do or suffer.' So we went and got on the ferry-boat and went back, and I never spoke to him; but I went with him all the way to his house.

"The next morning I heard that he and Mr. Hyrum were going to set off for Carthage to be tried. So I got a horse and went to Carthage before them, for I felt then that I cared for nothing but to see the prophet again. But I heard tell how, as they went along, their wives and their friends went with them part way, and they turned back two or three times as they were parting from them, for the prophet said that they would never see his face again.

"Governor Ford he met them at Carthage with a great to-do. He pledged the honour of the State that they should be safe, and he had the troops drawn upon either side, and he passed down between them with the prophet and Mr. Hyrum and showed them himself into the gaol. The prophet said that it was illegal to put them in the gaol, for it was a civil matter, and Governor Ford said, for I heard him, that it was because they would be safer there. I was standing just behind the line of soldiers jostling up with the crowd, and I heard the Governor say, 'I pledge you my honour, and the faith and honour of this State, that no harm shall come to you while undergoing this imprisonment.' So then they were shut in; but the crowd and the soldiers remained in the streets, and I heard enough to know that harm would come.

"The next morning the Governor went away from Carthage, to be out of it, and that day, in the afternoon, a mob of men with faces painted like Indians came out with guns, and we knew that their purpose was to murder the prophet. I went to the gaol and sat upon the steps, and the militia, which was called the Carthage Greys, came out, and halted, about eight rods from the gaol, and I thought at first that they would fire on the mob when they came, but they never moved, but stood and looked on. So the murder was done by them all in cold blood as well as by the mob."

"Did you see him die?" asked Susannah with white lips.

"If he was a relation of yours, ma'am, I can tell you that he died like a man. First I thought that I would spend what little strength I had left in fighting the mob at the door, and that they should not go in except over my body; but the gaoler opened the door in pretence of finding out what was the matter, for he was in the plot; so I thought that I would run up and give warning. But by the time I got to the door of the upper room where the prophet was, the mob was up behind me, so I never rightly knew what I did, for they knocked me down just within the room. There were four or five men with the prophet and Mr. Hyrum, and these kept the mob back for a few minutes at the door, but a bullet hit Mr. Hyrum in the head, and I saw the prophet leaning over him, and he said in a voice that was very sad, 'My dear, dear brother!'

"Then the prophet stood up quite calmly and pulled out a pistol and shot at the mob until all its barrels were discharged. His firing made the men hold back, for a good number of the mob were struck. Then they came on again until the door was literally full with muskets and rifles, but I was lying on the floor below the shots, so I saw them pass over my head. The very walls were riddled with them, and the prophet stood in the midst of the shots and threw up his hands towards heaven and cried, 'O Lord, my God.' Then, not knowing what he did, he staggered to the window, dying from his wounds, and he fell outside the window, and I heard that the mob out there propped up his body and used it for a target."

Susannah rose up with clenched hands and pitiful face, but she went out of the room, leaving the two men together. "Were you injured?" asked Ephraim of the stranger.

"Well, sir, I was bruised by being trampled on, but the gaoler got hold of me and dragged me into an iron cell and locked me in, and the next morning he came and let me out."

"That was a year ago," said Ephraim. "Have you been in Nauvoo since then?"

"Yes, I went back. I wanted to know, sir, what would come, and take my share of the suffering after seeing the prophet die so courageous; but, sir, the Church is sorely divided. I didn't like to say it before your lady, for I see that she's got some one she cares for amongst us, but there's a strong party among the apostles and elders that are worshippers of Baal, and are most evil in their conduct and practice, and are apostate, though they call themselves followers of the prophet. And Mr. Brigham Young is at the head of them. It's a bad thing that the Illinois militia is set out to fight against us and turn us out of the city without mercy, but it's a sorer thing that the greater part of our people, being ignorant, will follow Mr. Brigham Young; and he's bent on going west, sir, into the heart of the Rocky Mountains, where he can set up a kingdom of his own. His teaching is against good doctrine in two respects; he says that they will wax strong there until they can avenge the blood of their brethren who have been hunted and slain, and that the elders and apostles will live like the patriarchs of old, and have many wives, in order to build up the Church."

"And has the other party in your sect no strength to resist?"

"Very little strength, sir, except that God is on the side of the righteous; but Mrs. Smith, the prophet's widow, with his sons and many hundreds of us, will not give in to the evil, but will stay in Illinois and Missouri in face of the worst that persecution can do, for it was thereabouts that the prophet said that the Holy City should be, and he gave us no word to kill and destroy our fellow-men; and although perhaps he was led away and sinned sometimes as other men do, it is a scandalous lie to say that he thought to teach wickedness and falsehood to his Church."

"I wonder," asked Ephraim within himself, "if that is true, or what strange secret that troubled soul took with him to the other side of death?"

In the evening after the stranger was gone Susannah sat with Ephraim in the old doorway. Before them, mid the harvest fields, winding over hill and dale, lay the long white road which led to the hill of Smith's early visions—the road on which Susannah had set forth with Angel

Halsey on her wedding journey.

"You are a-weary, wife, tonight," said Ephraim. He smoothed the hair upon her brow. "You have exhausted yourself with long weeping, and yet—"

He did not say, "Have you reason to bemoan this man's tragic end?" for he knew that more sacred memories had caused the tears; of these some faint jealousy rose in his breast and kindness sealed his lips.

She told him the truth in very simple words such as loving women use.

"Today I seemed to see" (she laid her hand across her knit brows) "all the passion of it again, the wrong, the right, the misery—from the day that Angel and I went out with such young passionate desire to divide the right from the wrong. I could see Angel and my baby shot before my eyes as Joseph Smith was shot. It is terrible to see death come that way. But they are all three lying now in the perfect peace of death." She put her hand in his. "Then, dear, my mind came back, from the rage and terror of war. I thought of their peace and of you—how God has healed my life by your love, and given me such joy. Is he not able to provide for the healing of the nations?"

THE END